Summer with my Sister

LUCY DIAMOND lives in Bath with her husband
and their three children. When she isn't slaving
away on a new book (ahem) you can find her on
Twitter @LDiamondAuthor or on Facebook at
www.facebook.com/LucyDiamondAuthor.

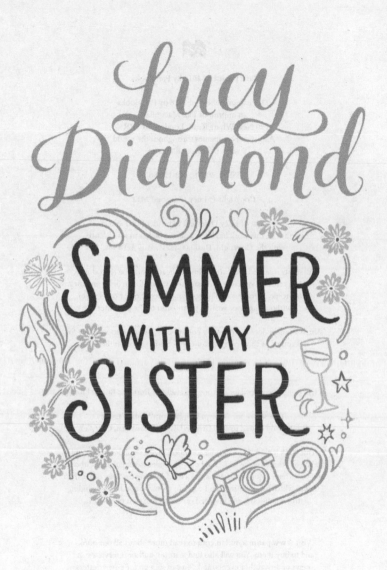

Lucy Diamond

SUMMER
WITH MY
SISTER

PAN BOOKS

First published 2012 by Pan Books

This edition published 2016 by Pan Books
an imprint of Pan Macmillan
20 New Wharf Road, London N1 9RR
Associated companies throughout the world
www.panmacmillan.com

ISBN 978-1-5098-1109-0

Typeset by Set Systems Ltd, Saffron Walden, Essex
Printed and bound by CPI Group (UK) Ltd, Croydon, CR0 4YY

Visit **www.panmacmillan.com** to read more about all our books
and to buy them. You will also find features, author interviews and
news of any author events, and you can sign up for e-newsletters
so that you're always first to hear about our new releases.

*For my sisters, Ellie Brothwell and
Fiona Mongredien, with lots of love*

Acknowledgements

Thanks to Nicky Adams and Simon Trewin, who helped with ideas for this novel at its earliest stages; to Kate Harrison for friendship, feedback and words of wisdom; and to Victoria Walker for letting me talk through plot problems along the way. Thanks also to Martin and Andy Powell for their long conversation about what cars my characters should have. (Sorry I couldn't squeeze in a Jensen Interceptor – another time!)

I couldn't be more grateful for the fabulous and insightful editorial feedback provided by my editor, Jenny Geras, and my agent, Lizzy Kremer. Thank you. You have both made this book infinitely better than it started out. I'd also like to thank the rest of the team at Pan Macmillan – in particular Chloe Healy, Ellen Wood and Michelle Kirk for all their hard work, as well as for being the loveliest people to drink cocktails with. What more could an author want?

Thank you to Hannah, Tom and Holly (the coolest children ever); to my parents, who have befriended every

Acknowledgements

bookseller in the Midlands on my behalf; and to Phil, Saba, Ellie, Ian and Fiona, for spreading the word and always being so supportive. And I couldn't write these books without my husband Martin's pep talks, plot brainstorming sessions and all-round cheerleading. Thank you so much.

Finally, a massive thank you to everyone who's bought one of my books and taken the time to email or write to me about it; I appreciate it so much. I hope you enjoy this one.

Prologue

As soon as she heard her parents driving away, she picked up the phone and called him. Her heart was racing. 'They've gone,' she said. 'Fancy coming over?'

'Too right,' he said, and a whoosh of heat went through her like a lit match in petrol. 'I'm on my way.'

She replaced the receiver, feeling heady and restless, pacing around the living room while she waited for him to arrive. *Hurry up, hurry up, hurry up.* She was going to lose her nerve if he didn't get there soon.

Two minutes later he was knocking on the door, the front wheel of his bike still spinning in the drive where he'd dumped it. She caught her own reflection in the hall mirror as she went to let him in, and her eyes were bright, her cheeks pink. This was it.

They snogged deliciously in the doorway for several passionate minutes in full view of the neighbours. It felt thrilling and dangerous. Anything might happen. Mrs Lindley's curtains twitched in disapproval across the road, but

Polly couldn't have cared less. Flicking the Vs at the nosey old bat in a glorious fit of defiance, she went right on kissing him, tingles of desire shooting around her body.

They'd never had sex in her parents' house before. Tonight was the night.

'Hello, gorgeous,' he said as they broke apart. His voice was husky, his pupils flooded with lust.

'Hi,' she said breathlessly. 'Come in.'

She took him by the hand and led him through to the living room, her heart bouncing, her skin prickling. She was seventeen years old, and what was about to happen that night would change everything.

Chapter One

Twenty years later

It was seven o'clock one April morning and the sun was edging above the City of London. The sky was streaked all the shades between shocking pink and palest apricot as the early Tube trains rumbled below the streets, a booming percussion twenty metres underground. Up in the gleaming office buildings, lights flickered on at the windows as if a vast machine was coming to life, and cleaners pushed whirring Henry Hoovers along soulless beige corridors. Elsewhere in the flats and houses sprawling out from the city's pulsing radius, millions of people rolled over in warm beds, dreamed, snored, spooned against their partners, pressed the Snooze on the alarm clock, or tended to early-rising children through squinty, barely seeing eyes.

Polly Johnson was a step ahead, already fully prepared for battle. Her skin had been scrubbed in a steaming power shower and was now hidden beneath a severely cut charcoal-

3

grey trouser suit and crisp white blouse. Her shoulder-length caramel-coloured hair was scraped back in a business-like bun. Her face was a mask of foundation and concealer — damn those dark circles below her eyes, they were becoming harder and harder to disguise — with a slash of red lipstick added like war paint. Laptop, killer heels, glossy handbag: tick, tick, tick.

She strode into the glass atrium that was the reception area of the Waterman Financial Corporation, raised a hand in curt greeting to the receptionists, slapped her pass key on the turnstile and pushed through its clicking metal barrier, the only arms that ever held her these days. Then she headed for the lift. *Going up.*

Polly Johnson had risen to the top of her game in a smoothly orchestrated crescendo over the years. No, that sounded as if it had all been laid on for her. It hadn't. She'd had to fight and hustle every single step of the way there, elbowing past all the other high-achievers, treading on the heads of those weaker and slower in her scramble for glory. She'd stacked up the hours, slogging away doggedly without holidays, weekends and parties; without a social life full stop, let's face it. Barely pausing for breath, she'd forced herself one notch higher on the career scale, and then another notch, and another. Female colleagues had peeled away meanwhile, veering down the motherhood path, only to find their career options collapsing at the doors of the maternity unit. Not Polly. Work took precedence over family and friends and lovers. You wouldn't catch Polly stepping off the gravy train for anything.

Now she was up there with the big guns, senior product consultant for Asset Liability Management and Funds Transfer Pricing in the Risk Management department. Admittedly, it was a lot to fit on a single business card. When she'd last seen her family, back at Christmas, their eyes had collectively glazed over as she'd told them her new job title, as if she was speaking a foreign language. They didn't look so confused when she told them how much she'd be earning, though.

'*How* much?' her dad had yelped, almost falling head-first into the sherry trifle.

'Bloody hell,' her mum had said faintly. 'Well done, love. That's amazing.'

It felt like redemption, that moment, as if all the things that had gone wrong in the past had been absolved. Gold star in the good books for Polly!

Clare, of course, had had to spoil things by making a barbed remark about bankers' bonuses being obscene, but Polly had blithely ignored her. *I win, you lose,* she'd gloated privately, staring her down. Jealousy was so unattractive. 'More champagne?' she'd asked everyone sweetly, flourishing the fat green bottle. There was only ever one answer to *that*, of course.

It had mattered more than she'd expected, the approval of her parents. It was only when she'd seen their awestruck faces that she realized how much she'd been trying to prove to everyone, them most of all. The money was great, sure, but it was success that she ultimately craved: glory, achievement, a power-packed CV. It was being able to show everyone she could do it, that she wasn't a waste of space. Since Michael had died . . . Well, she wanted to be doubly successful, put it like that.

And, thought Polly now as she strode into her office and saw the sky turning pinky-blue over the domed roof of St Paul's and the early-morning sunlight glinting off the windows and rooftops of the city before her, she'd made her point. She'd hit every target with precision accuracy, she'd bloody well earned the accolades, pay rises and promotions, not to mention the luxury South Bank apartment overlooking the Thames, membership of the most exclusive clubs in London, a silver sporty Merc that boy-racers eyed with jealousy, and a vast wardrobe stuffed full of designer clothes to die for. Oh, and one humdinger of a bonus heading her way very soon too. Which was just as well, really, because she'd overstretched herself financially with some hefty stock-market investments recently. You had to be in it to win it, though, right?

*

Polly's assistant Jake arrived at eight o'clock that morning with her usual espresso. He was tall, posh and nice to look at, and knew better than to be late when it came to something as essential as coffee. She'd sacked people for less.

He set the cup carefully in front of her and she grunted, not taking her eyes away from the monitor. 'Um ... Polly, there are a few things I need to check with you,' he said, clipboard and pen at the ready. 'You've been asked to speak at the Risk Management Solutions conference next month—'

'Tell them I'm busy,' she cut in, swearing under her breath as she made yet another correction onscreen. She was checking the research done by Marcus Handbury, a junior consultant, for an important meeting next week. One page in, and she'd already had to rewrite several lines and highlight three instances of poor grammar. Slack, slack, slack. Marcus was one of those pretty-boy public-school types who'd always had everything handed to him on a plate. Just because he had connections with all the right people, it didn't give him the right to be sloppy with his work.

'Secondly, Henry Curtis has been in touch again, wanting to meet ...'

Polly's ears pricked up. 'Lunch or evening?' Henry Curtis was a big cheese in a hedge-fund organization and had been making noises lately that he wanted to poach her. He'd made a beeline for her at a recent conference in New York, and had lavished her with attention. Flatteringly, he knew all about the coup she'd pulled off beating Carlson International to a major global account, and had gone on to butter her up like the proverbial parsnip. Mind you, the dirty gleam in his bloodshot, appreciative eyes as they roamed her suited flanks made Polly wonder if he was after more than just her business experience. Hmmm. Despite ticking several of Polly's perfect-partner boxes – rich, successful, attractive – he was officially too old for any romantic liaisons, being forty-six. (Forty-four was her upper age limit. Anything older, and men developed a whiff of approaching-fifty midlife crisis, which put them out of the running. In men, as in life, only perfection would do. Not that she had any *time* for relationships, of course.)

'Evening,' Jake replied, his pen hovering above his page. 'Should I book something?'

'Tell him lunch will have to do,' she said crisply. 'Maybe one day next week? Book a restaurant near here.' She'd have Curtis make the effort, get him to prove how keen he was, she decided. Not that she was in a hurry to jump ship, but it was pleasing to be asked, wasn't it?

Jake ran through a couple of other things, flagging up a liquidity-risk briefing that needed approving, various items on the board-meeting agenda, and a potentially interesting new client who'd approached the firm. 'Oh, and finally,' he said, 'it's your niece's birthday on Wednesday. Is there anything in particular you'd like me to send her?'

Polly waved a hand. 'Just ... something pretty,' she said carelessly. She wasn't certain exactly how old Clare's daughter, Leila, was now (ten, perhaps?), but Jake was good at choosing presents. He'd picked out an amazing couture dress for Clare's birthday last month, and the most stylish Paul Smith cufflinks for her dad's retirement gift. He was sure to find something appropriate. He had time to browse around after all, unlike Polly herself.

'That's everything then, thank you,' Jake said, bowing his head a little as he left the office.

'Not a problem,' Polly said automatically. Those three words had become her personal mantra over the years. Nothing was a problem to her – one merely had to apply logic or determination (or hire the right staff with the necessary skills) and anything could be resolved. Jake, for instance, obliterated many of Polly's problems. He arranged her dry-cleaning, her diary, her bill-paying, he sent flowers and birthday cards to people on her behalf, he booked in her car to be valeted ... How did anyone manage without a Jake in their life?

*

'Cheers!'

'Cheers!'

Twelve hours later Polly was in the Red House, a private members' club near Liverpool Street, full of other City types talking shop over cocktails and criminally expensive wines. She was in the fifth-floor bar, as she so often was these evenings, finding it impossible to go straight home after the relentless hustle of a long, hectic day without a drink or three first.

Clinking champagne glasses that night with Polly were the two Sophies, Richenda, Josh, Matt and Johnny. She wouldn't go so far as to say that any of them were friends, but they were all useful contacts. Like her, they were regulars in the Red House, high-fliers in the banking world who shuffled billions of pounds around without a second thought. Like her, they'd set their smartphones down on the table in front of them with almost religious solemnity, pouncing whenever emails buzzed through as if the financial industry depended on their cheetah-like reaction times. Polly had worked with the blonde Sophie at HSBC, and knew Richenda from a hot and dreary training week in Singapore that they'd both sweated through early on in their respective careers.

'Down the hatch,' said Johnny, with a lascivious wink at the brunette Sophie, 'and up the sn—'

'Oh, *Johnny!*' she hooted, elbowing him so hard he almost spilled his drink.

Ugh. Johnny was a pig. He'd tried it on with Polly once, had lunged at her and stuck his horrible, meaty tongue down her throat after one too many at a drinks party. If his thinning hair and ruddy, salami-like complexion hadn't already seen him struck off her list, his atrocious manners and that disgusting, thrusting tongue would have made him a goner in a heartbeat. Repulsive as he was though, he was also head of communications for a huge rival corporation, and thus someone she needed to keep onside. She forced a laugh, as did everyone else around the table. Nobody wanted Johnny to think they'd had a sense-of-humour bypass.

The other Sophie, who had ice-blonde hair, a sour-puss mouth and a caved-in face as if someone had accidentally deflated it, began to talk about the Risk Management Solutions conference and how she'd been asked to give the keynote speech.

'I got a call from them too, about speaking there,' Polly felt obliged to put in. 'Turned it down, unfortunately. Too busy.'

Sophie coolly raised an over-plucked eyebrow. 'Yes, I heard they were trying to fill a space,' she said. 'Julian Leighton was in that slot, had to pull out. So they've been in touch with you, have they?'

Polly flinched. Sophie was making it sound as if she'd been contacted as a last resort. 'Well, *ages* ago,' she lied. 'Almost forgotten about it, to be honest. I find it so hard to keep track of all these requests.'

'Oh, I *know*,' Richenda put in, her dark corkscrew curls bobbing like springs as she nodded. 'I've been *besieged* since my team won the Financial Bridging Award.'

'Did you win an *award*?' Mean Sophie muttered sarcastically under her breath. 'You should have said.'

'My PA has to run two diaries for me now, it's *crazy*,' Richenda went on, not seeming to hear the jibe. 'But what can you do?'

What could you do indeed? Everyone looked sage at the question, although they all knew they wouldn't have it any other way. The thrill of the chase, the adrenalin rush, the clammy hands and pumping heart when the market was on the rise – it was addictive, and worth any amount of stress.

A BlackBerry beeped and all eyes returned to the table immediately, everyone on constant high alert for business news from the American offices. Same old, same old, thought Polly with a smile to herself. Just how she liked it.

Later – two in the morning later – Polly stumbled into her flat, kicking off her shoes and rubbing her aching calves.

She really must catch up on her sleep at the weekend, she vowed, feeling battered with exhaustion after another gruelling day. The thing was, with a job like hers, you could never clock off at five and go home. Just as important was being a player, being seen out in such places, pressing the flesh, staying in the loop. And it had been worth going along tonight. Matt had had some interesting news about GlobalGo, the sportswear company that had scaled the heights of success at high speed, only to be freefalling now. He predicted they were going to be wound up any day, which could have repercussions for some of Polly's clients. 'Another one bites the dust,' Johnny had said knowingly. Business was business.

She fell into her enormous luxury bathroom, which was at least as big as most people's main bedroom, and snapped on the spotlights. Eww. Not looking pretty, Polly, she thought, catching a glimpse of her reflection in the vast rectangular mirror that hung above the stone basin. Her skin had somehow taken on a greyish tinge lately. Crow's feet were appearing beneath her eyes, nestling above the dark rings that never seemed to fade. She tutted, peering closer at the mirror itself. The bloody cleaner had left a smear on the glass again. Shoddy – she'd have to have a word with the agency about that. Polly was convinced the cleaner had been slacking off lately. The bed didn't seem to have been made quite right, either, the other week, and Polly was sure someone had helped themselves to her Crème de la Mer moisturizer. It wasn't good enough.

She slipped on her silk pyjamas, dimmed the lights in her bedroom, and climbed into her enormous bed, with its drifts of feather pillows, the softest Egyptian cotton sheets and the luxuriously thick duvet. She set her alarm, pulled on her lavender eye mask and then let herself sink into the bed's embrace. She was asleep within seconds.

Tuesday started just like any other day, with the six o'clock alarm and a drilling hangover. Into the shower, down with some Nurofen and a kick-arse coffee, clothes on, make-up on, then a takeaway breakfast from the deli on the way to the Tube.

'You look tired, love,' the guy behind the deli counter said sympathetically as he made her espresso. 'Reckon you could do with a holiday.'

Polly gave a hollow laugh. Holidays were for wimps. She smiled mirthlessly as she took her breakfast and walked to the Tube station, mentally running through her day ahead. There was a board meeting at eleven, a client meeting at two, cocktails at five for a PR do, and a dinner function with clients at The Ivy. Oh yes, and Hugo Warrington wanted to see her at ten for a chat. No doubt he was going to congratulate her on the Spelman account she'd netted last week. Maybe he would even jack up her bonus on the back of it. Hugo Warrington was the company chairman, the beating heart of WFC. He was fifty years old, enormously rich, and so ruthless you could practically see a dorsal fin through his Savile Row suit jacket. She liked the idea of a cosy chat with him, just the two of them. It was about time he recognized precisely how much clout Polly Johnson had.

On the Tube, off the Tube, into the office, up in the private lift that only management were allowed to use. Another round of ball-breaking, hustling, schmoozing and million-pound transactions was about to begin. Bring it on.

Hugo Warrington's office was on the floor above Polly's. The floor of power. Up there, the carpet was so thick a war could break out and nobody below would notice a thing. Up there, the walls were wood-panelled, as if this was an exclusive members' club – which frankly it *was*. Up there, Warrington's team of PAs looked like they'd been mass-produced: chic, lithe women with perfect nails and the steely power that came from being gate-keepers to the fortress.

'He's expecting you,' said the humourless redhead whose desk was outside Warrington's office. 'Go ahead. Can I get you a coffee, or . . . ?'

'No, thank you,' Polly replied, striding briskly past the clone. She was hoping she might be treated to something fizzy once she made it over the threshold. Rumour had it Hugo Warrington had a *very* well-stocked private fridge.

She knocked on the door and went inside. Warrington's inner sanctum had an even more clubbish, intimate feel, with its dark green walls lined with bookshelves and tasteful ornaments, and his beast of a mahogany desk. A golf trophy gleamed ostentatiously behind his head, while a decanter full of ruby-coloured liquid and a collection of cut-glass tumblers sat a discreet distance to his left on a polished silver tray.

He was behind his desk, frowning at a computer screen, piggish eyes screwed up in a flabby face. At Polly's entrance, he motioned her over. 'Take a seat.'

'Thank you,' Polly said, tucking herself neatly into the black leather chair opposite his. He smelled of cigar smoke, pungent cologne and wealth.

'Now, Polly, I know you've worked hard for us over the years,' he began without preamble, scratching his jowls with stubby fingers. 'You've built up a solid client base, you've shown commitment and professionalism, and you've certainly earned your place on the board.'

Polly felt the hairs on her arms stand on end as she listened to him. Oh my goodness. Praise from Hugo Warrington himself. Result! He was going to give her a *massive* bonus, she could almost smell it. Maybe even promotion. Get in!

'However,' he went on, and that single word was enough to banish her visions of showering banknotes and luxury treats. *However?* Had she heard that correctly? 'We find ourselves in difficult times, as you know. The financial world has changed. Stability is at an all-time low, and businesses everywhere are looking to make cuts.'

There was a sudden tightness in Polly's throat as the words sank into her brain. Ripples of alarm spread through her. Why was he saying this to her? What, exactly, was he building up to?

'We at WFC have had to take a long, cold look at our figures, and unfortunately they aren't as good as we'd like,' he said neutrally. He might have been discussing the weather, or reading the shipping forecast, Polly thought, agitation needling inside her. 'And so it is with regret that we have been forced to make a structural reorganization of the firm, which will unfortunately result in redundancies across the board.'

Redundancies. Shit. She hadn't seen that one coming. Was he looking to get her view on suitable candidates perhaps, or . . . ?

'I'm sorry to tell you, Polly, but your position is no longer viable here at the company,' he said. 'We're letting you go.'

Chapter Two

Clare Berry was drowning. No matter how hard she kicked out against the water or how desperately she flailed with her arms, she kept being pulled below the surface, with the tantalizing shimmer of daylight remaining just out of reach above her head. Her lungs were bursting, her heart was pounding and black spots danced before her eyes, but she had to keep trying to push up to the surface and breathe . . .

Then she woke up in a damp sweat in bed, panting and gasping, her hands weakly scrabbling at thin air, a sob escaping her throat. God. That bloody dream again. How many times had she had it now?

She glanced at the clock. Quarter past five, still dark outside. She had to go back to sleep, must try to dream about something nice this time, something unthreatening and lovely, like fluffy kittens or roses blooming or . . . Yikes. She was turning into Julie Andrews, with her list of 'favourite things'. Any minute now she'd start cutting up the curtains and stitching playsuits for the children, and then she'd officially be demented.

Punching the pillow into a more comfortable shape, Clare rolled over and shut her eyes, but sleep evaded her and the usual worries crowded in like vultures circling. Steve hadn't sent her any maintenance money for the last two months – she was going to have to chase him up, and that was always so much aggro. Threatening red gas and electricity bills had slithered through the letterbox within the last few days and she still didn't have a clue how she was going to pay them. It was Leila's birthday tomorrow, and the bike Clare had been hoping to nab on eBay had gone to a higher bidder at the last frantic second. Alex had been in trouble at school again for fighting, and his teacher had said, all-too-patronizingly, that in her opinion it was because he didn't have a 'good male role model in the family home'. To top it all off, the dog had worms.

No wonder she kept dreaming she was drowning. There was no need to call in Dr Freud to analyse that. She *was* drowning – drowning in stress and guilt and useless-parent feelings. The roof of the cottage was leaking, slugs were annexing the vegetable plot and destroying her lettuces, and the chickens, Babs and Marjorie, had some horrible infection that was making their feathers float off in drifts, and their eyes yellow and gummy-looking. (Why on earth had she agreed to take the wretched birds off Jay Holmes in the first place? Because they were rescue battery hens, and because she was rubbish at saying no to anything, that was why.)

An outsider stumbling upon Clare's life might see the cottage, the vegetable garden and the chickens and assume she was living in a rustic, rural paradise. From where Clare was sitting, though, it was about a million miles from *The Good Life*. The Crap Life Where Everything Goes Wrong was more appropriate. Any second now, the proverbial wolf would burst through the door, licking his lips and brandishing a knife and fork, chicken feathers billowing in his wake.

Clare groaned and pulled the duvet further up around her ears. It had been a tough twelve months, ever since Steve had, in true midlife-crisis style, announced that he was leaving her for a hairdresser called Denise who lived in Basingstoke. He'd met her on the Internet, apparently, and it had been love at first click. Well, good riddance to the idiot. She should never have married him in the first place.

Oh, it was no use. She was never going to be able to fall back to sleep now. She'd get up and make herself a cup of tea, Clare decided, and try to think positively about the good things in her life, instead of lying in bed fretting about those she had no control over. She wrapped herself in her dressing gown and padded downstairs.

Reasons to be cheerful ... Okay. Well, she had two amazing children whom she absolutely adored and doted on. Her parents were both still fit and healthy and she got to see them all the time, as they lived down the road. The village itself – that was another reason to be grateful. She'd lived in Elderchurch her whole life and never wanted to leave. Why would she? It was picture-postcard perfect, with its sweet tumbledown cottages made of red Hampshire brick, the best pub in the world and all her friends. Friends: yet another reason to count her blessings. Whatever happened, she had Debbie and the girls on her side, always had, always would have. And she had a job! Working as a receptionist in the doctor's surgery might not be the most brain-boggling career choice in the world, but it fitted in with school hours, her colleagues were (mostly) lovely, and at least every day was different.

So what if she hadn't got the bike Leila had wanted on eBay? She'd spent ages the night before making a chocolate fudge birthday cake (Leila's favourite), and her dad had said he'd seen a second-hand bike advertised in the paper the other day. That might do instead. It would be all right.

She poured boiling water into the teapot, feeling slightly better. Children, parents, friends, home, a job ... Okay, so she might be feeling temporarily downtrodden, but all the big things were there in place, the things that mattered. Bills, a lying ex, disease-ridden pets, trigger-happy eBay rivals ... they were minor irritants in the grand scheme of things. 'We're doing okay really, aren't we?' she said to Fred, their soppy old mongrel, who was curled up on his blanket in the corner. He thumped his tail sleepily as if agreeing. 'It could be a lot worse.'

It was then that she noticed the trail of brown crumbs on the slate floor, and the cake tin lying under the table with its lid off. 'Oh, Fred,' she said, hurrying over in dismay. 'Fred, you didn't eat the cake, did you?'

Fred's ears flattened at the change in her tone of voice and he hunched lower in his bed. Clare didn't know whether to shout in rage or burst into tears when she saw that he'd somehow nosed the lid off the tin and scoffed the entire contents. 'Oh, great. Just great!'

Tears pricked her eyes. 'I should give you away to the dogs' home, you worm-ridden fleabag,' she fumed, hands on her hips, utterly despairing. 'So much for man's best friend,' she wailed. 'I thought you were meant to be on my side?'

Fred whined, his eyes liquid and mournful. Then his guts gave an alarming-sounding gurgle ... and the next moment, before she could react, he'd thrown up everywhere: foul-smelling chocolate-brown puke that splashed over Clare's feet.

It was clearly going to be one of those days. Again.

★

Two hours later and the house had swung into its usual morning routine. Ten-tomorrow Leila sat bleary-eyed at the breakfast table, absent-mindedly spooning cereal into her mouth. Her body was definitely there in the kitchen, but her mind was still back in bed, caught in a dream. She always appeared wild and dishevelled first thing, her blonde hair a crazed tangle that looked as if she'd spent the night frenziedly backcombing it.

Meanwhile, Alex, aged eight, had decided he no longer liked any kind of cereal that they had and was turning up his nose at the granary toast, because of the dreaded 'bits' that freckled it. 'Can I have pasta instead?' he asked.

'No,' Clare snapped, feeling every minute of her too-early start. Why hadn't she tried harder to doze off again? She was going to be grouchy and baggy-eyed all day now. 'Toast or cereal, what's it going to be?'

'What about if I cook it myself?'

'No, Alex, I said no. Toast or cereal?'

'I don't WANT toast OR cereal. I said I want PASTA!' He kicked petulantly at the table leg and scowled at her, his brown eyes blazing beneath his shock of dark hair. God, he looked just like his dad when he sulked.

'I *am* listening to you,' Clare said patiently. 'I know you want pasta, and I heard you say you didn't want toast or cereal. But toast and cereal are what we've got for breakfast.

That's what we always have for breakfast. So which is it going to be?'

'Pasta,' he said, looking her straight in the eye. 'That's what it's going to be.'

Paging Mary Poppins . . . paging Mary Poppins . . . a voice trilled in Clare's head. If only. She glanced out of the window in the vain hope that the smartly dressed nanny was floating down with her umbrella, spit-spot. She wasn't. The only thing coming down from the sky was the sheeting rain. Wonderful.

She took a deep breath and tried not to think about what Steve and Denise might be doing right now, in their mock-Tudor house with the flouncy peach curtains. They didn't have kids (yet) so were probably still asleep, cuddled up together, her in some hideous nylon camisole, him in his M&S boxers, one hairy leg pushed manfully over her. He was very hairy, Steve: chest, back, legs – privately it had always rather repulsed Clare. She wondered how Denise felt about the issue. Maybe she'd taken one of the salon's waxing sets home with her to strip him of his fur, to render him a plucked chicken instead?

Ugh. She wished she hadn't just thought of that. Now she had the image of her ex-husband, naked and pimply, and . . .

Blinking the ghastly image away, she realized Alex was

staring defiantly at her, still waiting for her to respond. She half-expected a klaxon to sound, signalling that the daily Battle of Breakfast had now reached stand-off stage.

'Well, you'll just have to go hungry then,' she snapped. She couldn't be bothered today. Just could not be arsed to go through the whole rigmarole for the seven-hundredth time. Let him go to school with an empty stomach for once, it wouldn't kill him. It might even make him think twice about these ridiculous breakfast demands next time. 'Leila, can you eat that a bit quicker, love? It's nearly eight o'clock.' Once again her daughter had managed to drag out a single bowl of Shreddies for almost thirty minutes. That had to be some kind of art form, surely? She'd end up as an installation in the Tate if she didn't watch out.

'I'm going to have a shower,' Clare mumbled, pulling her dressing gown around her and heading upstairs. As she went, she heard Alex's grudging reply – 'Oh, OKAY THEN, I'll have cornflakes. If I HAVE to' – and smiled to herself. One day she'd laugh about this with him. If they were still on speaking terms, that was.

The surgery was busy that morning. There were two different bugs currently doing the rounds, and the patients in the waiting room were either clutching their stomachs and looking peaky or hacking up their throat linings in a revolting cacophony of coughing. 'Morning,' Clare said, sitting down at her desk and switching on the PC.

'Morning,' said Roxie, her colleague, who was twenty-two. She had peroxide-blonde pigtails and wore a salmon-pink, chiffon, cap-sleeved blouse with an enormous bow at the neck and a short peacock-blue skirt covered in mismatched buttons. Roxie had studied fashion at college and was now saving up to go travelling with some mates. She was economizing by making her own clothes, bleaching her hair with Domestos and using the surgery broadband for her extensive Internet and phone needs. 'You all right?'

Clare paused for a split-second as she debated going into a full-scale moan about the dog's vomming episode, but then clocked the chocolate-chip muffin that Roxie had brought in for breakfast and decided it was kinder not to. 'Not bad,' she said. 'You?'

'Hungover and knackered, and a bit tender in the old nethers, if you know what I mean.' Roxie winked. 'Richard insisted on it three times last night. Him on top, me on top, then doggy-style. He could not get enough of me, I'm telling you. Yes, can I help you?'

Clare was always deeply impressed by how Roxie managed to segue so smoothly from spilling saucy sexual exploits into being Miss Butter-Wouldn't-Melt for the patients. An elderly gentleman was at the counter, his eyes rheumy behind thick glasses, and his liver-spotted fingers trembling as he unwound his scarf.

'Benson,' he said. 'Nine-thirty for Dr Aardvark.'

Roxie's lips fluttered as if she wanted to giggle and she pinched them quickly together. Clare took over. 'Mr Benson for Dr Arkwright, yes, okay, take a seat.'

He shuffled away and sat on a blue plastic chair, then sneezed into a voluminous white handkerchief.

'Go on,' Clare urged. 'You were telling me about Richard. Which Richard is this?'

'Oh, you know, the fit one who used to be in *Spooks*,' Roxie replied. 'He was a right dirty bugger. Very athletic. I was squealing like a pig within five minutes. The neighbours started banging on the wall after a while to shut me up.'

'Ahh,' Clare said, putting the kettle on. 'Sounds good. Did you see *Corrie*, by the way?'

'Yeah,' Roxie admitted. 'And *Masterchef*. Then I went to bed with the new Jilly Cooper. God, real life is boring sometimes.'

'Isn't it just,' Clare agreed. 'Cuppa?'

'Cheers.'

The surgery where Clare and Roxie worked was in the small town of Amberley, a few miles from Elderchurch. There were five doctors and two practice nurses, and various clinics operated within the centre as well. Tuesday – today – meant the baby clinic, and the one day a week that Clare worked right through until six o'clock. Clare's mum would pick up Leila and Alex from school on Tuesday afternoons and spoil them rotten for three hours. It was an arrangement that everyone was happy with.

'Morning, ladies,' came a voice just as the phone rang.

'Good morning, Amberley Medical Centre, how can I help you?' Clare said, picking it up and blushing as Luke Brightside strolled into reception.

'*Morning*, Luke,' Roxie cooed, batting her eyelashes at him. 'Looking very handsome there today, if I may say so.'

'Looking very ... colourful yourself there, Roxanne,' he bantered in return, rolling his eyes comically at Clare as he walked by, a sports bag slung over one shoulder. She felt herself light up inside at his smile. For all Roxie's cheeky flirting, he *was* looking handsome. He always looked handsome. Luke was one of the GPs and he was *lovely*. He had such a kind face, such understanding, interested eyes and such a deep, sexy voice, she could see why he always had so many female patients flocking to see him. It was enough to make Clare fake an illness herself, the thought of Dr Brightside's tender bedside manner being lavished on her. In fact, she was getting a hot flush just imagining it ...

'Hello? Are you there?' came a petulant voice down the line, and Clare jerked back to the real world.

'Sorry, yes, I'm here,' she replied hastily. 'Did you say

you wanted an appointment? Let me see when we can fit you in.'

Debbie called mid-morning when she knew Clare would be on her break. Debbie had been Clare's best friend since they were both five years old and had met on their first day at Elderchurch primary school. She still lived in the village too, with her husband Will, four kids, a horse and two dogs. If Clare's life was the rural idyll gone wrong, Debbie's was the real McCoy, with the Aga and the Labradors and full acceptance from the horsey crowd, not to mention the successful husband and happy children. It hadn't always been so easy for Debbie, though – she'd had her first daughter, Lydia, when she was only sixteen, and had been chucked out of school. Then her boyfriend had done a bunk and joined the army, and Debbie had been left high and dry. Things had turned around for her, thank goodness, ever since she'd met Will, although she never took any of it for granted.

'Wotcha,' she said now. 'Just ringing to see if you want a hand on Saturday, or are you all set? I don't mind being your glamorous assistant, or I can have Alex for you, if he can't stomach the house being invaded by all those screeching girls, or . . .'

Clare laughed. Saturday was Leila's party and she was having seven girls from school round for the afternoon. Leila's dream party had originally been to invite the whole class to a roller disco at the village hall, but even when Mr Button, who did the hall bookings, had offered it to Clare at half-price and Debbie had put forward Will's services as DJ, it was still going to cost an arm and a leg, when you added in the hire of disco lights plus food for thirty children. Clare had persuaded Leila to scale things down slightly, so they were now having an 'Arts and Crafts' party at home. Clare was going to make bath-bombs with the girls, and had picked up some clear plastic boxes in the pound shop that they could decorate with acrylic paints, then fill with their bath goodies.

'I would love a glamorous assistant,' she confessed. 'An extra pair of hands would be fab. I can't help feeling this birthday is doomed, though.' And she poured out everything that had gone wrong with the bike, and the cake, and how she wasn't even sure that Steve was going to remember it was his daughter's birthday, and whether she should phone him to remind him, or, if he *had* actually remembered, whether her call would be an insult.

'Oh, mate,' Debbie said sympathetically. 'Ring the brainless berk, I would. The worst that can happen is he'll be narky with you. And so bloody what if he is. It's a lot better than Leila getting upset because she thinks he's forgotten her, right?'

'That's true,' Clare said. She glanced at her watch. 'I'd better go. Cheers, Deb. See you tomorrow.'

She'd text Steve later rather than phone, she decided, ending the call. That way he wouldn't be able to hear the desperation in her voice. That way she wouldn't have to hear *his* voice either and be reminded how happy she'd once been with him. Keep looking forward, she told herself. The future is bright. You just can't see it yet, that's all.

That night when Clare got home, sugar-loaded kids in tow, there were two things waiting for her on the doorstep.

One was a pastel-pink box that the delivery guy had left tucked behind the dustbin. Clare pulled it out to see 'Little Miss Luxury' on the address label and guessed, with a groan, that this was her sister's birthday present to Leila. Little Miss Luxury indeed. What would it be: another expensive, dry-clean-only dress with hand-stitched beads around the hem? Maybe some over-the-top jewellery that Leila would no doubt swap with one of her mates for a packet of felt-tips. Clare could lay money on the fact that it would be nothing that pony-mad tomboy Leila would be remotely interested in. Oh, well. That was Polly for you.

The second item on the doorstep was a battered-looking Quality Street tin with a Post-it stuck on the lid. 'Open when Leila isn't looking,' Clare read in Debbie's handwriting. She carried it into the kitchen and gave Fred a stern look. 'Keep away from this, if you value your life,' she warned him, and prised off the lid. Inside was a Victoria sponge with thick buttercream icing, decorated with chocolate buttons and rainbow sprinkles, and sandwiched with jam and whipped cream.

She felt like running across the field and kissing Debbie. Thank God she had her friends when everything else in her life was going tits-up.

Chapter Three

Polly wasn't quite sure how she managed the walk of shame out of Hugo Warrington's office, after his life-shattering bombshell. Somehow her legs worked robotically, one foot after the other, to take her back to the sanctuary of her desk.

Meanwhile her mind was racing with panic. Oh my God. Oh. My. Actual. GOD. She'd lost her job. She'd *lost* her *job*. How had Warrington put it again? She was being 'let go', that was it. Let go, like an animal released into the wild. Like this would liberate her. Like she should be grateful! The thing was, she didn't *want* to be released into the wild. She didn't want to go anywhere. She wanted to stay in her safe, warm cage — office, rather. Her PC, her phone, her filing cabinet . . . these were all the cornerstones of her world. These things *were* her world. What did she have, without this place? She spent more time here than in her actual apartment; she often ate dinner here, she'd even slept here occasionally on the stylish grey sofa when she was up against a deadline. And to have it all taken away from her, pulled out from under her feet ...

She clutched at the table, dizzy and light-headed. Shit. She hadn't seen that one coming. She'd had absolutely no idea. Usually you got a premonition of bad news at the firm: call it the inner radar, call it the twitching feelers, but generally you heard the whispers being passed along the grapevine. This time – nothing. Not even a knowing look. Twelve years of her life she'd given this place and they were just opening the door and pushing her out again, without a second thought. *Bastards.* Was she even going to get her bonus now? Christ! She needed that money; had already accounted for most of it. They'd better bloody cough up, or ...

She grimaced. Or what? She wasn't sure she had many options all of a sudden.

She buzzed through to Jake. 'Get me a coffee,' she said crisply. 'And make it a strong one.'

Damn. What was she going to do? Warrington had told her she had an hour to gather her things and leave the office. One measly hour. She'd wasted ten minutes already just staring around wide-eyed in horror, frozen to the spot as if rigor mortis had set in.

Her door opened and a burly guy from security appeared with an empty box. 'This for you, darling?' he asked. 'Need a hand clearing your stuff?'

Polly drew herself up to her full height, which, on these

particular heels, was an impressive five foot ten. 'No,' she said frostily.

He shrugged and dumped the box on the desk. 'Your call. Personal stuff only, all right? Everything else belongs to the company. We'll check it on the way out.'

He'd check it on the way out. Polly flushed. Like she was a common criminal, sneaking off with company secrets and juicy dossiers. The *nerve* of the man. She felt like throwing his wretched box in his porky-pink face. That would show him.

The door closed and Polly eyed the box. That was it? She was meant to fit twelve years' worth of belongings into *that*? He had to be joking. Did he not realize just how long she'd worked here? She could fill it five times over without breaking a sweat. She shut her eyes for a few seconds, fists clenched at her sides. Then she took a deep breath. She'd better get on with it.

When Jake came in with her coffee, he stopped and stared. 'What ... what's going on?'

Polly paused from unhooking a framed certificate on the wall. She'd already taken down the outfits that hung on the back of her door in case of an emergency meeting or a last-minute-invitation to a do. The wine-coloured dress, sparkly black shrug and slate-grey bouclé jacket were now slumped over her desk like dead bodies. 'I've got the boot,' she replied with a hollow laugh. 'Been made redundant.'

Jake looked from Polly to the box and then back at Polly. 'Really?'

She nodded, feeling small. Worse than small, actually — insignificant. Just one little cog that was being removed from the machine after spinning diligently as part of its mechanism for what felt like forever. 'Yep. Got to leave by eleven, Warrington said.'

'Bloody hell. So ... so what happens now?'

'Well ...' She paused and shook back her hair. She mustn't let him see how rattled she was. 'Well, I'll get something else, of course. With all my contacts, there's bound to be—'

'I didn't mean *you*,' he said, talking over her. Was that scorn she could detect in his voice? 'I meant, what's going to happen in the department? What does this mean for me, for the rest of us?'

'For you?' She stared at him, taken aback. Of all the self-centred things to ask. 'Well, I don't know. I'm afraid I hadn't thought about you,' she said, sarcasm biting into her words. 'I dare say they'll find something for you to do.'

He wasn't listening, though. His face was still and pensive, as if he were tuning into some telepathic thought-wave beamed to him from elsewhere in the building. Then his expression cleared. He smiled. 'Ah, okay, I get it. Marcus was dropping hints the other day about me and him being a good team. Said something about a new position opening up for him. I bet he'll be moving up the ladder, with you going.'

Polly stiffened. 'Marcus Handbury?'

'Yeah. He's been acting mysterious for a few days. Reckon Warrington must have lined him up to take over your work once you've gone.'

'But he can't just have my job if I've been made redundant!' she cried. 'It's not meant to work like that.'

He shrugged. 'Well, they'll call the position something different then, won't they? That's what they usually do.'

His tactlessness made Polly reel. 'Jake ... I've lost my *job*,' she said tartly. 'You could at least show some sympathy.'

His face hardened. 'Sympathy?' he echoed. '*Sympathy?* You're joking, aren't you?' His lip curled. 'This is the best news I've had all year.'

She took a step back, bewildered. She never usually felt bewildered. It was an unfamiliar and distinctly unsettling experience. Why was Jake being so rude? 'I ... I ...' she croaked, eyes bulging. 'I don't understand.'

He gave her a tight, flinty smile. 'I have bust a gut for you over the last few years,' he said, his voice loaded with contempt. 'I've not just been your PA, I've been your shit-shoveller too, doing all your dirty work: your dry-fucking-cleaning, your bloody bill-paying, buying presents for your sodding niece and nephew and Uncle-Tom-fucking-

Cobley . . .' He shook his head, his gaze never leaving hers. 'It's not been the most fun job, you know, but I've done it without complaining. I've done it even though these things have not been in my remit. And yet you've never said please. You've never said thank you. You've never even asked anything about me, about how I'm doing. You're like a fucking replicant. So no, I'm not sorry you're leaving. Good-fucking-riddance, that's what I say.'

He stormed out, leaving Polly staring after him. She swallowed hard. 'Th-th-thanks for the coffee,' she stammered, but the words fell uselessly into the silence of the room.

Thirty minutes later Polly had finished packing. It hadn't taken as long as she'd anticipated. It turned out she had surprisingly little that belonged to her. A few mugs. A spare pair of tights. A half-eaten bag of Haribos. Gum. A packet of paracetamol. Clothes. Certificates. A couple of personal cards sent by satisfied clients. That was the sum total of her twelve years in the place. The collection of items had barely filled the box, after all.

Once she'd collected everything together, she gazed around at the filing cabinets full of documents she'd lovingly written, reports she'd painstakingly compiled, letters she'd dictated, contracts she'd signed . . . All for nothing, now.

Those files and folders would be inherited by Marcus-effing-Handbury within hours, by the sound of it.

She was gripped by a surge of vengeful feeling. How easy it would be to steal a wedge of sensitive documents, she thought, a memory stick with the juiciest negotiations, a folder of incriminating emails, passwords to different accounts ... She could do it. She could stitch up Waterman's good and proper, and why the hell not, after the appalling way they'd treated her?

Then she drooped, remembering the security guard's warning about how he was going to check her belongings on the way out. That was why.

Still, a memory stick was small enough to conceal somewhere about her body, wasn't it? She could hide it under a tissue in her pocket, or down in her shoe. Hell, she could tuck it in her knickers, even; they were hardly going to strip-search her. Were they?

She hesitated. Polly was used to taking risks throughout her career, calculated risks, which usually resulted in a lot of money. So the big question was: did she have the balls to attempt to rip off her own company?

Yes, she did, actually. She most certainly did. Polly Johnson wasn't going to be made to look a fool by anyone. She'd have the last laugh, she thought, clicking the mouse to awaken her PC from standby. She'd forward a whole bunch of stuff to her personal email account and then ...

Oh. That was strange. She couldn't get into the company email system any more. A box with 'Unauthorized user' had appeared onscreen. Unauthorized user ... had they locked her out of the email network already? They had. The bastards!

Sod it, if they were going to play hardball, then so would she. She'd go the whole hog and put some stuff on a memory stick, she decided. In for a penny, in for the whole redundancy package. She tried to open a document, but again, the words 'Unauthorized user' appeared. Her courage shrivelled away inside her and she leaned back in her chair, feeling defeated. They'd locked her out of the whole system, she realized. It was as if she were pressing her nose up against the window of the building, no longer allowed to see inside. God, that hurt. How could they be so mistrustful, so defensive? It wasn't as if she'd been about to bring them down, steal all their secrets, attack from the inside, was it?

Well, all right, she had been tempted. So much for that, though. It clearly wasn't going to happen. Just for a second she was seized by the mad impulse to grab some of the folders from the filing cabinets and chuck them out of the window, watch them flutter down to Bishopsgate, pages fluttering in the breeze, like doves released by a magician. Then she could hurry downstairs and retrieve them from the pavement, and—

'Ready for the off?'

The security guard had appeared in her office again; had walked straight in without knocking. She was about to reprimand him for his lack of courtesy, but then remembered. She no longer had that sort of right around here.

'Just about,' she said, hoping he hadn't noticed the deranged way she'd been eyeballing the filing cabinet.

'Right, let's be having you then.'

She rolled her eyes, seething as she picked up the box and followed him out. He was actually going to escort her off the premises. Worse, he was using phrases like 'Let's be having you', as if he thought he was some kind of hot-shot cop, when he was just a jumped-up security guard, getting a kick out of someone else's misfortune. How pathetic.

Still, at least he had a job.

The walk through the open-plan area of the department to the lifts felt like the longest journey Polly had ever made. Everyone was staring. 'Oh my God, are you leaving? Have they *sacked* you?' cried Gloria, an ageing secretary who seemed to have been with the company since it had been established in the nineteenth century.

'Redundant,' was all Polly could get out through gritted teeth.

Gasps went from assistant to assistant like a breathy breeze around the room. *Redundant? Did she just say redundant?*

Jake was at the photocopier as she approached the lift. She'd have to walk right past him. Should she stick her nose in the air and flounce by, or stop and thank him for his work, say goodbye?

She hesitated and then, at the last moment, he looked up at her with what seemed to be gloating in his eyes. 'Bye Polly,' he said, his lip puckering in a smirk.

Any words of thanks she might have spoken vanished instantly from her tongue; any olive branch was immediately smashed into bits. He could whistle for thanks now. She completely ignored him and strode on towards the lift, her heart pounding.

'Bitch,' she heard him mutter, and the blood throbbed hard beneath her skin.

She had never been more relieved to see the lift doors part before her. She stepped into the waiting metal box and kept herself rigid and upright until the silver doors closed and they plunged to the ground.

'Going down,' the disembodied voice announced.

Goodbye, seventh floor, Polly thought in a daze. Goodbye, Jake and Gloria and all those assistants whose names I never bothered learning. Goodbye, corner office; goodbye, fabulous view over London. I'll never see you again.

'Ground floor,' came the voice from the lift's speakers, and the doors shuddered apart once more.

Polly felt wobbly on her heels as she stepped numbly into the reception area, where the security guard led her to a small side-office. Goodbye, life, she thought. I'm going to miss you.

Once the contents of her box had been examined (talk about humiliating), she had to hand over her security pass, her laptop, her company credit card and, worst of all, her BlackBerry. It felt like having a limb removed. Goodbye, BlackBerry. I really loved you.

'Sign here please, Miss Johnson,' the security guard said, passing her a pen and showing her the dotted line. 'Thank you,' he went on, as she shakily scrawled her signature. 'That's it, then.'

That was it? Polly blinked. She'd been removed from her office, had her possessions – okay, the company's possessions – stripped from her, and she was now being shown the door, all in the space of a few hours? Where was the humanity in these people? How could they dismiss her so quickly, as if she were nothing to them?

She remembered with a lurch the last round of redundancies two years ago. She'd gazed on dispassionately as a middle manager, a junior analyst and a couple of assistants had lost their jobs in the same morning. An uneasy silence had skulked around the department while they weepily packed up and left. The sombre atmosphere lasted several hours, and then afterwards it was as if the remaining staff were demob happy – laughing too loudly at the smallest of jokes, relief painted in broad strokes across every face, that it wasn't them who'd just been binned. As for Polly, she hadn't paid the whole thing much attention, other than to put on a grave face when the job losses had been discussed in board meetings earlier. Shit happened. Hell, in her job she'd advised numerous companies to make countless redundancies over the years. Privately she hadn't cared. They had been numbers on a page.

Now it was as if those numbers were springing off the page, materializing into human form one by one, person by person. Her. She envisaged the seventh floor exchanging the same nervous banter in the wake of her departure – the rather-her-than-me expressions, the there-but-for-the-grace-of-Mr-Warrington reflections. They wouldn't care for long, just as she hadn't. She would be forgotten by the afternoon, with all the excitement of Marcus moving into her office. Bloody Marcus Handbury. She felt like making a break for it past the security guard and rugby-tackling him in the corridor, pelting him with her fists.

'Miss Johnson?' the guard prompted, and she jerked back to the here and now.

'Right,' she said. 'So ... that's it? No exit interview or anything?'

He shook his head. 'The HR team will contact you with

the official redundancy package, plus information about claiming benefits or . . .'

Polly glared at him and he ground to a halt. Claiming benefits? What was the man *talking* about? 'Very well,' she said curtly. 'Perhaps you could call me a cab home.' Her voice brooked no argument; it was the least the stinking company could do, now they'd stolen everything else from her.

'Of course,' he said, dialling a number and speaking a few words into the phone. He turned back to her. 'Your postcode?'

'SE1,' she replied, trying to load it with as much haughtiness as she could muster. Her apartment on the embankment seemed like a glittering refuge all of a sudden. She would barricade herself in there, get into bed and pull the duvet over her head, block out the rest of the world for as long as possible.

Maybe she would wake up and this entire morning would have been a bad dream. She hoped.

She barely noticed the London streets flashing by as the cab took her back over the Thames to her flat. She kept glancing at the contents of her box – the tights, the sweets, the smart clothes – still unable to believe what was happening. As the driver pulled up outside her building, she wondered for a moment if she would have to pay for the journey (surely Waterman's had stumped up for the cab fare, hadn't they?), but thankfully the driver merely produced a chit for her to sign and didn't charge her.

She remembered to thank him — Jake's words ringing dreadfully in her ears — then let herself into the apartment block and took the lift to her floor. Bloody hell. Her legs were shaking, her head was spinning, her eyes were filling with tears. She blinked fiercely. *Don't cry*, she ordered herself. Stuff them. If they didn't appreciate her, there would be plenty of other people who did. Henry Curtis, for one, the guy who'd been pestering her to meet him for dinner. He'd be first on her list of contacts to call. He'd snap her up in an instant.

She fumbled with her key in the apartment door, the box of stuff balanced awkwardly on her hip. She'd held herself together remarkably well, given the circumstances. Not a sniffle, not a tear, not even an argument. Such dignity, such control. But then her self-congratulation gave way to doubt. Why hadn't she put up a fight? Why hadn't she made a defence case more forcefully to Warrington, told him the company couldn't afford to lose her? Instead she'd been so numb with the shock that she'd taken everything they'd thrown at her without a murmur. What an idiot she'd been.

Well, the first thing she was going to do when she got

in, she thought, finally managing to shove open her door and walk through, was—

Someone screamed. Polly screamed too, dropping the box so that it thumped down onto the carpet. There was a strange woman brandishing a Hoover nozzle at her, with a ferocious look on her face. Then the woman clapped a hand to her chest and laughed in relief. 'Ah! You are she? You are lady, Miss Johnson?'

Polly gathered herself. Oh, Christ. The cleaner. Exactly what she *didn't* need right now, some strange woman in her flat, who couldn't even speak proper English. 'Yes, I am Miss Johnson,' she said in her talking-to-foreigners voice, loud and over-enunciated. She bent down and picked up the box. 'Look,' she said wearily, 'just go, will you? I want to be on my own.'

'I am Magda,' the cleaner said, without being asked. She was in her twenties at a guess, slim and slight in tight grey jeans and purple Crocs. She had bobbed dark hair with a bright-red streak in one side, lots of earrings and an attitude. 'Soon finish.'

'No, finish *now*,' Polly ordered, irritation spiking through her. Stupid woman. Today of all days was not the right time for the cleaner to start arguing with her.

Magda shrugged. 'I no mop floor yet,' she said. 'And why you here, Miss Johnson? You have holiday?'

'No, I don't have ... Look, just push off, all right? Leave! I don't care about the mopping. Just leave me in peace.'

Magda stared coolly at this blotchy-faced, high-pitched, shrill woman standing there in her suit and heels. So she thought she could look down on Magda, did she, just because Magda was the unlucky one who had to clean her toilet and scrub her shower? How dare she start playing the big lady to Magda, who sweated, who slaved, who slogged, and all for a miserable pittance? Ha!

Magda folded her arms mutinously across her chest. 'I am here for three hours,' she said. 'I stay for three hours.'

'Oh for crying out loud,' Polly yelled. 'Is this about your poxy pay? Fine, I'll pay you for three hours then. Do I look like I care about an extra half an hour, or whatever it is? Well, I don't. So ...'

But Magda didn't appear to be listening. She'd dumped the Hoover nozzle right there on the floor and was shrugging on a denim jacket that she'd left on the hall table, along with a tiny khaki shoulder-bag.

'Okay, I go,' she said, pausing a moment to check her hair in Polly's large hall mirror. 'No need to shout at me, Miss Johnson. I only want to do my job.'

Cool as anything, she walked past Polly, nose in the air, and out the front door. Polly shut it thankfully after her, only realizing then that she had no idea where she should put the Hoover away.

She leaned against the front door and closed her eyes for a moment. Now what?

It was weird being at home on a Tuesday. It was still only eleven-thirty and the rest of the day stretched blankly before her. Twitchy and restless, Polly wandered through the empty rooms of her flat, seeing it all through new eyes. Her enormous black leather sofas and the flat-screen plasma TV . . . she'd hardly used them, now that she thought about it. She wasn't the sort of saddo who sat and watched TV on her own every night, after all; she was always out with the gang in the Red House, or at a function or launch or evening drinks, mingling her butt off, toasting the latest success. Even at weekends she tended not to slob out in here; she'd often end up in the office, promising herself that she'd catch up for a few hours there, only to blink and realize that it was somehow seven in the evening and she'd spent the whole day at work again.

And now every day was going to be shockingly empty, just like that. A two-minute conversation with Drongo Warrington and her life had imploded. What was left for her to do?

She sat experimentally on one of the sofas. Quite comfortable really. She kicked off her heels and tucked her feet up underneath herself. Even better. She stared around the room wonderingly. What did people *do* with themselves all day, when they didn't have a high-powered job in the City? Clare, for example, her sister. She only worked a few measly hours a day and spent the rest of the time mooning about at home. Doing what, exactly? Cleaning? Washing? Ironing the kids' school uniforms?

Polly shuddered. Poor thing; she couldn't imagine anything worse. She stood up, about to check her emails, before remembering that she no longer had a BlackBerry. Or the company laptop. Christ. She sat down again, putting her head in her hands. Talk about a blow, losing all those contacts in one swoop. Why had she never thought to back them up? She had to get hold of some new kit immediately.

But first ... Hell, this was the first actual day off she'd had in months. How did she work the TV again?

Chapter Four

'Happy birthday to you,
Happy birthday to you,
Happy birthday dear Leila
Happy birthday to you.'

'Make a wish,' Clare urged as she, Alex and her parents finished singing. Leila leaned forward, her face softly lit by the ten flickering candles, then blew out all the flames in one breath.

Leila shut her eyes, and Clare saw her lips twitch as she murmured something to herself. What was she wishing for? World peace, the biggest slice of cake, or something even more important, like those trainers she'd been eyeing up in JJB Sports?

Clare sniffled, softening with love for her beautiful ten-year-old daughter, who'd been born in this very room in the birthing pool they'd hired for the occasion. Steve had really wanted her to give birth in the cottage hospital twelve miles away – he didn't want to see all that blood and gore in his own house, he said – but Clare had put her foot down. She hated hospitals, after what had happened with Michael. She wasn't going anywhere.

And so Leila Grace Berry had made her way into the world in their warm, candlelit kitchen, the heart of the home. When she'd finally slipped between Clare's legs into the pool, Clare had pulled her up through the water to take her first breaths. 'Hello,' she'd said, half-laughing, half-crying as she clasped her baby's soft, wet head against her body. 'It's me, it's Mummy. Hello.'

Tears appeared in Clare's eyes at the memory and she smiled across at her girl, that baby who'd grown up into this bewitching creature with such a cloud of blonde dandelion-fluff hair, cat-like green eyes and freckles like fairy kisses all across her nose. Her girl, who'd been with her in the world for ten years now. She hugged her with a sudden fierceness. 'Happy birthday, darling,' she said.

'Uh-oh,' Alex warned. 'Mum's getting all soppy. Here we go: boo-hoo, wah-wah.' He scrunched his hands into fists and pretended to rub his eyes like a toddler. Everyone laughed, and Clare ruffled his hair.

'Thank goodness we've got this cake to stop me blubbing,' she joked. 'Who wants a slice, then?'

'Me!' chorused the children with such gusto that Clare's dad, Graham, pretended he'd gone deaf in one ear.

'Flipping 'eck,' he grumbled. 'That was almost as loud as Grandma's snores. Better make it a big slice for me, I need something sweet for the shock.'

Karen, Clare's long-suffering mum, rolled her eyes. 'Ignore grumpy Grandad,' she told everyone. 'He's telling porkies again; I think he's losing his marbles in his old age. I'd love a slice, please, Clare. It's not every day your eldest granddaughter hits double figures now, is it?'

'It's not,' Clare agreed. She was planning to have a massive wedge of cake herself; Debbie was brilliant at baking. Sod the image of denim shorts flashing past her eyes. Sod her bumpy, cellulite-pocked thighs and her soft, squidgy belly that would never be bared in a bikini again. It was a special day, and special days required cake. And so far, today had gone remarkably well. Somehow or other (via Debbie, probably) Jay Holmes, the village wide-boy, had heard that Clare was after a bike for Leila's birthday and had turned up last night with a rather knackered-looking girl's chopper.

'I know it's not much to look at right now,' he'd said apologetically as Clare's eyes flickered doubtfully over the tatty blue paintwork, spattered with mud, and the worryingly balding front tyre. 'But I reckon we could do it up between us, don't you?'

'What – now?' Clare had asked, unconvinced.

He'd shrugged. 'Why not? We can scrub her up, and I've

got some old bits of paint we could use: lilac, rose, turquoise...' He pulled them out of a carrier bag like a conjuror producing rabbits. 'Worth a go, isn't it?'

'And how much is this going to cost me?' Clare asked, folding her arms across her chest, leaning against the doorjamb. Knowing Jay, he wasn't doing this out of the goodness of his heart.

He shrugged. 'Fifty quid? Forty-five, if you help clean it up.'

Clare hesitated. Forty-five pounds was going to be a stretch. 'Forty?' she tried.

He thrust his hand towards her all too keenly; she immediately wished she'd started the bargaining at ten pounds lower. 'Done,' he said, pumping her hand up and down. The porch light was reflected in his dark eyes, like sparkles. He was good-looking, Jay, if you liked that sort of thing. Clare didn't. He was too rough and ready for her, too unshaven and scruffy, with black wavy hair that was well overdue a cut, and a hole in his jeans. 'Are you going to let me in then, or are you going to leave me standing out here all night?'

She laughed. Four years older than her, Jay was a charmer, and she didn't trust him as far as she could throw him, but you couldn't help liking him all the same. 'Go round the back,' she said. 'I'm not having this muddy thing wheeled through the house.'

'Got it,' he said, vanishing into the shadows.

She let him in through the back door, and they propped the bike against the kitchen table while they scrubbed the frame and Jay pumped up the tyres.

'How's your sister?' he asked after a few minutes of companionable silence. Hilarious as it might seem now, back in the sixth form Polly and Jay had been boyfriend and girlfriend, for almost a year. A more incongruous pairing you couldn't imagine these days, of course. She could just picture the look of disdain on Polly's face if she clapped eyes on Jay now – hilarious.

'She's all right,' Clare said dismissively. 'Making squillions of pounds in the Big Smoke. Haven't seen her for months; last time was Christmas, when she just bored on about her job and annoyed Mum by making so-called important calls all the way through *Gavin & Stacey*.'

Jay shook his head, looking amused. 'True Londoner now, isn't she?'

'You can say that again,' Clare replied. 'Turns her nose up at us bumpkins big-time.'

The bike was cleaning up nicely. The grips on the handlebars had been grimy and greying, but were becoming brighter and whiter as she set about them with a scrubbing brush. The wheels spun easily, once Jay had oiled them. The leather saddle, however, was cracked and old, and looked beyond repair. 'Hmmm, I wonder . . .' Clare murmured, rocking back on her heels and thinking. She had an ancient lilac fake-fur bag upstairs that she'd been meaning to customize for Leila. If she cut it up instead, the fabric would make a perfect seat-cover for the bike. 'Back in a sec,' she said, hurrying out of the room.

It was gone ten o'clock by the time they'd finished painting and primping the bike. Its frame now gleamed metallic lilac, the tyres were pumped up, and Clare had made a furry cover for the old saddle. 'It'll need new tyres before too long,' Jay said, peering at them closely. 'This front one is pretty shot, but it'll do for a while. I'll keep an eye out for you.'

'Cheers,' Clare replied. She could have hugged him. Instead she took two twenty-pound notes from her purse and handed them over. 'You saved the day,' she said.

By morning the paint was dry, and Leila's scream of excitement echoed around the house when she saw it there in the kitchen. 'Oh, wow! What a cool bike,' she said. 'What a cool ... um ... weird sort of bike,' she added as she drew nearer it, her eye taking in the distinctive chopper frame and the furry saddle. 'Thanks, Mum.'

So yes, Clare thought, passing her daughter a slice of birthday cake, it had turned out all right in the end. She'd pulled off another budget birthday somehow, without anyone feeling hard done by, even if some of the 'presents'

Leila had unwrapped had been promises Clare had written out and wrapped in sparkly paper and tinsel.

I promise ... to take you for the longest bike ride ever, with a huuuge picnic at the end of it!
I promise ... you can invite THREE friends round for a sleepover next weekend. Pizza and DVD included!

She'd found a couple of pony books in mint condition in the charity shop in Amberley, and a pretty charm bracelet for only two pounds from the same place. She'd spun out the presents by making them part of a treasure hunt around the house, and Leila had loved solving the clues and rushing to the next hiding place, still in pyjamas and dressing gown. You didn't have to spend a fortune to make things feel special.

The phone rang just as she was about to bite into her cake. 'Do you want to get that, birthday girl?' Clare asked.

Leila jumped up. 'I bet it's Dad,' she said. 'Or Aunty Polly.'

Clare and her mum exchanged glances. 'Don't hold your breath,' Clare muttered as Leila ran to grab the phone. Polly had come up trumps this time on the present front, with a Roberto Cavalli pink silk dress complete with ruffles, an enormous sash and a fake-fur hem. Leila had burst out laughing when she'd opened it this morning; it was about as far removed from her tomboyish style as it was possible to get. Polly might well splash the cash – Clare had once looked up the price of another outfit she'd sent, to see that the dress alone had cost over three hundred pounds (think what you could buy with that in Primark!), but she wasn't so good on the actual aunty stuff. There would be no phone call from her, no actual personal contact involved, you could bet the matching Cavalli beaded pumps on it.

'Hi, Dad,' she heard Leila say and looked over to see her daughter's face wreathed in smiles. 'Thanks. We're just having the cake.'

Clare felt a bitter-sweet ache inside. She still missed having her husband around, however much she tried to tough it out alone. On days like this, especially, she would have loved him to be there too, to share his daughter's special celebration. It broke her heart that he could have rejected all of this to go off with bloody Denise. She picked up her cake and then put it down again. Suddenly she'd lost her appetite.

Still, Leila was smiling. Steve had remembered to phone. That was what mattered, wasn't it?

Saturday began as usual with the children's swimming lessons in Amberley. Clare had 'history' with Amberley

Leisure Centre and could never walk into its hot, chlorine-tangy reception without a flashback to her youth. She'd been a good swimmer from the word go – it was the one and only talent she had that her brother and sister couldn't beat her on. When you were the third and youngest child in a family, such things were important.

She'd joined the Junior Dolphins club at Amberley, had trained and raced there four nights a week between the ages of nine and fourteen, perfecting her technique, steadily improving her personal-best times. She learned how to control her breathing, how to execute the perfect butterfly stroke, how to tumble-turn, how to dive. By the age of eleven she was representing the club in county trials, and was picked for the county squad when she was thirteen. There had been talk of special coaching, and vague, optimistic mentions of international championships, the Olympics even.

Then Michael had died, and everything changed. She'd never swum again, apart from one single emergency, which had caused her life to swerve in a whole new direction.

'Two for lessons, please,' she said, flashing their passes as they went past the doughy-faced woman on reception who was on the phone.

She helped Leila and Alex change and handed them over to their teacher, then wandered up to the spectator area to watch them. Leila was a confident, easy swimmer. She was fast and clean in the water, and her technique was naturally good. Her teacher, Ben, had suggested that she join the Junior Dolphins club (they still called it that, twenty years later), but so far Clare had put off making a decision. Maybe when Leila's ten, she'd been telling herself for the last year. She'd have to come up with a new excuse now.

Alex wasn't as competent as his sister in the water. He tended to panic and flail about nervously whenever he was out of his depth, legs churning, his pale, skinny body wrestling to stay afloat. Clare found herself watching him like a hawk, ready to yell out to the lifeguard that he needed help at any given moment. He was doing all right today, though, she noted thankfully.

It was through swimming that she'd met Steve in the first place, that fateful holiday in Gran Canaria with the girls. They'd been just twenty then, her, Debbie and Maria, and it was Debbie's first trip away from little Lydia, who was having a holiday of her own with Debbie's parents in Bournemouth. The three mates had jetted off with their bikinis, clubbing outfits and high heels, then proceeded to large it up good and proper in the Old Town every evening, drinking sangria cocktails and dancing flirtatiously with the swarthy Spaniards and the drunk, sunburned Brits. Clare had had her eye on a dark-haired Mancunian bloke in particular – they'd snogged for hours in a corner of the sweaty, pulsing club one night, and she was hoping for a rematch.

The following evening she and the girls were on their way out to their favourite nightclub, their heels clicking through the stone paths of the pool complex, the air still warm and scented with almond blossom. Then Clare spotted the body in the water.

It was about nine at night and the pool area was deserted by then, the white plastic sun loungers stacked up at one side to await tomorrow's scantily clad bodies, a lone orange armband bobbing in the children's pool, the rushing waterfall slide silenced and still. And there he was, a limp figure in the main pool, face-downwards.

'Shit!' Clare exclaimed, adrenalin pumping through her when she saw him. A single heartbeat later, she'd kicked off her shoes and instinctively dived in.

It was the first time she'd swum in six years, but her body remembered what to do. With three swift strokes she'd reached him and tried to flip him over, so that his head was out of the water. The man was a dead weight, fully dressed, unmoving, but the shock of the freezing water and the enormity of the situation lent her strength. She dimly registered Debbie and Maria screaming for help and then, after several increasingly desperate attempts, Clare managed to haul him over so that he was lying on his back.

His eyes were shut; she couldn't tell if he was breathing. And oh, he was so bloody heavy.

She towed him to the side, keeping his head above the water. His body was inert and his weight dragged her down. No way, something inside her said grimly; we are both getting out of this pool, and that's that.

People came running to help, thank God. Diners from the restaurant, a waiter, some other men. They helped Clare heave him out onto the spongy green AstroTurf, and the waiter crouched down and tipped the man's head back to administer CPR. Black spots were dancing before Clare's eyes now; she was on the verge of a panic attack and her breath felt shallow. In the nick of time, a pair of strong hands grabbed her beneath her armpits and pulled her out, shivering and dripping wet onto the side of the pool, her silky black minidress clinging to her like a second skin. It had cost a bomb in River Island too, that dress, she remembered thinking at the time. Then someone put a blanket around her and she passed out.

The man survived, thanks to Clare's instinctive bravery. It turned out he'd been drinking all day and had decided to take an impromptu dip, unknown to his mates. 'You saved my life,' he said shakily to Clare when she saw him later on in hospital. 'You've got to let me take you out for dinner sometime, it's the least I can do. I'm Steve, by the way.'

'Clare,' she'd replied.

You could look at his rescue as some kind of atonement for what had happened to Michael — that was what Debbie and Maria kept saying. Clare didn't see it like that, though. One right didn't cancel out a wrong. Didn't come close.

Nonetheless, it was strange how fate brought people together. There had been hundreds of holidaymakers staying at the hotel that week — maybe even a thousand. Clare might never have met Steve if they hadn't taken that particular route through the hotel that night; if Maria hadn't done one of her last-minute outfit changes, making them ten minutes later than usual; if . . . if . . .

It could have turned out so differently. She might have hooked up with the Mancunian and be living up north with him and a clutch of flat-vowelled dark-haired children by now. She might even have fallen for one of the locals (that heroic waiter perhaps) and decided to settle in Gran Canaria for the rest of her life. But then of course she'd never have had Leila and Alex, and they were worth any amount of marital disappointment that she'd suffered with Steve.

She was grateful to him for them, at least. Overwhelmingly grateful to have them, to love them, to be their mum. All the same, if she ever came across her ex-husband in a drowning situation again, next time she might be tempted to carry on walking.

Chapter Five

Polly felt as if she had been dumped in a parallel universe. There might be the same anxious face as ever staring back from the bathroom mirror, but Polly wasn't sure who the person in the reflection was any more.

For so many years her job had defined her, it had completely shaped her life. The long hours, the corporate uniform, the meetings, the number-crunching, the conferences, the kudos, the glamour, the top-whack salary – that was her. She'd always had an office to go to, always had a diary stuffed with appointments for months in advance.

All those things had gone now, in the blink of an eye. What, Polly wondered, was left? London, Paris, New York, Hong Kong . . . the world had suddenly shrunk to the space within her flat.

The first day of her redundancy she'd tried to act as if everything was normal. She'd abandoned the TV when she couldn't find the remote (that wretched cleaner must have hidden it somewhere) and decided to be proactive instead.

Treat this whole incident as a challenge, she'd instructed herself. Jump straight back on that horse before it tramples you into the mud. She'd fired up her computer and unearthed her CV, then spent an hour or so buffing it to perfection, adding every shred of experience and expertise she could think of. During her career she'd had to sift through hundreds of other people's CVs and application letters over the years. She knew how to make hers utterly killer.

She nodded with satisfaction when she'd got it to her liking. Damn, she was kick-ass on paper. Almost as kick-ass as she was in person. Getting another job was not going to be a problem for Polly Johnson, not with this document in her armoury.

The next task was to hunt for the perfect new employer. The big four were always hiring and firing, and she knew plenty of names in them all, thanks to her years of tireless networking. She'd pull a few strings, milk her contacts and get her CV in to the very best in-trays, just see if she didn't.

It was only a matter of time.

'Hi, yeah, could you put me through to Alison Rothman. This is Polly Johnson.' She perched on the edge of her seat, tapping her pen impatiently as she waited to be connected. 'Alison, hi, it's Polly Johnson from W— It's Polly Johnson here,' she said, correcting herself at the last second. She wasn't 'Polly Johnson from Waterman's' any longer. Her name felt odd without the usual addition, as if she'd been abruptly shorn. 'Just putting the feelers out that I'm looking to take on a new challenge at a different firm,' she went on breezily, 'and wondering if ... Oh.' The words dried on her tongue. 'Really? Okay. Do you think ... Oh. All right then. Thanks, Alison. Let's hook up soon, yeah? Bye.'

Damn. CVDS weren't hiring. In fact, Alison said, they were undergoing a similar reshuffle involving redundancies. Not a good time to be jumping ship, babe, Alison had said in her breathy, Sloanesville voice. Polly didn't think it worth mentioning that she'd already been pushed overboard.

Still, she'd wing her CV to the HR department anyway, mention her old friendship with Larry Truman, the Vice-President of the European Investment Banking division, see if that stirred any sparks. There *was* no old friendship of course, they'd merely sat next to each other at a conference dinner in Zurich about five years ago, but it was better than nothing.

She picked up the phone and dialled again. 'I'd like to speak to Henry Curtis,' she said in her most clipped tones. You had to talk to receptionists like that, she'd learned, not wuss about with a simpering 'please' and 'thank you', otherwise they didn't take you seriously. 'It's Polly Johnson.'

She heard the line buzz and then ring. She had a good feeling about this. She was sure Henry Curtis had wanted to poach her – he'd be delighted that she was a free agent now. She smirked. Show me the money, Henry, she imagined herself ordering him. Show me the goddamn money!

A young female voice answered. 'Henry Curtis's office, this is Sasha speaking, how may I—?'

'Put me through to him, please. Polly Johnson,' she interrupted.

There was a moment's hesitation. Polly imagined Little Miss Sasha quivering on her swivel seat. 'Um ... ahh,' she said tentatively. 'We've already had word from Waterman's about the meeting being rearranged, so ...'

Polly frowned. 'What are you talking about?'

'Mr Curtis is booked in to see ... ahh ... Mr Handbury now next week. It's very nice of you to let us know that the situation has changed, though, thank you.'

Polly opened her mouth, but her powers of speech seemed to have deserted her. 'Er ...' she managed after a moment. 'If Henry is around for a chat, I could perhaps—'

'Mr Curtis is very busy, I'm afraid,' Sasha said. Was she actually *typing* while she spoke? So rude. 'Thanks, anyway. Goodbye.'

'I ...' Polly tried, but there was just a click, and then the dial tone burring in her ear. She sat there smarting for a few moments. That turncoat, Jake! He'd wasted no time in delivering news of Polly's redundancy to Big Cheese Curtis, then. And the receptionist couldn't get rid of her quickly enough, either.

Screw them all. She'd send Curtis her CV anyway. He'd probably be mortified if he knew how unprofessional his assistant had just been. In the meantime ... She pulled up another phone number onscreen and began dialling. Let's see if Alan March at Ernst & Young had better news for her.

By the end of the day Polly had contacted everyone she could think of, but the story seemed to be the same everywhere. Nobody was hiring. Everybody was firing, or 'letting staff go', as Hugo Warrington had so delicately put it. 'I'd sit tight if I were you, Poll,' Hilary Armstrong from Andersen had advised plummily. 'Give it a year before the market settles.'

But Polly didn't have a year, she felt like screaming into the mouthpiece. She didn't even want one week without a job, let alone any longer. Someone *had* to take her on; she was too good for them not to. She'd been a grafter her whole life – experience like hers was a valuable commodity in the volatile world of banking. More to the point, now that she wasn't going to get her bonus, she needed some bloody money.

She turned off the PC, her shoulders stiff from where she'd hunched over it for so long, her eyes red and sore. God, it was quiet in here. She suddenly longed to see another human being, to hear the buzz and laughter of conversation around her, to moan about the mutha of a day she'd just had. More to the point, see someone who might be able to point her in the direction of her next career path.

She dialled the number of a cab firm and booked a car to the Red House before she could change her mind.

Walking into the Red House was like walking into a comforting embrace: the smell of perfume and cocktails, the pop of champagne corks, the whoops and cheers of a group of City boys . . . it was exactly what she needed. The opulent red velvet walls were like a womb around her; she was back on her home turf after the disconcerting events of the morning. It made her feel that the rest of the day might possibly have been a hallucination brought on by overwork. For those few short moments, as she strode towards the bar, it was as if the world was still spinning on its rightful axis, and everything was going to be okay.

She waited at the bar, gratified that it was just the same as ever. She knew the faces of the bar staff better than those of her own family, could recite the bar menu backwards if you asked her to. She knew exactly what she was going to order too: a bottle of the vintage Taittinger, a chicken-Caesar salad and some of the house-special spicy potato wedges. She would fill her glass with the best kind of bubbly and celebrate a new start. A new chapter. Okay, so she had no idea what this new start was going to *be*, but it was worth celebrating, Polly reckoned. Change was good, wasn't it? She tried not to think about the phrase 'drowning one's sorrows' while she waited to be served.

Who was in tonight then; anyone she knew? She scanned the room beadily. There was a group of male banky types, none of them familiar to Polly, discussing something earnestly around a champagne bucket. A hatchet-faced silver-haired woman and her tweedy male companion – they looked a bit scary and unapproachable. Ah, there were a couple of people she vaguely recognized from the business pages: brick-cheeked Charles Quarry, who was obscenely rich and very well connected; helmet-haired Selina Constable, the formidable CEO at the London office of Hartson International; and Elliot McCarthy, the rangy, dynamic New York banking mogul, currently stirring things up at Drake & Foreman.

A plan appeared in Polly's mind in the very next second. It was simple. She'd go over there and introduce herself, press a business card into each of their palms and persuade one of them – all of them – that they'd met their new company star. Jackpot!

She'd just have a swift drink first, she decided as the barmaid laid out a slim champagne glass and a silver ice bucket, and uncorked the Taittinger. She'd bolster her nerve, run through a few killer lines in her head, then seize the moment. Oh yes.

Polly took herself over to a table near Charles Quarry and his cohorts and sipped her champagne thoughtfully. Damn, that first mouthful was good: cold and dry and fizzing on her tongue.

Hi, I'd like to introduce myself, she rehearsed mentally. *I'm Polly Johnson and have been working as a senior investment banker at Waterman's Financial for twelve years. I'd love the chance to discuss employment opportunities with you some time, may I give you my card?*

Ugh. It was too vague, too undirected. Maybe it was better to target just one of them, zero in on a single member of the group rather than throw herself randomly at them all. Elliot McCarthy would probably be the most interesting of the three to work for: he was a maverick, a true entrepreneur who played hard and took risks, yet always came up smelling of roses. And money. Lots and lots of money.

Perhaps she should go in with some flattery first; soften him up. *I've always admired your work ethics* – actually no, better not. She seemed to remember some dodgy ethical practices that had been swept under the carpet by his people, now she thought about it.

I've always admired your drive and ambition; it's so great to have you in the UK. I love what you did with the Hudson Link account. Slightly creepy, but in her experience millionaires liked that kind of gushing. The detail was good too; showed that she did actually know what she was talking about, that she hadn't just pulled the compliment from thin air. Flattery *and* depth – good. Okay, that was her intro sorted. What next?

'Chicken Caesar and wedges?'

She lifted her gaze to see a waitress setting her food in front of her. Polly's stomach rumbled violently as she smelled the hot spicy wedges and the Caesar dressing ribboning the salad, and she realized she hadn't actually eaten anything since breakfast that morning. She'd been too pumped, too adrenalin-fuelled to think about food until this moment, and now her tastebuds were about to go into overdrive. Right, okay. So she'd just eat this lot, *then* she'd approach the bigshots at the table nearby. She glanced over to see Elliot McCarthy pouring more champagne into their glasses and all of them laughing at something. Good. They were in high spirits at least. Hopefully that would mean they'd be receptive to a spot of ingratiation.

She hungrily forked her food in, barely tasting it as she thought hard about what, exactly, she should say to Elliot. It would be amazing, landing a job with him. A-*mazing*. That would show Hugo Warrington that she was a player. Imagine if she could persuade Elliot to somehow buy out Waterman's, and then she could – *would*, more like – suggest a few redundancies of her own. Oh, yes. Redundancy number one: Warrington, that was a given. Out on his big wealthy ear, and good riddance to him. Redundancy number two: Marcus-frigging-Handbury, who had no doubt spent the afternoon arranging his personal belongings in her office, with an annoying smirk on his posh pink face. As for the traitor Jake, maybe she'd spare him the chop, but humiliate him by giving him the most dire, dreary, menial tasks possible. She'd crush him beneath her Ferragamos – just watch her.

Polly waved as she saw the two Sophies, Johnny and Richenda sauntering in, loaded with laptops and briefcases. It was weird being there without hers. She had missed her BlackBerry's bleeps and vibrations all day, had stretched out a hand to check it countless times already before remembering it had been taken away from her. Note to self, she thought: first thing tomorrow, buy a new one. Got to keep in the loop, still be seen as a player. How was she going to explain the fact that she didn't have hers with her now, in fact? Surely they'd notice that her phone was missing from its usual place on the table. It made her feel underdressed, as if she'd come out without make-up on, or any shoes.

'Hi,' she called out. 'Come and join me.'

In the next instant, she regretted her words. Seeing their faces en masse gripped her with panic. Could she tell them she'd lost her job? Could she actually bear the looks of pity, the smug glee that might sparkle in blonde Sophie's eyes? They'd bombard her with questions and it would be horrendous trying to keep her cool throughout, maintain some kind of confident composure, especially when she still didn't have a clue what lay ahead. If she pretended nothing had happened, everything would go on as normal. Wouldn't it?

Then she remembered her fruitless phoning around earlier that day, the increasing despair with which she'd sent off email after email with her CV and a polite covering letter. On the other hand, she needed all the contacts she could get.

She flicked her gaze sideways to the bigshot table. They were deep in conversation now, laughter muted, all expressions serious as they leaned in towards each other. She had to embark on her schmoozing mission with them before too long, she reminded herself. *Hi, may I introduce myself?* Adrenalin surged through her at the thought. She would do it. It was fate. And oh, how she'd laugh about it later. *Well, I lost my job out of the blue — yes, I was shocked — but by close of play I'd already lined up something even better. You know me!*

'Hi Polly, you got here early today,' blonde Sophie said, sitting next to her, sharp eyes scanning the half-drunk champagne bottle, as if already suspicious of Polly's reasons. 'Don't tell me you're slacking off now, because I won't believe a word of it.'

Polly smiled, a fixed fake smile. 'Delegation is the new

black,' she said, tapping her nose. The others laughed. Sophie didn't, but then she was a humourless robot and never did. Polly reckoned she might have got away with that one. Turn the focus on everyone else, she decided. She'd always been an expert tactician. 'So, how are you guys?' she asked lightly. 'Richenda, how did your presentation go today?'

Richenda looked pleased to be asked and started describing in full Technicolor detail her pitch and presentation to an important new client she'd been chasing for the last few weeks. Not wanting to be outdone, Johnny soon weighed in with the awe-inspiring deal-making he'd worked his magic on that day, and the nicer Sophie told everyone some gossip she'd heard about Santander. Yack, yack, yack. Lucky for Polly that they all loved the sound of their own voices. Lucky for Polly that they were arrogant enough not to think of asking her anything in return.

It was all going okay, she thought, draining the last of her champagne. (Christ, had she finished that bottle already? She felt as if she'd barely started.) Perhaps now would be a good time to wander across and mingle with the big *fromages*. There was nothing to lose, and her friends would be well impressed if she just moseyed on over to them and started chatting. She could already imagine their raised eyebrows, their astonishment. *Is that really Elliot McCarthy Polly's talking to? I didn't know she knew* him.

She stood up suddenly, but her movement was clumsy and she managed to knock over her empty glass. 'Oops,' she giggled, picking it up again. Her hand felt as if it was made entirely of thumbs. Shit, everything was swaying. She clutched the table for support, trying to right herself.

'Everything all right, Polly?' asked Nice Sophie, tilting her head on one side. (What was Nice Sophie *doing* in the business world? Polly had wondered before. She was far too ... well, *nice*, frankly.)

Polly was about to reply, yes, of course, never better, when her eyes locked with those of Marcus Handbury who'd just walked into the room, and she froze. She didn't seem able to drag her gaze away for a horribly long few seconds. Her insides turned cold and the bar seemed to list sideways as if she was on board a ship. Marcus-effing-Handbury. The last person in the world that she wanted to see.

He was coming over. Shit, he was actually coming over, his gaze still firmly on hers. She felt trapped amidst the others, the table blocking her from running away. Aargh. What should she say? How should she act? Panic bubbled up inside her and her knees felt uncharacteristically weak.

'Polly, hi.' He'd reached the table now, and the conversation halted abruptly. Everyone swung round to gawp at him.

A scarlet stain of embarrassment crept up Polly's throat and into her face. 'Hi,' she said coldly.

'I just wanted to say, I'm sorry about how things have panned out,' he said. He was one of those tall, solid rugby types, Marcus. The sort of person you could cannon into and they'd barely twitch. He had a plain, fleshy face and sandy hair, slightly thinning, she noted spitefully. 'Really gutted for you, but no hard feelings, yeah?'

No hard feelings. He'd just shafted her for her job and he had the nerve to say 'No hard feelings'? What did he think she was, some kind of cyborg?

She swallowed the lump of anger that had risen in her throat. *Don't lose your cool.* 'Whatever,' she said, affecting a disdainful shrug and staring past him.

The others were looking from Marcus to Polly in confusion, not following. 'What's this all about?' Richenda asked. 'What's happened?'

Blonde Sophie leaned in closer, sensing blood was about to be shed. 'Yeah, what's happened?' she asked in faux concern, as sincere as a politician.

Marcus looked taken-aback. 'Oh,' he said. 'Well, Polly's redundancy. I've been moved up as a result, so, you know, kind of awkward, really . . .'

To be fair, he did look genuinely pained at the situation. Not half as pained as Polly felt, though. She was trembling with the sheer awfulness of it all. 'Kind of awkward' was the understatement of the flaming year.

'Shit, you've been made *redundant*?' Richenda asked in

horror. Her voice seemed to echo around the room — redundant-redundant-redundant — and Polly cringed. 'When did this happen?'

'Why didn't you *say*?' Nice Sophie asked, her blue eyes boggling. 'Bloody hell, Polly. What a nightmare!'

'It's not a big deal,' Polly replied, waving a hand in what she hoped seemed a casual fashion. Richenda made a grab for her glass just before that got knocked over too. 'To be honest, I've got something way more exciting lined up,' she lied, tapping her nose once more. It was becoming her signature gesture tonight. Any minute now she'd go to tap her nose again and she'd find that it had shot out twenty centimetres like Pinocchio's.

'Oh yeah? What's that, then?'

Polly wished Mean Sophie didn't have to sound quite so disbelieving. She tipped her head right to indicate Elliot McCarthy's table. 'I've got an in with Elliot,' she said loftily. 'I was just about to go and discuss things with him when you lot arrived actually, so if you'll excuse me a minute...'

'What, now?' Nice Sophie looked concerned. 'With Elliot McCarthy? Polly, don't you think you're a bit' — she hesitated, clearly agonizing over whether to offend Polly or potentially save her — 'you know ... a bit *pissed* for a discussion with him right now?'

'Of course not,' Polly said, trying to disentangle herself from the table. She stuck her nose in the air, not making eye contact with any of them. Sod 'em. They were nothing to her. *Watch this, losers,* she commanded in her head as she stumbled towards Elliot McCarthy. Watch and learn. This is how Polly Johnson likes to operate – she scents blood and goes straight in for the kill.

'Hi,' she said, and then her mind went horrifyingly blank as the bigshots turned their impassive, who-the-hell-are-you? faces on her. Shit. What was his name again? 'Emily McCartney?' she blurted out before she could stop herself. 'May I introduce myself as your biggest fan, Polly Johnson. Hi there.' And then, with exquisite timing, she swayed on her heels and toppled clumsily into his lap.

Some hours later Polly opened her eyes and then immediately clamped them shut again, as blazing sunlight scorched her eyeballs. Ow. *OW.*

Her head throbbed in agony. Her mouth felt as if someone had hoovered out all of the saliva and coated its lining with fur. Her stomach was churning as if she was about to—

Oh God. Polly staggered off her bed and just managed to make it to the bathroom before spewing violently into the toilet. Ugh. She heaved again and dry-retched a few times, trying to spit out all the bits of sick that were trapped behind her teeth. Disgusting.

She lay on the bathroom floor whimpering, the stone floor cold against her hot cheek, not even having the energy to reach up and flush the loo or get some water to rinse her mouth. She felt as if she might die, right there on the tiles. Help. How had this happened?

She paged blearily back through what she could remember of the night before, cringing as a series of dreadful images flashed into her head. Marcus humiliating her in front of her friends. Humiliating herself in front of Elliot McCarthy and his companions, who just happened to be pretty much the most influential people in the City. Being asked to leave the Red House by the management, after Elliot McCarthy had complained to the staff about her.

She winced, remembering how they'd tried to manhandle her out of the building when she'd refused. Hell, she'd never be able to show her face in there again. And then what? She vaguely remembered being in another bar, somewhere (where?), drinking gin after gin and pouring her heart out to someone (the barman? complete strangers?), but the details were fuzzy – she couldn't make out her surroundings, other people's faces. As for how she'd got home again, it was a complete mystery. Shit.

She lay there for some time on her bathroom floor, not sure whether she was going to throw up again or not, but oddly comforted by the tiles beneath her face, as if there was no further to fall. This is what rock bottom feels like, she said to herself, and shut her eyes.

The whole day was a write-off. So much for continuing the bombardment of HR directors with her epic CV and bullet-pointed letter; it was all she could do to drag herself onto the sofa with the duvet without dying of hangover pain. She lay there for a few hours feeling mortified. How would she ever be able to go back to the Red House, after making such a spectacle of herself? And how would she ever be able to look the Sophies, Richenda and Johnny in the eye, without crying with embarrassment? She might as well face facts: her career was down the toilet, along with gallons of her alcoholic puke.

The only good thing that happened all day was when she found the TV remote, placed neatly in the wooden drawer of the coffee table. This at least meant that she could lie there watching Phil and Holly on *This Morning*, followed by *Loose Women* and Paul O'Grady. After several hours she found the strength to make herself a cup of tea. Other than that, she only bothered moving to change channels. What else was there left for her to do?

*

Several days passed in this vein, although none in quite such a hungover, alcohol-laced vein, thankfully. Oh, she made a few token efforts to check her emails, just in case anyone had replied to her job-seeking attempts with an interview or a welcoming pair of golden handcuffs but, unfortunately, the only responses she had were pro-forma rejections, informing her there were no suitable vacancies at the present time.

She clicked on the FT website several times a day, desperate to stay in the loop – old habits died hard – but whenever she checked out her investment portfolio, its worth seemed to have shrunk even smaller. *You've got to play the long game,* she remembered telling clients time and again. *No such thing as a quick fix.* She was starting to doubt the wisdom of her own words, though. Since her bonus had been snatched away at the eleventh hour, she didn't want to play a long game. She needed her shares to start rising again, fast. She needed a quick fix just as badly as a smackhead, damn it.

When she wasn't on her PC, she spent the rest of her time stretched out on the sofa, feet up, glued to daytime television. Why had no one told her how brilliant daytime television was? She already felt like Phil and Holly were old friends, and the Loose Women were the funny, sympathetic best mates she'd never had. She was getting good at spotting the bargains on *Bargain Hunt* too. And wasn't it cosy, just staying in her pyjamas all day? She felt as snug as an unemployed bug in a rug.

By the third day she'd wised up to planning ahead. She didn't want to face the rest of the world yet, so she ordered a food delivery online, full of all her favourite treats. Well, why not? It was about time she took things easy, chilled out for a change. She deserved a break after almost twenty years of pressing her nose against the business grindstone, and she was one hundred per cent convinced that a job would have turned up by the end of next week.

On Friday, when she'd been in the same pyjamas for four solid days, had just eaten cornflakes for lunch again (that Ocado van really couldn't come too soon) and was wondering if one o'clock in the afternoon was too early to have a tiny little glass of wine while she watched *Loose Women*, she heard a key in the door and nearly had a coronary in fright. What the hell?

She unswaddled herself from the duvet and leapt up from the sofa indignantly, heart pounding. 'Excuse *me*,' she began as her front door opened, 'but . . .'

Then she stopped, as she realized who the intruder was. That effing cleaner again.

Magda recoiled at the sight of Polly standing there, lank-haired and barefoot in what appeared to be quite grimy pyjamas and a dressing gown. 'Miss Johnson, you are here?' she asked in confusion. 'Again?' She blinked, taking in the sight of empty cereal bowls stacked up on the coffee table, the cold cups of coffee, the plasma screen TV blaring the *Loose Women* titles. 'You are ill?'

Polly hesitated. 'Yes,' she said after a moment.

'You want me go? Or I clean?'

Again Polly hesitated. She didn't want anyone else in the flat right now, she was enjoying wallowing on her own. She'd decided to take the rest of this week off, before throwing herself back into job-hunting again on Monday. Having the cleaner bustling about with the Hoover would break the spell, let the real world back into the bubble she'd created around herself.

On the other hand, the flat was kind of a tip.

'You can stay,' Polly said grandly, retreating to the sofa and pulling the duvet up under her chin again. If she didn't look at the cleaner, she might be able to pretend she wasn't there. She'd just concentrate on her programme, especially as an interview with Colin Firth was coming up.

'You want I make you drink? Something to eat?'

The cleaner – Polly had forgotten her name – was standing in front of her, blocking the TV screen. Polly twitched irritably and was about to shoo her away again when she processed the questions. Did she want a drink or something to eat? Actually, she did. She was paying the woman after all. 'A cup of tea would be great,' she said. 'I'm out of food unfortunately. Oh, and do make yourself one if you want,' she added as the idea occurred to her. 'I think the milk's gone a bit lumpy, so you might prefer it black.'

The cleaner began stacking up the empty cereal bowls, some of which had become rather whiffy. 'You have no one to look after you, eh? Is no good. I here now. Magda look after you, eh?' she said, casting a sideways glance at Polly.

Polly smiled thinly, wishing Magda would shut up and get out of the way of the television. She wasn't exactly in the mood for chit-chat, let alone with a cleaner. She said nothing, just stared pointedly at the TV, and after a while Magda took the hint and vanished into the kitchen.

Magda boiled the kettle and opened the dishwasher to load in the dirty crockery. A dreadful smell arose from the machine as soon as she pulled open its door. There was one plate and a few cups inside that sported dark fringes of mould. How long had they been sitting in there? 'Mój boże,' she muttered. 'My God, this woman is a disaster.'

She glanced around the upmarket white kitchen with its granite worktops, which had probably never seen a chopping board or fresh vegetables; its fridge, which was always empty, save for a pint of milk or maybe some champagne; the cupboards, which were largely bare. What a waste it all was, she thought, shaking her head. Maybe she'd got Miss Johnson wrong; maybe her apartment was often full of friends in the evenings – dinner parties, girls' nights, a lover who cooked for her – but she'd never come across any evidence to support this. Instead there was the lone wine glass, plate, knife and fork occasionally left in the sink. The packaging of a ready-meal for one in the bin. If this place belonged to Magda – ah, it would be so different. It would be a home.

She thought of her own kitchen: small and cramped, but decorated with her children's artwork and certificates from school, and full of good smells from the stews she cooked on cold days or the apple cakes the children liked to help her bake. Tomasz would sit at the small wooden table, dark head bent over his homework, while Kasia would perch on the worktop swinging her legs and chattering about her day.

Magda shut her eyes for a brief pleasurable moment, thinking of their smiling faces upturned like flowers, the warmth of their young bodies when they hugged her, their peaceful faces as they slept. This woman, Miss Johnson, she might have the fancy apartment that Magda's small flat could fit into twenty times over, the money and the big important job, but these things were nothing when you had nobody to care for you when you were ill. Poor Miss Johnson. Magda would not swap lives with her in a heartbeat. *Wcale nie.* Not at all.

Chapter Six

It was Saturday afternoon and Leila's party was in full swing. Earlier that day Clare had hung bunting around the kitchen, spread her nicest polka-dot oilcloth on the table, and set out mixing bowls and wooden spoons for Leila and her seven guests. The plan was to make bath-bombs and soap, and the girls were currently mixing sodium bicarbonate and citric acid together, white puffs of dust floating above their bowls as some of them stirred rather too vigorously. Clare went around spraying witch hazel into each bowl and got them to mix it in, then passed around a box full of scent bottles for the girls to smell.

'I've got lots of different fragrances you can choose from,' she said. 'Chocolate, vanilla, raspberry, lavender, lemon, English rose, sea-spray ... there should be something you like. Choose one each and I'll add a few drops to your mixture. Be very careful with the bottles, though, as some scents are expensive.'

'We're watching you like hawks,' Debbie joked, putting

her hands on her hips and peering around beadily at them. 'One spill, and you're out.'

The girls began oohing and ahhing over the scents, wafting them under each other's noses. Clare had been experimenting with bathtime goodies for a while, and really enjoyed making bath-bombs, bubble baths and soap. She'd got the idea last Christmas when she'd been stony broke and unable to afford proper presents for anyone but the children. She'd seen an article in one of the magazines at the surgery about easy crafts you could try at home, and had found the bath-bomb recipe there. They were so simple to make (and dirt cheap too) that she'd made her first batch that evening, adding lavender and dried rose petals to the mix, and wrapping them in colourful tissue paper tied with large bright ribbons.

She'd intended it to be a one-off, but then a few people had come back to her asking where she'd bought them, as they were so nice. When Clare had explained that she'd made them herself, they had promptly put in orders for more. Since then she had begun experimenting with bubble-bath mixture too, bars of soap and shea body-butter. She'd mainly given her products to friends and her mum to try out for free – she wasn't a hard-nosed business woman like her sister, after all – but already Debbie, Tracey and some of the other girls had come back and ordered more: paid for, this time. It was never going to make her a fortune but she found it relaxing, making her potions and bath treats in the evening and filling the house with yummy fragrances.

'Okay, so we're aiming for a wet-sand feel, guys,' she said now, coming around to check how their mixing was progressing. She added in fragrances for each girl, then opened jars of dried petals that they could sprinkle into the mix. 'Try squeezing a bit in your palm to see if it sticks together – when it does, you're ready to put it into the mould.'

'This is cool,' said Anna, Leila's closest friend, sniffing her mixture. 'Mine smells so chocolatey, it's making me hungry. Yum!'

Clare beamed, thankful that Leila's friends all seemed to be enjoying themselves. Some of the girls in her class had really over-the-top parties – hiring out Amberley Pool, for example, or taking everyone pony-trekking – and she'd worried that a home-based party might be too low-key. Hopefully this one would meet with peer approval. But then Carly Prince went and opened her big mouth.

'I'm not sure my mum will like this,' she said, peering disdainfully into her bowl. 'She only gets, like, really expensive stuff. The *proper* stuff?'

Meow. Clare exchanged a glance with Debbie. Carly Prince was the snobbiest girl in the class, and spiteful with it. If she wasn't showing off wildly, she was crushing somebody else. Why Leila wanted to be friends with her was beyond Clare, but the girl seemed to exude a powerful, irresistible magnetism that held her classmates in thrall.

Ignoring her, Clare passed around paper pill-cups so that the girls could press handfuls of their mixture into them. 'I thought bath-bombs were meant to be *round*?' Carly said, turning up her nose. 'Like, *bomb*-shaped?'

'Ahh, these are special ones,' Debbie put in quickly before Clare had to explain that the spherical moulds were quite fiddly to use.

'Yeah, these are going to look really cute,' said Anna – lovely loyal Anna – in the next breath, smoothing over Carly's abrasiveness.

Carly pinched her mouth together, annoyance flashing in her eyes. She dumped her mixture carelessly into the pill-cups, then glanced around the room for a new target. Her eyes fell on Leila, and Clare felt a shudder go through her.

'I can't wait until it's *my* birthday next month,' Carly sighed, tossing back her long, honey-coloured hair. 'Daddy said he's going to get me a new pony. I'm so excited.'

A chorus of envious 'Oooh's went around the table. Carly was the only child in the local school with that kind of wealth; nobody else could compete. Only a year and a half left of primary school, Clare kept telling herself through gritted teeth, and then no doubt Carly's parents would ship her off to a posh private school somewhere, leaving all the normal kids to go on to secondary school together. It couldn't come soon enough.

'So, what did *you* get for your birthday, Leila?' Carly went on, as Clare had known she would.

'I got this really cool bike,' Leila replied, half-turning to grin at Clare. 'Mum personalized it for me and put a furry saddle on; it's fab.'

Clare's heart seemed to swell at the pride in her daughter's voice. So there, Carly Prince, she thought. Money might buy you a pony, but it can't buy you a cool customized bike with a furry saddle stitched by your own loving mum.

'Awesome, where is it? Can we see it?' asked India, a tall vivacious girl with long red hair and a frenzy of freckles.

'It's outside. Can I get it, Mum?' Leila asked, wiping her dusty hands on her jeans.

Clare smiled. 'Of course you can, love,' she replied, and Leila darted out of the back door, blonde ponytail swinging. 'Now, who needs me to help them? I think we're nearly there.'

Clare was just squidging the last crumbs of Martha Stringer's rose-tastic bath-bomb into its paper cup when Leila reappeared, wheeling in her bike. It was a bit of a sight, Clare had to admit, with the tinsel Leila had insisted on leaving wrapped around the handlebars, and stickers now adorning it, but Leila was beaming gappily, so she didn't care what the others thought.

'Whoa,' said India. 'That's awesome. Such a gorgeous colour!'

'I love the saddle,' Martha put in, her eyes shining behind her glasses. 'What a cool style too. Really unusual.'

Leila beamed. 'It's great, isn't it?' she said.

Carly was staring at the bike, frown lines creasing her forehead. 'I used to have one like that,' she said slowly. 'Really similar. But it got nicked a few weeks ago – our shed was broken into and they took Daddy's Trek bike too.'

Clare swallowed. 'It ... it got nicked?' she echoed faintly.

'Yeah.' Carly came out from her place at the table to take a closer look. 'You know, the tyres look just the same,' she said. 'My bike was blue, not lilac, but apart from that ...'

Clare felt sick. This bike had originally been blue, she remembered. Surely that was just a coincidence, though?

'The seat was different,' Carly said, walking over and fingering the fluffy cover Clare had stitched. 'Mine was white leather, but it had got really cracked, and ...' Then she took off the seat-cover and gasped. 'Oh my God. This is *my bike!*' she cried, pointing at the worn white seat that had been exposed. 'This is my actual bike, the one that was nicked.' She whirled around accusingly and glared at Clare. She was only nine years old, but it was terrifying. 'Where did you get this from?'

'From a friend ... there must be some mistake,' Clare garbled, aware of her face turning crimson. Oh God. Oh *shit*.

Leila was looking baffled. 'Wait, you're not saying ... My mum didn't nick your bike,' she said indignantly. 'Did you, Mum? Tell her – you bought it for me, didn't you?'

It was one of those moments when the world seemed to stop turning, when she felt the stare of every person in the room weighing heavily on her. She was going to *kill* Jay Holmes when she got her hands on him.

Somehow she made it through the rest of the party without metamorphosing into the human equivalent of Munch's *The Scream* painting. It was an effort though, an awful, horrible slog of two hours with Carly's scornful gaze flicking between her and that wretched bike the whole time. Honestly, how could she have trusted Jay? How could she have blithely accepted that he'd picked up this bike, without asking exactly where he'd picked it up *from*? Of all the stupid, trusting people in the world, she had to be the most gullible muppet of all.

Just to make matters even more excruciating, the doorbell

rang halfway through the party and Clare opened the front door to see Steve there on the step. 'Thought I'd surprise the birthday girl,' he said jovially when Clare's face collapsed with dismay. 'All right if I join the fun?'

Fun? Clare was almost tempted to hand over her apron to him and leave him to it, while she pelted upstairs and hid in the wardrobe. She'd managed to fob off Leila and Carly with a line about the bike being second-hand (true), and that she was sure they could sort everything out (false) if there was a problem (no 'if' about it). She was dreading the arrival of Mrs Prince, though, and Carly's accusatory voice ringing out as she apprised her mother of the situation, no doubt at top volume in front of all the other parents.

Bloody hell. How did she get herself into these fiascos? And now, to top it off, here was Steve, striding past her into the house, booming, 'Where's my birthday girl, then?' as if he was the guest of flipping honour.

Clare heard Leila's squeal of delight and her racing footsteps, and then she'd thrown her arms around her dad's neck and he was swinging her up through the air, both of them laughing.

This party could not get any worse. Roll on five o'clock, when it would all be over and she could sink into a bottle of wine.

'I've had to leave your present outside because it's too

big to come through the front,' Steve was saying as Clare shut the front door, smarting.

Too big? What had he got her, an elephant? Denise had probably curled its sparse, bristly hairs or put a ribbon on its tail, she thought spitefully. Then her own bile made her stomach churn. At least he hadn't got her a knock-off bike, a voice retorted in her head. A knock-off bike stolen from the class snob, no less.

'Open the back door and have a look, babe,' she heard Steve say as he went into the kitchen. 'Hey! Hello everyone. Having fun? Ah. Hello, Debbie.'

'Afternoon.'

Clare hurried after them, just in time to see Debbie giving Steve a cool, appraising look as if to say, *Well, look what the cat dragged in.*

Ignoring Debbie, Steve flung open the back door. 'Ta-dah!' he shouted. 'What do you think?'

'Oh, wow,' Leila said, shooting an anxious look at Clare before staring outside again. 'Another bike – thanks, Dad!'

The smile slipped from Steve's face. 'Another bike?' he repeated.

Leila nodded. 'Yeah, Mum got me this one,' she said, pointing to where Clare had propped it against the far wall. She stepped outside, then reappeared with a mint-green racer, which was unmistakably brand spanking new and certainly hadn't been pinched from anybody's shed. 'Whoa,' she said, visibly delighted. 'Dad, this is awesome, thank you!'

Clare felt herself sag. Hadn't she been thinking only a few moments ago that this party couldn't get any worse? Somehow it just had. Much worse.

'Whoops,' Steve said nonchalantly, his eyes flickering over the chopper and then across to Clare. 'Communication-breakdown alert. I should have said. It's just that I knew Leila really wanted a bike, and I didn't think...' His unsaid words hung in the air and Clare finished the sentence in her head: *I didn't think you could afford one, Clare.*

Fair enough. She hadn't been able to afford one. Not until Jay Holmes had rocked up with a fell-off-the-back-of-a-lorry bike that she'd been dumb enough to pay forty flipping quid for.

'It's cool, Dad, honestly,' Leila said, ever the diplomat. 'I really like them both. And I can lend one to Anna so that we can go on bike rides together.'

'Even if one of the bikes is actually, like, *mine*,' Carly put in under her breath.

Steve heard her muttered comment – well, everyone heard her muttered comment, just as Carly had no doubt intended – and shot Clare a questioning look.

She shook her head. 'Later,' she mouthed. She'd explain

later, once she'd brained Jay Holmes with the rolling pin, she thought. First things first.

At last it was five o'clock and the parents began arriving to pick up their daughters. Clare had helped the girls decorate the boxes into which they'd packed the now-dry bath-bombs, and she'd tied ribbons onto them all while they ate the party tea.

'Mmm, it smells amazing in here,' Martha's mum Imogen said as she came into the kitchen. 'I can't wait to try one of these bath-bombs. You are clever, Clare.'

'She makes soap as well, and really nice bubble bath,' Debbie said at once. 'They make brilliant presents, if you ever need some.' She winked conspiratorially. 'Just saying, Im, because I know Clare's far too modest to blow her own trumpet.'

Clare blushed. 'Thanks,' she said to both Debbie and Imogen at once. Not everyone was out to get her, she reminded herself.

'That's good to know,' Imogen said. 'I'm hopeless at remembering presents, so I'm always dashing around trying to pick something up at short notice. Right, where's Martha? Come on, love, we need to go. Say thanks to Leila and Clare.'

It hadn't all been bad, Clare thought, relief rising within her as one by one the children departed. If it hadn't been for the bike debacle, she'd have considered the party a resounding triumph, bar some snipey snobbery from Madam Carly.

At that moment she heard Steve letting someone in the front door (he was making himself very at home here, she thought crossly, considering this wasn't actually his home any more) and then came the unmistakable voice of Mrs Prince. 'Parking's a nightmare in this street, isn't it? I don't know how you can bear not having your own driveway.'

Cringe.

Clare listened to Steve explaining that he didn't live here now, but yes, it was rather a pain, parking on the lane, and he was sorry if he'd hogged the space with his Beamer out the front there.

Double cringe. Clare pulled a face at Debbie. 'Brace yourself,' she muttered.

'Mummy!' cried Carly, rushing through to greet her. 'You'll never guess what, it's the weirdest thing. Leila's got my bike! You know the one that was nicked?'

Debbie looked at Clare. 'Where did you get it from?' she hissed.

'Jay,' Clare replied through gritted teeth. 'Hi there, Stephanie,' she said politely as Mrs Prince wafted into the kitchen in a cloud of pungent perfume. 'I'm afraid there's been some kind of a mix-up, if you'll just let me explain . . .'

Chapter Seven

Polly finally forced herself out of the apartment on Saturday to buy a newspaper and a stash of chocolate (somehow she'd managed to leave that off the Ocado list; what had she been thinking?) and the world felt an unfamiliar, chilly place when she stepped out into it. The colours around seemed harsh and dazzling. The rumble of buses jarred in her ears. People were bustling along the South Bank – tourists, families, smoochy couples arm-in-arm – and this mass of human life was overwhelming after the quiet solitude she'd been wrapped in. It made her realize how cut off she'd become, how isolated. She hadn't heard a peep out of Waterman's, save a standard goodbye letter and confirmation of their stingy redundancy terms. She hadn't heard anything from her so-called friends, the Sophies and Richenda, either, after that disastrous night in the Red House. Nothing. She'd been ditched, that much was obvious.

Head down, she walked at top speed to the corner shop, wanting to get this excursion over and done with so that she could be home again as quickly as possible. Going out had become stressful. The air felt too ... fresh. The sun was too glaring without tinted windows. How had it ever seemed normal to leave for work every day, to get on the Tube with all those crowds, to jostle and push, to *talk* to everyone? It was a relief to be back in her apartment, just her. Safe.

On Monday she'd crack on with the job hunt properly again, she'd promised herself. Monday morning she'd get up early, put on some power clothes and haul herself into the hottest headhunting agencies, brandishing a mint-fresh CV in their faces. She'd chase up everyone she'd already emailed her details to as well, see if she could muscle her way into an interview. She wouldn't rest until she had a new employer, a new office to call home.

But then on Monday morning when the alarm blasted her awake, she found herself rolling over blearily, slamming it off and going back to sleep until ten o'clock. Damn. How had that happened? She slunk guiltily out of bed and into the shower. Come on, Polly. Standards were slipping. Everyone at Waterman's would have been at their desks for hours already.

Right, into action. No excuses. Computer on. Coffee on. Phone on. She wouldn't even look at the TV until she'd networked her way around the entire City, even though *This Morning* was starting soon.

She'd felt sorry for herself for too long. 'Polly Johnson is back in town,' she muttered as she dialled the first agency.

Two hours later she was slumped in front of the television with the *Bargain Hunt* music playing. God, looking for a job was soul-destroying. There was simply nothing out there. Nothing! Her CV was with at least fifty people by now and she hadn't had even the slightest spark of encouragement in return. What was she meant to do, run along Bishopsgate naked, prostrating herself to Mammon? What would it take for someone to give her a break?

She was starting to sound desperate on the phone; she could hear it seeping through her voice. And every time she was fobbed off with those dreaded words, 'There's nothing at the moment, but we'll keep your details on file.' It was like some kind of dismal purgatory. It was starting to grind her down. One interview, one call back, that wasn't too much to ask, was it?

She heard the key in the door and felt like screaming as Magda came in, glancing warily over at the sofa. 'You are still ill, Miss Johnson?' she asked. 'Is bad, yes?'

Polly opened her mouth to say yes, but didn't even have the energy to lie any more. 'I lost my job,' she said bluntly. The words sounded awful said out loud; it was the first time she'd heard them from her own mouth.

Magda bit her lip. 'Is bad,' she confirmed. 'Sorry. My husband – the same.'

It was on the tip of Polly's tongue to say that actually, Magda, it probably wasn't the same. She doubted Magda's husband had commanded a six-figure salary like her, or was responsible for the humongous mortgage she had. It wasn't the same at all. The pained look on Magda's face stopped her at the last second, though. 'Sorry to hear that,' she mumbled.

'Yes,' Magda said. 'He is builder. No building work needed now. Is hard.'

'Mmm,' Polly said. 'Very hard. Not many jobs out there.'

Magda nodded sagely, removing her denim jacket. 'Something good come soon,' she said. 'I know it. Something good. Oh, Miss Johnson, you crying? Don't cry, Miss Johnson. Don't cry. Something good come soon.'

It was truly a new low, sobbing on the cleaner's shoulder like that. A hideous, unspeakable low. Magda had actually put her arms around Polly and held her while she wept. Talk about embarrassing.

After Magda had left, hot shame burned through Polly like a forest fire. This was unacceptable, she told herself. This was not on. She, Polly Johnson, did not indulge in this sort of pathetic behaviour. She hated herself almost as much as she hated Magda for the pitying expression on her face. How could Polly have fallen apart like that? In front of a *cleaner*, of all people?

Smarting, she phoned the cleaning agency immediately and made a complaint that Magda hadn't been respectful towards her. It was very unprofessional behaviour, she said, her voice trembling, and she simply couldn't put up with it any more.

'We're so sorry,' the lady on the other end of the line said. 'We'll send a different cleaner next week.'

Polly hesitated. Could she bear the thought of anyone else coming in, snooping about, seeing her in her hour of desperation? She couldn't. She'd actually rather wallow in her own stinking chaos and mess than suffer another sympathetic look from someone on the minimum wage. 'No, don't bother, I'm closing the account,' she said briskly. She'd hire someone else once she'd got a new position and was back with the high-fliers, she vowed.

If she got a new position, that was.

Six weeks passed, with little change. As the days went by, one after another after another, with still no job offer, Polly began to feel as if she were sliding down a hole, deeper and deeper, further and further away from the surface. It was getting harder to fake the smile, harder to make the effort.

Nobody was returning her calls. Nobody wanted her. News that she'd phoned Henry Curtis after a particularly alcoholic afternoon and called him an arsehole seemed to have spread through the industry like wildfire. She was becoming a joke. She couldn't bear it.

Credit-card bills dropped through the letterbox like hand-grenades. Ouch. They were eye-wateringly, *how-much?* astronomical. She received a rude letter from the mortgage division at the bank, saying she'd defaulted on that month's payment and needed to arrange payment within the next seven days, or else. Then her car was towed away after she'd parked on double yellows in central London, and when she went to pay for its release, her first two credit cards were declined. Thank goodness she had three others that still worked.

More bills arrived. She stopped opening the envelopes. If she couldn't see how bad the debt was, she wouldn't have to worry about what she owed. She stuffed them in a drawer and shut it. Out of sight, out of mind. She had given up looking at the stock market too. Two of the companies she'd invested heavily in had gone to the wall. The others were looking similarly precarious. If only she'd been given her bonus, none of this would have happened. But 'if onlys' counted for nothing.

Meanwhile she was still chasing up the recruitment agencies, trying to keep the fear from her voice as she felt the wolf coming ever nearer to her door. The bank phoned her several times and she had to pretend she was out. The mortgage people phoned and wrote again, telling her that she needed to contact them urgently about when she was going to make a payment. The flat began to collect dust and fluff in Magda's absence. Surfaces became sticky. And Polly dreamed that she could feel the wolf's hot breath on her face as it lay in wait, scenting fresh blood.

If she could just get a job, an interview, a short-term contract, *anything*, she might still be all right. She had to try harder. She had to set her sights lower. She looked in the Job Centre, exuding desperation from every pore, but they informed her she was overqualified for all their current vacancies. 'Look, I don't care, I'll do anything – well, anything that pays over forty K, at least,' she told the man behind the desk.

He gave her an 'are-you-for-real?' kind of look and pressed some leaflets about claiming benefits into her hand. She couldn't bring herself to even look at them though. Surely things weren't that hopeless?

No, she told herself. She would not go begging for handouts. Polly Johnson was made of tougher stuff. She redoubled her efforts. She wasn't beaten yet.

At the beginning of June she met her accountant, who told her, in no uncertain terms, that unless she got some money, and fast, the flat would be repossessed. The thought of potato-headed bailiffs with worrying biceps and merciless eyes sent a terrified shiver down her spine. 'You're going to have to sell up,' he said. 'Put the flat on the market and make a quick sale. Unfortunately, with the market having bottomed out, I doubt the value of the property has risen much since you bought it, but you should make just enough to clear your debts and keep the bank off your back.'

She felt as if she'd been slapped. 'So you're saying, that even if I sell the flat, I'll still basically have nothing until I get another job. Is that right?'

'That's about the size of it,' he said. 'Your investment portfolio is looking pretty sick right now; if you can avoid selling your shares, I would try to ride out the market. But you'll have to act fast with the flat – like, now. Oh, and you'd better start kissing ass with the mortgage guys too, tell them you're on the case and beg for more time. They should give you another month, at least, before they send the heavies round.'

Polly had left his office in a numb trance. She still couldn't quite get her head around the fact that her life had become so calamitous so quickly. Surely it hadn't come to selling her flat already? Where would she go? She didn't have enough money to stay anywhere; she would have to live on credit . . . but how long could she manage that?

And so along came the estate agents, a parade of spotty

blokes in nasty brown suits who left a foul stink of BO and cheap aftershave in their wake. With a last stab of hope, she asked the first how much rental she could expect from tenants, if she let the flat rather than sell it, but the figure he quoted didn't go anywhere near covering the colossal monthly mortgage payment. The last dregs of her optimism leaked out like the final stale gasp of air from a punctured balloon. 'Looks like I'm selling then,' she said, her voice trembling.

A life can fall apart surprisingly quickly, as it turned out. All those years of work, of building her career and a glitzy, luxurious life for herself in the capital ... it took far less time for the whole lot to implode. She plumped for the estate agent who quoted the highest asking price, the one who assured her he had clients queuing round the block to see properties like hers. Vince, he was called, and he looked every bit a Vince with his wispy moustache and slightly too-close-together eyes. 'I've got one cash buyer in mind who's very keen to move into this area,' he boasted, when she called him back to tell him that he could market the property. 'Vacant possession might just seal the deal.'

'Vacant possession ... You mean, I should move out?'

'If you've got somewhere to go, yes. Makes a property much more attractive, considerably reduces the buying chain.'

If you've got somewhere to go ... Oh God. But she didn't have anywhere to go! This was all happening too fast. 'I'll let you know,' she said guardedly.

'No problemo. I'll swing by again tomorrow with a contract, and take some photos. We'll have that apartment sold before you know it, Miss Johnson.'

'Right. Thanks.'

So it was really happening. The dream was over. Practically penniless and soon to be homeless, she was too depressed and scared to cry any more. Her luck had run out, as well as her money. Now what?

Well, there was one last avenue left open to her, if she could stand it. The nuclear option. She took a deep, sighing breath, then dialled another number. 'Mum?' she said. 'It's me, Polly. I need a favour . . .'

This was never part of the life plan, Polly thought as, just two days later, she heaved the last box of her belongings out of the apartment and down to the van below. This was not even Plan B. This was Plan Z, the very last resort. She'd arranged to have most of her furniture and non-essential possessions put in storage, not wanting to think about when she might see them again.

'That the lot, love?' asked her dad, taking the box from her and shoving it into the back of the van he'd hired.

'Yeah,' she said quietly. 'That's the lot.'

He slammed the van doors shut and put his arms around her. It was a hot, soupy day and she could smell his sweat, mingling with the quick ciggy he'd had when he first got there. He wasn't a man for cologne, Graham Johnson, just as he had no truck with moisturizer, or shaving enhancers, or any of the other male grooming products that regularly baffled him on the shelves in Boots. Soap, deodorant and a slick of pomade, that was all a man needed.

He clapped Polly on the back now, trying not to show how alarmed he was to see her in such a state. He'd always been so proud of his eldest daughter, had revelled vicariously in her career triumphs, boasting to all his mates about her vast salary and high-end lifestyle. True, she wasn't exactly the most daughterly of daughters. Karen phoned her every Sunday to see how she was, but apparently it was like pulling teeth, trying to engage Polly in conversation. He knew Karen and Clare minded that she had turned her back on them when she got her first City job, but he understood that she was ambitious. Secretly he admired her for it.

Now, though . . . now she looked pale, scrawny and limp, as if the life had been squeezed out of her. Her hair was greasy, she had spots round her mouth, and the spark was missing from her eyes. She looked defeated. Beaten. He wanted to wrap her in his arms and look after her. Well, he'd drive her back to Elderchurch and she could have the spare room for a while anyway.

'I'll just check I've not missed anything,' she said, wheeling away before he could give her that sympathetic look again. She couldn't bear her own dad thinking she was a loser.

Upstairs in the empty echoing flat, it already felt like some kind of dream, her having lived there at all. She'd actually had this incredible Thames view and cavernous living space, but she'd barely appreciated it. When she'd moved in she'd pictured herself throwing fabulous parties and swanky dinner dos, had imagined a lover throwing her onto her gigantic bed and rumpling the sheets with her. None of it had happened. Somehow she'd just been too damn busy, and now it was too late. The apartment's particulars were already up on the estate agent's website, and Vince had arranged an open day there this Saturday when hordes of interested buyers would tramp through, marvelling at the light and airy rooms.

She leaned against the cool cream wall, staring around unseeingly. Was this it, then? Would she ever return to London, or would she have to make do with the spare room in her parents' bungalow for the rest of her life?

A tear rolled down her cheek. 'I blew it,' she whispered into the hushed room. 'I totally blew it.' And then, because being here any longer was just going to make her cry and cry so hard that she didn't know if she'd be able to stop, she took a deep breath and walked out.

'Goodbye,' she murmured, pulling the door gently shut. She pressed her hand against the white-painted wood for a few seconds, then turned and walked away, her goodbye resounding in her head with every step.

Chapter Eight

Clare had been at work when she'd heard the news a few days earlier. She'd been updating the patient database – a grindingly tedious job that she and Roxie always put off for as long as possible – when her mobile rang. 'You'll never guess what,' her mum had gasped down the line. 'Polly's coming home for the summer.'

'*What?*' Clare had yelped, her head jerking in surprise.

'Yes! It's true,' her mum had said, breathlessly as if she was running back to London to get Polly herself. 'She's taken a sabbatical to do some research, apparently; goodness knows what this research is *about*, it went completely over my head when she tried to explain it. But anyway she needs somewhere quiet to work, she said. So she's coming to stay with us for a few months.'

Clare gaped. 'God,' she said. 'Really? A few months?'

She wasn't sure how to feel about this bombshell. It seemed so out of character, for starters, her brash, loadsa-money sister leaving the Big Smoke to camp out in their quiet, sleepy village. As for taking a sabbatical, that was even more out of the blue. Polly had always been welded to her job, her BlackBerry like a shiny plastic extension of her hand. How would she cope without the nine-to-five? It would be like transplanting a hothouse flower to a cool, rainy meadow.

'How come she's staying with you?' she blurted out. 'No offence, but I'd have thought Polly's style would be to hole up in a glamorous hotel somewhere, not . . .'

Her brain caught up with what she'd said and she trailed off, not wanting to offend her mother.

Karen Johnson merely laughed. 'Not slum it with us, you mean? Well, it did strike me as strange too. Maybe she's been missing my home cooking. She looked that skinny at Christmas, you could almost see the roast potatoes going down her throat. Wrists like Twiglets, bless her. I'll feed her up, you wait. Anyway,' she went on. 'Just wanted to let you know. I'm cleaning every inch of the spare room in preparation. You know how particular she is. High standards, and whatnot.'

'Mmm,' Clare replied, still digesting the extraordinary news. 'Mum, are you sure you've got enough room for her?' Her parents' bungalow was very modest after all, with barely space for the two of them and Sissy, their Yorkshire terrier, not to mention her mum's vast collection of knick-knacks, arranged on every available shelf and occasional table. Clare knew her mum had her sewing table set up in the spare room and, since she'd been forced to take early retirement from her job in Amberley library, she liked to sit there on sunny afternoons, sewing machine whirring and *The Archers* on the radio as she worked on a new patchwork quilt or pair of curtains.

'Well, it'll be cosy, put it like that,' Karen replied. She was perched on the sofa as she spoke and glanced along it, trying to imagine a third bottom parked there every evening – a fourth bottom, if you counted Sissy's. Poor Sissy would be miffed if she was suddenly relegated to the carpet; she always gave you that look, those big sad eyes, that Karen could never hold firm against.

The dog cocked her head as if reading Karen's thoughts and gave a little whine. *Please don't put me on the carpet.*

'I'll just have to chuck your dad out to his shed if it feels too cramped,' Karen joked in the end.

Clare felt her lips pursing. Her dad was sixty-six now and by rights shouldn't have to be chucked out anywhere, least of all for Lady Muck. 'Well, if there's anything I can do to help . . .' she said. 'I'd better get on now, Mum. See you later.'

She put the phone down. 'God,' she muttered again. Polly hadn't spent more than two consecutive nights in Elderchurch during the last twenty years. It was going to be very odd having her back. A few months, hey? Plenty of time for Polly to wind her up, big-style.

'You okay?' Roxie asked, looking over from the front desk. 'Your face has gone all scrunched up. Have you got trapped wind?' She pointed her pen at Clare authoritatively. 'Try sticking your bum out and bend your knees; you need a big old fart, that's all, Clare.'

Clare laughed. Despite her art degree, Roxie increasingly fancied herself as a medical expert, as if by working in close proximity to doctors and nurses she had somehow imbibed their knowledge by osmosis. 'Not wind, just ... news,' she replied, wrinkling her nose. 'My sister's coming back to Elderchurch for the summer.'

'Your sister? I didn't even know you had a sister,' Roxie exclaimed with interest. Then her turquoise-lined eyelids snapped open a fraction wider. 'Oh, wait, is she the one who always gives you mad presents? The stinking-rich one?'

Clare snorted. 'That's her,' she replied.

'Whoa. The prodigal daughter returns,' Roxie said, shuffling excitedly on her chair. 'What the hell has she come back to this dump for?'

Clare arched an eyebrow. 'That's what I'm wondering, Rox,' she said. 'You just hit the nail smack on the head.' She turned back to her computer screen, but the patient names kept jumbling before her eyes. Polly was coming back. Shit. This was all Clare needed.

*

115

'I sound really horrible, don't I? Like the worst sister in the world. But the thing is, I just don't want her to come back, Debs. Does that make me an evil person?'

Debbie eyed Clare over her mug. It was later that day and Clare had dropped round for a natter before the school run. The two of them were sitting in Debbie's warm kitchen, along with a pair of dogs snoozing comfortably in front of the Aga, and fresh coffee and home-baked shortbread on the table. Debbie, being Debbie, had painted the kitchen a warm vibrant pink, and the walls were full of children's artwork. Plants and bright vases jostled for space on the window-ledges and a colourful clutter of mugs, teapots and plates were randomly displayed on the old wooden dresser.

'No,' Debbie replied. 'It doesn't make you an evil person. It makes you an honest person.' She sipped her coffee. 'But it might actually be a good thing, her spending some time here. You can get to know each other again – start a new relationship.'

Clare snorted. 'Never going to happen,' she muttered. 'Not a chance. It's going to be one long mutha of a summer, I'm telling you now.' Then she caught the gloominess of her voice and felt mean. 'Oh, I dunno, maybe I'm being too pessimistic. Maybe you're right. Only ever seeing each other at Christmas doesn't exactly make for the best sisterly bond, does it?' She pulled a face. 'I kind of wish I hadn't sold all those awful presents she's given us on eBay, though. Do you think she'll be expecting Leila to be prancing about in that ridiculous dress? I really hope not, because I flogged it to some woman in Northampton last week. Ninety quid she paid for it too, the maniac.'

She nibbled her shortbread. Orange and chocolate-chip: yum. Debbie was an ace baker. 'It's just going to be weird, that's all. My sister, back here on Wednesday. I can't imagine it.'

'Well, if you're finding the thought of it strange, just imagine how freaked out she must be,' Debbie pointed out. 'Once word goes round that she's here, everyone will be noseying at her. The great Polly Johnson, back in Elder-church. We are not worthy!'

She bent over, arms outstretched as if worshipping a deity, and Clare giggled. 'I'm worried she'll be expecting a bit of that,' she confessed. 'You know: Return of the Golden Girl. Didn't she do well? How come *Clare* never managed anything more exciting than a job at the Amberley Medical Centre?' She broke off, aware of how bitter she sounded.

'It's not a competition,' Debbie reminded her, 'as I find myself saying to the kids at least twenty times a day. Honestly, I'm going to get a T-shirt printed up with that on, one of these days.' She mimicked herself, wagging a finger. 'It's not a competition. It's not a race. What's the magic word? No hitting. Stop fidgeting. Have you washed your hands? Eat those peas ... Aargh, I sometimes hear myself and feel depressed at what an old nag I am. What's happened to me?' She grimaced. 'Maybe your sister had the right idea, getting out of here and doing something exciting with her life. Better than turning into a boring old housewife like me.'

'You'll *never* be a boring old housewife,' Clare said in surprise. Apart from Roxie perhaps, Debbie was the least boring person she knew. She'd been a pink-haired punk at school with plans for art college, until baby Lydia had unex-pectedly arrived and put that on hold. Even though she was now a so-called respectable wife and mother of four, it was always Debbie who'd be at the helm of a raucous night out, a party girl through and through. 'You're lovely. And you've been more of a sister to me than Polly has, that's for sure.'

'But ...'

'But nothing,' Clare said firmly. 'Don't start wishing you were more like her, whatever you do. Once you've met her again, you'll realize that being like Polly is the last thing you want.'

On Wednesdays Clare worked an early shift at the surgery and was always the first person to arrive and unlock the building at eight in the morning, after dropping Leila and Alex at the school 'breakfast club'. She rather liked coming in early and getting everything straight before the patients arrived. She tidied the magazines, went through the answerphone in case anything urgent had come up, then sorted the post and left it in the doctors' in-trays.

The doctors arrived one by one, followed by Roxie, and the waiting room began to fill up. In came Frank Lullington, who was on the waiting list for a liver transplant. Next was a frazzled-looking mum and her sobbing, curly-haired toddler, who kept clutching one ear as if she was in a lot of discomfort. Then came Ellen Cartwright, who'd lost her husband to pneumonia the last winter and was heading rapidly downhill herself. The phone was ringing non-stop too and Clare's head began to ache, trying to juggle all the patients into the diary.

At one o'clock, just as the appointments were tailing off for the doctors' lunches, a text pinged on her phone from her mum. Short and to the point, it merely said: *She's here.*

No need to ask to whom 'She' referred.

And? Clare texted back furtively, dropping her phone in her lap as a heavily pregnant woman waddled up to her counter. 'Hello there, can I help you?' she asked.

'I've got an appointment with Dr Copper at ten past one,' the woman said, scarlet-cheeked and short of breath.

'Elizabeth Harris? Take a seat,' Clare said.

Her phone pinged again. *Looks awful. Twiglet all over. Face like a smacked bum. Why don't u pop in later with the kids?*

Clare grimaced. *Wow, Mum, you've made it sound so appealing,* she wanted to text back. *How could I refuse?*

She hesitated, her finger on the reply button. Popping round for a civilized cup of tea was going to be much harder than suffering her sister on Christmas Day. At least at Christmas you could have a gin and tonic permanently by your side and nobody thought the worse of you for it. At least at Christmas there was the distraction of presents and stockings and cheesy films to offset any awkwardness. Still, she was going to have to see her sister at some point, so it might as well be in the neutral territory of their parents' house.

'Fancy a cuppa?'

Roxie's cheerful voice broke into Clare's thoughts. 'Ooh, y—' she began, but Roxie interrupted.

'Fab, make us one while you're there then, cheers. Biscuit as well? Thanks, that would be lush. If you insist.'

'Roxanne Fetherington, you are a nightmare,' Clare said, laughing. 'Go on, then, just this once. Because you're so damn cheeky.'

As she got to her feet, an elderly gentleman shuffled to the reception desk. After some rummaging in his pockets, he brought out a sample-pot and placed it on the counter in front of Roxie. The contents were brown, and quite unmistakable.

'I'll get on with that tea then,' Clare trilled, stepping

away and trying to hide a gurgle of laughter at the appalled expression on Roxie's face.

Roxie, to her credit, managed to smile up at the old man. 'Do you bring gifts for all your girlfriends, eh?' she joked. 'Thank you. I'll treasure it.'

The old man winked at her. 'Popped it out fresh for you just now, darling. Still warm.' And with that, he turned and shuffled away.

'Well, that's just lovely,' Clare heard Roxie muttering, and giggled as she filled the kettle.

'Was that a *chocolate* biscuit you wanted with your tea, Rox?' she couldn't resist teasing.

'I am so making the tea next time,' Roxie replied. Clare peeped around the door of the little kitchen to see her gingerly manoeuvring the sample-jar into an envelope. 'Ugh. This job, honestly. Sometimes I wonder why I bother. And no, I don't want a chocolate biscuit. I've gone right off the idea now.'

Clare brought the mugs of hot tea over and quickly texted her mum back. *Okay. Will be there after school x*

She was a grown-up, after all. She could do it.

Chapter Nine

Polly had *meant* to tell the truth all along, truly she had. It was only when her mum had answered the phone and she'd heard that kind, concerned voice in her ear that she saw her own failings through the lens of her parents' eyes, and found herself unable to go through with the full story. The lies had come out instead – this sabbatical nonsense had flown out of her mouth like breath, and before she could say 'bullshit', her dignity had been restored within a matter of seconds.

She would be researching the impact on the company of new risk legislation, she'd said, a grandeur reappearing in her voice that she'd not heard for some time. Complete peace and quiet were essential, hence the move out of London. She was hoping that after she'd completed this research and handed it in, she'd be given promotion. With a bit of luck, she'd be heading up the division by October.

If there was any word of this that her mum didn't believe, it didn't show in her voice for a second. 'Oh, it'll be lovely to have you back,' she'd gushed. 'Graham, Graham, where are you? You'll never guess!'

Then, when her dad had turned up with the hire van, more lies had tripped out, every bit as fast as the first few. She had arranged for an agency to take care of the apartment while she wasn't there, she told him – well, it was kind of true, she supposed. The reason she was so pale? Oh, she'd been slaving away, burning the candle at both ends, as usual. She was looking forward to a more restful time in Elderchurch (the biggest lie of all).

Again, her dad seemed to swallow all of this down and had loaded up the van without a murmur. They'd driven away through the maze of London streets, and the lies had taken root. Polly was actually starting to believe them herself. It sounded much nicer, didn't it, a comfortable three-month sabbatical, rather than 'unemployed'. Meanwhile, she would secretly keep applying for vacancies, and hopefully they need never know the truth. Breathing space, that's what she'd just bought herself.

It was all too soon before Graham turned off the M3 onto the smaller roads that led deeper into the Hampshire countryside. It had been drizzling in London, but the big skies were clearing now, the clouds becoming fluffier and brighter as the sun burst around them. Polly stared dully through the mud-speckled windscreen. Usually when she came this way she was hurtling along in her foxy little sports car, not chugging down the road in a filthy old van. She felt a pang of missing her car. She'd loved zipping about in it, the top down, sunglasses on her nose. When she'd bought it, she'd imagined herself driving to meet a lover for weekends in country piles, glamorous hotels, days at the races. She'd hardly ever taken it out of London, though, had travelled mostly via cabs in fact.

'Not far now,' her dad said, breaking the silence.

She didn't reply. She knew it wasn't far now – she could tell because all you could see for miles around were fields and trees and hedges. Not a shop or apartment block or office building in sight. The thought made her feel queasy. The countryside seemed horribly alien after the bustling warren of inner and outer London, and she realized that she hadn't actually seen Hampshire in the summer for years, having only ever deigned to return at Christmas time.

She imagined her skin breaking out in hives. I am allergic to the countryside, she thought wryly. Living in Elderchurch for the summer was absolutely going to finish her off.

'Here we go,' her dad said, slowing to thirty miles per hour as they turned into the quiet lane that led to the village.

Polly tensed as they drove past the high hedges and through the awkwardly narrow stretch of the lane. There was the white farmhouse, stuck on the edge of the village, and then the first smaller cottages, some dating back to the fifteenth century, built of warm red brick with tiny windows and thatched rooftops. Jacky Garland from school had lived in one of them, she remembered, the image of going there for tea one afternoon surfacing from the depths of her brain. It was the first time Polly had ever had ginger beer, and Jacky's mum had baked fairy cakes with buttercream icing and fruit pastilles on top, like glittering jewels. They'd sat on the back step together, sucking the pastilles in companionable silence, the gritty sugar dissolving deliciously on Polly's tongue.

There was the church with the old wooden lychgate and worn stone path up to its heavy door. There was the village shop where she'd been caught nicking a Bazooka Joe bubblegum, aged seven, and had received a smacked hand for it. There was the stream where she, Michael and Clare had paddled on hot days, kicking great arcs of water at each other and squealing.

Oh God. It was like stepping back in time. Make it stop, Polly thought in anguish, trying not to look any more. Make it stop!

Graham bibbed the horn and raised a hand at an old lady, who smiled and waved back. Then her eyes fastened on Polly and widened in surprise. Polly wrenched her face away, her heart thudding. Was this what it was going to be like, then? Everyone staring at her, the fallen star? She imagined her mum had told the entire village that she was coming back. Oh, great.

They didn't know she was a fallen star, she reminded herself. She *wasn't* a fallen star. She was on a sabbatical to write up a very important, career-enhancing paper, so there!

She stuck her nose in the air, glaring out of the windows at the old schoolhouse and its parched playing field, the pub, the butcher's and the baker's. All they needed was the sodding candlestick-makers, she thought sourly, and they'd have the full set.

Graham turned down a winding lane. A string of modern houses had been built here, away from the older heart of the village. Nasty little 1960s semis, Polly thought contemptuously, with their manicured lawns and hulking caravans on the driveway. One caravan actually bore the name 'Marauder' and it was all she could do not to snort in derision. And here was bungalow valley down at the end, where the older villagers gravitated with their fruitcakes and greenhouses and silly little dogs.

Graham slowed the car and tucked it into the neat block-paved driveway of number fourteen. He pulled on the handbrake and put his hand on Polly's knee. 'Welcome back, love,' he said. 'Knowing your mum, she'll have the kettle boiling and lunch on the table. Come on in.'

Polly forced a smile, but she felt like crying. This was

really happening. She was actually back here in Elderchurch, in broad daylight, with hordes of gawping locals. She swallowed hard and held her head high. *Prepare to be wowed, Elderchurch*, she said to herself as staunchly as she knew how, and swung herself down from the van. *I'm better than the lot of you put together.*

'Hello, love.' Karen Johnson's smile simply couldn't stretch any wider as she flung her arms around her elder daughter. 'Good journey?'

'Fine, thanks,' Polly mumbled into her mum's silvery hair. Every time she saw her parents she was struck by how much older they were getting. It freaked her out that they were Grandma and Grandad to Clare's kids. She wished they could be preserved in time as their 1970s selves, wearing flares and scoop-necked tops and, in the case of her mum, a smelly blue sheepskin lined coat with toggles. Now look at the oldies they'd become.

'Come in, I've got lunch ready,' Karen said, finally letting Polly go. 'Kettle's on.'

Graham winked at Polly and she gave him a small smile in return. 'What's so funny, you two?' Karen demanded. Privately she was delighted to have them teasing her. It felt like old times, she thought, although she was shocked to see just how gaunt Polly had become. I'll soon have her rosy-cheeked and bonny again, she vowed, already planning the puddings and pies she'd bake in the months ahead.

Polly followed her mum into the kitchen. The bungalow looked different, she thought, then realized that she was unused to seeing it without all its Christmas clutter draped everywhere. No dinky tree with flashing fairy lights, no crepe-paper bunting crossing the ceiling (the exact same crepe-paper bunting they'd had since she was a child), no messy displays of Christmas cards that toppled over like dominoes whenever you opened or shut a door. The place seemed more subdued, she thought, although that suited her mood perfectly.

Sissy was yapping around her ankles and Polly fought the desire to kick out at the little mutt with her high-heeled sandals. She pressed her mouth tight shut so that she couldn't say anything she might regret.

In the kitchen a buffet lunch had been laid out on the table: sandwiches, sausage rolls, a tube of Pringles, and some home-made flapjacks with nubby pieces of glacé cherry. Polly blanched at the sight. She'd hardly eaten lately; the stress had taken her appetite, along with everything else. 'Thanks, Mum,' she said faintly, sitting down.

She hadn't grown up in this house – they'd lived a couple of streets away in a larger, semi-detached house with a swing in the back garden and guinea pigs in hutches. She and Clare had shared a room, whereas Michael had a smaller box room to himself. There had been much arguing and door-slamming it's-not-FAIR about the room arrangements, she recalled. She and Clare had physically come to blows on more than one occasion, largely due to Clare borrowing Polly's stuff without asking. She could still remember the fury she'd felt when Clare and her friends had helped themselves to her Coral Queen nail varnish, then spilled the rest all over her dressing table. 'It was an ACCIDENT,' Clare had roared, hands on her hips, as if that had made it any better.

She shut her eyes, not wanting to dredge up old memories. She'd rather leave the past firmly silted away beneath the now.

'Tired, love?' her dad asked, clapping her on the shoulder. 'Exhausting business, moving. Mind you, sounds like you've worn yourself out full stop lately, all your hard work.'

'Mmm,' Polly said, not meeting him in the eye. 'I have been putting in some long days, I suppose. But that's how it is in the City, Dad.' An image flashed into her mind of her stretched out on the leather sofa in her dressing gown, glued to *Bargain Hunt*, and she felt a twist of guilt in the pit of her stomach.

'Now don't hold back,' Karen said, as she set a steaming cup of tea in front of Polly. 'You tuck in. Have a spot of lunch, and then you can unpack.'

Polly nibbled a ham sandwich and tried to look grateful.

But oh, the cut and thrust of Waterman's seemed far, far away now. The gleaming towers, the corridors of power, her swivel chair, her desk, her phone ... She missed them as one did an old boyfriend, seeing only the romance and high points, forgetting the negatives and bad habits.

She chewed mechanically, barely tasting her sandwich as she wondered how on earth she was going to keep up this facade for three long months. *Whatever does not kill me makes me stronger*, she reminded herself. Although at that moment, she couldn't ever remember feeling so utterly weak.

'Hello Polly.'

Polly gulped. 'Clare, hi, how are you?' she said, mentally pulling a veil down over her face so as not to betray any emotion. Her hands shook as she and her sister embraced without warmth, touching each other for the briefest possible moment. She'd been dreading this.

She forced a smile at the children, trying not to appear too dismayed by how unkempt they both looked, Leila with her thick blonde hair tangled and falling loose from wonky bunches, Alex's school trousers about an inch too short and his shirt hanging out. Good grief. 'Hello kids, how are you? How's school?'

Leila gazed up through long eyelashes. 'All right,' she said politely, just as Alex replied, 'Boring' and scuffed at the floor with his shoe. This was immediately followed by, 'Have you made any cookies today, Grandma?' with considerably more interest in his voice.

Karen smiled fondly. 'I might just have baked a few,' she said. 'Why don't we all go into the kitchen and I'll make us a nice cup of tea.'

Polly sighed inwardly. Another 'nice cup of tea'. She was onto her fourth, and she'd only been in the bungalow three hours. Her dad had helped her heave all the boxes into the spare room and there was barely space there now to turn around. The single bed had been made with the same Snoopy duvet she'd had as a child – a far cry from her luxury king-size in London. She was surprised her mum hadn't left out some of her old Care Bears just to rub it in.

Back in the kitchen, she felt Clare's cool blue eyes hard on her. 'So what's this research all about then?' she asked.

Polly flinched, not liking her sister's sneering tone. 'It's quite complicated,' she replied crushingly, 'although if you're really interested, I'm going to be looking at the impact of some new risk legislation on the company, in particular market risk assessment.' It was complete nonsense – there *was* no new risk legislation that needed investigating as far as she'd heard, but Clare wouldn't be able to tell the difference. Blind her with science. 'And of course I'll be focusing on our insurance strategy, bearing in mind the emerging market trends.' Her meaningless twaddle had served its purpose. Clare was staring blankly, as if Polly had just spoken in tongues. Ha.

'Well, that makes absolutely no sense to me whatsoever, but it sounds utterly riveting,' Clare replied drily. 'Great fun. I'll look forward to perusing your report when you've finished.'

Polly was almost one hundred per cent sure her sister was taking the piss out of her, but felt herself flinch at the idea all the same. God. She would actually have to cobble some old crap together, she decided, just so that her cover story remained convincing. 'I'm afraid it's confidential at the moment,' she said brusquely. Up yours, Clare.

Clare pulled a face. 'Shame. I could have done with some light bedtime reading. Sounds right up my street.'

'Girls, don't start bickering,' Karen said automatically, putting the teapot on the table and pouring squash for the children. 'There. Isn't this nice?'

Nobody answered immediately. Leila and Alex were too busy stuffing cookies into their mouths, spraying crumbs everywhere as they chomped. Apart from their revolting scoffing noises, there was a tense silence and Polly realized she was digging her fingernails into her own palm. 'Thanks, Mum,' she managed to say tightly.

'Lovely,' said Clare with a meaningful look at Graham. He smirked back at her.

Polly scowled. Oh, right. Like that, was it? Clare had

always been Daddy's girl. She had the feeling that new battle lines were being drawn up, and tensed her body accordingly. If Clare wanted to start scoring points, then Polly would be ready to fight her corner.

Polly was surprised at how well she slept that night. As soon as her head touched the Snoopy pillowcase, she was out like a light, plunging into fathomless depths of sleep. Over the last few weeks she'd dozed fitfully, plagued by nightmares about debt and unemployment. Coming here felt as if she'd temporarily escaped such demons; she'd stepped into a safety chamber to which they had no access. After nine solid hours of slumber she was woken at eight o'clock by what sounded like rain thrumming against the wall, and rolled over dreamily flinging her arms out, only to almost topple straight out of bed. She clutched at the padded blue headboard to stop herself, fully awake now, heart jumping in panic.

Oh yes. Single bed. Snoopy duvet. Pink floral wallpaper. And that sound of pattering water was presumably somebody in the shower, just on the other side of the wall.

She sat up and stretched. It was strange waking up knowing that there were other people within the same four walls. Sure, she'd lived in an apartment block where there were other flats in the building, with other inhabitants living above and below her, but the walls had been so thick and soundproof she'd never heard anyone else.

Here, on the other hand . . . She groaned as she heard her dad begin singing 'Oh my darling, oh my darling, oh my DARLING Clementine' through the wall. Here, it was going to be cheek by jowl. Literally, she thought, recoiling from the wall, trying not to visualize her dad's bare bum-cheek separated from her face by just two inches of plaster and tiling. Ewww.

'Needs must' was becoming her most loathed expression.

Her parents were both retired and Polly was surprised to see them up so early in the morning. She'd envisaged being the sole early riser, breakfasting alone and then plugging into her so-called work while they lounged in bed. What did pensioners have to get up for anyway?

'So, what are you two doing today?' she asked over her plate of poached eggs, bacon and toast. Mmm. She'd forgotten how good her mum's cooking was. 'Do you usually potter about at home, or . . . ?' She didn't know, she realized with a jolt. She had no idea what her parents did all day, every day. It had never crossed her mind to ask.

They looked amused at the question. 'Well, your dad's playing golf with the lads this morning and I'm helping out at the playgroup,' Karen told her. 'I got into the habit when

Clare's two were there, and I still pop in a few mornings every week to lend a hand.'

'Oh,' Polly said. 'So you'll be out all morning, will you?'

'Yes, until midday,' her mum replied. 'Then I'm having lunch with Jean – remember Jean Garland? After that, housework and *The Archers*, then I'm meeting some of the girls in Amberley for coffee.'

'Oh,' Polly said again. She felt rather taken aback that her parents had such busy social lives, with 'the lads' and 'the girls' to hang out with.

'Then I'll do us all some tea – I've got chops for tonight – before I go out to my Bums-and-Tums class. Come along if you want. It's quite a giggle.'

Graham snorted. 'Get away, you daft woman, she'd be the only one under sixty if she goes there with you,' he said, rolling his eyes comically at Polly. 'She's got better things to do than hang out with a load of creaky grannies, right, love? She's probably dying to see some of her old mates, not yours.'

Karen cuffed him. 'Less of the "creaky grannies", thank you very much,' she retorted. 'Ignore your rude old father,' she went on to Polly. 'The offer's there, although I suppose he might be right for once in his life, and it would be more fun for you to catch up with your friends. I'll tell Jean you're back – I expect Jacky'd love to see you again.'

Polly tried to keep back her shudder. Spend an evening

with boring, plump Jacky Garland, who'd had braces on her teeth for most of the secondary school years, and who'd left school at sixteen to sweep hair clippings at A Cut Above in Amberley? Digging her own grave would be more 'fun'. 'Maybe,' she said, swigging the last of her coffee. 'Thanks,' she said, getting up from the table. 'Right, I'd better have a quick shower and crack on then.'

She was about to leave the room when her dad gave a theatrical-sounding cough. She turned questioningly.

'Your plate,' he said, indicating it with his head. 'Don't forget to put it in the dishwasher.'

Polly flushed and made to go back for it, but her mum rounded on him. 'Don't nag her, Graham, she's our guest,' she said. 'I'll sort that out when I've finished mine.'

'I don't think it's much to ask, for her to put her own plate in the dishwasher,' he replied as if Polly wasn't standing right there. He turned back to Polly. 'Many hands make light work, eh, Poll? Your mum's already got enough to do, looking after me.'

Karen elbowed him. 'Keep bossing us around and I might decide to *stop* looking after you,' she warned. 'Leave it, Polly, I'll do it.'

Polly could feel Graham's eyes on her, though, and daren't walk away from her breakfast things. She picked them up and stacked them in the dishwasher, then stalked out, cheeks flaming. Oh God. Told off by her dad already: the man who'd happily sat with his feet up for forty years, never lifting a finger while his wife fussed around him, fetching and carrying all his plates and cups. What had got into him?

She could hear her parents bickering as she unpacked her shampoo and shower gel in the small beige bathroom. 'You didn't have to say it like *that*, Graham. Let her settle in. I don't mind if she leaves her plate on the table, for heaven's sake.'

'Well, I do. I'm not having her making extra work for you. While she's under my roof she's got to pull her weight, and that's the end of it. Clare said she'd expect us to wait on her hand and foot the whole summer – and it looks as if she was right. I won't have it, do you understand?'

'Don't you start ordering me around, Graham Johnson. We hardly ever see Polly. Now she's back, I want to make a fuss of her, spoil her a bit. Can't you see she's exhausted? Give the girl a break.'

There was another snort from Graham, and Polly switched on the shower before she had to listen to his retort. She felt hot all over. So Clare had been bitching about her before she'd even arrived, had she? How unsisterly could you get? Clare was just jealous because she'd never done anything with her life, that was all. Clare was freaked out at the thought of Polly moving into her precious village, because their parents would probably start loving Polly best, now that she was on the scene.

After wedging the last of her favourite bubble bath and body lotion into the bathroom cabinet alongside – ugh – a large tube of haemorrhoid cream and some athlete's foot powder, Polly stepped into the weedy, drizzling shower and gritted her teeth. She had Clare's number, and her sister had better watch out.

Thankfully her parents were both on their way out of the house by the time she was dressed. 'If you get chilly, do put the heating on,' her mum began saying, opening the cupboard that housed the boiler, but her dad swatted her hand away from the thermostat the very next second.

'She won't get chilly, it's June, you silly old bat,' he said irritably. 'Leave her be, she doesn't want all your fussing. Am I right, Poll?'

Polly smiled weakly. 'I'm sure I'll be fine,' she said, not wanting to take sides. 'See you later.'

The door closed and Polly let out a sigh of relief. Finally, a chance to be on her own for a while. She hadn't realized how much tension she'd been holding onto until that moment. Her parents were lovely, in that slightly maddening parental way, but they did kind of cramp one's style. All their funny little routines: their cups of tea on the hour, her dad's tuneless whistling, the dog's annoying yapping ... It was a shame they'd left Sissy behind, she thought darkly, noticing the dog eyeing her from her basket in the kitchen, but you couldn't have everything.

Polly made herself a coffee, then prowled around the bungalow, Sissy trotting after her, as she debated where to set up her new workstation. It was like exploring a foreign country, one where she didn't belong. There was a small table in her bedroom, which her mum had originally suggested she might use, but it was now piled high with boxes, so that was out. The kitchen table wasn't the most practical, either – she'd never get anything done, with her parents traipsing in and out and interrupting her. Short of camping out in the shed, she'd have to use the living room.

'So long, mutt,' she said, dumping Sissy back in her basket and shutting the kitchen door behind her. The last thing she wanted while she worked was the dog gazing up at her with those huge, mournful brown eyes. She needed to concentrate, make the most of this time *sans* parents.

The living room had Artex swirls on the walls and ceiling, and faded burgundy velvet curtains hanging in swags at the windows. The soft plush sofa was a similar wine-red, but unfortunately just too far along the colour spectrum to match. It clashed, actually, Polly thought, wrinkling her nose, and the overall effect wasn't exactly helped by the floral blue arm-covers that her mum had added to cover the worn patches. A seascape painting hung on the wall, and Karen's collection of china animals paraded along the mantelpiece in between a gallery of photographs.

Polly eyed them from a distance. There was one of Clare's wedding: Clare in the naffest, cheapest-looking meringue ever witnessed, with shiny-faced Steve gurning gormlessly beside her. What had she ever seen in that pillock? Polly had known all along that the marriage would be a disaster. Catch her throwing everything away for a bloke? Never.

Her lip curled as she noticed the bridesmaids in long, dark-red dresses flanking the meringue. Clare hadn't asked Polly to be a bridesmaid. Not that Polly had *wanted* to, of course, but it wasn't exactly sisterly of Clare, was it?

There were some baby photos too: bald, chubby Leila with a single front tooth, and Alex brandishing a plastic spade on a windswept beach. A black-and-white photo of her parents' wedding. A family shot of the five of them back when Polly was about ten, on a carefree summer holiday somewhere in Dorset. And Michael's last-ever school photo.

Polly dragged her gaze away quickly, not wanting to look at him, not wanting to meet his eye, and think about what had happened. It was too late, though, and in the next second she was ambushed by a torrent of awful images, including one of her dad sobbing brokenly at the funeral. It was the first time she'd ever seen him cry, and the sight of that unbearable pain etched on his face had scarred Polly's mind like a branding.

Step away from the family photos, Polly, she told herself numbly.

At the other end of the room stood her dad's old Victorian desk, which had originally belonged to his great-grandfather. It was a rather splendid piece of furniture, made of solid mahogany, with four drawers on either side, topped with a green leather writing surface. It was completely out of place in a 1970s bungalow, of course, but there was something reassuringly sturdy about it. This would do for the time being. Turning her back on the photos, Polly went over and cleared the piles of letters and bills that littered the top of the desk and dumped them underneath, then briskly opened her laptop and switched it on. There.

She gazed out of the window while she waited for it to whirr into life. The back garden was her dad's pride and joy, filled with flowers and vegetables. She remembered helping him in their old garden when she'd been bored on summery Sunday afternoons as a child, whenever Michael and Clare had hatched some game that didn't involve her. Dad had had her pulling out clumps of pale flowering chickweed and watering the vegetable plot with the big green watering can, so full and heavy that it had bumped against her bare legs as she'd lugged it from the kitchen, spilling water on her feet in noisy glugs.

Right. Work to do. Staring out of the window wasn't going to get her anywhere. Polly clicked on the Internet connection and the browser opened on its usual job-hunting site. *Here we go again*, she thought, trying not to let the customary pessimistic feelings of doom sweep through her before she'd even begun.

Come on, Polly. Chin up. The sooner you can find a new job, the sooner you can get out of this hole.

That, alone, was more than enough motivation for her to lean forward and start clicking with renewed enthusiasm.

Chapter Ten

Two days later Polly leaned back in her chair, stretched her arms above her head and sighed. It was Friday lunchtime and her parents' house was deserted once again; they'd trekked off to a garden centre this time, making excited noises about bedding plants and bags of compost. Yes, it was thrills galore in Elderchurch, all right.

She'd been sitting here at the computer for the last forty-eight hours and had achieved precisely nothing – except perhaps a grudging respect for the fact that her parents both seemed to have a way more active social life than she'd ever managed. They were never bloody in the house! So much for looking after her, the firstborn, their *guest*. They were far too busy haring about all the time, enjoying themselves. There was something deeply wrong with that, in Polly's opinion. Selfish, even.

Her thoughts slid Londonwards, as they had done approximately every three minutes since her arrival in this dump. She hated imagining her flat sitting empty without her. Would anyone have been tempted by it yet? It was taking every shred of will power not to keep phoning the estate agents for an hourly update.

Now that she was here, miles from the city, it seemed even more of an impossible task to get herself back. She seemed to be going round in circles, visiting the same recruitment websites several times a day, only to see the same maddeningly small list of jobs on offer, almost all of them way too menial for her.

Oh, it was no good. She couldn't do this today. On the spur of the moment she decided that she'd brave it and go into the village, snatch a break and some fresh air (as much as you could call cowshit-smelling air 'fresh' anyway) and try to come up with her Plan B. Plan A – bagging herself a new job asap – didn't seem to be happening right now.

She stood up from the chair, then sat down again just as fast. Whoa, hang on a minute, she needed to think this through. Walking into the village might mean bumping into villagers. Having to engage in conversation. Being asked intrusive questions. 'What are you doing with yourself these days, Polly?'

She'd have to lie and lie and lie, keep up a fake, tight smile the whole time, her face aching with the effort. Oh God. Could she really handle that? Then again, the alternative was to sit dying a slow death at this desk for the rest of the day.

Sod it. She'd do it. She'd brave the outside world for half an hour, power-walking with her shades on so that nobody could look her in the eye. She might even come up with a good idea if she had a change of scenery. And anything was better than vegetating here for hours on end, until her parents returned, laden with nasturtiums and primulas, and brought her yet another too-weak coffee and some custard creams.

She went to put on her shoes and was joined in the hall by an excited, yapping Sissy, obviously thinking a walk was in the offing. 'Well, a walk *is* in the offing, but not for you, you little pest,' Polly mumbled, shoving her feet into a pair of Converse. Damn, the word 'walk' had sent Sissy into an absolute paroxysm of joy: running backwards and forwards in front of Polly, stumpy tail beating like a furry metronome, her big brown eyes full of hope.

Polly stepped over her, completely ignoring the dog's excitement, and eyed herself in the mirror. She wasn't exactly looking her best, she thought ruefully: her hair scraped back into a ponytail, yesterday's clothes on again and no make-up on her pallid skin. It wasn't like she had anyone to impress, though.

She went to the front door, but Sissy yapped louder than ever, racing dementedly around Polly's ankles as soon as she put her hand on the latch.

'Oh, all *right*,' Polly grumbled. 'But don't start getting any ideas. This is just a one-off, so that I look like I've got something to do, okay? Can your tiny canine brain understand that?'

She clipped the lead onto Sissy's collar and off they went.

It was a warm day, the sky swept clear of all clouds, and the sun glaring down like an accusing eye. Polly put her shades on and set off, Sissy trotting companionably by her side.

She was wearing an old T-shirt and a pair of indigo Diesel jeans that had somehow become so baggy on her that she'd had to cinch them in tight with a belt. The sunshine felt pleasingly baking on her bare arms, and after only a few moments she found herself raising her face to its heat, like a flower unfurling. Gorgeous. If one could ignore the hideous modern bungalows on either side and the eyesore caravans (as well as the Marauder, she'd also spotted one called 'Swift'; were the manufacturers *serious?*), she could almost be in Provence or Tuscany, the scent of lavender tickling her nostrils, a meadow of poppy fields on the horizon, a row of cypress trees swaying tipsily on the breeze . . .

The lead jerked as Sissy stopped abruptly. Polly turned and saw her squatting to crap on the pavement, and the vision of paradise vanished in an instant. Ugh. Disgusting.

What was she meant to do with *that*? She hadn't brought any doggy bags with her, hadn't even thought about such things. She dug into the pocket of her jeans, hoping there'd be something in there that she could use to wrap the turd in, in order to dispose of it. This was definitely the sort of place that was heavy on Neighbourhood Watch. If she dared walk away from Sissy's deposit, there would be twitching lace curtains and hands on hips. A local vigilante might even come knocking on her parents' door that evening. 'Thought I should bring it your attention that . . .'

Bloody hell! Stupid dog. Why had she been such a sucker as to fall for those pleading brown eyes in the first place? Now look what she had to deal with.

She dug further into her pockets (a used tissue, no, too small), before finally pulling out a long till receipt for lunch and drinks at the Bluebird on the King's Road, dated March, the last time she'd worn these jeans. That's right, it had been her birthday lunch, she remembered now. She'd stayed away from the office on Saturday for once and had asked a couple of colleagues to join her there. Somehow she'd ended up paying for everyone, though. That wasn't right, was it, when it was her actual birthday? Over two hundred quid, she'd spent, according to the till receipt. It had meant nothing to her at the time, of course, but now the sun made her feel ill. How could she have flung money around so brazenly? Two hundred pounds, just for lunch, for people she didn't even particularly like. She thought about how her parents always snipped out every money-off coupon from the newspaper, how they hunted down bargains and patched up any broken items, rather than buying replacements. Worst of all, she'd looked down on them for doing it.

The receipt in her hand felt like something she wanted to hide, something she never wanted them to see. Which was just as well really, considering what she was about to do with it.

'All this is fit for, Sissy,' she muttered, 'is your shit. Fit for shit, you could say.' Sissy turned away as if maintaining her dignity, while Polly gingerly manoeuvred the receipt under the offending article; ugh, it was still warm; she was *this* close to vomiting everywhere. Somehow (thank God) she managed to shovel it up with the paper and tipped the revolting parcel into the nearest wheelie bin.

Gross. She shuddered, feeling dirty and germ-ridden, and it was all she could do to go on walking. 'Don't do that again,' she told Sissy sternly as they continued along the road. 'I mean it. No more poos, thank you very much. Otherwise I regret to inform you that it'll be dog pie for dinner tonight.'

Sissy barked cheerfully – probably at the word 'dinner' – and Polly shook her head. This was not turning out to be the relaxing stroll she had anticipated.

Further along the lane they went. Now she was venturing into more familiar ground, and Polly glanced warily from side to side, recognizing friends' houses that she'd been into as a girl. There was Catherine Woolley's house, with the white garage and staring windows. The one opposite was where Peter Brooks had lived, she remembered. He'd been friends with her brother, and Polly had always detested his annoying, gappy-toothed grin and freckly face. He and Michael had pelted her with water-bombs in the garden one time when Peter had been round to play, and she could vividly remember the shock of being splattered in the face, drenched right through her T-shirt and shorts; could almost hear their joyful guffaws, her furious scream of 'MU-U-U-UM!' Little sods.

Thinking of Michael brought a pain to her chest, a pain that swelled and expanded like an inflating balloon. She never usually thought about her brother, preferred to block him right out of her head. Coming back here seemed to be sparking off all sorts of memories, though, things she hadn't thought about for years.

He'd always been laughing, Michael. That was what she remembered most about him. Right from when he was little, he'd had the most joyous, pealing laugh of anyone she'd ever met. Happy-go-lucky, they'd written in his school reports. He loved life, the newspaper report had said.

She swallowed, blinking back the tears. Oh God. *Michael.*

What would he be doing now, if he hadn't died? He'd been good at sports and making things – he'd loved helping their dad fiddle with the car engine, the two of them spending hours in the garage together. 'A proper little grease monkey,' Graham would say proudly when they emerged, both covered in oil and beaming with satisfaction. Michael was good at art too, and had painted an enormous silver, red and black mural on his bedroom wall: a wild, glorious mix of patterns and motifs.

'You'll be the one painting over it, if we ever need to sell this house,' their parents had warned, as the mural grew and grew.

But he'd been dead by the time the house went on the market. And it was all Polly's fault.

She dashed away the tears as she walked. *Don't think about him*, she urged herself. *Block it out. It's ancient history – just leave it alone.*

She was nearly at the centre of the village. There was the old church and the churchyard on her left, the cluster of shops just afterwards. She could hardly remember what she was doing here now. The so-called fresh air seemed to be choking her.

Up ahead, an elderly lady was coming towards her, dressed in faded blue slacks and a long-sleeved beige top. She had owlish spectacles and short silvery-grey hair cut in a bob, and there was a jaunty-looking Jack Russell at her side.

Polly's heart thumped as she eyed the woman through her sunglasses. There was something familiar about her; she'd definitely met her somewhere before.

The lady was peering down at Sissy, seeming to recognize her, and said something to her dog. *Oh look, here comes Sissy*, Polly imagined her saying, and a feeling of horror spread through her. Oh no. Here we go. The lady's eyes were gleaming and fixed on Polly now, an extra crease lining her forehead as she tried to place her.

Sensing an interrogation looming only seconds away, Polly veered off quickly through the lychgate of the churchyard and hurried inside. Phew. That was a close one. That was really close. The old woman had been practically opening her mouth to call out to her. *Are you ... are you Karen and Graham's daughter? I heard something about you coming back, how lovely!*

Polly put her arms around herself in relief and hurried along the path that cut through the neatly mown grass. The churchyard was a pretty, peaceful place. A gnarled yew tree spread its branches in the far left corner, making a gentle sighing sound as a breeze lifted and then dropped its limbs. Lichen-covered headstones, some shaped like Celtic crosses, others great slabs of stone with crumbling, curving tops, sprouted randomly in the grass. You could hardly read the names on the oldest stones, for their inscriptions had been weathered away by the centuries of wind and rain, but some dated back to the eighteenth century.

All those people who'd died, and been mourned for here. All those tears shed on this patch of earth, the church bells tolling sombrely in the background through funeral after funeral, loss after loss. It made Polly shiver, even though the sun was still sending out a scorching heat and she realized, with dismay, that she was heading for the so-called Garden of Remembrance, where her brother's ashes had been interred.

She knew her parents came here regularly to sit in the garden and speak to their lost son as if he was still part of the family. She hadn't been back once since the dreadful day of the funeral, though. Every Christmas for years after, her mum and dad had encouraged her to visit the grave in some horrible mawkish act of sentimentality, but Polly had refused each time. What was the point? Michael was gone. Standing on the ground where his ashes had been buried wouldn't change anything. He was still never coming back.

'Excuse me? Er . . . excuse me?'

Polly turned blindly at the sound of the voice. A pink-faced man was hurrying towards her with an air of apology. 'I'm afraid dogs aren't allowed in the churchyard,' he said, clasping his hands together in front of him. 'Would you mind tying – ?' Then he broke off, peering down at the terrier. 'Oh, is that Sissy? Are you Karen and Graham's daughter?'

Curses.

'Yes,' she muttered.

He thrust out a large pink hand. 'Joseph Mullins. I'm the vicar here at Elderchurch. Very nice to meet you. Are you here to see our Remembrance Garden?'

'Er . . .' She was so distracted by his vigorous handshake that she was temporarily lost for words. 'Yes,' she mumbled eventually. It felt churlish not to.

'Let me take Sissy for you then,' he said. 'I'll tie her up at the gate, okay? You just go on ahead to the garden – it's right at the back of the church.' He took the lead out of her hand, then shook his head, as if irritated with himself. 'What am I saying; of course you know where it is. Sissy will be perfectly safe at the front gate, all right?'

And before she could reply he had walked away with the dog and she was left there on her own.

Oka-a-ay. She really had to do this then. Thanks, Vicar. Thanks for pushing me into doing the one thing I didn't want to. Her stomach churned. *It's just a garden,* she told herself. She'd sit there for ten minutes and go home again. And, looking on the bright side, at least nobody would disturb her there.

She walked around the back of the church and followed

the path to a walled garden, pushed open the sturdy wooden gate and went in. Her heart banged inside her ribcage and she had to force herself to breathe normally. It's just a *garden*, she reminded herself again. Don't start freaking out.

The gate clicked shut behind her, but she hardly noticed. She stood there motionless for a few moments, letting her eyes wander about the space, her hands curled in defensive fists by her sides. The garden wasn't huge – about twenty feet square – but it was a riot of colour, with flower-filled borders all the way around. There was an apple tree and what she thought might be a plum tree, and a pretty wooden gazebo and bench, which had both been painted a soft green. There was a stone birdbath in the centre with a single white petal floating on the puddle of water there.

She walked slowly around the path, gazing at the tall, creamy lilies, the papery blue flowers of love-in-a-mist, the pom-pom-like dahlias, the first yellow roses with a blush of pink at the base of their petals, and the sprawling mauve hydrangeas. It was beautiful. Heavenly.

When she reached the gazebo she paused and then, as if her body was moving of its own will, lowered herself to the bench inside and sat there, breathing in the mingled flower scents and watching the bees weave patterns through a robust-looking buddleia.

Her mouth opened, her lips feeling dry. 'Hello Michael,' she whispered, holding her hands tightly in her lap. 'I ...

I'm sorry I haven't been around much. But I never stopped thinking about you.'

Tears plopped from her face onto her hands. Her fingers were trembling. *If that vicar dares come in now, I won't be able to bear it,* she thought fiercely. She imagined herself screaming at him to get out, to mind his own business, to leave her alone, peppering her language with all sorts of words that shouldn't be used in a churchyard.

He didn't appear, though. There was nothing to be heard except the faint soughing of the wind and the musical rattle of the branches on either side of her.

After a few minutes she felt herself relax. She leaned back against the bench and shut her eyes. *I'm sorry, Michael,* she said in her head. *I'm so very sorry. I'll never stop missing you.*

The wind caressed her face and it felt for a moment like the touch of a hand. She opened her eyes, but there was no one there. Just a pale-yellow butterfly that drifted over the wall and away.

Michael had been sixteen when he died. It had happened one Thursday in March, just an ordinary, average, drizzly March day, with no portentous bolts of lightning or bone-shaking earthquakes to herald his last day on earth. He'd had a bad headache for about a week, and Karen had booked him a doctor's appointment for the Friday, after he'd complained about the pain for several days. 'I've had migraines myself,' she'd said, dosing him up with more paracetamol. 'They're horrible things. You stay in bed and try to sleep.'

If only they'd known. If only there had been an earlier appointment. It had been no good booking him in for Friday. He was already dead by then.

Polly remembered feeling rather disbelieving of her brother's ailment at the time. She knew he had a ton of GCSE coursework he was meant to be doing and wondered if it was all an elaborate skive. She remembered (oh, the guilt) being dismissive of him when he could barely eat anything at teatime. 'On a diet, are we?' she'd mocked, raising her eyes to the ceiling as he miserably pushed his food around on the plate, one hand still clutching his forehead. 'This in aid of Julie Miles, by any chance?'

'Sod off,' he'd growled, kicking her under the table.

That night Clare was swimming in a gala. Clare was fourteen at the time and showing real promise as a sprint swimmer. 'We'll have you in the next Olympics, you wait,' her dad kept crowing as she won race after race. Clare's half of the bedroom that she shared with seventeen-year-old Polly was rapidly becoming papered over with certificates, while the mantelpiece gleamed with medals and trophies.

It was the Hampshire County Championships this time, held in Waterlooville, and both proud parents were taking

Clare. 'Keep an eye on Michael,' Karen had said, as they'd headed out to the car. 'He can have two more paracetamol at ten o'clock, all right? See you later.'

'Sure,' Polly said blithely, then as soon as she heard their car pull out of the drive, immediately dialled her boyfriend's number. 'Jay? They've gone. Fancy coming over?'

Jay and Polly had been inseparable back then. They were going to spend the rest of their lives together. After their A-levels that summer they planned to work somewhere until Christmas – hopefully Jay's dad would sort them out jobs at the brewery he worked for – and then intended to go inter-railing for six months, just set off with a backpack each and travel to Italy, Spain, Germany ... Jay had ambitions for them to have sex in every European capital city. 'We'll tackle the rest of the world later,' he vowed. The future stretched out like a ray of sunshine, bright and golden, full of promise and excitement and saucy contortions in foreign backpacker hostels. It was all going to be fantastic.

Jay duly arrived and the two of them had spent the evening on the sofa, indulging in what Amberley Leisure Centre called 'heavy petting' to the sound of *Pills 'n' Thrills and Bellyaches*, which was 'their' album. They'd had sex before – sticky knee-tremblers around the back of the youth club, daring entanglements at Jay's house when they were supposed to be at college, and once even in a bus shelter on the way back from a friend's party – but never at Polly's house. She felt weird about it, especially with Michael being there upstairs.

'He won't know,' Jay kept whispering hotly into her ear, as his hand crept up her T-shirt. 'If we're really quiet, he'll never know.'

She'd giggled. She couldn't resist. 'Go on, then. But we've got to be quick,' she muttered.

And so, fumbling and fondling, they'd removed one another's clothes and Polly had lain back on the burgundy faux-leather sofa, the vinyl cushions cold under her bare bum. Jay had wrestled with the condom and just then, over the sound of his rubbery manoeuvring and Shaun Ryder's drawl, she'd heard a cry. 'Polly? Polly!'

She froze. 'That's Michael,' she said, feeling very exposed and less sure about this whole idea all of a sudden. If her brother came downstairs now and saw her like this, oh my God, she'd absolutely *die*. He'd never let her forget it!

Jay grinned, condom-clad cock bobbing as he straddled her. 'Don't think about him,' he whispered. 'Think about this.'

Then he was kissing her, and Michael drifted clean out of her mind. And at some moment during Jay's thrusts and her muffled gasps, her brother died in a small bedroom upstairs, all on his own, just like that.

She didn't find out until it was too late. Once she and

Jay had cleaned themselves up, faces flushed, hair dishevelled, beaming at one another; once the soggy tissues had been plunged well into the kitchen bin so that her parents would be none the wiser; once the sofa had been given a quick wipe-over and the cushions plumped up again, only then had she remembered her brother calling out to her.

'I suppose I'd better go and see what Sickboy wanted,' she said, her eyes lingering on Jay's face. 'Back in a minute.'

And then nothing was ever the same again.

Polly gripped the edge of the bench, trying to push away the images of that awful night, but they kept hurtling into her mind as if it had only been last week.

It had been a cerebral aneurysm, the rupture of a bulging blood vessel in his brain, causing a massive haemorrhage. 'A time-bomb waiting to go off,' they'd said at the hospital. 'Incredibly rare. There was nothing anyone could have done.'

But Polly disagreed. If she'd got to her brother in time, if she'd run to him when he'd called out her name instead of prostrating herself for Jay, she might have been able to save him. She could have made everything different. It was all her fault.

Blindly she got up from the bench. Her breath felt shallow and difficult, and she put a hand to her chest as she walked. She had to get back to her parents' house, had to get away from this garden. The scent of the flowers seemed intoxicating now, overpowering. They made her feel queasy and faint.

Her mind still bursting with unasked-for memories, she stumbled through the gate and along the churchyard path to find Sissy. Sweat trickled down her spine and her tongue felt thick and uncomfortable in her parched, dry mouth.

Coming back had been a mistake, a terrible mistake. She grabbed Sissy's lead and all but ran to the bungalow.

Chapter Eleven

On Friday evening Karen knocked on Clare's back door and let herself in. 'Yoohoo, babysitter entering premises,' she yodelled.

Clare was up in her bedroom, trying to decide what to wear. 'Down in a minute,' she yelled, hearing the children's cries of 'Grandma!' and Fred's welcoming woof, then turned back to the mirror.

The jeans were giving her a bit of a muffin-top — she'd put on a few pounds lately. It was typical that she should be feeling blobby just when her sister had rocked up looking like a size zero. Mind you, Polly's gaunt, haggard appearance wasn't exactly scoring highly on the foxy stakes, either. Clare had found herself wondering if this 'research' that her sister had come to do was actually code for some horrible terminal illness. Polly's hair, which had always been enviably glossy and bouncy, was now dull and straggly, just hanging from her scalp. Her brown eyes looked like holes in her head, ringed with the dark circles of a poor sleeper, although they glittered with defiance, as if daring Clare to say a single word about her appearance.

It was only when Polly started speaking in that insufferably patronizing way of hers that Clare realized she was fighting fit after all, rather than on her deathbed. 'Fighting' being the operative word.

Oh, skirt it was, she decided, snatching it off the hanger. She was heading into Amberley for Roxie's birthday drinks and there would probably be hordes of Roxie's skinny young twenty-something friends there too. Next to them, she'd feel like a fat slab of mutton dressed as lamb in her jeans. Her legs were her best feature, even if they were still slightly streaky from a self-tanning disaster; she might as well show them off in a skirt rather than cover them up.

She dressed quickly, slapped on some mascara and lipstick and dabbed her wrists and neck with perfume. A few weeks ago she'd seen an article in one of the magazines at the surgery about making your own scent and she'd tried some of the recipes printed there. This fragrance was called 'Arabian Queen' and was a heady mix of orange, juniper, coriander and frankincense oils. It smelled fresh and exotic on her skin, and she was complimented on the scent every time she wore it. She'd already wrapped up a bottle of it for Roxie, along with a home-made bath-bomb, as her present. One day she'd be able to afford flash gifts for her friends, like Polly could, but right now everyone would just have to make do with cheap and cheerful.

One last look in the mirror. She fluffed up her shoulder-length brown hair, peered in at her eyes to check for stray blobs of mascara and bared her teeth to inspect them for lipstick. She wished she didn't look quite so nervous. Then she flicked off the bedroom light and ran downstairs to the kitchen, where she could hear Leila and Alex chattering away to Grandma, talking over one another in their eager-ness to tell her all their news.

Karen looked up as Clare came in. She was sitting at the table with Fred's daft head on her knee and a grandchild on either side. 'Hi, love,' she said. 'You look nice. Ooh, lovely perfume too,' she added, sniffing the air.

'Thanks, Mum,' Clare said. 'It's one I made – I've got lots spare, if you want a bottle of your own.'

'Yes, please,' her mum replied. She winked at the children. 'That'll give Grandad a shock, won't it, when I come in smelling all posh.'

Clare smiled. 'Kids, get your pyjamas on, I'll be up in five minutes to do your teeth.' She set the kettle to boil as they thundered upstairs. 'How's it going, then, with your new house-guest?' she asked, frowning as she noticed how weary her mum looked. She hoped Polly hadn't run her ragged.

'Well, it's taking a bit of getting used to,' Karen replied

delicately, stroking Fred's silky ears, 'but it's lovely to have her. She's working ever so hard, though. I haven't dared hoover or sit down and watch any of my programmes because she's sat there at the desk all day.' She shook her head, a web of fine lines creasing the sides of her mouth as she clicked her tongue. 'I wish she'd relax a bit, but she's ... Well, she seems very tense. Me and your dad have been tiptoeing around her. Your dad didn't even watch *Countdown* this afternoon. Went out and mowed the lawn instead, even though it didn't really need doing. And then Polly got all tetchy about the noise, so he shouldn't have bothered.'

'Hmmm,' Clare said. It irked her, her parents having to pussyfoot around Polly in their own home. 'Can't she work in her room? I mean, why does she have to hog the living room? Surely Dad should be able to watch *Countdown* when he wants to.'

'That's what he says,' Karen replied, scratching Fred under the chin. 'We've had a few barneys about it already. You know what he's like, the stubborn old mule. But we'll all get used to each other soon, I'm sure,' she added loyally. 'It's just ... different.'

Clare busied herself making the tea and didn't reply immediately. She knew her mum was so happy to have Polly back that she wasn't about to rock the boat in any way. That was understandable, given that Polly had all but estranged herself for so many years, but at the same time

Clare didn't want her sister to take advantage. 'Well, don't let her push you around, all right?' she said in the end. 'Tell her you'll stop her allowance if she doesn't behave. Or ground her!'

'Chance would be a fine thing,' Karen sighed. 'She's grounded herself. Not interested in coming out and meeting our friends. Not bothered about seeing Jacky Garland, even though Jacky invited her over, said she'd organize a little coffee morning with some of Polly's other friends from school so that they could all catch up.'

'What, and she said no?'

Karen nodded. 'Didn't even think about it before she refused flat out. What am I going to tell Jean now? It's very rude, especially when Jacky's going out of her way.' She shrugged. 'Probably seems a bit quiet here after London, though. She must miss all her mates. I've been trying to get out of her whether or not there's a fella on the scene back there, but if there is, she's not letting on.' She mimed zipping her lips. 'You know Polly, though. Always been the secretive type.'

'Mmmm,' Clare said. It was weird, she mused, how none of them had any idea what was happening in Polly's private life. Clare knew nothing whatsoever about her sister's relationships or friendships, hadn't a clue what she did in her spare time. She could have been married several times over, for all that the rest of the family knew. Her mum was right – Polly had always been secretive; a closed book, whereas Clare was completely the opposite. She had the worst face ever for playing poker, you could read every emotion she was experiencing from the expression she wore. It was kind of annoying sometimes, being so transparent, but at least she felt honest. What must it be like being Polly, so repressed and shut-off from the world? How could anyone bear to live that way?

'Edith Lindley said she'd seen her dashing into the churchyard earlier,' Karen said, raising her eyebrows meaningfully. 'I couldn't believe it, but she said it was definitely Polly. Well, it was definitely Sissy anyway, and I'm pretty sure nobody else was walking her into the village.'

'Wow,' Clare said, taken aback. 'She hasn't been there for—'

'Since the funeral,' Karen said quietly. They locked eyes. 'I've not had the chance to ask her about it yet. I hope she's all right.'

It was a twenty-minute drive to Amberley at this time of the evening, and Clare found a parking space in the Somerfield car park for her little battered Fiat. Driving there and back wasn't ideal, but she couldn't afford the cab fare, and it was too far to walk. It meant she couldn't drink either, which was a pain. On this sort of occasion where you were thrust into somebody else's circle of friends, not knowing any of them, a bit of Dutch courage really helped. Still, she was so skint she couldn't afford Dutch courage anyway. She'd have to dredge up some of her own instead.

Roxanne was having her birthday drinks in The Fox and Goose, a smart, upmarket bar on Amberley's main street. It had been styled with mellow lighting, ironic flock wallpaper and elegant, chintzy sofas set around solid wooden tables. Some of the walls were rough stone, while others were hung with vibrant paintings, wrought-iron sconces bearing thick white candles and, bizarrely, a black-and-white cowhide.

There was already a crowd when Clare walked in, and a buzzy Friday-night atmosphere. She scanned the place for her friend and began to make her way through the tables of shiny-haired women and smart-casual men, trying not to feel intimidated. It was certainly a far cry from the King's Arms in Elderchurch, the sole pub in the village, a cosy, comforting place of worn velvet banquettes and dark wood, where Stu and Erica, the landlord and landlady, presided over the beer pumps like everyone's favourite aunt and uncle.

She craned her neck, trying to catch a glimpse of the birthday girl. Where was she?

'Clare, is that you?'

A deep voice just behind her left ear made her jump, and Clare swung around. Then she blushed. Luke Brightside was standing right there, inches away, smiling down at her. He was tall with rather rumpled dark hair and grey eyes and . . . and he was far too young and handsome for the likes of Clare, she reminded herself firmly.

'Oh good,' he said. 'It *is* you. I hate walking into places like this on my own. Where do you suppose Birthday Princess is then?'

Clare smiled, grateful to have been spotted. He smelled nice: fresh, woody and masculine. Then she realized he was waiting for her to speak. 'Um . . . I don't know,' she gabbled stupidly. Heat rushed into her face. God, she was so obvious. Middle-aged single mother hitting on the young handsome doctor. How sad could you get?

'Let's brave the meat-market together, shall we?' he joked.

'Let's,' Clare said. 'Eyes peeled for the Birthday Princess.' And to cover her awkwardness at being in such close proximity to Luke, she promptly strode away from him into the crowd.

After a near miss with a gin-and-tonic spill, then almost treading on someone's dainty Grecian-sandalled foot with her own great clodhoppers, Clare spotted Roxie holding court in a corner at the back. She was wearing a satsuma-coloured, tight, ruched dress complete with matching feathery hairband perched in her curled blonde hair, high pink heels and about a gallon of mascara. On Clare, the outfit would have looked monstrous, but Roxie was so supremely confident in herself that the whole look screamed fabulous.

'Clare! Luke! Ooh, hello,' she squealed. She was sitting against the wall, surrounded by a gaggle of women drinking lurid cocktails, but crawled inelegantly under the table to get out and greet the new arrivals.

Clare laughed as Roxie emerged, brushed herself down and flung her arms around each of them in turn. 'Thank you so much for coming,' she said, beaming. 'Did you arrive ... together?' She raised an eyebrow as if scenting gossip, and Clare shook her head.

'Just met at the door,' she said, pressing the gift bag of presents into Roxie's hand. 'Here. Happy birthday, lovely.'

Luke handed over a card. 'Happy birthday, Roxie,' he said. 'Sorry, I'm hopeless with presents, but let me buy you a drink at least.'

'Oh, you don't have to, Luke,' Roxie demurred, batting her eyelashes. 'But go on then, it is my birthday, so I'll have a Kinky Pink please, thank you very much.'

Luke laughed at her breathless delivery. 'A Kinky ... Pink. Okay. I can do that,' he said. 'Clare, how about you, what would you like?'

Satin sheets, fresh strawberries and your naked body was on the tip of her tongue. 'A lime and soda,' was all she said, though. 'Please.'

He walked away and she had to stop herself from sighing with out-and-out lust. Get a grip, Clare. She was glad that she wasn't having an alcoholic drink now; she'd only get overexcited and make a tit of herself. That was one thing she did *not* want to do in front of Dr Brightside.

'Ah, when you two arrived together like that, I thought something exciting might have happened,' Roxie teased.

'As if,' Clare replied, pulling a face. 'Are you having a good time then?'

'I certainly am,' Roxie replied. 'See that guy over there – don't stare! – in the lavender shirt with the cropped hair? I've got my eye on him. Planning to kidnap him and take him back to mine later, see if he'll give me a birthday treat.'

Clare slid her gaze along to where a good-looking man in his early twenties sat with a couple of mates. He wore a garish shirt (Clare would have said purple, but she supposed 'lavender' sounded more tasteful) and had unusual green eyes (colour contacts?) and a swarthy, unshaven jaw. Just looking at it made Clare imagine how prickly it would be to be kissed by him when that jaw was sandpapering against your face, but she decided it was better not to say so. 'Nice,' she commented. 'So, are you going to introduce me to your friends then, or what?'

Roxie introduced her to Davina, Maz, Coco, Jodie, Amelie, Izzy and ... oh, Clare had lost track by Izzy. She smiled, feeling dazed, as one by one these gorgeous young creatures stopped nattering and turned to say hi to her. 'Hi, everyone,' she said with a silly little wave. 'Um ... mind if I sit next to you, Coco?'

'It's Jodie, but sure, go ahead,' Jodie replied, tossing her sleek chestnut mane over one shoulder.

Clare was saved from having to initiate an awkward conversation by Luke reappearing and plonking a large pink cocktail in front of her. 'Sorry,' he said cheerfully, 'I completely forgot what you said you wanted, so I bought you a Kinky Pink as well. Roxie! Here's your drink.' He sat next to Clare and raised a pint of lager in her direction. 'Cheers,' he said. 'Nice to be out with you for a change. We never get the chance to speak much at the surgery, do we?'

'No,' Clare said, eyeing her cocktail warily. It looked dangerously alcoholic. 'Um ... What's in this, do you know?' she asked. 'Only I've got the car; I'm going to drive back tonight.'

'Oh God, sorry,' he said. 'My memory's so crap. People tell me things and seconds later it's vanished from my head. What was it you wanted? I'll go back to the bar.'

Clare hesitated. She had twenty-five quid in her purse, which was meant to last the weekend. She really didn't want to dip into that for a taxi, which would probably cost fifteen pounds. And while she mustn't get over the limit, at the same time she didn't want to have to explain all this to Luke, as she was worried that she'd come across as a total wet or, even worse, a skinflint. 'Don't worry,' she said. 'One drink will be fine. And thank you.'

'Are you sure?' he asked. 'I don't mind. We can always give it to Roxie, she'll be happy to neck them both, I bet.'

Clare made some rapid calculations. She wanted to get Roxie a drink, and would like to buy Luke one too, now that he'd got the first round. That would probably come to the best part of a tenner. If she dragged this Kinky Pink out and then just drank tap water, she'd be all right. 'No, it's fine,' she said. Decision made, she sipped it. 'It's lovely, thanks.'

There was a small silence as they looked around. Then they both started talking at once.

'So, do you know . . . ?'

'So, whereabouts do you . . . ?'

He laughed. 'Go on, you first,' he said.

'I was just going to ask if you knew if anyone else from the surgery was coming along tonight?' Clare said. There were five doctors at the practice – Angela Copper (forty-something, married with two teenage daughters), Marcus Walter (as delicate and blond as Luke was strapping and dark; Lancastrian, gay), Edward Arkwright (approaching retirement; grizzled and grumpy) and Hilary Manning (a pale fifty-something who looked like a librarian, was devoted to her four cats and had the kindest, gentlest voice Clare had ever heard). Of all of them, the only likely contender was Marcus, but Roxie was so unpredictable that she might well have asked Dr Arkwright down for a few flaming Sambucas.

'Your guess is as good as mine,' Luke said. 'I think Marcus is in London this weekend, and Angela said something about having friends over for dinner. As for Hilary and Edward...' He grinned. 'Somehow I doubt it. In the nicest possible way, of course.' He swung his head around to take in the circle of friends around Roxie. 'What's the plan for tonight anyway? Roxie said something terrifying-sounding about going to some godawful club later on – are you planning to tag along?' He pulled a face. 'Please say you're not. I can't bear those places any more. They make me feel such an old fart.'

Clare spluttered with laughter. Luke Brightside was so *not* an old fart. 'Don't give me that!' she told him. 'I bet you're younger than me. And no, I'm not going on to a club. I've—' She was about to say her mum was babysitting and she'd promised to be back by midnight at the latest, like the Elderchurch Cinderella. Something stopped her, though. She didn't want to be mumsy right now, blathering on about babysitting and children. 'I'm more of a pubber than a clubber these days,' she said instead.

'Oh, me too,' he replied. 'And I'm thirty-four, so I must be ... oh, at least ten years older than you.'

His eyes were twinkling, he was teasing her, but it was

nice. 'Thirty-*four*?' she repeated, pantomiming horror. 'Oh God, well, I take it all back then, you *are* an old fart. I'm a mere spring chicken at thirty-three, you see.'

They both laughed and it felt so cosy, so intimate, that for a second – for a mad second – she felt a pulse of attraction between them.

'Clare,' Luke said, leaning in a fraction closer.

'Yes?' She was all but shivering with excitement.

An unmistakable buzzing and trilling sounded from her bag. She'd turned her phone up to loud so that she'd hear any calls above the sound of the music. 'Um . . . is that your mobile?' he asked.

She tore herself reluctantly from his gaze and bent down to find it. 'Sorry,' she said. 'Just a sec, I'll turn it off.' The caller display read 'Mum' and she hesitated. It was probably only something silly about whether Karen could give the leftover sausages to Fred, but . . . 'Sorry,' she said again, 'I'll be two seconds.' She pressed the green button. 'Hi, Mum, is everything okay?'

'Oh, thank goodness,' came Karen's flustered voice. 'It's Leila, I think you'd better come back. She's been sick in her bed, and she's burning up.'

Clare felt as if someone had thrown a bucket of icy water over her. 'I'll be there as soon as I can,' she said, rising from her seat. 'Sorry, Luke, I've got to go, my daughter's ill.' She stared around in search of Roxie, but saw that she was in the middle of some outrageous story or other, judging by the shrieks coming from her audience. 'Tell Roxie I've had to go, will you?'

Then, without waiting for an answer, she grabbed her bag and hurried out of the pub.

Chapter Twelve

'Clare! Wait!'

She was pounding along the street, the warmth of the pub fading from her cheeks, the shout only dimly registering in her brain amid a tangle of swirling worries. Typical, wasn't it, the one night she dared go out and her daughter fell ill. The one night she wasn't there, guarding her babies. Bad mummy. Negligent mummy. She had to get home as fast as possible. Thank goodness she had the car.

'CLARE! Wait!'

Footsteps thudded behind her and then Luke was at her side. 'I'll come with you,' he offered, his eyes liquid in the filmy evening light. 'We can stop at the surgery, grab a medical kit, I can check her over for you. If you want me to, of course?' he added, less certainly.

'Would you? Oh God, that would be brilliant, thank you,' she panted gratefully. 'My car's just in here,' she added, pointing at the car-park entrance on their right. 'Thank you. She slowed to a jog, putting a hand to her chest. She was wheezing like an old boiler and probably scarlet in the face, but who cared. Who fucking cared. All she cared about was her daughter.

This was what happened when you weren't watching all the time, she thought miserably. This was what happened when you took your eye off the ball for a second, allowed yourself to be distracted by ridiculously pink cocktails and ridiculously handsome doctor colleagues. This was what happened when you swanned off to a swimming gala, insisting both parents came with you, leaving your ill brother behind, only for him to —

She felt as if something was squeezing her heart in an iron grip. *Don't go there. She's going to be okay.*

Clare unlocked the Fiat, her fingers shaking on the key. 'Thanks, Luke,' she said as he folded himself into the small car. 'I really appreciate this. I'm probably completely over-reacting, but...' She gave a false laugh as she started the engine, willing it to fire up first time. Result.

'But she's your daughter, and it's not worth taking a risk,' Luke finished gently.

She swallowed. 'Yep,' she said. She turned on the head-lights, released the handbrake and drove away, her usual caution deserting her. Thank God she hadn't drunk any more than a few sips of the cocktail. Thank God Luke was with her too. It was one of the things she hated most about being a single parent — trying to make medical diagnoses and decisions about her children on her own when they were ill or injured. How she longed to have someone else there to say, 'I think he's fine, it's just a bump' or 'Let's get her down to A&E' so that it wasn't solely up to her to make the call. Clare always felt as if her mind froze with hundreds of possibilities at the slightest rash or temperature or tummy ache. Was it meningitis? Pneumonia? Gastric flu?

Worse was when one of the children had a headache. It was all she could do to prevent herself roping them to her side, not wanting to be apart from them for a single second until they felt better.

Aneurysms were hereditary, she knew. If the same string of genetic code was present in her children as had been in Michael, then—

She snapped her attention back to the road. She was driving too fast. 'Sorry,' she said. 'My brother died young,' she went on by way of explanation. 'I get kind of twitchy about ill children.'

'Shit, Clare, really?' The sympathy was coming off him in waves. 'How awful. What happened?'

'Cerebral aneurysm,' she said tightly, not trusting herself to say anything else for a moment. She pulled in at the surgery and left the engine running. 'And it was all my fault.'

He stared at her and shook his head. 'No,' he said. 'No,

Clare. An aneurysm isn't anyone's fault. Ever. Wait there and I'll just grab some kit. I'll be right back.'

She sat there numbly, the indicator still ticking as he scrambled out of the car, unlocked the surgery and was swallowed up in its darkness. The lights blinked on and she saw him disabling the alarm, then running into one of the treatment rooms.

He was back in the passenger seat in less than two minutes, and she drove off while he was still clipping his seatbelt in.

'Sorry,' she mumbled again. 'I shouldn't have gone on like that about my brother. It's just there in my head whenever one of the kids is ill.'

'Well, that's entirely understandable,' he said. 'And I'll give you a lecture about how it couldn't possibly have been your fault another time. Tell me about your daughter now, though. What do you know?'

Clare started reciting back what her mum had said, but her mind had travelled to the pool in Waterlooville. There she had been, racing costume, white rubber cap and goggles on. Lane four. She and the other girls in her heat were standing at the edge of the pool, knees bent, poised to spring, waiting for the countdown. Under-fourteens butterfly, one hundred metres. Her favourite event.

She was trying to empty her mind as her coach had

taught her, to focus only on her body, her beating heart, her pumped-up energy, the strength and power in her arms and legs. She could do this. She could win it. And if she could just knock a second off her personal best, then—

'Could Mr and Mrs Graham Johnson please report to Reception?' came a crackly voice over the tannoy, and Clare had jerked out of her thoughts in surprise. 'That's Mr and Mrs Graham Johnson, please report to Reception.'

Then came the official's command. 'On your marks.'

The other girls bent into their starting positions, heads tucked in, hips high, fingers dangling by their toes. Clare copied after a moment, feeling distracted as she glimpsed her parents making their way through the rows of spectators. They were going to miss her race. What was going on?

'Get set . . .'

Five bodies tensed on their blocks. Clare couldn't concentrate. The voice *had* said Mr and Mrs Graham Johnson, hadn't it? Could there really be two Graham Johnsons in the building? Was everything all right?

BEEP!

The signal went and everyone dived in, Clare's body working automatically as she threw her arms forward and took off, entering the water cleanly. *Focus, Clare, focus.* She powered down the pool, trying to push her parents from her mind. *Think about this. This race. Your arms and legs, nothing else.*

It was no good. Her concentration had deserted her. She'd finished fourth, a full five seconds off her personal best. Afterwards she'd hauled herself out of the water and raced to find someone who'd tell her what was happening, only to hear the most devastating words anyone had ever said to her. Michael's dead.

Whatever Luke said, it *was* her fault Michael died that night. Her mum had wanted to stay behind and look after him, but Clare had pulled a strop, stamped her foot even, saying that these were the County *Championships*, didn't Mum *care?*

If only she'd kept her mouth shut and gone with just her dad. If only she'd had the sense to think that of course her mum cared; she just cared about Michael too.

Too late for 'if only' now, though.

'Here we are,' she said thankfully as they reached Elder-church and she turned into her street. For a moment, she felt self-conscious at the idea of Luke seeing her ramshackle little cottage. He probably lived someplace much grander, being a doctor. But again, who cared? All that stuff was irrelevant right now. 'Come on in.'

The house was quiet as they entered. 'Mum?' Clare called softly.

'In here,' came a voice from the living room.

They went in to find Leila and Karen on the sofa, Leila lying with her head on Karen's lap as they watched *Kung-Fu*

Panda on DVD; Fred at their feet, as if guarding the young mistress from any more germs. 'Mum,' croaked Leila, her eyes fever-bright in her flushed face. 'I've been sick.'

'Hello, love,' Clare said, rushing over and putting a hand on her daughter's clammy forehead. 'Poor old you, Grandma told me you were poorly. Dr Brightside's here, he's going to have a look at you. Mum, have you met Luke before? Luke, this is my mum, Karen.' The words were gushing out of her in a torrent.

'Yes, we've met,' Karen said, smiling up at him. She'd been to the surgery for her arthritis a number of times, but always booked appointments on days when Clare wasn't working. She didn't want her to worry.

'Hi,' Luke said politely, but his eyes were on Leila and he crouched in front of her. 'Hello, Leila. Can you sit up for me? Let's see what your temperature's like.'

He popped the thermometer into her mouth and felt behind her ears for swollen glands. 'Good girl,' he said.

Clare perched on the arm of the sofa and held Leila's hot sticky hand while Luke checked her tummy for spots (none, that was good), read her temperature (one hundred and one, not so good) and peered into her mouth and ears.

'I don't think there's anything to worry about,' he said after a few minutes. 'Nothing is seriously wrong, it just looks like a virus to me. Give her some Calpol to bring down the fever, and make sure she has plenty of fluids.' He smiled at Leila. 'The best place for you now is bed, young lady,' he said. 'Have a nice long sleep and hopefully you'll feel better in the morning.'

Clare's heartrate began to subside from its nervous gallop; she felt dizzied with relief. 'Thank you,' she said, squeezing Leila's hand. 'I'm so grateful. I'll just sort Leila out, then I'll give you a lift back to Amberley.'

'There's no need, honestly.' He rose to his feet. 'You stay here. I can call a cab.'

'Definitely not,' Karen said. 'It'll cost a fortune, this time of night. I'll run you back, Luke, my car's just outside. That way Clare can stay here with Leila.'

Luke looked awkward. 'Are you sure?' he said. 'I don't want to put you out.'

'You won't,' she said firmly. 'It's the least we can do.'

Clare's relief that Leila was okay was now giving way to huge embarrassment that she'd torn Luke away from his Friday-night drinks to her shabby little cottage when nothing was even badly wrong with her daughter. Look at him there, so tall and handsome, in his nice going-out shirt and aftershave, the doctor to the rescue ... and for what? A piddly virus and a botched, ruined night, cut short because of a paranoid, hypochondriac, sad old mum.

'Sorry about this, Luke,' she said, remorse coursing

through her. 'I shouldn't have dragged you out, I just panicked. I owe you one, all right? I'll – I'll bring you extra coffees all week. It was really kind of you.'

He smiled. 'Hey, you didn't drag me anywhere,' he reminded her. 'I followed you and invited myself along, remember? But I'll take you up on the free coffee thing all the same,' he added, his eyes crinkling at the edges. He looked as if he was about to say something else when his phone beeped and he looked at the screen. 'Ahh,' he said.

'Everything all right?' Clare asked.

Luke dragged his eyes away from the phone. 'Yep. That was Corinne,' he said. 'Finished her shift early.'

'Corinne?' Clare echoed, feeling her heart contract.

'My girlfriend,' he said. 'She's a nurse in Salisbury,' he added for no particular reason. 'I'd better go,' he went on, turning to Karen. 'Are you absolutely sure about giving me a lift? You're not just being polite?'

'Of course I'm sure,' she said, getting up and smoothing down her skirt. 'Let's go. Goodnight, Clare. Goodnight, darling.'

'Give me a ring if she's not well again by Sunday,' Luke said to Clare on the doorstep. 'Here, this is my mobile number.'

Clare felt worse than ever as he scribbled it down. Luke had a girlfriend. Corinne. A sexy piece in a nurse's uniform, no doubt. Damn it. Damn it! She cringed as she thought how gooey-eyed she'd been at him in the bar earlier. Horrendous or what? He'd probably have a good old laugh with Corinne about it later on. *Talk about a desperate housewife,* he'd say. *Totally delusional!*

No. He wouldn't say that. He was too nice. But all the same ... Thank God she hadn't drunk all of that cocktail. The evening had been embarrassing enough without her getting sloshed and fawning over him even more.

She gave Leila some Calpol, put her back to bed, sent Roxie an apologetic text explaining her sudden disappearance, then slumped in front of the television feeling a total fool. Why did everything always go wrong for her?

Not at all, Luke had said when she'd thanked him for the thousandth time. *Better to be safe than sorry when it comes to children. I'm just glad there's nothing seriously wrong.*

His niceness curdled inside her, somehow making things even worse. Oh well, she thought glumly, leaning her head back on the sofa and shutting her eyes. At least it had nipped her tragic little crush in the bud before she made an even bigger fool of herself. At least now she knew where she stood.

The following morning Leila seemed much better, if a little wan and washed out, so Clare decided a quiet day at home would do them all good. She and the children baked cookies together, then they found homes in the garden for the young strawberry plants her mum had brought round the night before. After a restorative cookie or two all round ('just to test them'), Clare did some weeding while Leila read an *Artemis Fowl* book in the shade, and Alex played a rowdy game of football with Fred. She was growing some plants that she could use in her bath products – lavender, mint, rosemary, chamomile – and was cultivating some baby cucumber plants because she'd read about a cucumber-and-lemon shampoo that was meant to be amazing. She sat back on her haunches and nibbled a peppermint leaf in the sunshine, feeling slightly more cheerful. Who needed a man around the place, anyway? She and the kids were doing just fine without one.

On Sunday they went to Clare's parents for lunch, as they had done every Sunday for the last ten years or so. The only difference today was that Polly was there. Somehow having that one extra person at the kitchen table altered the dynamic completely. The children seemed more subdued, her mum was getting flustered about the gravy, and even her dad wasn't whistling while he carved the chicken. He always whistled while he carved the chicken – admittedly a tuneless, rather irritating drone of a whistle, but it meant he was happy at least. Not today.

Clare made everyone drinks and helped carry the dishes of food to the table while her sister sat there, Princess Polly, not lifting a finger. Not even making conversation with her niece and nephew who were whispering furtively together, their heads bent low.

'Is that everything? Then help yourselves,' her mum said, a rather strained expression on her face as she sat down.

Polly looked less peaky, Clare noticed, eyeing her across the dishes of roast potatoes and vegetables as she spooned peas, carrots and green beans onto her children's plates. ('Not *that* many peas, Mum,' Alex moaned, but she ignored him.) Her sister's face actually had some colour to it now, Clare saw, rather than the deathly pallor it had had a few days earlier. But there was still a haunted look about her eyes and huge dark rings around them, as if she wasn't sleeping well.

'How's work?' Clare asked when it became obvious that Polly wasn't about to offer up any conversational openings herself.

Polly looked down at her plate. 'Not bad,' she muttered, sawing at a piece of chicken breast. 'You?'

God, was that all she was going to give? Clare bristled, not wanting to let her sister off the hook that easily. Couldn't she see how rude she was being? 'Have you got much done since you came here?' she persisted. 'I guess you must be at the preliminary stages, right?'

'Mmm,' Polly said, not looking at her.

There was an uneasy silence. 'She's been working ever so

hard,' Karen put in brightly, pouring gravy. 'Hours and hours she's sat there.'

'Even yesterday, when I was trying to watch the cricket,' Graham said. He rolled his eyes in an aiming-to-be-affectionate manner, but his annoyance came across loud and clear. 'Not that it was any great loss,' he mumbled as an afterthought. 'England were woeful.'

'Wow, working on a Saturday,' Clare said, watching Polly closely. 'That *is* dedicated.' She raised an eyebrow at her dad. 'Must be where we've gone wrong all these years. Monday to Friday just doesn't cut it, if you want to get to the top.'

Polly's face tightened, but she said nothing. Somehow this annoyed Clare even more than if she'd retaliated to the goading. She was just about to push further, get some kind of rise out of her sister, when her mum changed the subject.

'Remind me, Leila, what day is your assembly next week?'

'Thursday,' Leila said through a mouthful of potato. 'It's going to be so cool – we're doing it on the Tudors, and we've found out all these gross things about Tudor punishments.'

Clare tuned out as her daughter went into grisly detail about thumbscrews and ducking stools. She kept an eye on

Polly, though, who was still eating with her head down, as if anticipating a session with some thumbscrews herself. *I'm watching you*, Clare thought, her eyes narrowing. *I don't know what you're up to, but I'm watching you.*

Princess Polly sat there on her skinny, lazy arse while Clare and her mum cleared the plates and dishes away, and she went on sitting there while the crumble was served, eaten and cleared away too. 'Doesn't she do *anything* to help?' Clare fumed as she stacked the dishwasher later on. 'Honestly, Mum, you've got to tell her. She can't treat this place – your *home!* – as some kind of hotel. I mean, is she even paying her way? Has she offered you any money towards food and everything?'

'No, and I wouldn't take it from her even if she did,' her mum replied stoutly. 'She's my daughter, Clare, I can't begrudge her a few meals and a bed, not when she's asked so little from us for all these years. I'm her *mother*. I want to look after her.'

Clare nodded, her lips pursed. Fair enough. She could understand her mum's point of view. What she didn't understand was how Polly could think it was in any way okay to let her parents wait on her hand and foot. 'Leave those,' she told her mum, who was filling the sink with hot water to clean the roasting tins. 'Me and Polly will do them. POLLY!' she yelled before Karen could argue. 'Give us a hand with the washing up, will you?'

'I'll make some coffee then,' Karen suggested, as Polly shuffled into the kitchen, a sulky look on her face.

'No, you won't,' Clare told her. 'You've been slaving away all morning making lunch for everyone. Go and put your feet up and read the newspaper. We'll do the coffee once the washing up's done.'

Karen hesitated. 'Go on,' Clare ordered. 'Shoo. And shut the door after you, too.' *Polly and I are going to have a little chat,* she thought grimly, squirting washing-up liquid into the bowl.

Polly, meanwhile, looked coldly furious about being bossed around. You could tell she wasn't used to it.

'Look,' Clare said shortly, dumping the saucepans into the foamy water. 'I think you're out of order, doing your Lady Muck thing here. Mum and Dad aren't loaded, you know. Has it even crossed your mind that they might not be able to afford an extra person in the house? Have you offered them any money, some kind of contribution towards your three-month stay?' She scrubbed at the metal steamer furiously. 'Let me guess ... No.'

'It's none of your business,' Polly said, glaring.

'Oh yes, it is,' Clare replied. 'It *is* my business when I see my own parents being pushed out of their home by you.

They're tiptoeing around you, trying not to disturb you … Why do you think they're never in? Poor Dad has missed all his favourite programmes, according to Mum. Well, it's not on. It's their *home*.'

'Do you think I don't know that?' Polly exploded. 'Don't fucking remind me!'

'I still can't work out what you're actually *doing* here,' Clare retorted, slamming the steamer on the drainer in a splatter of suds. 'Why on earth aren't you doing your poxy research in your own flat?'

'Because I can't concentrate there,' Polly said. 'I needed to get out of London, to … to …' She was floundering, waving the tea towel in agitation. 'To clear my head.'

There was an edge in her voice, an anxiety that gave Clare pause. 'Well, why didn't you just book yourself into a luxury hotel then?' she replied after a moment. 'Seems to me that you'd have been much happier with room service and a pool and what-not. Why come back here?'

'Because … Look, what difference does it make to you anyway?' Polly was crumbling. Clare felt a mixture of curiosity and horror at the sight of her perfect, polished sister looking so disconcerted for once.

'What difference does it make? Every difference, when it affects the lives of – ' Clare broke off as Alex trailed into the kitchen. 'Not now, love,' she told him. 'I'm just talking to Aunty Polly.'

'No, you're not, you're shouting,' he said, his eyes darting between them with interest. 'Can I have a chocolate biscuit?'

'No! For heaven's sake, Alex, you've just eaten a massive lunch,' Clare snapped, more impatiently than she normally would have done. 'Can you give us a minute, please,' she said, in a softer voice. 'We're ... in the middle of something.' *And it's just getting interesting,* she thought. 'Close the door after you, good boy.'

There was a strained silence once the door had clicked shut. Clare's heart was beating quickly as she sluiced out the potato pan. 'Look, I get the feeling there's something you're not telling us,' she said evenly. 'You might as well come out with it.'

Polly rubbed hard at the steamer with a tea towel, even though it was already quite dry. She remained mutinously silent.

'Have you split up with someone – is that why you've run away from London?' Clare guessed. It would explain a lot about her sister's gaunt appearance and stand-offishness, she thought, if she was secretly nursing a broken heart.

'No,' Polly said, unable to help a sigh escaping with the word.

'Well, what then? What in God's name is it? Are you ill?'

The door opened before Polly could reply and their dad stuck his head round. 'Everything all right in here, girls?'

'Fine,' they chorused untruthfully, neither of them looking at him.

He shut the door again. The atmosphere between them
was now so tense that Clare's head was starting to ache.

'I'm not ill,' Polly muttered. 'I . . .'

She paused and an awkward silence thickened. Clare
pressed her lips together, scrubbing at the roasting tin, while
the clock ticked loudly on the wall behind them. *I'm going to
find out the truth if I have to shake it out of her*, she thought
ferociously. *I knew there was something going on. I knew it.*

'If I tell you,' Polly said in a low voice, uncharacteristically nervous. 'If I tell you, you've got to promise not to tell
Mum and Dad. I mean it. You've got to swear on your life.'

Clare stared at her in alarm. Wow, this sounded more
serious than a broken heart. Was Polly in trouble? Was she
on the run from some heinous crime, or allegation? She
blinked and then nodded. 'Go on, then. I promise,' she said.

Polly's mouth buckled as if she were on the verge of
tears. She swallowed hard then held her head up and looked
Clare in the eye. 'I've lost my job, Clare,' she said. 'I've lost
everything.'

Clare stared at her in astonishment. 'You've . . . lost your
job?' she repeated dumbly.

'Yes,' Polly said.

Clare was still staring. 'But, this work you're doing . . .'
She frowned, her brain not computing.

Polly shrugged. 'Is a big fat lie,' she said. 'I'm just trying to get another job. Didn't want to tell Mum and Dad.' She glared. 'And you mustn't tell them either. You did promise!'

'Yes, of course. I mean, no, I won't tell them. Shit, Polly.' Clare bit her lip. She still couldn't take it in. Of all the things for her sister to say, she hadn't been expecting this one. 'Shit, I'm sorry, I had no idea. I thought—'

'Yeah, I know what you thought,' Polly said. 'I know exactly what you thought.'

'But . . . Oh God. So you've lost your flat too?'

Polly's dark eyes glittered and for an awful moment Clare thought she was about to cry. For the first time in years Clare was struck with the impulse to put an arm around her sister. It felt . . . weird.

Polly swung her head away haughtily as if she'd rather die than have anyone's sympathetic arm around her. 'Yep. I've had to put it on the market,' she said, her tone brittle.

'Fuck. I'm really sorry to hear that.'

'Are you?' Polly's voice was a disbelieving sneer.

'Of course I am!' Clare cried. 'I know we haven't exactly got on very well, but I'm not made of stone.'

There was a pause that stretched between them like a crevasse. Feeling awkward at her sister's palpable vulnerability, Clare turned back to the roasting tin. 'What are you going to do?' she asked after a moment.

'Find something else,' Polly mumbled. 'What choice have I got?'

'What, and stay here indefinitely?' Clare asked.

Polly gritted her teeth. 'Clare, I've got nowhere else to go,' she said, losing her patience. 'I've got no money left. And I'm trying to find another job, but it's not fucking easy, you know?'

'What about friends – couldn't you stay with one of your friends in London? Or . . . ?' Clare floundered under her sister's ferocious scowl. 'I guess not,' she muttered.

Polly was drying a saucepan, but it somehow slipped from her fingers, clattering to the floor. As she bent to pick it up, Clare noticed the thinness of her shoulders, the misery on her face. She looked broken; a far cry from the strutting show-off she'd been for so many years.

I'm not made of stone, she'd said just two minutes earlier. But the truth was, she'd hardened herself to Polly over the years. Who wouldn't? What with her disastrous hen night when Polly had turned her nose up at Clare's friends and slunk away early from the nightclub, then Clare's wedding to which Polly had arrived rudely late and sat there at the back of the chapel with her shades on looking bored the whole time, and, then worst of all, the births of her children, about whom Polly had shown a hurtful lack of interest. It was enough to turn anyone against their own flesh and blood.

But all the same, Polly *was* her sister. The only sibling she had left.

Clare put the last tin in the drainer and tipped the water away. They both watched as it swirled around the sink and gurgled down the plughole, then Clare took a deep breath. 'Look,' she said awkwardly. 'I think Mum and Dad are finding it hard having you staying.'

'*They're* finding it hard? It's not exactly a picnic for me either, you know!'

Clare gritted her teeth. Even when she was being offered refuge, Polly still had to be such a snob. She was on the verge of changing her mind, retracting the offer before it had even been made, until she saw the wobble of Polly's lip. One tiny movement that belied her superiority.

Oh, just say it, Clare. She'll probably say no, and then at least you can go home with a clean conscience. She owed it to Michael, at least, to try and patch things up. She'd let *him* down, to her everlasting regret; she couldn't leave Polly stranded in her hour of need too, however hateful she was being right now.

She swallowed, trying to put a pleasant expression on her face. 'So ... why don't you stay with me and the kids instead?' she said.

Polly stared. 'I ...'

'I mean, you'd have to pull your weight obviously; it wouldn't be like staying here, where Mum's done everything for you,' Clare put in quickly. There was no way she was going to cut Polly the same amount of slack her parents had. 'You'd have to muck in, help out around the place.' Then, seeing how stunned Polly was looking (God, she was actually speechless with gratitude), she softened. 'But, yeah. You can stay. The kids won't mind bunking in together for a while, just until you're straight again.'

'But . . .' Polly was still staring. 'Is this some kind of trick?'

Clare blinked. That hadn't been the response she'd been expecting. *Thanks, Clare, I really appreciate this. Thanks, Clare, that's so kind of you.* Ha. To think she'd actually believed there had been *gratitude* on her sister's face. Disdain, more like. Suspicion. Well, sod her then.

She folded her arms across her chest, feeling defensive. How dare Polly be so sniffy about her extremely generous offer? 'Well, it's up to you anyway,' she said coldly. Polly's lip curled. Rude bitch, thought Clare with increasing fury.

'I . . . I'll think about it,' Polly muttered.

Chapter Thirteen

Yeah, right, Polly had thought. Stay at Clare's and have her little sister patronize and pity her? Not in a million years. Clare had always envied Polly's success – it was obvious she couldn't wait to gloat endlessly about her downfall. Dream on, Clare. *I'll think about it*, she'd said, just to shut her up, although she didn't intend to give it another second's thought. But then, the very next day something awful happened.

She was working in the living room – well, all right, clicking furtively onto the estate agent's website to look longingly at the photos of her flat, in between cruising the recruitment websites for the zillionth time – when she heard a strange sound. A faint, muffled sound of distress. She stiffened, straining to hear. Was it the stupid dog, trapped in a cupboard somewhere? A bird that had fallen down the chimney?

Frozen in silence, ear cocked, she listened hard. There it went again.

She was the only person in the house; her parents had been in a slightly subdued mood that morning and hadn't talked much about their plans for the day. Grateful for the silence, Polly hadn't bothered asking what they were up to, but had heard the front door shut behind them and her dad's car drive away an hour or so ago. So who was making that noise?

She slipped off her chair and padded across the room, dread thickening inside her. Oh God, what if a bird *had* flown in somewhere and was beating around the room, frantic to get out? She had a thing about birds – their weird beady eyes, their clawed feet, those prehistoric beaks. There would be feathers and crap everywhere; she'd have to go out and pretend she hadn't heard anything, to avoid having to clear up the mess herself.

The sound was louder now, and Polly's heart lurched. It wasn't a bird. It was somebody crying. Somebody who sounded very much like her mum. Oh shit. *Now* what was she supposed to do?

She hesitated helplessly, knowing that Clare, of course, would have rushed in, arms outstretched, the angel of comfort. But Polly was no angel of comfort. She was a shamble of awkwardness and stood paralysed for a few moments, without a bloody clue what to do next.

She walked slowly to the doorway, hoping the crying would subside. To her dismay, the volume increased. Actual sobs were coming from her parents' bedroom now. Oh, help. If only she'd gone out to work in the garden, or taken the wretched dog for another walk. She couldn't do this, she couldn't comfort her own weeping mother, she didn't know where to start.

She had to do something, though.

She knocked tentatively at the closed bedroom door. 'Can I come in?'

There was no answer. That probably meant 'No', didn't it? Her mum wouldn't want to be disturbed if she was having a moment. Polly was about to creep away in relief when she heard a quiet, tearful 'Yes'.

Damn.

Karen Johnson was always upbeat and cheerful, always smiling and warm. That was who she was; that was her way. Today, though, she was crumpled on the bed, her face blotchy, her eyes streaming with tears.

Polly sat beside her and gingerly put a hand on her mother's heaving back. 'Mum, what's up?'

To her astonishment, Karen seemed angry to be asked. 'What's up?' she mimicked, her voice shrill. 'What's *up?* Do you really not know? It's the thirteenth of June, Polly. Don't tell me you'd actually forgotten?'

All the breath seemed trapped in her body for a moment. Of course she knew. Of course she hadn't forgotten. The thirteenth of June was Michael's birthday. She'd lost track of the days since she'd been here. 'Oh God,' she said, choking on the words. 'I didn't realize.'

'He would have been thirty-five,' Karen sobbed. 'Thirty-five years old. Married with kids, maybe. But we'll never know.'

She covered her eyes as she wept, and Polly felt dumb-founded with guilt and uselessness all over again. This was horrendous. She wanted her mum to stop crying – now, please – or if not that, for them to be able to cry together, to share the grief. But neither option seemed possible.

She patted her mum's arm. 'It's all right,' she tried saying feebly. 'It's all right, Mum.'

It wasn't all right though, and they both knew it.

The image of Karen weeping haunted Polly for the rest of the day. She had no idea that her mum still carried around such raw, painful grief for Michael; she'd assumed everyone had just blotted him out from their memories, like she had. Obviously not. That evening Clare and the children came round again for tea, and there was a cake with candles, which they lit with great ceremony. Clare was quiet and thoughtful, and even Graham's eyes were suspiciously red-rimmed.

'We miss you, Michael,' they'd chorused, clinking glasses of wine. Clearly this was a ritual that took place every year.

Polly's face had burned with shame. She'd always tried to treat June the thirteenth as an ordinary day, albeit one to be got through as fast as possible. But candles were still burning brightly for Michael in this part of the country, and had been for the last twenty years. It made her feel hollow inside, like she was a bad person.

Thirty-five years old, her mum had sobbed. *Married with kids, maybe.* Unlike his older sister, who'd messed her life up completely, Polly thought miserably in bed that night.

The next morning, though, her parents seemed to have clicked back into normal mode. Her mum gave her a hug at breakfast time and apologized for her tears the day before. 'His birthday always gets me,' she said breezily, 'but I'm fine again now. Coffee?'

Polly accepted with a certain amount of wariness, but she needn't have worried. Her mum was humming as she buttered toast, and her dad was laughing at something on the radio, as if the mourning and misery of the day before had been a mirage, a dream.

Her heart ached for them unexpectedly. Was this how they coped then? Papering over the cracks for most of the year, with this deep well of sadness always there beneath the surface?

Perhaps she'd been naive to think that life had been continuing as normal for them all these years. Why hadn't she noticed?

She munched her toast grimly. She already knew the answer to that one.

'Clare, it's me. Polly. Hi.'

It was Wednesday afternoon, and Polly had finally cracked. She couldn't bear another morning waking up to her dad's shower-singing, another day averting her eyes from the photos of Michael on the mantelpiece, another mug of dishwatery instant coffee. She was also fed up with *Waterloo Road*, *Lark Rise to Candleford* and all those other abysmal programmes that her parents devoured. And she never wanted to go through the deeply cringeworthy experience of 'a nice chinwag' with Jacky Bore of the Year Garland and her daffy old bat of a mum again, after Karen had insisted on inviting them round for coffee.

'Hi, Polly, how are you?' came her sister's voice down the phone.

Polly sighed. 'Going insane,' she confessed. That was the truth. She was starting to hate herself every time she told her parents a lie about her 'work'. The walls were closing in around her too, tighter each day. 'I was wondering . . .' She licked her lips, suddenly hesitant. 'Is your offer still on?'

'About moving in? Er, yeah. Sure,' Clare replied. 'I was going to ring you anyway. I've found you a job.'

'A *job*?' Polly lowered her voice, aware that she'd just

squawked the word in her shock. 'What ... what do you mean?'

'It's not a big career move, I'm afraid,' Clare said cheerfully. 'But it's something to tide you over at least. I mean, I do need you to chip in with money for food and stuff if you're going to be staying, Polly. I'm even more skint than Mum and Dad, and can't subsidize you.'

'Right.' Polly swallowed, trying to push back the ginormous lump that seemed to have lodged itself in her throat. She had a horrible feeling that her sister had her over a barrel. 'So ... what is it, this job?'

'I'll tell you later. When do you want to come round?'

'Tonight?' Polly said glumly.

'Don't sound too excited, will you? Yeah, all right. Tonight's fine. Not like I've got anything else to do. Listen, there's something in the oven that I'd better check on, so I'll see you later, bye.'

And that was that. Polly sat for a few moments on the bed, wondering if she was doing the right thing. She wasn't at all convinced that this 'job' her sister claimed to have found her would be up to much. She doubted it would pay even a fraction of her last salary, and she couldn't believe there were any financial or business-related positions up for grabs in either Elderchurch or Amberley. Unless Clare had wangled her some freelance accountancy perhaps, or maybe even some consultancy work further afield ...

Polly grabbed a suitcase and began stuffing clothes into it. She'd missed work so badly, she realized. Missed using her brain, making calculations, solving problems. Hell, she'd even missed putting on a suit and full make-up every morning. Even if she had to take a small step down the career ladder, this job of Clare's might just be what she needed.

'A cleaner? A fucking CLEANER? Tell me you're joking.'

Clare shook her head. It was eight o'clock, the children were in bed – now both sharing Leila's room, which had caused a good forty minutes of mutiny on either side, before Clare had had to resort to bribery – and she'd just heaved her sister's last case up to Alex's room, which was Polly's new (and definitely temporary) abode. 'I thought you'd be pleased' was all she said.

This was not strictly true. Clare had known damn well that Polly would not be in the slightest bit pleased about the suggestion that she work as a cleaner for the local pub, but as far as she was concerned, beggars could not be choosers. Especially when beggars were about to stay with their kind, patient younger sister and needed some means of paying their own way.

'*Pleased?* Are you taking the piss?' Polly felt as if she'd been slapped in the face. How dare her sister suggest such a ridiculous thing as her, Polly Johnson, taking on that kind of menial, revolting and probably disgracefully badly paid job? She didn't even know *how* to clean – and never wanted to learn, either. Cleaning was something other people did, end of story.

'No, of course I'm not,' Clare retorted. 'Don't be such a snob. Look, I wasn't joking when I said I needed you to pay your way here. I'm surviving on a shoestring, Polly. No money. And when you're skint, you can't afford to be picky.' She leaned back against the sofa. 'You don't have to take the job. It was only an idea, okay? Just something you could do to earn a few quid while you're waiting for a better offer. But if you're too high and mighty to put on a pair of Marigolds, then – '

Polly ground her teeth together. High and bloody mighty indeed. She'd only been in Clare's grotty little house half an hour and already her sister was trying to rub her nose in it. That hadn't taken long. 'I'll find my own job, thank you very much,' she growled.

'Suit yourself,' Clare said, swinging her legs up onto the sofa and turning her whole body away. A moody silence was on the verge of descending, but then she flicked the TV on with the remote, and brightened. 'Oh, brilliant, *Florida Mansions*. Do you ever watch this?'

It was on the tip of Polly's tongue to say a scornful 'No', of course she didn't watch that sort of trash, but during her meltdown period immediately after losing her job she'd actually watched this programme quite a lot. 'Sometimes,' she muttered, sitting down next to her sister.

At least she could enjoy some tacky telly here at Clare's, she thought, trying to get comfortable on the knackered old sofa. She could feel its springs through the cushion, and the wooden backrest through the thin padding – neither was a good sensation. The cottage wasn't exactly palatial, with its low ceilings and tiny rooms, and Clare might not have the best creature comforts in the world, but at least there was the glorious *Florida Mansions*, a programme so brainlessly bad that the phrase 'guilty pleasure' might have been coined for it. She sighed and leaned back, staring at the screen as the garish titles began spooling.

'What a knobber,' Clare said, guffawing gleefully as one of the characters in the soap – Jed, a brainless hunk with muscles so pumped up they'd surely been inflated – got completely the wrong end of the stick in a conversation with Marcella, the quirky redhead who'd just moved into their apartment block.

'I know,' Polly said, unable to help a snort of amusement herself. 'Total doofus.'

'Isn't he? Did you see that one a few weeks ago when he was trying to get the job with what's-her-name? Tina, at the car warehouse? Cringe or what?'

'Oh God, I did!' Polly said. 'I could hardly watch. Tina's face!'

Clare spluttered. 'Gotta love him, though, especially when he doesn't actually speak. I wouldn't kick him out of bed for eating crisps, put it like that.' She leaned forward to put the remote down on the coffee table and, as her T-shirt rode up, Polly noticed a small bluebird tattoo at the base of her sister's back. God! When had Clare got *that* done? Did their parents know about it?

'He so *would* eat crisps in bed,' she said, dragging her eyes back to the screen, where Jed's cheerfully gormless face had fallen at the realization (at last) that he'd totally put his foot in it with Marcella. 'But, yeah, I suppose that could be overlooked. As long as he shared them with me, of course.'

'Yeah, and put the packet in the bin afterwards,' Clare added. 'That drove me nuts about living with Steve. He never seemed to get the hang of bins; he'd always drop stuff wherever he was, as if he thought the litter fairy would pop by and pick up after him all the time. As for dirty clothes ... God. My life is so much better for not having to pick up his smelly pants and socks off the bedroom floor every day.'

'Ewww,' Polly said, wrinkling her nose. Not that her own personal hygiene standards had been particularly high recently, but all the same. Men's dirty pants and socks: *ewww*.

The titles flashed up to signal an ad-break and they fell

silent for a moment. It was as if they'd been in a cosy shared bubble while their programme had been on, which had now popped. 'Do you miss him?' she asked as a gaudy pizza advert began blaring. She was surprised at her own question – she and Clare didn't generally go anywhere near personal stuff.

'Sometimes,' Clare said, fiddling with her bracelet. 'At Christmas I did, and the kids' birthdays; you know, those full-on happy-family times. And when he's not there for things that matter to the kids, like their school concerts or sports day, and I can see on their faces that they're wishing he was there, that's horrible. I feel a sort of ache, as if something's not right. But on the whole...' She lifted her chin up defiantly. 'No. We're doing fine without him.'

There was silence for a few moments and Polly scrabbled about desperately for something to say – something that wouldn't sound patronizing or ineffectual. What did she know about bringing up two kids on her own, though? Bugger all.

'I never liked the way he tried to put you down,' she blurted out before she could stop herself.

Clare's eyes narrowed. 'What do you mean?'

Tread carefully, Polly. 'I mean, he seemed to hate it when you had any kind of success or triumph,' she said. 'Like the Christmas you made Mum and Dad that amazing mosaic picture and he came out with a mean comment about buying them a "proper" present next year when you had more money.'

Clare flushed. 'I'd forgotten that,' she mumbled.

Polly hadn't. It had been painful seeing Clare's look of pride crumple into embarrassment when Steve came out with his snarky remarks. Mum and Dad had protested, saying how lovely the picture was and how long it must have taken Clare to make, and it *was* lovely, even Polly had to admit as much, despite despising home-made gifts in general. Unfortunately it seemed that Steve had already destroyed what pleasure she'd had from giving it to them.

'And then there was that time, another Christmas it must have been, when Leila was only tiny and—'

'All right, all right,' Clare snapped. 'No need to dredge all that up now.'

'I was only—'

'Yeah, I know. But let's not go there.'

Oops. Okay, so slagging off the ex was still off the agenda. Luckily Polly thought of the perfect thing to say instead. 'Oh, I forgot! I've brought you some wine as a thank-you for having me. Shall I open it?'

'Yes,' said Clare with audible relief in her voice. 'Good idea.'

*

One bottle of Ernest and Julio's finest later (the village shop wasn't exactly laden with quality vintages) and Polly felt she and her sister might just be approaching some kind of peace treaty. First they'd bonded over *Florida Mansions*. Then had come the discovery that they were both addicted to *Flying High*, the sexy-pilot series that had been repeated recently. And finally, when they had moved on to tumblers of Clare's emergency gin ration, they'd come over all confessional. Clare had admitted to breaking their mum's prized porcelain doll at the age of six (Michael had got the blame at the time, despite him hotly denying having anything to do with it) and Polly had fessed up to nicking fifty pence out of the collection plate at Sunday school, back when she'd been nine and desperately saving up for roller skates.

The topic of money must have jogged Clare's drunken memory, because the next thing she said was, 'So are you going to think about that job at the pub then?'

And just like that the new-found confidence between them splintered and broke. Polly twisted awkwardly on the uncomfortable sofa – she was so going to have backache the next morning – and scowled. 'No! I already told you! I'm . . .' She thumped a fist down on the arm-rest. 'I'm not interested in that kind of work. I want to go back to London, not hang around in this poxy place any longer than—'

She broke off, slightly scared by the look of fury that

had appeared on Clare's face. Ahh. Maybe she shouldn't have called Elderchurch a 'poxy place' quite so bluntly.

'Well, I'm sorry that this isn't up to your usual standards,' Clare fumed, getting unsteadily to her feet. 'And I'm sorry you're not even going to *try*, when a perfectly good job is going begging right on the doorstep. I should have known you'd turn your nose up at it; just as you've always turned your nose up at everything here, your whole flipping life. The sooner you go back to London, the better for everyone.'

'Oh, don't be like that, I didn't mean—' Polly tried, but Clare had already flounced out. Seconds later there were thunderous footsteps on the wooden staircase and Polly guessed she'd stormed off to bed. Goodnight to you too, Clare.

Polly leaned her head back in irritation. Deliberate antagonism, that was her sister's game; goading Polly and trying to humiliate her with this wretched cleaning job.

Well, she'd be damned if she let it get to her. Clare could shove her stinking Marigolds up her own jacksy, Polly thought savagely, draining the last of her gin. And from now on, she could bloody well keep her nosey beak out of Polly's business too.

Polly tossed and turned under Alex's alien-patterned duvet that night. Luminous miniature planets dangled disconcertingly above her head from the ceiling, a Wallace and Gromit clock ticked loudly, and there was a distinct pong of socks emanating from under the bed. The Ritz this was not. 'The Pitz, more like,' she muttered, rolling over for the umpteenth time.

The sooner you go back to London, the better for everyone, Clare had said. Yep, Polly thought. Couldn't have put it better herself. She'd never moan about city life again when she returned there. The smog, the traffic, the crime – she'd embrace them all like long-lost friends. As for the thought of a new proper job, with her own desk to sit at, a PC, an assistant ... She'd be the dream employee, given half a chance.

If only she could *get* that half-chance ...

Tomorrow I'll wake up and someone will have emailed saying they want to interview me, she promised herself. *Tomorrow, things will start to turn around: I'll spot a new vacancy for my perfect job, I'll be headhunted, my phone will ring and it'll all begin to fall into place. I don't need a crappy cleaning position. I can do better than that. I WILL do better than that.*

'So there,' she said out loud. She punched the *Pirates of the Caribbean* pillowcase into a better shape and rolled over. Positive visualization, that was the key. She had to keep telling herself that her luck would change any day soon. The alternative was simply too dreadful to contemplate.

Chapter Fourteen

'Alex SNORES,' Leila announced grumpily at breakfast the next day.

'No, I don't.'

'Yes, you do.'

'No, I *don't*.' Kick.

'Yes, you DO.' Push.

'Oh, stop bickering, for God's sake,' Clare snapped. She had a thrumming headache right behind her eyes (whatever had possessed her to break into the emergency gin like that?) and had nearly cracked the bathroom mirror with her rough-as-sandpaper reflection when she'd peered into it just now. Polly no doubt was still sleeping it off, the lucky cow. That was if the quarrelling niece and nephew hadn't just woken her, of course.

'How long till I can get my own bedroom back anyway?' Alex grumbled, pulling a hideous face at his sister.

'A few months, not that long,' Clare said, trying to appease him. Damn, they were nearly out of coffee, she noticed, foraging fruitlessly for a new jar in the cupboard. 'We're just helping her out for a while, that's all. That's what families do.' She tried to keep a kindly tone to her voice, but couldn't help hearing a ring of sarcasm through it. She hadn't been best pleased to come down that morning and find the gin bottle still there on the coffee table with its lid off, and the glasses either side of it too. Her glass still had an inch of gin in it, she'd noticed, with rising fury. What if one of the children had thought it was water and glugged it back? Had it not occurred to Polly that she should have tidied them away before taking herself off to bed?

Obviously not.

'A few *months*?' Leila wailed. 'Oh, great. That's like nearly Christmas!'

'No, it isn't,' Clare said. 'It's only for the summer. It might even be less time than that.'

'Can't Alex sleep with Babs and Marjorie? Or in the kitchen?'

'No, he can't. Look, Polly's family. My *sister*. It's nice to have her staying.' The words sounded unconvincing even to her own ears. Last night's conversation hadn't exactly ended nicely.

'Huh,' Leila grumbled. 'I don't think so. All she ever says to us is *How's school?* Who cares about school? She's a rubbish aunty. She never even buys us *sweets*.'

'Yeah,' Alex agreed. 'I'm never letting *Leila* stay with me when I'm a grown-up. Sisters stink.'

'Not as much as poo-pants brothers,' Leila retorted. 'And there's no way I'd *want* to stay with you anyway.'

'Good, cos you're not invited,' Alex said, sticking his tongue out. 'EVER.'

'Just eat your breakfast, you two,' Clare sighed, buttering more toast and putting it on the table. She hadn't had enough sleep the night before to be very patient today. The evening had been surprisingly good fun to begin with, once Polly had got over her initial huff about the cleaning job at the pub. They'd actually had quite a laugh together, even bonded about various telly hunks they both fancied, and the conversation had flowed as easily as the wine.

Then, unfortunately, she had to go and open her big trap about the cleaning job again and it had all gone wrong. Worse than wrong, in fact; she'd ended up tearing a strip off Polly about her bad attitude. That was gin for you, it always made Clare arsey.

She munched her toast thoughtfully. Maybe she'd been a bit harsh. For most of the evening Polly had seemed humbler, less cocksure than in past years, as if the redundancy had knocked out half of her confidence. There must have been some devil in Clare that had been unable to resist that unnecessary swipe, upsetting the delicate balance they'd just arrived at.

'Alex!' she roared, suddenly catching sight of him feeding the dog under the table. 'That toast is for you, not Fred. Hurry up, we've got to go in fifteen minutes and you're not even dressed yet.'

School mornings were usually painfully observed rituals of hustle and hurry. As a single parent, it had to be that way – she couldn't rely on anyone else to get them all ready and out of the house. Once breakfast had been eaten and the table cleared, clothes had to be thrown on, teeth and hair brushed, bags checked for permission slips, homework or reading books, and then at last they'd be into the final straight of shoes and coats if the weather was bad, or suncream and sunhats if the sun was actually showing its face.

Clare knew from bitter experience that if one single link fell from the chain – if the hairbrush couldn't be located immediately, for instance, or one of them remembered at the last minute (as they were annoyingly prone to do) that oh yeah, they were meant to be coming to school dressed as a book character today, or whatever – then the whole routine would collapse. No mercy. And so, when she realized her sister was locked in the bathroom taking a long shower when she'd have liked a quick hose-down herself, not to mention the fact that none of them had brushed their teeth yet, she could sense that the morning was on the brink of unravelling completely.

She banged on the door, impatience sparking. 'Are you going to be long in there?'

There was no reply, except for the sound of pouring water. 'I need a wee,' Alex said, shifting from foot to foot.

'Well, you'll have to wait, or go in the garden, I'm afraid,' Clare said wearily.

'But I need a poo as well.'

Clare took a deep breath and banged on the door again, louder this time. 'HURRY UP!' she bellowed through the wood. She felt like thumping her head against it too. Rules were going to have to be set down regarding bathroom availability times, she could see, as well as rules about leaving open gin bottles around the place.

Great. Her new lodger was going to love that.

Thursday was Clare's day off, so once she'd finally hustled the kids off to school (teeth still unbrushed unfortunately, and with her having to make do with a stand-up wash at the kitchen sink – *nice*), she wandered home, trying to shake off her bad temper by running through the list of things she needed to tackle that day. A supermarket run, clothes washing, hoovering, tracking down Leila's lost trainer (what on earth had she done with it?), a long walk with Fred and general house-cleaning and tidying duties. That would do.

She rather liked Thursdays, even though they consisted mainly of domestic chores. It was the sense of catching up on herself, of having a breather to put everything in order once more, before the chaos had a chance to explode again.

She was glad not to be going into work for other reasons too. She'd felt embarrassed the entire week about what had happened with Luke the Friday night before. The more she thought about it, the more hysterical she became in her memory of that evening, wild-eyed and frenzied, fingers like claws as she dragged Luke into her car, driving like a lunatic and garbling all that stuff about Michael to him. Shit. What must he *think* of her? Talk about how to make a fool of yourself. He'd been as friendly and nice as ever since then, asking how Leila was and waving away Clare's apologies, but she still found herself turning pink every time he came near her. It was toe-curlingly horrendous.

She let out Babs and Marjorie, the chickens, who strutted down their ramp, beady-eyed. 'Thanks, ladies,' she said, reaching into their house to collect two warm eggs. 'At least I can count on you pair.'

Carefully carrying the eggs, she pushed the back door open to see Polly in the kitchen crunching her way through a bowl of cornflakes with a mean-looking black coffee by her elbow. Clare took in the spilled milk on the table, the trail of sugar crystals from the bowl, and Fred with his greedy head under the table to gobble up the stray cornflakes there, and felt cross all over again. 'Morning,' she said shortly, putting the kettle on.

Polly jerked in surprise at Clare's appearance. 'Shouldn't you be at work?'

'Day off,' Clare said. 'There are eggs here, if you want them,' she added, putting them in the fridge. She opened the cupboard to take out the coffee, just before she saw the empty jar on the worktop, lid off, a scattering of granules freckling the surface. 'Ahh. Did you use the last of the coffee?'

'Yeah,' Polly said. 'I'll get some more later on. I think you're out of milk too, unless there's another secret fridge that I haven't tracked down yet.'

Clare smiled tightly. 'No secret fridge,' she confirmed.

'What was all that banging about this morning, by the way?' Polly asked, spooning in more cornflakes. 'Do the kids always make that sort of racket?'

'That was me,' Clare said, feeling her jaw stiffen. 'That was me, banging on the bathroom door, because we needed to brush our teeth. And poor Alex nearly wet himself on the way to school because he was bursting for the loo.' She folded her arms across her chest. 'If you could try to avoid having a long shower at that time in the morning, I'd really appreciate it. We're always in such a mad dash to leave on time as it is, without . . .'

Polly rolled her eyes up to the ceiling and Clare wanted to throttle her.

'All right, all right, I didn't realize,' she said huffily.

'Right,' said Clare as the kettle whistled to a crescendo of boiling – uselessly now, as it had turned out. 'Well, I guess I'll hit the supermarket then. Is there anything in particular you want?'

'Some proper coffee,' Polly said at once. 'Oh, and some nice shampoo. I like that Salon Class stuff, you know, in the silver bottles?'

Clare knew, all right. The most expensive range on the shelves, no less. Did Polly expect her to shell out for that, as well as her posh coffee? Clare narrowed her eyes. Like hell she would. Her sister would be getting supermarket own-brand 2-in-1 shampoo and would have to lump it. 'Sure,' she said, turning away so that Polly couldn't see the irritation on her face. She grabbed her handbag and car keys and strode towards the door, with Fred trotting hopefully after her. 'No, you're staying here, matey, sorry,' she said, patting him. 'I'll take you out later. Unless...' She eyed Polly. 'Maybe you could take Fred out if you've not got anything to do?'

Polly shook her head. 'I'm going to be busy,' she said. 'Sorry.'

Clare was reminded of the *Little Red Hen* story she'd read to the children when they were younger. 'Well, I'll just do everything myself then,' she muttered, slamming the door behind her.

'I never thought I'd say this, but thank God I'm working today,' Clare sighed the following morning, sinking into her chair behind the reception desk.

Roxie goggled at her. 'Er ... who *are* you? You might look like Clare Berry, but you sure as hell don't sound like her.'

Clare managed a smile. 'Well, it is me. Just about. A demented version of me, who's desperate to get out of the house and away from my house-guest, that's all.' She shook her head. 'She is driving me MENTAL.'

Roxie, who was wearing her hair in Princess Leia-style coiled buns over her ears and sporting a lime-green short-sleeved blouse with silver heart-shaped buttons, and a hot-pink frayed denim miniskirt, looked amused. 'What happened? She hasn't found out you flogged her daft presents on eBay, has she?'

'No, and if you ever meet her, you mustn't tell her,' Clare said. 'She's just got no idea about living with someone, that's all. She's worse than a bloody man! She never tidies up after herself, she spends hours in the bathroom every morning when we're trying to get ready for school, she doesn't lift a finger to help, and she's practically colonized the kitchen with her so-called "work".' She made little quotation marks in the air with her fingers and snorted. 'Although I caught her watching Jeremy Kyle when I came back with the shopping yesterday morning, so she's not exactly pressing her nose to the grindstone.'

'LOVE Jeremy Kyle,' Roxie murmured, rather inappropriately.

'The irony is,' Clare went on, ignoring the interruption, 'that I was moaning on to her about how crap and lazy Steve used to be around the house, and she was giving me all this sympathy – like, oh, how awful, what a nightmare. And it turns out she's even *worse*; something I didn't think was humanly possible!'

'Morning, Luke,' Roxie cooed just then, batting her false eyelashes, which were so long they sent a small breeze across the reception counter.

'Morning,' Clare mumbled, embarrassed to be caught whinging on so heatedly.

Luke seemed distracted as he went by. 'Morning.'

Roxie began whistling 'Always Look on the Bright Side' rather pointedly, but he took no notice and went into his office. 'What's up with him then? Has he got spikes in his undercrackers or something?' She patted Clare's arm. 'Don't worry, honey. I'll make you a nice cup of tea and tell you my exciting news. That'll cheer you up.'

Clare smiled wanly, wondering if Roxie's exciting news

meant sordid tales of an imaginary bunk-up with Jake Gyllenhaal or Orlando Bloom this time. Still, it would be a welcome change to have someone else make her a drink, at least. Polly had only been staying two nights, but already Clare felt as if she was running a café-cum-guest-house. 'Thanks,' she said, clicking on the appointment list for that day and answering the phone. 'Good morning, Amberley Health Centre, can I help you?'

'So,' Roxie said without preamble a few minutes later, plonking a steaming mug in front of Clare and perching on her swivel seat once more, 'the exciting news is ... I've gone and got you some business, hopefully. I know, I'm amazing; I'm the best, you love me. You don't need to say it, that's a given.'

'What do you mean?' Clare asked, eyes on her computer screen as she typed in a new appointment.

'I *mean*, my Aunty Kate came to stay with us last night,' Roxie said, twirling on her chair. 'Have I ever told you about her?'

'No,' Clare said, wondering where on earth this was going. An old lady had come to stand at the counter, her eyes rheumy. 'Morning, Mrs Atkins, do take a seat,' Clare said. 'Dr Copper will be with you in a minute.' She turned back to Roxie. 'Who's Aunty Kate?'

'She's a buyer for Langley's,' Roxie went on. 'You know Langley's, that funky hotel chain?'

'No,' Clare confessed. 'Funnily enough, I haven't been to any hotels lately, funky or otherwise.' She scrolled down the list of patients they had booked in for the morning. It was going to be non-stop today, she could tell already.

Roxie ignored her sarcasm. 'Well, they're pretty cool. Glamorous, but funky – kind of like vintage meets art school. Anyway, they're opening a new boutique hotel not far from here, in Lovington. It's a new direction for them too, this one, according to Aunty Kate: what they're calling "Home from Home". The idea is that you feel like you're staying with a bohemian, ever-so-slightly eccentric mate, not in some bland corporate-clone hotel.'

The phone rang just then and Roxie took the call. Then, as she was hanging up, the other phone rang, so Clare answered. Then three patients came in for their appointments, and the post arrived and had to be signed for.

'Go on,' Clare said, when all this had been dealt with. She had absolutely no idea why Roxie was embarking on this anecdote featuring glamorous hotels, but was interested all the same. 'Don't tell me,' she guessed. 'Your Aunty Kate has offered to put my sister up for a while in one of these lovely hotels, take her off my hands. No – even better, she's decided to let *me* stay there for a holiday and I'm going to be pampered from top to toe. Am I right?'

'Not quite,' Roxie said. 'But listen. She's a buyer for the chain, so she's been in charge of kitting out the new hotel with all its furniture, bed linen, cutlery ... oh, everything. Can you imagine? Being paid to *shop*, like, as your *job? Well* jeal'. Anyway, because it's Langley's, it's really fun, funky stuff too. Like, the crockery looks kitsch and mismatched, not your bog-standard white IKEA stuff, and ...' She caught Clare's eye and cut to the chase. '*So* she's got to source a load of toiletries too, for the hotel bathrooms.' She grinned. 'And that's where you come in.'

Clare blinked. 'What?'

'She's sourcing a new range of toiletries for the Lovington hotel,' Roxie repeated patiently. 'She said she's after a local company preferably, organic if possible, really high-quality stuff, but a bit different from the norm. So I told her I knew just the person to supply her. You!'

'ME?' Clare laughed at the joke, then stopped as she saw the hurt expression on Roxanne's face. 'You're not serious?'

'DUH! Of course I'm serious!' Roxie's eyes were sparkling with excitement beneath their pearlescent aquamarine eyeshadow. 'Your stuff is lovely. I showed her my perfume (I couldn't show her the bath bomb you gave me because I've already used it and it's down the plughole), and I think she was impressed. You would be perfect for Langley's, I reckon – I mean, it's not super-posh, like terrifying-posh, where the likes of me and you would be scared of using the wrong knives and forks and what-have-you, but quirky and cool, and ... you know. Nice. Just like you.'

Oh, bless her. Clare couldn't help feeling touched by her friend's enthusiasm, but shook her head slowly all the same. 'That's really sweet of you, Rox, but honestly, my little business is just a kitchen-table sort of thing. It's only a bit of fun, for family and mates, it's not like I'm in it as a serious company, or anything . . .'

The phone was ringing and Roxie snatched it up. 'Amberley Medical Centre, can you hold for a moment?' she said politely. She clapped her hand over the receiver and gave Clare a stern look. 'Well, I think you should give it a go. What have you got to lose?' And before Clare could formulate a reply, she'd uncovered the phone and was speaking into it once more. 'Sorry about that. How can I help you?'

After much badgering, Clare finally agreed to think about the idea. 'Your aunt's never going to want my stuff,' she kept telling Roxie weakly, but Roxie wasn't having any of this defeatist approach.

'How do *you* know?' she replied each time in bracing tones. 'She might! And wouldn't it be amazing if she did?'

'Yes, but . . .'

'Look, Clare. This is a really cool opportunity to expand a bit. She's back next week and has lined up some meetings with other firms. If you could get a few samples together by then — say, a bubble bath, shampoo and soap — and come up with some costs, she'll listen to your pitch.'

A pitch? Costs? This was sounding more like *Dragons' Den* by the minute. Clare shook her head. 'I really don't think—'

'No need to decide now. Let me know on Monday,' Roxie told her airily. She elbowed Clare. 'And don't say I never do anything for you.'

'Thanks, Rox, but—'

Roxie picked up the ringing phone before Clare had a chance to progress the 'but' any further, and stuck her tongue out. 'Amberley Medical Centre, how can I help you?'

Clare clocked off at two-thirty and, by the time she'd driven home, she'd pretty much written off the whole hare-brained idea. Roxie was lovely for thinking of her, but really, it was just plain daft to imagine her little home-made toiletries would ever be professional or perfect enough to be stocked by a fancy, upmarket hotel. She wasn't a business-woman, end of story. The whole thing was a silly pipe dream that you might indulge yourself in for a few minutes, but nothing more than that.

She returned to discover a sea of mess in the kitchen: papers dumped in haphazard piles on the table amidst empty coffee cups, a plate with sandwich crumbs, a soggy, browning apple core and a Diet Coke can. Polly's caffeine intake obviously hadn't fuelled her with any energy for tidying, Clare thought peevishly. No surprises there. There were even – ugh – splats of chicken shit on the floor too, where Polly must have left the back door wide open. Babs and Marjorie loved an excuse to wander into the house, and clearly they'd had some kind of party in here today. Brilliant.

Clare sighed in exasperation. It was not only completely bloody annoying that her sister saw her as some kind of char, it was also deeply hurtful. Clare had actually been really kind, opening her door to Polly and inviting her in. God knows what had got into her. If she knew back then that having Polly to stay was going to result in this kind of chaos, she'd have kept her mouth shut. Why couldn't Polly show even the slightest hint of gratitude that Clare had put her family life through a complete upheaval to make room for her?

Still, she shouldn't have really expected anything different. Even when her sister had lost her job, she couldn't do it quietly like most people – oh no; she had to go the whole hog, had to lose everything spectacularly and cause a gigantic fuss. And, of course, everyone else had to fall in with her wishes, cosset her like some kind of victim. Well, there wasn't going to be any more cosseting in this house, she thought grimly. Not if her sister kept treating the place like a hotel.

As if on cue, Polly walked in, still wearing her pyjamas. She had no make-up on and didn't even seem to have brushed her hair. 'Oh, hello,' she said, as if surprised to see Clare there in her own kitchen. 'How was work?'

'All right,' Clare said shortly, whistling to Fred, who was dozing under the table. 'I'm going to walk the dog and get the kids from school,' she said. 'Unless you've already walked him today?'

Polly looked down at her pyjamas pointedly. 'Well, no,' she said. 'Did you want me to?'

Clare gritted her teeth. 'Might be helpful now and then if you did,' she said, trying to keep her voice even. 'And even more helpful if you could keep the back door shut, to stop the chickens coming in. That lot will need cleaning up before Leila and Alex are home.'

She pointed at the offending dirty protest, and Polly's mouth dropped open in disgust.

'Oh, and by the way, I'm going out tonight,' Clare went on. 'Meeting a couple of the girls in the pub, if you fancy joining me?'

Polly's expression said loud and clear that she'd rather chew her own arm off. 'I'll pass on that, thanks,' she mumbled.

'Okay,' Clare said. Just as she'd thought. Of course Polly would turn her nose up at going out with Clare and her friends, like she'd always done. 'Well, I'll let Mum know there's no need to bother coming round to babysit then.

Save her a trip out, if you're going to be here anyway. See you later.'

Polly was about to protest, but Clare had already stepped carefully across the floor and was through the door, with Fred lolloping after her. Gotcha. Outside in the warm scented air Clare grinned, relishing the appalled look that had appeared on her sister's face. Ha. The sooner Polly wised up to the real world, the better for everyone.

That night Clare met Debbie, Tracey, Maria and Jane at their usual table in the King's Arms. They all knew each other from school except for Jane, who'd married Maria's brother Neil a mere ten years ago and was therefore still something of a newcomer by Elderchurch standards. Not that you'd ever guess. Jane worked in the post office and knew everything there was to know about everyone. She had a heart-shaped face, curly dark hair, an always-laughing mouth and the most voluptuous cleavage in the village. She was also prone to giving away Chupa Chups lollies to children when they were kicking off in the post-office queue. It was no wonder everyone loved her.

While Jane was plump and jolly, Maria was skinny, sallow and more serious. She was getting over her husband's recent spot of infidelity, but with three children between them she was determined to get things back on the straight and narrow, however fraught life currently was at home. She worked in sales for a coffee chain and spent most of her waking hours on the M3.

Finally there was Tracey, who was funny and sarcastic, onto her third marriage, and with a fourteen-year-old daughter and one-year-old twin boys keeping her busy round the clock. 'A teenager *and* teething toddlers, aren't I the lucky one?' she said, rolling her eyes.

It was when Debbie was uncorking the second bottle of Pinot (the first had vanished almost immediately) that she leaned over to Clare. 'Oh, I nearly forgot. My mum would like to order some bubble bath from you. The rose one, if that's okay.'

Clare flushed with pleasure. It still gave her a thrill every time someone asked for one of her products. 'Sure,' she said. 'I'll drop a bottle round for her. Funny you should mention that,' she went on before she could help herself, 'because . . .' Then she stopped, wishing she'd kept her mouth shut. That was the wine talking. Why repeat what Roxie had said? It wasn't as if she was going to take it any further.

'Oooh!' Jane said, spider-lashed eyes widening. 'Dramatic pause alert! What is it? Don't leave us in suspenders.'

Clare's face flamed as they all gawped at her. 'Nothing. Forget it.'

Debbie folded her arms across her chest. 'Spill,' she ordered. 'You can't tease us like that. What's nothing?'

'Boots have been on the phone, wanting Clare's secret recipes,' Tracey teased. 'Don't tell them, Clare. Not until they've agreed to pay more.'

Clare laughed. 'I wish. No, it's nothing like that. Just...' And then, because they were still looking at her so expectantly, she haltingly told them what Roxie had said, feeling a complete plonker for having mentioned the situation at all.

'Oh, wow,' Maria said at the end. 'Langley's are *nice*. We had a conference at the Langley's in Brighton last year – sooo cool. It was like a Regency palace with chandeliers and chaises longues, but with funky bright artwork everywhere too.' She leaned forward eagerly. 'Have you sorted out a meeting then? If you want a hand polishing up your pitch, I can help you.'

'Well...' Clare fiddled with a beer mat. 'That's why I shouldn't have even started talking about it, because I'm not going to do it.'

'What?' screeched Tracey.

'Get away,' said Jane. 'Pass up an opportunity like this? You can't!'

'Why not?' Debbie asked. 'You've got nothing to lose by just *meeting* her.'

Clare lifted her glass to sip her wine, but realized that somehow she'd already swallowed the lot. Tracey noticed and topped her up with a generous splash from the bottle. 'Well...' Clare began again. She hated being the centre of the conversation like this. Usually she took up a more comfortable place on the sidelines, rather than being thrust into the spotlight. 'Well, I just know she won't want my titchy little range,' she said in the end, trying to laugh it off. 'I mean, I'm hardly Molton Brown, am I?'

'Yeah, but she wants somebody local,' Maria replied. 'And original. Looking at it from a sales point of view, you've got a great story too: local mum, growing her own ingredients, starting off the company in her kitchen ... what's not to love?'

'I agree,' Jane said. 'How exciting.'

'You've got to do it,' Tracey put in, leaning forward. 'This could be your big break, Clare. You could be the next Anita Roddick!'

Clare smiled faintly. 'I don't think so,' she said. 'Really. I can't turn up there with my little bottles of stuff, handwritten sticky labels on them, and try to pass myself off as a serious businesswoman. I just can't.'

Debbie's eyes sparkled. 'Then maybe you need a designer,' she said. 'Me! I could work up some gorgeous designs for you and print some labels, no problem. What do you say?'

'I...' Clare felt taken aback. They were taking this seriously, she realized. 'The thing is, I'd be expected to talk about costings and stuff...'

'Get that sister of yours on the case then,' Debbie said. 'She's a business geek, isn't she? She can do all that for you.'

'I'm telling you, lady, if you don't say you'll do it right now, Team Clare will have to stage an intervention,' Jane warned.

Team Clare. How lovely was that? There was a sudden wetness in her eyes. These women had been by her side throughout her failing marriage and divorce; they'd been the loyal, loving sisters Polly had never been to her. Just having their encouraging, smiling faces all gazing at her was enough to make the last of her resistance crumble away. They were right. What did she have to lose, except perhaps her dignity when the Langley's woman turned her down? She might as well try. 'Okay, then,' she said. 'Why the hell not? I'll give it a go.'

And as her friends cheered and clapped her on the back, poured her more wine and started planning the whole pitch in earnest together, Clare felt an unfamiliar feeling sweep through her. She couldn't put her finger on it immediately, then realized. Excitement. That was it – excitement!

Chapter Fifteen

Polly was not the least bit happy about spending her Friday night babysitting the children. The cheek! Who did Clare think she was, swanning off and leaving her to it like that? Taking advantage of Polly's good nature ... taking the piss, more like.

'Feel free to go out any evening *you* want, obviously,' Clare had said, checking her lipstick in the mirror.

'Who with?' Polly had glowered. 'I don't have any friends here any more.'

Clare had raised an eyebrow. 'Hmmm. I wonder why that is,' she'd said sarcastically. And before Polly could retaliate, she'd wished them all goodnight (with a rather annoying jauntiness about her, frankly) and vanished off to the pub.

It was seven-thirty and the evening stretched ahead like a minefield. Bloody hell. She hated kids!

'Can you read me a story?' Alex asked.

'A story? Can't you read it yourself?' Polly snapped. 'And anyway isn't it time for bed now?'

'Time for bed NOW?' Leila repeated, tossing her hair with a great deal of scorn. She was wearing a skull-and-crossbones T-shirt, a glittery pale-blue scarf around her neck and denim shorts over striped footless tights. Somehow, she looked way cooler than Polly had ever looked, at any age. 'As if! Aunty Polly, it's not bedtime for *hours* yet. Mum lets us stay up until nine at the weekend.'

Polly narrowed her eyes. 'She didn't say anything about that to me,' she retorted. 'Isn't nine o'clock a bit late for a nine-year-old?'

Leila scowled and threw herself onto the sofa next to Polly, making her aunt bounce up in the air. 'I'm TEN,' she said witheringly, folding her arms across her chest and looking the image of Clare.

'And I'm fourteen,' Alex said, doing a headstand in the middle of the floor and crashing over. Polly winced as his feet missed the television by inches.

'I might be a decrepit old aunty, but I'm not stupid,' Polly said. 'You are definitely not fourteen. And are you sure you're allowed to do headstands in here?'

'All the time,' Alex assured her, kicking his skinny legs up again. His pyjama top slid down to his armpits, revealing his pale belly. 'I'll stop if you read me a story, though.'

This time he keeled over perilously close to the coffee table and Polly sucked in a horrified breath. Clare would kill her if she came back to discover her precious son had broken his legs doing forbidden gymnastics under the so-called care of his aunt. 'Oh, go on then,' she grumbled. 'What story do I have to read, then? *Baby Bunny and the Big Boo-Boo* or something awful like that?'

'That's not a proper book,' Leila said loftily. 'You just made it up.'

'I'm not a *baby* anyway,' Alex said, getting to his feet, his cheeks pink. 'I don't even *like* stories like that. Mum's reading me *Harry Potter*.'

Leila examined her fingernails. 'Oh, Aunty Polly won't be able to read that,' she said. 'I'd choose something else, Alex.'

'What do you mean, I won't be able to read that?' Polly fired back. 'I can read, you know!'

'Yeah, but Mum does really good voices for all the characters,' Leila said, with a crushing sideways glance. 'She does it *properly*.'

'*I* can do good voices!' Polly retaliated, stung. '*I* can do it properly!'

Leila looked disbelieving, but said nothing, as if she were far too polite to argue.

'Here you are then,' Alex said, plopping an enormous tome into Polly's lap. 'We're up to chapter seven.'

From the smirks her niece and nephew were now exchanging, Polly had the distinct impression she'd just been conned. This looked set to become the longest evening of her life. With a weary glance at the clock – still only seven-forty, unfortunately – she began to read.

The last time she'd read anything aloud to anyone had been a presentation she'd made at a conference in Zurich back in February. There her audience had been suited and groomed, they'd listened politely, taking notes and nodding in key places. Applause had pattered around the room afterwards.

Now look at her: stuck on the most uncomfortable sofa in the world, with a child either side leaning against her and a book about wizards in her hands. Where was the glory in that?

Nevertheless she was surprised to realize, after only a few pages, that she was actually rather enjoying herself. The story was pretty good, and she found herself getting quite into the action and even doing her best spooky voices when they were required. When it came to the cliffhanger at the end of the chapter, she paused, unsure whether or not to go on.

'Another one!' Alex demanded. 'Pleeeease?'

'You're not doing too badly,' Leila said kindly. 'Considering you've never read anything before. Can we have one more chapter? Please?'

Polly hesitated. If the truth be told, she was quite keen to find out what happened next herself. 'Oh, all right then,' she said. 'Just because I'm feeling extra kind.'

The next chapter was a funny one, and Leila and Alex both burst out laughing at several points. Polly found herself laughing too — as much at their delighted reactions as anything else. They were definitely a more gratifying and easily pleased audience than the ones she'd previously spoken to in sterile conference rooms around the globe.

'This is great,' she said, at the end of that chapter. 'I can't believe I never realized this *Harry Potter* thing was so good.'

'Haven't you read *any* of them before?' Leila asked, looking aghast at such an omission from her aunt's life. 'Truly?'

'Nope.'

'You must have seen the films though,' Alex said. 'Everyone's seen the ... You *haven't*?' he exclaimed as Polly shook her head. 'Whoa. I thought everyone in the whole world had. We have, loads of times.'

'I know!' Leila bounded off the sofa, her face alight. 'Let's watch the first one now. We've got the video, Aunty Polly. Can we? You'll love it. You so, so will.'

'Well...' Polly glanced at the clock. Five to eight. If it was still another hour before bedtime, she might as well stick a film on to kill a bit of time. She could finish reading the *FT* on her laptop while they watched it, and send them up to bed when it was nine o'clock.

'We could have POPCORN! I know how to make it,' Alex said. 'Go on, Aunty Polly. We can bring down our duvets and lie on the floor with the lights off while we watch, that's what we usually do when we have a cinema night.'

'Pleeeeease?' they chorused.

'Oh, all right,' Polly said, defeated by their enthusiasm. 'Just for a bit then. But at nine o'clock you're both going straight up to bed, all right? That's the deal.'

At half-past ten that evening Polly carried a sleeping Alex upstairs to bed, while Leila trotted beside her. 'And remember, you must promise not to tell your mum how late you've been up,' Polly whispered guiltily 'Otherwise she'll give me a smacked bottom and take my pocket money away.'

Leila giggled. 'I promise,' she said, skipping into the bathroom and parking herself on the toilet in full view of Polly. 'Wait, what about Alex's teeth?'

Polly, who'd swung away at the sight of her niece with her knickers around her ankles, hesitated. 'Well ... one night without brushing them won't do him any harm,' she decided, creeping into the dark bedroom and treading on something hard and knobbly. Ow. What sort of insane person left *Lego* on their floor, for heaven's sake?

'I think you should make him do a wee, though,' Leila called. 'He might wet the bed otherwise. You know what boys are like.'

Again Polly hesitated. Actually, she didn't know what boys were like any more. Not really. In fact, until this evening she'd lost touch with what children were like, full stop, having avoided them like the pox her entire adult life. She looked down at her sleeping nephew, who was surprisingly heavy in her arms, given what a skinny thing he was. His long, dark eyelashes fluttered on his cheek and a tiny smile flickered on his lips as if he was having the nicest possible dream. She'd truly meant to get him and Leila into bed by nine, but then the film had turned out to be so much fun that nobody could quite bring themselves to stop it. And then Alex had fallen asleep right there on the floor, curled up on the duvet pile like a sweet little dormouse.

'Um . . .' she said in answer to Leila, turning back towards the landing. Sweet and dormouse-like was all very well, but she did not want to make her nephew 'do a wee' as his sister had suggested. She had no idea how one went about such matters and seriously did not want to find out.

'Just wake him up,' Leila advised, flushing the toilet and washing her hands. She dried them, then came out of the bathroom and leaned over her brother's sleeping body. 'Alex! Hey, Alex,' she hissed, prodding him. Then she pinched his nose. 'Alex!'

He woke up, squirming and kicking out, and Polly put him carefully on the floor. 'Are you okay? It's time for bed, Alex. Just ... um ... go to the loo quickly, then I'll tuck you in.'

She left him to it while she went downstairs to fetch their duvets. When she came back up, the children were thankfully both in their beds and Alex was already asleep again. She covered him up, and then Leila, and was about to walk away when Leila suddenly wrapped her arms around Polly's neck and hugged her. 'Tonight was fun,' she said drowsily.

Polly blinked in surprise. Fun? At the start of the evening she'd been desperate to get the children in bed and out of sight. But somehow or other she'd ended up quite enjoying herself. 'Yes,' she replied. 'I suppose it was. Goodnight.'

'Night,' Leila murmured, her eyes closing.

Polly turned off the light and stood in the doorway for a few moments listening to them breathing. It gave her a strange feeling inside – a sort of ... *warmth*.

Then she shook herself briskly. Warmth, indeed! She was overtired, that was all. Worn out by looking after those monkeys all evening. She took herself off to bed, hoping to fall asleep before Clare got back and had the chance to quiz her about how the babysitting had gone.

*

Clare was in a strange mood the next day, and crashed around in the kitchen with a face like thunder, despite it being a sunny Saturday morning. 'Is it too much to ask,' she began the second Polly ventured into the room, 'for you to actually clear up the mess you make in here?'

Ahh. There was the popcorn pan she'd left on the side, along with the unwashed hot-chocolate mugs that she'd dumped in the sink.

'I mean, I know you're not *used* to picking up after yourself; I know you probably had a housekeeper or a fleet of staff to do all that for you in London, but—'

'Good morning to you too,' Polly said frostily, stalking over to the kettle. 'I hope you had a good evening in the pub while I was babysitting your children.' Touché. Have some of it back, Miss Up-Yourself, she thought, watching Clare falter mid-rant.

Clare's shoulders sagged. 'Sorry,' she muttered. 'Fair enough. And thanks for looking after the kids. Were they okay? Leila said you watched *Harry Potter* with them.'

'They were fine,' Polly said, wanting to gloss over the mention of the film and how late they'd stayed up. 'How about you? Good night?'

Clare began wiping the table, her back turned. 'Yes,' she said after a while. 'Just the usual – the same girls I always meet up with, but –' She clammed up and Polly glanced over at her curiously.

'What?' she prompted. 'You've gone all mysterious. Did something happen?'

Clare wrinkled her nose. 'No, not really.' She paused, then shook her head. 'No, nothing. Probably had too much to drink, got a bit carried away.'

Polly watched her, puzzled, wondering what Clare was not saying. Was there some bloke on the scene maybe that Clare didn't want to tell her about? Some juicy village gossip she'd decided not to share? *Interesting.* Polly would have to keep an eye out for what it could be. Something was going on, that was for sure.

'We've had lots of interest since the open day, although people are saying the price is a little on the high side. Don't you worry, though, Miss Johnson, I'm sure someone will snap it up very soon. Trust me.'

Polly sighed as she ended the call to the estate agent. Trust him? If only. So now he was saying the price — *his* price, don't forget — was too high. Great. She shut her eyes, trying to make the calculations. If she lowered the price a fraction, she would still break even, according to her accountant, but then again no one ever actually *paid* the asking price, did they? She couldn't afford to reduce it by much; she'd be left still in debt. Bloody hell. She leaned back in the deckchair, trying not to wail out loud.

The garden was providing solace at least, even if Vince hadn't been able to. With Clare and the children out at swimming lessons, Polly had had a nice quiet hour sunning herself out there with Fred at her feet and the next *Harry Potter* to read (Leila had pressed it into her hand over breakfast, telling her she was totally going to love it). It was rather nice living somewhere with a garden, it had to be said, especially when it was turning out to be such a warm and sunny summer. The flowers smelled glorious, the bees were murmuring busily to themselves and the sky was still an early-morning misty blue. She'd never really done this in London, she realized – just sat outside with a book, letting her mind wander. For the vast part of the last twenty years she'd been inside air-conditioned buildings, barely noticing the weather, let alone the seasons changing.

She watched as a cabbage-white butterfly danced through the air before her eyes. In the past she'd never envied Clare anything, had always disagreed profoundly with every life decision her sister had made. Stay in Elderchurch all her life? No way. Marry Steve? You must be mad. Take the most boring job ever, to fit around your kids? Not in a million years.

It was strange, realizing that actually there was one thing she envied her sister for now: this garden, and the calm serenity that came simply from sitting in it. Mind you, she didn't envy her the chickens, she thought, noticing them strutting about, picking their feet up as if they were goose-stepping, stopping to peck at the ground now and then. They gave her the creeps.

'Yoo-hoo!' came a voice just then. 'Clare! I've got you some – Oh. You're not Clare.'

So much for calm serenity. Polly stared at the old lady who'd just wandered into the garden, brandishing a bunch of carrots. 'Hello,' she said coldly.

'Aha! You must be the sister, am I right? The *grand fromage*, as our French friends would say.' She tapped her nose, her bright-blue eyes mischievous sparkles in her leathery, wrinkled face.

Polly had no idea who this batty old bag was, swinging those carrots by their long frilly leaves as if they were an organic flail. 'I am Clare's sister, yes.' *Now bugger off.*

'Well, it's lovely to meet you, my dear. I am Agatha. Clare's neighbour?'

'She hasn't mentioned you,' Polly said rudely.

'Oh, thank heavens for that! Too polite to tell you about me getting locked out all the time and talking to my plants and whatnot; that *is* a relief. Anyway. Carrots – incoming. Catch!'

And before Polly could react, Agatha had thrown the bunch of muddy carrots straight into her lap, showering soil all over her bare legs. Then she wandered away, humming to herself in a high pitch.

Polly stared after her. 'Everyone in this village is bonkers,' she muttered.

'Isn't it wonderful?' Agatha called back over her shoulder, obviously having overhead.

Babs — or was it Marjorie? — came clucking inquisitively around Polly's legs, and Polly swung the carrots at her in annoyance. 'And you can bloody well get lost as well,' she hissed. 'Go on, shoo!'

Once Clare and the children were back, along with a powerful whiff of chlorine, Clare draped the wet costumes and towels on the washing line and went into the kitchen, saying something about a picnic lunch. Something struck Polly as odd, but she couldn't put her finger on what it was.

Leila bounded over, wet hair swinging, her feet slapping in purple Crocs. 'How are you getting on with the book, Aunty Polly? Are you enjoying it?'

Polly smiled at her. Her niece was actually proving to be rather sweet. 'It's great,' she replied. 'Very exciting. How was swimming?' she asked.

'Cool,' Leila said, throwing herself upside down in a handstand. She was wearing a red T-shirt with a snarling dragon on it, khaki combat trousers and a silver skull wristband. 'We're starting lifesaving skills. We had to dive right down at the deep end to try and pull out this dummy. It was so heavy! Hardly anyone could do it, but *I* did.'

'Well done,' Polly said as her niece flicked gracefully over into a backbend. 'Just like your mum. She was always a brilliant –' Then she realized what the odd thing was. Only two costumes on the washing line. 'Didn't your mum go in the pool today?' she asked in surprise.

Leila turned herself right way up again. 'No,' she said, scratching at an insect bite on her ankle. 'She never goes in. I don't think she likes swimming.'

Polly pushed her sunglasses up onto her head and stared at her niece. Didn't like swimming? Clare? 'That's weird,' she said. 'She used to love it. You know she used to be really good at it, right? Swimming for the club and the county, winning loads of races and . . .' Her voice trailed off at Leila's blank face. 'She never told you?'

Leila shook her head. 'No,' she said.

'What sandwiches does everyone want?' Clare bellowed through the kitchen window just then and Leila skipped away to put in her order.

'That's really weird,' Polly murmured again. Swimming had always been a massive part of Clare's life. It *had* been her life for a few years when they were teenagers, in fact. It had annoyed Polly that their shared bedroom always had a lingering pong of chlorine, thanks to Clare's obsession with the pool; it had driven her mad, too, whenever Clare had set the alarm for some ungodly hour in the morning so that she could sneak in an early practice before school. She'd been so tireless and motivated about it, though – amazingly so, now that Polly looked back. She'd cycle to Amberley pool on her own before anyone else in the family was up, swim a mile or so, then cycle back and get ready for school.

Polly couldn't remember why Clare had stopped swimming now. Puberty maybe. Perhaps she'd started to get embarrassed about her changing body, or hadn't wanted to be different from her friends any longer. Maybe she'd stopped because she'd got interested in boys?

She heaved herself out of the deckchair, figuring she ought to lend a hand – even *she* could make a sandwich or two without blowing the place up.

'Anything I can do to help?' she asked, entering the dingy kitchen and blinking after being out in the sunshine for so long.

Clare did a double-take, then gave a chuckle.

'What?' Polly asked. 'What's so funny?'

'Nothing,' Clare said, passing her a bowl of slippery-looking hard-boiled eggs and a dollop of mayo. 'Some help would be great, that's all. You can mash these. Thank you.'

*

After a picnic lunch in the garden, ably assisted by Fred, the sky clouded over. Clare was just suggesting that they all go out for a bike ride, now that it was cooler, when a woman with hennaed hair cut in a pixie style, loads of children and a crazed lurcher appeared, and the place basically exploded with noise. The dogs barked hysterically, the children swarmed everywhere and Polly found herself reeling in horror from the din. Clare's life really was *noisy*, she was starting to realize. And there were always so many *people* involved in it.

'Hello, I'm Debbie,' the henna-haired woman said cheerfully, seeing Polly on the picnic rug. 'I'm Clare's interfering friend, who's come round to nag her again about Langley's.'

Debbie, that was it. Polly remembered her from the wedding. Chief bridesmaid, no less, when everyone knew that a *sister* had the divine right of being chief bridesmaid. Even now, the demotion rankled.

Clare had turned red and glanced across at Polly, as if Debbie had just spoken out of turn. 'Um...' she stuttered.

'And I've brought some designs for you to look at,' Debbie went on breezily, seemingly unaware of Clare's discomfort. 'I thought I might as well get stuck in straight away, run a few ideas past you. I ordered Will to take the kids out all morning, fired up the Mac and...' She trailed off and glanced from Clare to Polly. 'What? Why are you looking at me like that? Is this a bad time?'

'No, no,' Clare said quickly. 'I just ... Cold light of day and all that. I think we probably got a bit overexcited about the whole thing last night. I'm not so sure it's a good idea any more.'

Debbie stared at her. 'Not so sure? Overexcited? Oh, give over, will you? Tell her, Polly. Langley's are going to love her!'

Polly stared at Debbie, then at Clare, wishing someone would enlighten her. The only Langley's she'd ever heard of was the boutique hotel chain, but they obviously weren't talking about *that* Langley's. She doubted anyone from Elderchurch had even heard of that Langley's. 'I'm not following,' she said with a polite laugh.

Debbie gave Clare a severe look. 'You haven't told her, have you?' she said, as if she were scolding a child. 'Clare Berry, what are you like! Well, I'll tell her then.' She sat down on the picnic blanket and turned to address Polly. 'Your sister has got a chance to make some serious dosh with her bath products and she's wussing out about it. That's what this is all about.'

'I'm not wussing out, I'm being realistic,' Clare argued, although there was already more than a hint of defeat in her voice.

'Um ... I'm still not following,' Polly said. The conversation was starting to irritate her.

Debbie, after another pointed look at Clare, filled Polly

in on the whole matter. 'You're a businesswoman, aren't you, Polly? You'll back me up, and tell your sister that she'd be mad not to try the pitch, won't you?'

Polly was taken aback. Clare — pitching for business? Had she just heard that right? It seemed incredible. Were those unlabelled bottles of goo in the bathroom something to do with this sideline of her sister's then? Polly had assumed they were some ghastly potions the children had concocted. 'Er . . . yes,' she managed to say after a moment. 'Yes, of course you should try, Clare. Langley's are a good firm, they're performing very strongly at the moment. I've stayed in one of their hotels before — in York, I think. A bit unusual; not your traditional hotel fare, to say the least, but that seems to be their strength, from what I can gather.'

Debbie grinned at Polly as if they were conspirators. 'Well,' she said, before Clare had a chance to speak again, 'I think that means you're outvoted. Now then. Designs.' She held up an A4 envelope and pulled out a sheaf of paper. 'I realize I've taken a bit of a liberty, because I know you haven't actually decided on a name for your brand or anything, but . . . what do you think of Berry Botanicals?'

'Berry Botanicals,' Clare repeated, as if testing the feel of the words. Then she nodded. 'Sounds healthy and fruity, and it's got my name in. Perfect!' She leafed through the sheets of designs that Debbie had brought and gave a little cry. 'Oh wow,' she said. 'They're gorgeous, Debs.'

They all peered at the papers. Debbie had created a silhouette pattern that looked like a vine, with flower shapes and different fruits appearing between the branches. She'd worked the pattern so that a horizontal oval space was empty in the centre, apart from the words 'Berry Botanicals' and then, in smaller letters underneath, 'Rosehip Shampoo'. In an even smaller, handwritten font below, following the bottom curve of the oval, was written 'Made for Langley's, with love'. She'd run the pattern through with different colour schemes and fonts, and overall the effect was striking and very pretty.

Polly had been silent for a while. She couldn't quite get to grips with the insane idea of her sister trying to pitch her home-made bubble bath to Langley's. To *Langley's!* It was, quite frankly, ridiculous. Her instinct was to pour cold water on the whole thing and tell Clare in no uncertain terms that she was making a fool of herself. But something stopped her from saying so.

'What do you think of the designs, Polly?' Clare asked.

Ah, they'd remembered at last that someone with a bit of business nous was actually there. She pretended to consider them. They were actually kind of attractive, she had to admit. 'Is it slightly too girly, I wonder?' she mused. 'You do get a lot of businessmen staying at hotels like this. I'm not sure they'd go for pink flowers, for example.'

'Good point,' Debbie said. 'Perhaps if we stick to darker

blues and greens as backgrounds then, just picking out a bright red or turquoise with the lettering. That should make it more unisex.'

'And we can zing the names up a bit,' Clare added. 'Rosehip Shampoo, Lime Bubble Bath – they're not sounding all that exciting at the moment. But overall I think they're going to look amazing. And I think *you're* amazing too,' she said to Debbie, sounding choked. 'I can really imagine my toiletries as actual ... well, you know, *proper* toiletries, like you see in the shops. And I love my brand name.' She giggled. 'I can't believe I just said "my brand name". Me, with a brand name!'

Despite her cynicism about the whole hopeless project, Polly felt her lips twitch in a smile. Her sister was being way, way too emotional about this – she'd never make a tough old businessbird like Polly – but she looked so thrilled and excited, that it was ... well, it was rather touching actually. And kind of infectious too. At least something interesting was happening around here, for a change.

Chapter Sixteen

Clare felt as if she were on board a runaway train as Berry Botanicals began to take shape. It was all happening so fast! Over the course of the afternoon she and Debbie brainstormed the names of sample products and came up with Ginger Ninja Bubbles, Limelight Shampoo and a soap bar called Vanilla Thriller, then later on she picked Polly's brains about how to go about producing a costing. During the course of Sunday she made up some samples for the pitch, stirring and sniffing, trying and testing. If she was seriously going to go through with this, she wanted everything to be perfect.

On Sunday evening, when the children were in bed, Polly helped her work on her pitch. As Clare had absolutely no experience in this sort of thing, her sister's advice and suggestions were a total godsend.

'She'll be looking for your bottom-line figures, how flexible you can be, how quickly you can supply her with what she wants,' Polly coached her. 'The costs we pulled together last night actually stack up pretty well, as you've got such low overheads, so try and be confident. You're offering a decent-quality product at a reasonable price; you're local; and you're using ingredients you've grown yourself, where possible – these are all bonuses.'

Polly was speaking to her differently all of a sudden, Clare realized. Gone was the aloof scorn and patronizing air. The dynamic between them now felt more like one between colleagues, working towards the same goal. To say this was an improvement was the understatement of the century. 'Do you think I should tell her much about myself?' she wondered. 'I mean, I don't exactly have much of a business history.'

'Just focus on the positives, put a spin on your words to make it all sound good. So rather than saying you've got zilch experience, phrase it that you're a new start-up and Langley's would be your major customer – they'll like that sort of exclusivity. Also, let her know that you're willing to work with the company on what they want; you're not rigid about what you can and can't produce.' Polly patted her sister's hand. 'It'll be fine, I promise. Let's just put some bullet points in this document . . .'

They were sitting at the table in the kitchen with the laptop between them, and Clare was struck by a massive wash of gratitude for everything Polly was doing. 'Thank you,' she said quietly. 'Seriously, I wouldn't have a clue about the business side of things. Not a clue. I wouldn't be able to do this on my own.'

Polly went on typing for a moment, then pressed the Return key with a flourish. 'It's the least I can do,' she said with a self-conscious laugh. 'You're putting me up – or, rather, putting up with me – so until I get back on my feet financially and can pay my way, I'm happy to contribute some business ideas. More than happy.'

'Well, I really appreciate it,' Clare said.

There was another odd silence and then Polly changed the subject. 'I've been meaning to ask: is that a tattoo I spotted on your back the other day?'

'My bluebird? Yeah,' Clare replied. 'Me and the girls got matching ones when we turned thirty. I think it was Tracey's idea – she was worried about turning into an old fart.' She laughed. 'Now we're just old farts with crap tattoos, so I'm not sure it's any better really. Still, I love it. Makes me feel like part of a team, if you know what I mean.'

She reached around and touched the bird on her back, remembering the day they'd ventured to the tattoo parlour in Andover together, giggling like schoolgirls. They'd settled on the bluebird as a symbol of happiness and freedom and had taken it in turns to be inked, yelping at the pain as the needles buzzed through the design. Afterwards they'd found a wine bar and toasted each other with glasses of cold Sauvignon Blanc, before dashing back to pick up the children, laughing about what the other mothers would think of them turning up, stinking of wine, with scabby tattoos on their backs. *Her team*, she thought with a smile, remembering the way they'd all backed her in this Langley's idea. God, she was lucky to have friends like that.

Polly was silent, and Clare wondered if she was missing her friends in London. Perhaps it was insensitive to go on about the girls in front of her, when she must be dying to get back to her own gang.

'Have you got a tattoo?' she asked. 'I bet you have. Go on, what is it? A pound sign tattooed on your bum or something?'

'No!' Polly spluttered. 'I wouldn't – I couldn't. Far too much of a wuss.'

'You, a wuss? I don't believe that for a second.' The idea made Clare snort. Polly was without doubt the most confident, headstrong person she'd ever met. She was surprised the word 'wuss' was even in her vocabulary.

Polly wrinkled her nose, but her smile was empty of feeling. Once again, Clare wondered what on earth was going on in her sister's head.

On Monday Roxie's first word to Clare was an arch 'Well?'

Clare grinned. 'I'm up for it.'

'YESSSS!' screamed Roxie, much to the surprise of Luke,

who'd walked in at that moment. She high-fived Clare, beaming. 'Woo-hoo! That's so exciting.'

'Wow,' Luke said, pausing and staring at them both. 'What have I just missed? Are we all getting a pay rise or something?'

'Oh, it's nothing to do with *this place*,' Roxie said, rolling her eyes as if that was the last thing she'd ever be squealing about. 'Clare's going into business,' she announced grandly.

Clare squirmed beneath Luke's look of curiosity. 'It's not that big a deal,' she said, feeling her face flare with hot colour.

'Oh yeah? Sounds a big deal to me,' Luke replied. He seemed bemused. 'Go on, then. What sort of business? Are we looking at the next Richard Branson, right here in Amberley?'

'Don't be so ridiculous,' Roxie scoffed. 'Clare's much better-looking than him!'

'I don't think he meant—' Clare said hurriedly, just as Luke said, 'Well, I know *that*,' and gave her the most disarming wink.

'Clare makes totally gorgeous bubble baths and smellies,' Roxie said, sounding every bit the proud mamma. 'And, fingers crossed, she's going to supply Langley's – you know the hotel company? – with her stuff!'

'Really? Wow,' Luke said. 'That's amazing, Clare.'

'It's not definite,' Clare mumbled, wishing Roxie hadn't

bigged her up quite so much. It was going to be horribly embarrassing when she didn't get the commission and had to admit as much to Luke and everyone else to whom Roxie had blabbed. 'In fact it's not even remotely *likely*, but . . .'

'Play your cards right, Luke,' Roxie went on coyly, looking up at him through her mascara-clumpy lashes (a striking lilac colour today), 'and she might even give you a free sample.'

He smiled. 'I'd better behave myself then, hadn't I, and do some work. Don't want to fall behind with my patients before I've already started.'

He went off, whistling, and Roxie elbowed Clare. 'He *so* likes you.'

'He doesn't,' Clare snapped back, feeling flustered. 'He's got a girlfriend anyway; he's not allowed to like anyone else.'

Roxie snorted and slapped her forehead. 'God, Clare Berry. Sometimes I can't believe you're actually more than ten years older than me, when you come out with crap like that. DERRRR! He's a *bloke*. With a willy ruling his tiny little brain!' She shook her head despairingly. 'Honestly, woman, you need to—'

'Roxanne! Clare! Could you keep it down out here, please?' came a clipped and rather cross voice just then.

Clare turned guiltily to see Dr Copper glaring daggers at them.

'There are ill people in the waiting area. They do not want to hear you giggling and screeching,' she went on. 'I've already had one complaint this morning about all the noise you're making. I don't want to have to apologize for your behaviour again, is that clear?'

'Sorry,' Clare said, dropping her eyes.

'Yes, Miss,' Roxie muttered under her breath, like a naughty schoolgirl. As soon as Dr Copper had walked away again, she fished out her phone and started jabbing at the buttons with practised speed. 'I'll just wing Aunty Kate a quick text. Tell her to give you a call and arrange a meeting.' She chuckled to herself. 'Richard Branson will be asking you for tips once I've finished meddling, you wait.'

Clare arranged to meet Roxie's Aunty Kate (she mustn't actually call her that out loud, she kept reminding herself) the following Thursday at the site of the new hotel. When the day came, she put on her one and only suit and a pair of Polly's L.K. Bennett black patent heels. The shoes were actually half a size too big, but since they were a million times smarter than anything she owned, she stuffed the toes with toilet paper and vowed to make do. Then she packed up her documents and samples in a smart little briefcase (also borrowed from her sister) and rehearsed what she was going to say one last time in front of the bedroom mirror.

She looked awful, pale and tense, as if she were a victim in a slasher movie, rather than a business winner.

'All set?' Polly asked. 'Honestly, don't worry. Keep it professional and succinct, show her the products and figures, job done.' She patted her arm when Clare didn't respond. 'Do you want me to come with you?'

Clare smiled wanly. 'I would love you to come with me,' she replied. 'I would love you to stand there and do it all for me, while I cower in the car. But at the same time I want to do it myself.'

'Of course,' Polly said. 'This is your baby, I'd feel just the same. Well, good luck. Ring me when you get there if you need a pep talk. And try to enjoy it.'

Enjoy it? Clare felt as if she was going to puke as she started up the Fiat and drove away. She still wasn't convinced that this wouldn't be a total waste of everyone's time but ... oh, what the hell. Nothing ventured, nothing gained, as they said. And if it all went pear-shaped in the actual meeting, then so be it. At least she might finally have gained a few respect points in her sister's eyes for getting that far at all. There was a first time for everything.

Lovington was about thirty minutes away by car, buried deep in the leafy Hampshire countryside. Clare knew the roads around there pretty well, but nevertheless the hotel took a bit of finding, as there were no signposts at the entrance yet. After a lot of reversing and swearing and a panicked call to Roxie, she finally tracked the place down, about half a mile along what she'd originally thought was a country track. The track was bumpy and potholed and definitely in need of some TLC, but was lined with magnificent spreading cedar trees that arched above her, casting dappled light through the windscreen. After a while she turned a corner and saw the hotel building in front of her and sucked in her breath, nearly stalling at the sight of so much grandeur.

It was an old manor house, built in warm red brick with two rows of large arched windows and a rampant wisteria on its front. Looking up, Clare could see clusters of twisting chimneys on the rooftops, and smaller attic windows in what must have once been the servants' quarters. There was a circular driveway in front of the house with an ornate stone fountain in its centre, and Clare could imagine horses and carriages arriving there in years gone by, the horses' breath steaming in cold mornings, footmen and maids on the front steps of the house . . .

It was glorious. Far too glorious for the likes of her, she thought in the next second, biting her lip. Feeling a little sick, she tucked her Fiat out of sight behind a builder's van, then turned off the engine. This was it. The daft pipe dream had become bricks and mortar, and was standing right there in front of her.

She read through her proposal one last time, applied some fresh lipstick and practised a confident smile in the rear-view mirror. *You can do it, Clare.*

Okay. Time to get moving. With trembling legs, sweaty hands and a heart that was pumping like a piston engine, she clambered out of the car, then tottered across the driveway in her unfamiliar heels and up the formidable stone steps.

Inside the hotel's main entrance some major decorating and refurbishment was under way. A couple of men were papering the walls with a tasteful eau-de-nil stripe, while Clare could hear the rasp of a saw and thunderous hammering elsewhere. The hall had clearly once been fabulously grand, with a broad wooden staircase sweeping up to the first floor on the left, and an old chandelier still glittering from the ceiling. Clare could imagine wonderful parties and balls taking place here over the years, beautiful young things arriving in their finery, beaded flapper dresses and cigarette holders, champagne glasses clinking, crackly old gramophone records playing...

Her reverie ended abruptly as one of the builders began a tuneless whistle. Oh yes. Business meeting. So where was she meant to go?

Just then there came the brisk clip-clop of high heels along a corridor and a forty-something woman with a dark, glossy bob appeared. She was wearing a neat grey suit and a very loud turquoise shirt with pointy collars.

Clare swallowed. 'Hi,' she said, plastering on a bright smile and walking towards the woman. 'Are you by any chance Kate Hendricks? I'm Clare Berry.'

'Clare, hello, perfect timing,' the woman replied. 'Yes, I'm Kate. Sorry about this,' she went on, gesturing around the half-decorated hall, 'but we're in a state of flux, as you can see. Come with me, I'll take you somewhere a bit quieter, where we can chat.'

Clare followed Kate along a wood-panelled corridor. 'It's a gorgeous building,' she said timidly, peeping through the open doors that they passed and glimpsing ornate ceilings, huge sofas with the plastic wrapping still around them and heavy velvet curtains tied back in swags. 'How old is it, do you know?'

'Most of it is seventeenth-century,' Kate replied. 'It belonged to the same family for generations, apparently. The gardens are amazing around the back, too. It's going to be fantastic when we've worked our Langley's magic on the place and are up and running.'

'When are you planning to open?' Clare asked.

'Hopefully September,' Kate said. 'I expect Roxie's told you that this particular hotel is going to be the first we've opened in this part of the country, which is why we're so keen to source local products where we can. As well as its being a hotel, we plan to expand it to become a country club too, which members can use.' She stopped at a door on the right of the corridor and led Clare into a large, light room, which had duck-egg blue wallpaper patterned with hummingbirds. There was a generous fireplace on the far side, with an impressive black marble mantelpiece, and there were huge leaded windows, which looked out onto an ornamental garden where Clare could see a woman clipping the hedge. There was also a vast bright-pink slouchy sofa heaped with cushions – the sort of sofa you could spend a whole day in quite happily. Elsewhere there were chunky shelves crammed with books, a large vase of lilies and gypsophila, and a couple of overstuffed armchairs in a Liberty fabric on either side of a small table. It was all gorgeously, tastefully done – the modern and the vintage working perfectly together.

'Wow,' Clare sighed, unable to help feeling an impostor here, stunned by the wealth and grandeur everywhere she looked. This was not her world, and probably never would be, either. She felt like a kid with her nose pressed against a sweet-shop window.

'Lovely, isn't it?' Kate said. 'We haven't finalized the artwork for this room yet – I've been meeting local artists who are interested in having their paintings featured – but this is the kind of style we're going for throughout the hotel.'

'It's amazing,' Clare said. 'Just the right balance between traditional and ... fun.'

'That's exactly what we're aiming for,' Kate said, sounding pleased. 'Luxury with a twist. Old-school glamour meets modern bohemian, with a relaxed feel. We want our guests to be completely at home here.' She gestured towards the armchairs. 'Have a seat. Can I get you a tea or coffee?'

'A tea would be lovely, please,' Clare said. She felt a stab of longing inside as she perched in the armchair. Now that she was here, and had seen what a cool place the hotel was going to be, she wanted desperately to be involved.

Kate made a quick call to order some drinks then sat opposite Clare. 'So,' she said pleasantly. 'Shall we start by looking at your product line?'

Clare was glad that Kate made no reference to Roxie during their conversation. She'd been worried beforehand that she'd be taken less seriously for the unconventional manner in which this interview had been arranged. She'd dreaded getting any hint from Kate that this was all a favour for her demanding niece, an annoyance that had to be dealt with as quickly as possible, and had almost wanted to pre-empt her with an apology for taking up her time.

Polly had told her several times, in no uncertain tones, that this was absolutely out of the question. 'If you can't treat this as a viable business proposition, then she definitely won't,' she had said. 'Do not — I repeat, do not — go in there with any kind of hangdog, sorry-I-exist look on your face and start talking yourself out of the deal before she's had a chance to make up her mind. You're better than that.'

With her sister's words ringing in her ears, Clare did her best to bite back any self-deprecation and instead set her sample bottles on the table in front of Kate, and began telling her about their natural ingredients and how she'd arrived at the formula for each. She spoke haltingly at first, her words sounding strained and unnatural to her own ears, but she was on safe ground at least, discussing her potions and how she'd concocted them. She knew her stuff backwards and, after a couple of minutes, felt herself begin to relax and speak more easily. 'I'm only a small business,' she confessed, 'and if you were to choose me as your supplier, the hotel would be my biggest customer. But that would mean, of course, that I could be flexible to your needs, and I'm more than happy to create exclusive fragrances and products as you wish.'

Ooh, that sounded good. Just as she and Polly had rehearsed! Kate was nodding appreciatively, Clare noticed, with a prickle of excitement. For all her earlier certainty that this was pie-in-the-sky and nothing would come of it, she now felt the yearning ramp up inside her. She really wanted to do this.

Kate picked up the Ginger Ninja bottle and smiled when she saw the 'Made for Langley's, with love' line on the label. 'Nice touch,' she said. 'Lovely designs too, very fresh and eye-catching.' She unscrewed the cap and sniffed the contents. 'Mmm. I like it. Not too feminine, either, which is a plus. Okay, thank you for talking me through what you've got. I'll take the products away if I may, to show my team. Can we discuss costs now?'

Once the meeting was over, Kate led Clare back down the corridor, with its last tantalizing glimpses of Wonderland, and out through the main doors. In the driveway an Audi the colour of gun metal was pulling up smoothly, the gravel flinging itself beneath the heavy wheels, and as Clare said her final goodbyes to Kate, the car parked in front of the hotel and two women got out. Dressed in tailored business suits with crisp blouses, perma-tans and perfectly coiffed hair, they carried Mulberry bags and exuded waves of power and expensive perfume.

Was this the competition? Clare's heart plummeted around her ankles. Shit. She had no hope then. No hope whatsoever.

'Ah, I think these are my next ladies,' Kate said, removing her hand from Clare's. 'Thanks again, Clare. I'll be in touch,' she said a little distractedly, before fixing a new smile on her face to greet the recent arrivals. 'Hello there. I'm Kate Hendricks, can I help you?'

'Good morning, Kate, I'm Jacqueline Wade and this is Annabel Palmer-Thompson,' Clare heard. 'We're from Brownes.'

Clare tried to give her rivals a professional, business-like smile as she passed them on the front steps, but – unused to wearing heels, let alone too-big heels – her ankle chose that exact moment to give way and she staggered, losing her balance and falling all the way down the steps onto her hands and knees in the gravel.

'Oops,' she heard one of the glamazons say, with what sounded horribly like a titter behind a manicured hand.

'Oh goodness, Clare, are you all right?' Kate cried, hurrying down after her. 'Some of the steps are a bit uneven, I should have warned you, I'm so sorry . . .'

'I'm fine, thanks,' Clare said, getting quickly to her feet before Kate felt obliged to help her up. Her tights had ripped and her palms felt punctured from the sharp little stones, but the embarrassment was far worse than the pain. She could feel them all watching: the impeccable women from Brownes no doubt smirking at her imbecility, and

Kate probably wondering if she had a drink problem. Shit. What a clumsy oaf she was. What a prat-falling, useless idiot!

'Sorry,' she muttered, her face fiery, as she brushed herself down, deliberately keeping her back to the other women. To top it off a crumpled length of toilet roll was now hanging right out of one shoe and she shoved it back in with her foot, feeling more gauche than ever. *Don't cry, don't cry.* 'Thanks again,' she managed to say and hurried off, praying her wobbly ankle would make it as far as the car. Stupid heels. Loathsome heels!

'Okay...' she heard Kate say uncertainly behind her. 'Bye then. Take care.' There was a delicate pause. 'Now then, would you two like to come in? I've been looking forward to seeing your products.'

And in they went through the old oak doors, a strong scent of Chanel lingering in their wake.

Clare let out a groan. Bollocks. Big, hairy, dangling, *sweaty* bollocks. What a total fuckwit she was. What a klutz! She'd done okay in the meeting too, she'd actually come out with a few coherent sentences and not muffed any of the figures. And then to go and blow it by falling over, bum in the air, knickers probably flashed for all the world to see, face in the gravel like an utter twenty-four-carat loser. Why had she ever agreed to this ludicrous meeting in the first place? That little trip down the steps had reminded her of her place, all right – sprawled on the ground, while the proper business types of the world stepped over her prone body and were handed a big fat contract.

It was only the horrific prospect of being discovered weeping in her crummy old Fiat by elegant Kate that gave her the will to turn the ignition key and start the engine.

Chapter Seventeen

Sorry, there are no results that match your search criteria.

Unfortunately we have no vacancies in your field. Please try again soon – our recruitment database is updated regularly.

For the last time, no jobs here for you. Just give up and admit you're a failure, yeah?

Polly was going cross-eyed from staring at the computer screen for so long. For all their boasting about regular updates, the job websites were starting to look brain-achingly familiar, and soul-crushingly hopeless when she scanned them every morning. There was the Market Risk Data analyst job that sounded good, until you looked at the pay. Then came that same old project-manager post, also working in the Market Risk area, which she'd already applied for (still crossing those fingers, but the company seemed to have extended the deadline date, which was worrying). A couple of jobs in Brussels. Something in

Edinburgh. Short-term contracts, some as short as a week, but these were no good to her now that she no longer had a home in London. To enable a move back she needed something meaty, a proper contract that she could show to prospective landlords of lovely flats . . .

Oh God, she missed her flat. She missed living alone. Being at Clare's was . . . well, to be fair, it wasn't quite as dreadful as she'd anticipated, but there were certainly no mod cons here, no breathtaking views of the city skyline, no bustle and buzz of the capital's energy. It was turning out to be harder than she'd thought to get anything done here, what with her parents dropping in for coffee and a chat all the time, as well as batty Agatha and her frequent visits, involving more offerings of manky root vegetables.

She forced her attention back to the laptop screen. Face it, she said to herself, there were just no jobs suitable for her right now. Nothing. Even Clare's business prospects looked more enticing than Polly's – although after the dismal expression on her face when she'd returned from the Langley's meeting last week, nobody was banking on that little venture coming to fruition. But still, at least Clare had some *hope*, some kind of way forward. Polly's way forward seemed to be completely barred right now. She was never going to get a new job at this rate; she'd never be able to return to London, she'd have to stay in Elderchurch for ever and ever and would die here, a bitter and miserable old crone.

Her phone rang, jerking her out of her torpor. The estate agent's number was flashing on the screen and she pressed the connection button hungrily.

'Hello?'

'Miss Johnson? Vince here. How are we today?'

She pulled a face. 'We're very well, thank you. How are things?'

'Good, good. Listen, I'm ringing with a bit of news. We've had an offer on the flat – very nice couple, short chain, they're good to go. The offer's quite a bit lower than the asking price, though.'

'How much lower?'

He paused dramatically. If he'd been there in the same room as her, this was the moment she'd have punched him in the face. 'Forty grand lower.'

'*Forty grand?* They can fuck off.' She slumped back in her chair, sick with disappointment.

Vince was chortling as if she was joking. She so wasn't joking. 'Okay, Miss Johnson, you've made your thoughts on that pretty clear. I'll get back to them with the bad news.'

She screwed up her face as the call ended, wondering if she'd just made a mistake. But no, they were taking the piss with such a rubbish offer. She had to sit tight, wait it out and hope they'd come back with a higher figure. 'Oh, please come back with a higher figure,' she moaned out loud. Fred, who was slobbing out beneath the table, pricked up his ears and gave a little whine as if sympathizing.

Polly turned back to her laptop, but it was no good, she couldn't concentrate now. She switched it off, then got to her feet, the chair screeching as it scraped across the floor. 'Sod this for a lark, Fred,' she said. 'Let's get some fresh air, shall we? Have a little walkie?'

Fred scrambled out from under the table immediately, his tail wagging, and Polly knelt down to hug him. She was becoming quite fond of Fred, even if he did smell heinous most of the time. It was nice having someone – okay, *something* – who was always pleased to see her, and could be counted on for a cuddle when she felt miserable and lonely. 'Come on then,' she said, clipping the lead to his collar. 'Let's stretch our legs and have a wander.'

Propping her big shades on her nose Polly set off with Fred at her side, his tongue out in a big doggy smile. It only took minutes to get out of the village, clamber rather inelegantly over a wooden stile, and then she was in a lush green field dotted with buttercups and clouds of ox-eye daisies, with large swaying oaks and chestnut trees at the far end.

She smiled to herself. All those boring family walks she'd endured as a child, with her dad reeling off the names of every tree, plant and bird they passed, must somehow have lodged themselves deep in her subconscious. She could still name most types of tree with the same certainty she had about identifying the parts of her own body. Not that she'd needed such arboreal knowledge very often in London, admittedly.

The grass swished against her jeans as she walked across the meadow. She, Clare and Michael had spent half their summers here, splashing in the icy stream, climbing the trees and swinging from the branches, making dens and camps with their friends, taking picnics, playing cricket . . .

'Those were the days, Fred,' she said, letting him off the lead and patting his hairy brown coat before he gambolled away. Happy times. She tried to recall which tree it had been that Michael had fallen from and broken his arm – perhaps that vast horse-chestnut, laden with white candle-like flowers. She could still remember the cry he'd made as he'd slammed against the ground, the sick-making bend in his arm that looked so horribly wrong. Clare had been dispatched to the nearest house (Mrs Warren's, that was it) to phone their parents, while Polly stayed with Michael, holding his other hand, frightened by how dark his freckles looked against the ghostly white of his face, scared by how fast her own heart was racing and by the injured-animal whimpers he made at intervals.

Oh, Michael. She wished she could hold his hand again and tell him how much she wished he hadn't died. She wished she could tell him how sorry she was.

'Well, look who it is! Fancy seeing *you* here.'

She turned in shock to see a man in front of her grinning, his dark eyes twinkling beneath the shock of black hair. Oh my God. It wasn't, was it? Where had *he* just sprung from?

'I heard you were back in Elderchurch, Poll.' He peered at her, suddenly affronted. 'Don't say you don't remember me?'

Didn't remember him? Of course she remembered him. She was remembering, right then, having sex with him on her parents' sofa, the night her life fell apart. 'Hello, Jay,' she said, her mouth dry. 'I ... Long time no see.'

'Very long. Must be ... what, twenty years?'

'Something like that.'

There was an awkward pause. The sun suddenly felt too hot on Polly's face and she was glad she was wearing enormous sunglasses, which hid her eyes and disguised the fact that she had absolutely no make-up on. If only there was something to hide her scruffy ponytail, and the old jeans and pink top she'd bunged on earlier as well.

'So ...' she said. 'What have you been doing in the last twenty years then?' The answer certainly wasn't spending time on his appearance – that was obvious. He had a few days' worth of stubble, his hair needed cutting and he was in raggedy jeans and old trainers. What a hobo.

He shrugged. 'Bit of this, bit of that. Travelled for a while. Worked in Australia with a few mates.'

She hadn't been expecting that. 'Oh, nice. Sydney?'

'Perth. Nothing that exciting – labouring work, mostly, but I loved it there. Then Rachel and I got married . . .'

'You *married* her? Big-Tits Lewis?' Rachel Lewis was the girl Jay had hooked up with after they'd split. She'd had better boobs than Polly, and her family owned a villa in the south of France. Polly couldn't imagine *what* Jay had ever seen in her.

'Yeah, I married Big-Tits Lewis,' Jay said drily. 'Not for long, though; she went off with another bloke. That's all water under the bridge now. No kids. How about you?'

'I'm in finance,' she said, drawing herself up to stand slightly taller in her tatty flip-flops. 'I've worked all around the world, but have been in London for the last twelve years. Busting balls in the City, earning a fortune, you know . . .' She gave a short laugh. He *didn't* know, obviously, but she couldn't help wanting to rub it in. *I'm better off without you, mate.*

He shook his head. 'Clare's been keeping me up to date,' he said. 'I heard you were one of those buy-sell types, all suited and booted.' Was it Polly's paranoia, or was he casting a smirky eye up and down her current outfit? 'All sounds a bit stressful to me.'

She tossed her head. 'Not at all. Personally I thrive on big business – in fact, I'm finding it a real chore being here in Nowheresville. I can't wait to get back to city life.' She stuck her nose in the air and scanned the field for Fred, who was frolicking happily with a waggy-tailed mongrel. Jay's waggy-tailed mongrel, at a guess. It looked about as scruffy and charmless as him. 'Fred! Come here, boy,' she yelled, completely ineffectually as it turned out, when Fred paid no attention whatsoever.

'Nowheresville, eh?' Jay chuckled, much to her annoyance. 'Oh well. See you around.' He put two fingers in his mouth and gave an ear-splitting wolf-whistle. Both dogs turned immediately and galloped across the meadow. 'Good girl,' he said, reaching down to pat his dog, who seemed to have half a stinking cowpat on her feet. 'Come on then, let's go.'

Without another word he turned and stalked off, his dog gazing adoringly up at him as she trotted alongside.

Polly glared, her feathers well and truly ruffled by the encounter. Honestly! What a prat. What a total jerk. What had she ever seen in *him*? The nerve of him, the way he'd been so dismissive of her. Contemptuous, even.

Well, she'd been right to dump him after Michael had died. And good riddance to him as well.

The conversation kept replaying in her head like a jammed recording, though, as she strode away. Oh God, why had she felt the need to boast to him about her glittering career, for heaven's sake? Who cared what he thought anyway? She flushed as she remembered the mocking way he'd described her job: *buy-sell, all suited and booted*, or however he'd put it. That was plain bad manners, and sour grapes too no doubt, because he'd never done anything with his life. As if she would start criticizing him for his career – labouring in Perth and what-have-you – even though she had every right! No. She had manners. She had a bit of courtesy. Unlike him, the ... *tosser*.

Bloody Jay Holmes. And bloody village life! More than ever she missed the anonymity of London, where you could safely wander around without having to worry about bumping into ex-boyfriends. Not that there'd been many of those, of course. The night Michael died had put paid to that. How could she have a relationship with Jay or anyone else when she was responsible for her own brother's death? She didn't deserve it, end of story.

She'd reached the other side of the meadow now and walked into the shady refuge provided by one of the chestnut trees, leaning against the trunk, grateful for its support. If only he hadn't caught her off-guard like that, the conversation might not have gone so wrong so quickly. But he'd taken her by surprise, and she'd been boastful, and then he'd been sarcastic ... Why had they reacted to one another that way? And why was she letting it get to her so badly, letting *him* get to her? She'd barely thought about him for years, she was certainly not about to start raking up old history and heartbreak now.

Sod it, she thought, heading back to Clare's with the dog. She'd rather take a job in Brussels than spend any longer than she had to in the vicinity of *him*.

The phone was ringing when she got back and she scrambled to unlock the door and get into the house. The reception for her mobile wasn't always brilliant in the village, so she'd given Clare's landline number to several companies recently in her contact details and had subsequently been pouncing every time it had trilled.

'Hello?' she panted into the receiver, adrenalin buzzing around her. Would it be Vince the estate agent again, calling with a better offer? Or, even better, a headhunter who'd found a post that was absolutely perfect for her? This conversation could well be the first link in a chain of events that would pull her all the way back to good old glorious London town. Take *that*, Jay Holmes, and shove it!

'Hi, is that Clare?'

Disappointment sank through her like ink in water. She couldn't speak for a second. 'No, this is Polly,' she replied eventually. 'Clare's ...' She glanced up at the clock: two-forty. 'Clare's on her way back from work right now, she should be home in a few minutes. Can I take a message?'

'Please,' the woman said. 'This is Kate Hendricks from Langley's. Let me give you my number.'

Ooh, a call from Langley's. Polly was so startled for a moment that she didn't have the wherewithal to grab a pen and take down her details, and had to ask the woman to repeat her number. Surely this was good news? Would she really be phoning if it was a big fat no to the pitch? It was on the tip of her tongue to try and glean some crumb of information, some hint about what was happening, but she managed to hold back. No. This was Clare's news to be told. All in good time.

'Okay, I'll pass that on,' she said, her brain teeming with questions. She hung up and stared at the phone for a few seconds. Well, this could be interesting.

Clare had come back in a right state from the meeting last week with torturous tales of falling down steps, toilet roll dangling from her shoe and tittering Barbie competitors. Polly had been as kind as possible and had tried to say all the right sympathetic things, but inside her head was a flashing neon sign that said: WRITE-OFF. Reading between the lines, Clare had no chance.

But what if the pitch hadn't been as disastrous and doomed as Clare had predicted? Polly swallowed. She wasn't quite sure what she'd think if Clare had actually gone and swung a deal.

No. Surely not. The call-back was probably just because

this Kate woman was the aunt of Clare's friend Roxanne. Simple courtesy as a favour to her niece, perhaps providing a bit of much-needed feedback. Thanks, but no thanks; we've decided to go with a proper company, which actually does this for a living – like professionally? Don't give up the day job, whatever you do.

Polly sat down at the table once more and dutifully checked her laptop for new emails or job alerts, but it was hard to concentrate when she kept glancing out of the window for Clare's car returning. She scrolled through her in-box with an increasing sense of déjà vu. A rejection, an acknowledge-ment of an application, her new log-in for yet another finan-cial-recruitment website, another rejection and a newsletter from Waterman's that she was still signed up to. Nothing whatsoever leaping out to say: GOOD NEWS, POLLY!

When was *anyone* going to say 'Good news, Polly!'? It had been such a long time.

At last there came the familiar chug of Clare's old banger as it swung into the drive. Polly couldn't wait any longer and ran through the back door to greet her. 'She's just phoned. The lady from Langley's. Wants you to ring back.'

Clare's eyes went very round as she stood there, a hand flying up to her mouth. 'Oh, gosh. How did she sound? Did she say anything else?'

Polly shook her head. 'No. Just could you call her. I've got her number for you.'

'God,' Clare said with a nervous laugh as they went into the house. 'I've gone all jittery. I wasn't expecting her to phone. I thought it would be a Dear John letter in the post: thanks and everything, but we don't want to work with someone who puts toilet roll in their shoes.'

'Well, I know, I thought the s——' Polly began, then broke off quickly before she could put her foot in it. 'Ring her and see,' she urged.

Clare put her hand on the phone. 'It's probably a no, right? I should just get it over with.'

'Do it.'

Clare punched in the number while Polly leaned against the kitchen counter, her arms folded across her chest. She couldn't help feeling jittery herself now as she heard the burr-burr of the ringtone.

'Hi,' Clare said, her cheeks turning pink. 'This is Clare Berry. May I speak to Kate Hendricks, please?' She pulled a hideous eye-rolling face at Polly. 'Oh, Kate, hi. I gather you called me?'

Polly held her breath.

'I see. Uh-huh ... Right.' Then Clare gasped, her whole body jerking in sudden shock. 'They *did*? You *do*? Oh, wow! That's wonderful!'

Oh my *God*, thought Polly, incredulous. She'd only gone and bloody got it.

Clare's eyes were like stars and her mouth kept dropping

into an O of amazement. 'Yes, of course,' she said, scribbling some figures down in a daze. 'And when would you need them by?'

Whoa. Polly couldn't believe what she was hearing. No way! Her little sister – one of the suppliers for the new Langley's hotel? Her little sister going into business with a national hotel chain, while Polly was stranded on the scrapheap? She felt sick with jealousy, right to the middle of her stomach. Oh ... *bollocks*. This was so unfair.

'Okay, fine,' Clare stammered. 'Of course. I'll be in touch. Look forward to it, Kate. Thanks again, bye.'

She put the phone down, then screamed. 'She loves the products, she thinks they're a great fit with the Langley's brand. It's a YES!'

Despite her all-consuming, stabbing jealousy, Polly dredged up every last scrap of self-control and managed to throw her arms around her sister. With stupendous will power, she even managed some magnanimity. 'That is AMAZING, Clare!' she cried. 'God, well done. You did it!'

Clare was laughing and then she was crying. 'Fuck, this is mad,' she said. 'Seriously mad. I didn't just imagine that, did I? She really did call? Shit!' She clutched at her head. 'And now I've got to produce three months' supply of everything, plus she wants to meet me next week to talk about further options.' She looked stricken. 'What the hell have I just agreed to? I won't be able to do it!'

'Wow, three months' supply — so we're talking hundreds of soaps and bubble baths?' Polly said, taken aback. It was a massive order, way beyond what they'd hoped for in their plans. 'And you said you could deliver that? Whoa.'

'I know.' Clare's face crumpled. 'I'm never going to manage it, am I?'

No, probably not, Polly thought. But her leadership instincts came to the fore. 'You *are*,' she told her sister. 'And I will help you. Now sit down and tell me every single thing she said. Then we'll start drawing up a plan of action.'

The following morning Polly woke feeling bleary-eyed and thoughtful. Clare had invited their parents and her friends over the night before, and she'd asked them all to muck in with her new venture. The magnitude of what she'd signed up to was obviously beginning to sink in, especially when Polly pointed out that suppliers would need paying in advance and there might be a cashflow situation. It was all very well snipping bits of lavender out of the garden when she was making a few tubes of hand cream for her mates, but when she was being asked to make *nine hundred* mini bottles of shampoo and bubble bath and nine hundred bars of soap ... Well, it didn't take a genius to realize that it was all going to add up to one long mutha of a shopping list. An expensive mutha of a shopping list at that.

Talking about costs up front had sobered Clare right up. In fact she had changed the subject pretty quickly, Polly had noticed, skimming over the details as if she couldn't quite bring herself to confront them head-on. The problem was, there *was* no money to spend on supplies. Clare was skint, she was always going on about how much Steve owed her, in between stressing out about not being able to afford new school shoes for the children or the gas bill.

Despite her somewhat ungracious feelings towards Clare's career, Polly did genuinely wish she could help out financially. When she thought of the piles of money she'd squandered over the last few years – stupid money on stupid things that meant absolutely zilch to her now – she could have kicked herself for not squirrelling more of it away, for not allowing herself a buffer of savings. All those times she'd lavished money on so-called friends (so-called friends she hadn't heard a peep from since she left London, incidentally) – *Oh, this one's on me. My round – no, I insist!* – and as a result it meant she couldn't do the same for her skint, scrabbling-for-coins sister now, when she really needed help. Even if Vince rang back that day and said that someone had offered the full asking price on her flat, the money would take weeks to come through, of course, with the surveys and whole legal shoobydoo of the property purchase process.

It had made her feel pretty lame. Pretty shallow. And

boy, hadn't she felt the weight of everyone's expectations last night when the subject of money came up. Her parents had both looked straight at her, obviously waiting for her to pipe up that she'd cover Clare's costs, no problem. But she hadn't been able to say any such thing, which had made her feel such a miserly cow. Her ears had burned after they'd gone, and she was sure it was because her parents and Clare's friends were bitching about what a tightwad they thought she was, all the way down the road.

Her own sister, and she can't even put her hand in her pocket!

I thought she was meant to be loaded as well.

Always the rich ones who are the stingiest, isn't it? Typical.

It was no good. She was going to have to pull her finger out and make some kind of contribution to this Langley's endeavour. She *had* to, otherwise she'd be hounded out of the village by Clare's angry mates, brandishing flaming torches as they ran.

And so, with a heavy heart and a dragging reluctance in her step, Polly headed out that morning, well aware that what she was about to do marked an all-time low in her career. She'd called Vince in the hope that he'd had a better offer on the flat, but he hadn't heard anything yet. She'd double-checked her last remaining shares and bonds before she came out, just in case they were miraculously on the up and she could cash some in, but no; they were little more than worthless right now. Another gigantic waste of money. Another humongous cock-up in Polly Johnson's laughable personal financial management. For a so-called risk expert, the risks she'd taken with her own money hadn't exactly paid off.

It was crushing how dire things had become. She never would have believed it six months ago, but yes, she was actually walking towards the King's Arms at eleven o'clock in the morning. And yes, in all seriousness she was fully intending to swallow her pride and ask about that cleaning job. Although when she did venture inside, blinking in the gloomy half-light, she very nearly lost her bottle and asked for a large glass of Chardonnay to swallow instead.

Dutch courage. She'd never been more in need of it.

The landlord looked surprised to see her walking in, bang on the stroke of eleven. They'd only just opened and he was poring over the sports pages of the *Mail*, which he'd propped against the beer pumps, with a steaming cup of coffee by his side. She felt as if she was interrupting something.

'Hi,' she said, clearing her throat awkwardly. 'Are you the landlord here?'

'I certainly am,' he replied, eyeing her. He was burly and

short-necked, looked as if he'd once been a rugby player with his broken nose and solid arms. He turned the page of his newspaper, still gazing at her. 'Who wants to know?'

She swallowed. Could she really go through with this? Had she truly sunk to this new low?

Then she remembered the disapproving looks exchanged between Clare's friends last night, the surprised disappointment in her parents' eyes when she hadn't volunteered a cash injection for the fledgling business. 'Um ... I'm Polly. Clare Berry's sister. Karen and Graham's daughter.'

'Ah.' His interest piqued, he stood up a little straighter, newspaper forgotten. 'The high-flier returns.'

She hesitated. *The high-flier crash-lands and wrecks the plane, more like.* 'Um ... something like that,' she said. 'Only ... well ...' Oh God, this was excruciating. 'Can you keep a secret?'

He leaned forward and tapped his nose. 'A pub landlord has many secrets,' he assured her.

She made a split-second decision. He looked trustworthy enough, she supposed. A decent bloke. It was a risk she'd have to take. Another one.

'Okay,' she said. 'You've got to promise not to tell my mum and dad, right? Or anyone else. Seriously. But I've kind of fallen on ... hard times.' She swallowed again. It was like a confessional. 'And I was wondering if the cleaning job here was still free?'

Chapter Eighteen

Over the next few weeks Clare attempted to take control of her new business and get things rolling. Karen and Graham lent her five hundred pounds so that she could put in an initial order of ingredients and, with clammy hands and a gnawing terror inside, she applied for a bank loan of another two thousand pounds. Polly had done the sums and assured her that she would be able to pay it all straight back, plus the interest, once she'd delivered her first order to Langley's. (If they approved it, of course. Clare was not even *going* there with thoughts of failing their quality-control tests.) She'd met Kate again at the hotel and had shakily co-signed a purchase-order agreement, binding her to deliver three months' supply by the last week in August – eight weeks away. If the hotel and their customers were satisfied with the products, Kate said they would then extend the contract, after which time either side could renegotiate terms.

'We're so proud of you,' Karen had said tearfully, when Clare had showed her the contract the Sunday after her meeting. She, Polly and the children had gone over for a barbecue, and Karen had splashed out on Prosecco for all the grown-ups, and lemonade for the children.

Her dad was at the barbecue, merrily charring the sausages, and raised his tongs at her in a salute. 'Two businesswomen in one family,' he'd cried. 'Thank goodness you both inherited your old dad's brains, eh?'

Even Polly had been nice about Clare's bit of success. Complimentary, no less. 'This is going to be amazing, Clare,' she'd said, with what sounded suspiciously like genuine warmth in her voice. 'Well done. And if it all goes to plan, you'll be quids in. You can take the kids on an awesome holiday when the dust has settled.'

If it all went to plan. For such a small word, the 'if' carried an almighty weight. Clare still wasn't entirely sure how she was going to manage to pull this off, and was already having sleepless nights with worry. But the thought of an awesome holiday was a sweetener, at least. She, Leila and Alex had endured a week's camping in Dorset last year, where the rain had sheeted down relentlessly. They'd spent more money on drying clothes and sleeping bags in the campsite launderette than they had on suncream or ice lollies. The word 'awesome' hadn't really been appropriate.

Whereas the idea of jetting away somewhere hot, lounging on a beach, feeling sunshine on her skin again ... Well, that definitely worked as a carrot on a stick.

A routine developed. She worked her hours at the surgery as usual, cooked dinner and looked after the children, then once they were in bed at eight, began work all over again in the kitchen, with Polly as her assistant. The bottles and soap moulds she'd ordered had arrived, and if the two of them really went flat out, they could make up two batches of bubble-bath mixture – fifty small bottles' worth – and a batch of twenty soaps, which had to be left to harden overnight. Lydia, Debbie's eldest, who had just finished her A-levels, came along to help when she could and proved to be a bit of a star in the production process. 'I won't be able to pay you until I'm paid myself for the order,' Clare had said, wringing her hands. Luckily Lydia had been sanguine about the situation. 'No worries,' she'd replied. 'It's my uni fund. Stops me spending it before I've left home, I suppose.'

It all meant long days of hard work, but Clare got a massive thrill from seeing her finished bottles building up, box by box. Her parents and friends pitched in whenever they could, and both Roxie and Luke asked her regularly for updates. God, she was lucky to have them all helping her, she thought frequently. Tracey hadn't been joking when she'd called them Team Clare.

Still, she wasn't there yet, not by a long chalk. With the end of term imminent, she had the usual working-mum juggling act to contend with for six weeks, which was always tricky. She'd signed Leila and Alex up for week-long drama and football clubs in Amberley, and her friends and parents had agreed to look after them at other times. She also wangled some shift-swapping with Roxie and put in for a fortnight's annual leave in August, hoping fervently that she'd be able to spend some of this time doing fun things with the children. It was going to be a strange old summer, all right.

That weekend it was Steve's turn to have the children. Usually Clare felt somewhat vulnerable about him coming to the house and taking the children away, but today she realized she felt different and wondered if it was because her new-found ally, Polly, was going to be in the house with her. Clare wasn't daft; she'd seen the way Polly had flinched when the Langley's phone call had come. She knew her sister envied this piece of success that had come her way, and she had wondered if Polly might descend into an almighty sulk over it, or perhaps try to belittle the business. But Clare had been wrong. Against all expectations, Polly had mucked in just as much as anyone else and had worked really hard. The initial tension that had simmered between them now seemed to be melting away, and Clare was surprised and happy that Polly seemed to be the newest recruit to her team. Who would have thought it?

Steve hadn't exactly seemed delighted to see Polly again. They'd never hit it off in the past: she'd looked down her nose at him, and he thought she was up her own bum. 'Fridge-knickers' he'd always called her behind her back.

Good one, Steve, Clare thought now, remembering this; if a woman makes you feel intimidated, put her down by implying frigidity. What had she ever seen in the bloke? It was becoming harder and harder to remember.

'Morning,' Polly had said coolly when he walked into the kitchen. She was making coffee, but didn't offer to pour him a cup.

His nostrils quivered at the mingled aromas of coffee, ginger, vanilla and lime, and his eyes swerved around the kitchen with interest, taking in the boxes of bottles stacked in a corner and the supplies of Castile soap flakes and liquid glycerine. 'What's going on in here then?' he asked.

Nosey sod. 'Work,' Clare said shortly. 'And if you don't mind, I need to get on.'

'What do you mean, work? What *is* all this stuff anyway?' His lip had curled; she'd always disliked the way he did that. So supercilious. Well, she wasn't going to give him the chance to sneer at her business, she decided, so she ignored his questions.

'Leila! Alex! Dad's here, hurry up!' she yelled. 'See you on Sunday,' she added pointedly to him, walking out of the room.

The door closed behind the three of them ten minutes later and Clare braced herself, ready for the usual feelings of desolation to overpower her. It had been awful, the first few times Steve had taken the children away for his weekend 'contact', as the custody agreement termed it, leaving her all on her own, rattling around the place. She'd felt as if her heart had been ripped out. Even now, over a year later, she still wasn't used to the deep, empty silence that swallowed up the cottage whenever they were away overnight.

This weekend, at least, she was not on her own and had more than enough to keep her occupied. Count your blessings, Clare.

'Are you okay?' She felt Polly's hand tentatively alight on her back.

'Yeah. Let's get stuck in,' she said briskly.

'Is he always like that when he comes to pick up the kids?' Polly asked, donning an apron and opening the kitchen windows to let in a breeze. The hot, heady smell of honeysuckle drifted through. It was rampant all over the back wall at the moment, thick with fat bumblebees, its delicate pink-and-white flower heads open like mouths towards the summer sun.

'What? A prick?' Clare replied. 'Yes, unfortunately. I look at him and can't believe I ever fancied him now, let alone was madly in love with him.' She shook her head. 'Weird, isn't it, how that happens. How can you think the world of someone and know them so intimately once ... and then want nothing else to do with them, six months down the line.'

Polly looked blank. 'Um . . . I suppose,' she said, opening the freezer door and pulling out the trays of soap they'd made the night before. She prodded one delicately. 'These look good.'

Clare eyed her curiously. Why was she being so obtuse? 'You *suppose?*' she echoed. 'I know you've always kept your private life private, but there must be some vile ex-boyfriends lurking in your past, surely?'

'Not really.' Polly had her head down and was carefully pushing the little soaps from their moulds. Clare could smell their sweet vanilla fragrance as they slid onto the table.

'Don't give me that,' she scoffed. It was like picking at a scab, pressing Polly in this way. A reluctant scab that didn't want to be prised off by anybody's fingernails, but Clare couldn't help herself. 'There must have been *someone* you loved. Someone you were really close to. Wasn't there?'

Just for a second Clare thought she'd glimpsed a wistfulness clouding Polly's eyes, a rarely seen uncertainty about her face. Then down came the shutters and she shook her head. 'Nah,' she said airily, as if she didn't care. 'I was always too busy for relationships.'

Too busy. What a cop-out. Since when did having a full-on job have to preclude any other kind of life? There must have been a degree of choice in the matter for Polly to have shunned all relationships completely. That was if she was telling the truth, of course. Clare didn't believe a word of it.

'Right,' she said diplomatically after a weighty moment.

'I mean, I have *dated* a lot, I have had *sex* with men,' Polly added. 'I'm not saying I'm a born-again virgin. But they were just dates. And just sex. I never really bothered getting to know any of them. I certainly never *cared* about them.'

'Oh,' Clare said, not sure how else to reply. What an awful, horrible thing to admit to. And Polly said it as if she couldn't give two hoots about the situation, as if she wasn't bothered either way that she'd never really loved anyone. Clare couldn't imagine anything more depressing. Better to have loved and lost, in her experience, even if it had meant marrying Steve.

'I guess I've never been the settling-down type,' Polly said, popping out the last soap from the mould and taking the trays to the sink, where she set about washing them with a good deal of splashing.

And that, Clare thought, was all she was going to get out of her sister on *that* subject. She wasn't sure whether to pity or admire Polly for it. It wasn't a way of life she'd have wanted, though.

The two of them began work in earnest. Clare put some

music on and started melting soap flakes, feeling herself slowly beginning to relax at the prospect of a child-free weekend. She would miss Leila and Alex, of course – she always missed them – but this was the first weekend ever that she hadn't gone straight upstairs after they'd left to sit mournfully in the desolate silence of their empty bedrooms, wondering what they were doing without her, how many treats and goodies Steve and Denise were lavishing on them, if Alex would be sick on the way home or if Leila would return fired up with talk of pony-riding and go-karting and all the other things Steve had shelled out for her.

Once they came home again, Clare always struggled not to ask questions about the life Steve and Denise led in Basingstoke, even though part of her was desperate to know everything. 'Denise wears make-up at breakfast time,' Leila had once said (rather scornfully, to Clare's relief), but this fact alone had been enough to keep Clare awake that night, miserably tossing and turning as she imagined the radiant Denise in her skimpy silk dressing gown and a full face of creams and powders to start the day.

Her phone buzzed just then and she saw that a text from Steve had appeared onscreen. *Back home and all OK. Will call later. S*

Paranoid as she was about her children's well-being, she'd asked him all those months ago to let her know when they'd arrived safely on these contact weekends, just so that she wasn't fretting. But why did he need to call her later? He never usually rang. Did he have some big piece of news that he wanted to break, which he'd bottled out of doing in person that morning?

A few months ago Alex had come home and mentioned that Denise had vomited twice while they'd been staying there. There had been a considerable amount of relish in his voice at the grossness of the situation. 'It was *disgusting*. You could hear the puke coming out into the toilet, like this . . .' And as he'd launched into a demonstration of gruesome fake-retching noises, Clare had been gripped with the fear that Denise was pregnant; and then of course her mind whirled immediately through all the possibilities: the new baby Berry, cosseted and cooed over, dressed in ridiculous Baby Dior outfits by image-mad Denise. Loved more than Leila and Alex . . .

Steve hadn't announced any pregnancy news, though, and there had been no further word from the children about Denise having a bump, or showing scan pictures to them. Maybe it had just been a tummy bug, or maybe Denise had been too early in the pregnancy to want to announce anything yet. Steve had made no bones about the fact that the two of them were keen to start a family, though. He'd actually said those words: *Start a family*. As if he didn't already have one of those.

One thing was for sure, she'd have to practise sounding delighted when Steve broke the news, if she was to stand a chance of avoiding the dread in her heart spilling into her voice.

As it turned out, there was no joyful announcement of baby news. Instead Steve was ringing about something entirely unexpected: her neglectful parenting.

'I've been talking to the children and I'm shocked at what's been going on there,' he began without preamble. 'It's not on, Clare. It's just not on.'

It was as if he was speaking in riddles; it took a few seconds for her brain to actually decode his words. Even then they made no sense. 'What?' she asked in bewilderment. 'What are you talking about?'

'I'm talking about you setting up a factory for your *business*' – he seemed to spit the word down the line as if he couldn't bear the taste of it – 'in our *kitchen*. Exposing our *children* to dangerous *chemicals!* It's bang out of order, Clare. It's absolutely unacceptable.'

Her mouth dropped open in astonishment as, once again, she needed a moment to decipher this absurdity. 'Wait a minute,' she said, appalled that he could even suggest such a thing. 'It's not "your" kitchen, just as it's not any of your business what I do in there.' She shook with anger. How dare he criticize what she was doing? If anyone was out of order, it was him, one hundred per cent.

'That's where you're wrong,' he said. 'It *is* my business, when it affects my children.'

The sanctimonious tone of his voice filled her with fresh rage. *His* children now, were they? Oh, this was rich, coming from him, the man who needed reminding when *his* children's sodding birthdays were. 'They are not being affected in any way,' she retaliated, struggling to keep her voice sounding even and calm. 'There are no dangerous chemicals whatsoever. And they are not being neglected, thank you very much. What sort of person do you think I am?'

'Has your sister put you up to this?' he replied. 'This business bullshit? Well, I'm not happy about it, Clare. Not happy at all.'

'Not happy about what? Me making a half-decent crust for *our* children, for a change? I'd have thought you'd be grateful. You're the one who's always been so reluctant to contribute any maintenance money. You're the one who's left me skint and struggling for so bloody long.'

'Oh, so it's all my fault, I get it.' His voice dripped with sarcasm. 'I've pushed you into the whole thing – yeah, right. You should listen to yourself, Clare, you're full of shit. And I'm getting onto my solicitor about this, first thing on Monday morning.'

She sat down heavily on the arm of the sofa, feeling as if she'd been punched in the stomach. 'Your *solicitor*? Why the hell do you need to talk to your solicitor?'

'Because I don't think it's right that you're running a business – manufacturing these goods, creating fumes and dust, and God knows what else – in the kitchen where my children live,' he snapped.

'But it's not doing them any *harm!*' she shouted. She was shaking now, shaking with rage, but also fear of where this was going. 'There *are* no fumes or dust, there's no danger to them whatsoever. Can't you see, you fucking moron, that—'

Click. He'd hung up on her.

She clutched at her chest, unable to catch her breath for a moment. Why was he doing this? And why did he have to be such an arsehole about it?

'What the hell's happened?' Polly asked, coming into the room wide-eyed, her hair up in a towel turban. 'I could hear you over the noise of the shower.'

Tears stung Clare's eyes and she had to swallow hard before she could speak. 'Steve,' she said, her fists still clenched so tight that her fingers were blanched of all colour. 'Kicking off about my work being a health hazard to the children. Like I'd ever put them in the way of any harm, Polly. Like I'd ever do anything that could possibly hurt them!'

'What?' Polly's eyes nearly fell out of her head. 'What's he playing at? He knows how much you care about them. He's talking total crap.'

'I know, but, according to him, he's going to his solicitor about it,' Clare said hoarsely. She put her head in her hands. 'And then what? I've no idea what that'll mean for us.'

'He's full of hot air,' Polly said, sitting next to Clare and putting an arm around her. 'Ignore him, he's being a wounded alpha-male because he's just cottoned onto the fact that you might be going somewhere with your business and that terrifies him.'

But Clare wasn't so sure she *could* ignore him, however wrong he was. She sat there trembling and numb, wishing she'd never let her children out of her sight that morning. The only crumb of comfort was that her sister was with her, telling her everything was going to be okay. If only she could actually believe that.

Chapter Nineteen

If Clare's star was on the rise in terms of career glory, then Polly's seemed to have fallen completely from the sky and burned itself to a crisp. For the last three weeks she'd been employed as a cleaner at the King's Arms. This was what she'd been reduced to.

When she'd set off for her very first shift, sick with disappointment that her life had come to this, she'd had a flashback to the last time she'd gone to work, wearing her best suit and killer heels, briefcase in hand, striding into Waterman's. Now look at her: in jeans and an old T-shirt, with her hair in a ponytail. She wasn't exactly dressed for success any more.

Still, there was actually something rather pleasant about seeing Elderchurch at this early hour, she realized. It was only ten to seven, but there was a light, bright freshness in the air, the sky was a pale clear blue, and you could tell it was going to be another corker of a day. Funny how you noticed the weather more in the countryside. She glanced over at the fields beyond the village and was rewarded by the sight of a bird of prey – a sparrowhawk? a kestrel? her dad would be able to tell her, if he was here – gliding magnificently on a thermal high up in the cool morning sky. Beautiful. You never saw *that* on your London commute.

Erica, the landlady, let her in and showed her the ropes. There seemed to be an awful lot of ropes. Not only was Polly expected to hoover the lounge and restaurant area, but she also had to mop the tiled floor behind the bar, empty and scrub disgusting-smelling slop trays, polish the brass, wipe down the tables and heave the trolley of empty bottles round the back. She didn't dare tell cheerful, plump Erica that she had never worked a Hoover before; instead she agreed to everything and got on with it as best she could. By the end of the shift she stank of bleach and was ready to collapse, but she'd actually earned some money for the first time in months. The only way was up.

The days passed by and Polly dutifully got up every morning and went to work her shift. She knew the drill by now, had mastered the wretched Hoover and knew its temperamental ways. She could polish up the bar brasses until they gleamed, could spot a stray pork scratching at twenty metres, and had stopped feeling quite so sick at the stench of the empties. In some ways she actually preferred ploughing through a short period of intense physical work to spending hours at a computer screen, clicking and typing like a machine. This way she could make a visual difference, she could bring order to chaos and feel a certain amount of satisfaction at her efforts . . .

She laughed to herself. Listen to her, bigging up her cleaning job, like it was some massive career achievement. Yeah, right. If Magda, her old cleaner in London, could see her now!

The thought was an uncomfortable one. It had to be said that Magda had become something of a thorn in Polly's side, ever since she'd started work at the pub. Whenever she thought back to the inhuman way she'd treated the Polish woman, it made her cringe. Magda had shown nothing but kindness to her – the sympathy she'd offered when Polly had broken down in tears, for example; the way she'd been gracious enough not to ask awkward questions, and had worked so hard for all that time without any word of thanks. And for what? For Polly to call the agency and complain about her, demand that she be sacked. How could she have behaved so callously? How could she have done it, knowing as she did about Magda's own financial worries?

If Magda could see me now, she'd probably spit in my face, Polly thought glumly one morning, dragging out the Hoover and plugging it in. She'd probably laugh her socks off. See how the mighty had fallen!

The only solace was the knowledge that she'd changed so much since then; there was no way she'd dob someone in like that when their only 'crime' had been to attempt to comfort another human being. There was certainly no way she'd ever look down on a cleaner again, either, or anyone employed to do menial tasks. She knew just what a slog it was, and how little you got paid for it.

'She works hard for her money,' she began singing over the roar of the Hoover, pushing the nozzle under the tables and into the corners. 'So ha-a-a-ard for the money . . .'

Then she screamed in shock as she turned and saw a man standing right in front of her. Clutching a hand to her chest, she switched off the Hoover, then wilted in dismay as she realized a split-second later who it was. Oh, bollocks. Of all the people.

'No need to stop singing on my account,' he teased.

'Jay,' she said, aghast. 'God, you made me jump. What are you doing here?'

He laughed. 'What am *I* doing here?' he echoed. 'I could ask the same of you. Is this a spot of moonlighting in between multi-million pound financial transactions then?'

Shit, oh shit, oh shit. Well, her cover story about the sabbatical had been well and truly shot down in flames now. She sighed, hating the way he was smirking. Oh, he was loving this, wasn't he? Couldn't wait to blab it about the village, no doubt. *You'll never guess WHAT* . . .

'It's a long story,' she said after an agonizing pause. 'But basically . . .'

She screwed up her face in despair, unable to finish the sentence. She wanted nothing more than to blag it, to fob him off with another line but the way he was looking at her so intently was disarming. She wouldn't be able to get away with it.

Her shoulders slumped. 'You don't want to know,' she muttered.

'Oh, but I *do*.' Course he bloody did. Couldn't wait to crow. 'I'm intrigued. Last thing I heard, you were busting balls. Now you're busting dust.' He leaned against the bar, still with that infuriating grin. 'Come on, tell me. I'm all agog.'

She glared at him. 'I haven't time, I've got to get on with this,' she said, switching the Hoover on again. *If I ignore him, she thought, he'll go away again. He'll vanish and we can both pretend this never happened.*

She turned her back and carried on pushing the nozzle doggedly to suck up the scattered crisp shards, bending down to snatch up a discarded Scampi Fries packet. *He's not there. Just block it out. Don't think about him any more.*

But then the Hoover let out a sorrowful whine before falling completely silent. She whirled around to see that he'd flicked it off at the socket and was setting two stools at a table, with worrying closeness. 'Sit down,' he said. 'And tell me all about it.'

She glanced around, wary of Stuart or Erica coming in

and seeing that she'd stopped working. 'I can't,' she said. 'Look, I know you think this is hilarious, but I do actually have a job here, and I've got loads to do.'

He just laughed again. 'You don't get it, do you?' he said. 'Didn't you know? I work here too. Well, for the brewery, anyway. I'm the area manager, so I guess that makes me your boss. And I'm telling you to sit down.'

Polly stared at him, uncomprehending for a second, before his words began jigsawing into place. Oh God. His dad had been high up at the brewery back when they'd been teenagers, she remembered. So Jay had followed in his footsteps and was now area-bloody-manager ... Aargh. Monstrous. Jay Holmes, lording it over her? How excruciating could you get. 'Oh,' was all she said dismally.

He patted the stool next to him. 'So. What happened?'

She couldn't think of anyone she less wanted to tell about her painful fall from glory, but there seemed no way around it. She sat down wearily and propped her elbows on the table. 'I fucked up,' she said bluntly. 'Lost my job, lost my flat, lost my whole life. Okay? Satisfied? So, well done. You win. I hope you enjoy telling the rest of the village all about it.'

She didn't look at him, couldn't bear to see the gloating on his face. 'Bummer,' he said mildly, and she felt a hysterical laugh building inside her.

'Is that all you can say? *Bummer*?' Her voice sounded wild.

'Don't you see: I lost it all. I'd done really well – I was at the top of my game. I had a corner office! I had this amazing flat overlooking the Thames! I ... I had a silver Mercedes!'

She swung her gaze to his, daring him to mock. He shrugged. 'Yeah, I heard you'd done well,' he said. There was a pause. 'So, they made you happy, did they, your corner office and your amazing flat and your silver Mercedes?'

She hated the way he was repeating her words. 'Well, of *course* I was happy,' she retorted, but there was no mistaking the hollow ring to her answer.

Had she been happy? It was a tough question to answer. She'd loved the work – yes. The satisfaction of achieving and the peer recognition had made her happy. But the lifestyle; the so called friends who'd dumped her like a shot once she was made redundant; the paranoia in the industry about who was competing against you, who was snapping at your heels ... That hadn't been so good. And then she remembered how lonely she'd felt in her big empty flat, and in all those hotel rooms she'd stayed in around the world. Suddenly her prized corner office didn't seem quite the be-all and end-all it once had.

'Well, you know,' she added after a moment. 'As happy as anyone is.' Then she felt defensive. What was it to Jay-effing-Holmes, anyway, whether or not she was happy? 'So

I take it *you're* happy, are you?' she retaliated waspishly. 'Being area manager, just like Daddy: that's you set up, right?'

He shrugged. 'To be honest, it's taken me a while,' he said. 'I was drifting around for years, couldn't stick at anything, always looking for the next exciting thing, you know?'

She nodded. She'd never drifted in her life (apart from the last couple of months), but she could relate to that grass-is-greener driving force. It had urged her on constantly too, pushing her towards more power, more glory, more money.

'Then I came home to Elderchurch and hooked up with all my old mates. Went back to the brewery and actually tried to make a go of it, for the first time in years. Believe it or not, I got sucked into that corporate thing for a while myself.'

Polly snorted. Jay in a suit and tie? She couldn't even picture him shaving that stubble off for a business meeting, let alone donning cufflinks and shiny shoes. Right now he was wearing tatty jeans, a moss-green T-shirt and knackered Converse on his feet. Not exactly your traditional mana-gerial ensemble.

'I know – unbelievable, right? And it took me a few years to realize that I was doing it for all the wrong reasons. My dad had always worked hard at the brewery, and this was me trying to best him. Then I was promoted to area manager – higher than he'd ever got – and almost overnight I went off the whole thing, just like that. I was putting in really long hours, driving miles every day, tons of paperwork … it wasn't fun.'

'So what happened?'

'Well, it just hit me one day. What was the point of busting a gut when I never had time to see my mates, or take the dog for a long walk, or even sit and play my guitar? Those were the things that made me happy, and I was working so hard I never got the chance to do any of them. So I quit.'

'You *quit*? So you're *not* area manager any more?'

'I tried to quit, but they wouldn't have it,' he said. 'So basically we came to an agreement. I could go down to four days a week and keep my job. Suits me. Four days a week I'm a corporate slave, and the rest of the time I'm my own man.'

'Right.' Polly wasn't sure why he was telling her all this. Rubbing her nose in it? 'And today you're … a corporate slave?' she said, eyeing his appearance doubtfully.

He laughed. 'Can't you tell?' he teased. 'No big meetings, though, just supervising the lads on the delivery run, and catching up with a few of the landlords. No point dressing up for that.'

'Well, good for you,' she said, getting to her feet with a

certain briskness. 'But now I should get on with the hoovering.'

'Look, I didn't tell you all that to score points,' he said, getting up with her. 'And I won't tell anyone your secret, Polly, all right?'

'Mmm,' she said, picking up the Hoover. *Whatevs*, as Leila would drawl.

Jay put his hands in his pockets and stood there for a moment. 'I've just got to get this delivery signed off and go through the accounts with Stu,' he said, 'but after that ... What are you doing later?'

She narrowed her eyes. Why did he want to know *that*? 'I'm helping Clare out with some work she's got on,' she replied. 'And applying for proper jobs.'

'Tonight?'

'Er, nothing,' she replied warily.

'Fancy having a drink? Catching up properly?'

Her eyes boggled. Was this some kind of wind-up? She was there, after all, in skanky old clothes, no make-up and a baseball cap covering her crap hair, and she'd just confessed to having lost everything. And he was asking her out for a *drink*? She searched his face for a smirk, but his brown eyes were expectant and – yes – sincere.

She hadn't had a night out in weeks. It would actually be great to get out of the house for an evening, even if it was with him. 'Okay then,' she said, shrugging. 'Not here, though, if you don't mind.'

'Sure,' he said. 'I'll pick you up at eight. We'll take a spin down Memory Lane.'

Memory Lane? Polly was not fond of Memory Lane at the best of times, let alone with *him*. She was about to blurt out that actually she'd just remembered she *was* busy this evening after all, and wouldn't be able to make it, but he'd already walked out whistling to himself.

God. What had she just gone and got herself into *now*?

On the way home to Clare's her phone rang. Vince. 'Good *morning*,' he boomed. 'I've got some very good news for you today, Polly. Another offer!'

She stopped dead in the lane. 'Yeah?' she asked. It was so long since she'd had any good news that she felt wary of his declaration. *Please let this one be a decent offer*, she prayed. *Please, Vince, give me a break.*

'Oh yes,' he said. 'Ten grand below the asking price. And get this: cash buyers, too!'

'Wow,' she said. This was a vast improvement on the last offer at least. And a cash buyer would speed everything up. She tried not to think of the fabulous view from her flat, the one she'd never see again. 'Okay,' she said quietly.

'You're accepting the offer?' She could just imagine him preening himself as he spoke, chest puffed out with satisfaction.

'Yep,' she said. 'I'm accepting the offer.'

'Cool! I'll get straight back to them with the news. You have a good day now.'

'Cheers,' she said, ending the call. So that was that. Now they would start the property search and instruct their lawyers to draw up contracts. The wheels were turning at last. No going back, Polly.

She sighed, and went on walking.

Once back at Clare's, Polly looked up the number of the cleaning agency she'd used and called it. Time to make amends. 'I was ringing to see if you've still got a cleaner on your books called Magda,' she said, perching on the kitchen table. 'A Polish woman?'

'Can I ask if you're one of our clients, please?' the snooty-voiced receptionist wanted to know.

'Er, not any more,' Polly replied. 'I used to be for years but ... Anyway. That's not the point really. I just wanted to know if Magda's still there, as I'd like to send her something. She might have been ... um ... sacked a while ago, though, so I wanted to check first.'

There was a delicate pause. 'I'm afraid I can't give that

sort of information out over the phone, if you're not a client,' came the smooth reply. Hoity-toity. 'We have a lot of ladies working for us and we have to respect their privacy.'

'I only want to send her a letter thanking her for her hard work,' Polly said, swinging her legs under the table in frustration.

'I'm sorry, I can't help you,' said the jobsworth, not sounding sorry in the least.

'Oh well, up yours, then,' Polly said and jabbed the red button on her phone to end the call. Honestly! She was just trying to do something nice. Why did people have to be such idiots?

The back door opened and Clare walked in. 'There, kids dropped off for the day, so . . . What's up?' she asked, seeing Polly's thunderous face.

'Just the world conspiring against me,' Polly replied, chucking her phone down onto the table in disgust. 'I was trying to say sorry to somebody I hadn't appreciated in the past, but got fobbed off by a snotty, jumped-up little . . .'

'Don't hold back.'

'. . . *madam* who was completely unhelpful instead.'

'What, she hung up on you? How rude. I always say I've got something in the oven if I'm trying to get rid of someone,' Clare confessed. 'Much more polite.'

Polly laughed. 'That's what you said to me that time,'

she realized aloud. 'When I rang you about moving in. You said you had to go, you had something in the oven.'

Clare clapped a hand to her mouth guiltily. 'Oops, did I? Sorry. No offence.'

It might have irritated Polly a few weeks ago, finding out that her sister had made excuses not to speak to her, but things had changed since then. Now she found it quite funny. 'None taken,' she said, wrinkling her nose. 'Anyway, *I* hung up on *her*, the snotty cow. Which felt good, but now I've probably blown my chances of getting to speak to this ... person.' Polly slid off the table and pulled her pay packet out of her jeans pocket. 'Here, have this, by the way.'

'What is it?'

'Money from the pub. I know it's not much, but ... have it. I've just accepted an offer on the flat too, so fingers crossed I'll be properly solvent again soon.'

'Oh, wow – you've sold your flat? That's good news ... isn't it?'

Polly shrugged. 'I suppose. Yes,' she amended, trying to sound positive. 'At least it means the mortgage company will be off my back. But it feels weird, too. Another bridge burned.'

Clare nodded. 'I can see that. Bitter-sweet.' She gave Polly's arm a squeeze. 'It doesn't mean you can't ever go back to London, though,' she added. 'There'll be other flats.'

Polly gave a half-smile, grateful for the comforting words. 'Yeah.'

Clare opened the envelope, pulled out the notes and handed half of them back to Polly. 'Thanks,' she said. 'But let's split it. You can't give me all of this if you're skint too. Go and treat yourself to ... I dunno. That expensive shampoo you like, or something. Go crazy in the hair aisle.'

Polly hadn't been expecting that. She'd been looking forward to making a contribution to Clare's funds at last; she'd felt so guilty that she hadn't been able to before now. Clare refusing to take it all came completely out of the blue, and she was just about to protest when she remembered her conversation with Jay. Ah, yes. She didn't want to go out with him and not have any money on her. How would that look? 'Actually, you're right,' she said slowly. 'I'll need some of this later.'

'Later?'

'I'm ...' Polly felt uncharacteristically shy about telling her sister. 'I'm going out.'

'Oh, yeah? Who with?'

'With Jay, actually.' She wasn't sure why she'd added the 'actually'. All it did was make her sound coy and defensive. 'Don't look like that,' she cried as Clare raised her eyebrows. 'It's just a drink and a chat, that's all. He saw me in the pub this morning and I ended up telling him about my torrid situation of homelessness and joblessness. He must have felt sorry for me, because he suggested a drink. And I must be a total mug and a half, because I said yes.'

'Ooooh!' Clare was beaming, her eyes sparkling with amusement.

'Don't start Ooh-ing me,' Polly warned, but she felt giggly too all of a sudden. 'It's only a drink. We'll probably argue the whole time. I bet it's just one massive wind-up so that he can take the piss out of me.'

Clare was shaking her head. 'Nah,' she said. 'He's always carried a bit of a torch for you, I reckon.'

'No way.'

'Yeah, definitely. He's often asked about you over the years. Certainly never forgot you.'

Polly squirmed. 'I don't know about that,' she scoffed, turning away and fiddling with her laptop. 'Probably just didn't like being chucked. I bet he's been dying to get back at me ever since.' Mind you, if that was the case, he'd already done it, by seeing her at her lowest: cleaning the King's Arms. God, he must have loved discovering what a disaster zone her life had become.

She clicked on the browser, not wanting to think about that any more, and brought up a list of recruitment agencies. 'Oh, by the way, I'm planning a day up in London soon,' she said, changing the subject. Talk of Jay and carrying torches was making her feel flustered. 'I'm trying to arrange some face-to-face meetings with recruitment consultants again, see if that will gee them into action.' She bit her lip. 'Look, I know it's putting you and the kids out, me being here. They must be getting fed up sharing Leila's room, and I know I'm in the way, so . . .'

'It's fine,' Clare said. 'Really. Especially as you've helped out so much with the business.' She put on her apron and heaved out the bag of soap flakes. 'You're welcome to stay the whole summer. I mean it. So don't feel you have to dash off on my account.'

'Thank you,' Polly replied. 'I'll just ring a few agencies now and book some appointments, but then I'm all yours.'

'Polly,' Clare said, a strange expression flitting across her face. 'That person you wanted to say sorry to – who was it?'

Polly's mouth turned up in a small, tight smile. 'Just . . . Nobody,' she said. 'I'll figure it out.'

That evening, as Polly started to get ready for going out, she found herself wishing they'd agreed on a more specific venue. A spin down Memory Lane, Jay had said, which sounded more and more ominous. She hoped that didn't mean revisiting all the dreadful old boozers they'd frequented as underage teenagers: The Green Man, The Dog and Duck, The Chequers. They'd spent many evenings snogging in those particular beer gardens with their half-pints of lager, and fake ID cards in their pockets, just in case.

What should she wear? Most of her clothes were still boxed up in her parents' garage, but she'd brought a few nice things with her to Clare's, on the off-chance she'd get to wear them again. Her red sparkly Karen Millen dress, maybe? No. It was too over-the-top for anywhere round here. She'd last worn that at the office Christmas party last year, when she'd got completely hammered on tequilas.

How about the vintage-style peacock-blue dress with a full Fifties skirt? She had some great heels that went perfectly with it, but again, it was perhaps too much. What if Jay appeared looking as scruffy as he had done both times she'd seen him so far? She'd feel completely overdressed.

Rummage, rummage ... what else did she have? It was like sorting through someone else's collection of clothes, it had been so long since she'd worn anything pretty. There was the dusky pink Jigsaw maxi-dress that she'd worn to the Summer Ball last year ... No. It was too long for her and she didn't want to go stumbling arse-over-tit tonight, thank you.

'Wow, are these all yours, Aunty Polly?' came Leila's voice just then. She was standing in the doorway, eyes wide at the sight of her aunt surrounded by so many colourful clothes.

'Yes, I'm trying to decide what to wear tonight,' Polly replied. 'Come and help me.'

Leila picked her way across the floor. Alex's bedroom looked unrecognizable now, with designer outfits draped all over his alien duvet and across the threadbare carpet, like an Aladdin's cave of eveningwear. 'Whoa, I like this colour,' she said, picking up a deep-purple silk blouse with a long, looping bow at the neck. 'Dunno about that ribbony bit, though. Too girly. Nah.' She began sorting through a pile of dresses. 'Don't you have any trousers?' she asked. 'Or shorts?'

'Ye-e-e-s,' Polly replied. 'But I was thinking a dress or skirt might be smarter.' She cocked her head to look at her niece, who looked distinctly unimpressed at this answer. 'You're not a fan of dressing up, are you? I can tell.'

'Ugh,' Leila said. 'I hate dresses and skirts. You can't do gymnastics properly in a skirt, everyone can see your knickers.' Then she looked pained, as if a thought had just struck her. 'I mean, well ... like, sometimes people have sent me really nice dresses for my birthday and that...'

Aha. 'Leila,' Polly said. 'Remind me: did *I* send you a dress for your last birthday?'

Leila nodded, eyes down as if she was worried she'd just put her foot right in it.

'Was it really really horrible?' Polly asked. 'It's okay, you can tell me.'

Leila caught her aunt's amused eye and nodded again. 'It was *frilly*,' she said with a shudder. No other words were needed.

Polly felt a pang of guilt that she'd never bothered to find out if her niece would actually *like* a horrible, frilly dress, before blithely telling Jake, her former assistant, to order her one. How rubbish was that? She hadn't had a clue, just as she'd known nothing about Alex, Clare, her parents even. She'd shunned them all, when they'd turned out to be the nicest people you could want to know. The years she'd spent cut adrift seemed a horrible waste of time all of a sudden. 'I promise I'll never buy you another stupid frilly dress ever again, okay?' she said, with a catch in her voice. 'Not unless you ask for one.'

'Well, that is *never* going to happen,' Leila said confidently. Then she grinned. 'I'd really like a hamster, though . . .'

Polly laughed and gave her a hug. 'Would you now,' she said. She sat back on her heels, surveying the mass of clothes once more, then pulled out a crumpled mint-green shift dress from the bottom of one of the cases, which still had the price tag in the back. Two hundred quid it had cost in Selfridges – and that was the sale price. When she thought how hard she'd worked to earn a measly sixty pounds from the pub that week, it made her want to throttle her former spendaholic self.

'Hmmm, I like the colour,' Leila said generously. 'But you couldn't wear it with jeans, could you?'

'No, you couldn't wear it with jeans,' Polly agreed sagely. 'But do you know what?' she went on, 'I've worn nothing *but* jeans lately. I'm really sick of jeans. So I think this will do the trick for tonight.' Bubbles of excitement began popping inside her as she got to her feet. 'To the ironing board, and don't spare the horses!'

At eight o'clock there was a knock on the door and Polly felt besieged with nerves. She'd showered and shaved her legs. She'd ironed the dress and zipped herself into it. She'd dug out a simple silver necklace and a pair of high-heeled sandals and had pivoted uncertainly in front of the mirror in the full outfit, with both Leila and Clare assuring her that the ensemble worked, even without jeans. Then she'd blow-dried her hair, made up her face and spritzed herself with some of Clare's perfume. She felt *great*.

'Hi,' she said answering the door to Jay. 'I'll just grab my bag.'

He'd scrubbed up pretty well too, it had to be said. Gone was the stubble, gone were the tatty clothes and Converse. Instead he was wearing dark jeans and a short-sleeved red shirt. Something about his tanned, muscular arms covered in dark hair gave her goose-bumps. Memory Lane was becoming a more appealing destination by the minute.

'Oh,' came Leila's disgruntled voice from behind her just then. 'Aunty Polly, you're not going out with *him*, are you?'

'He's in Mum's bad books,' Alex said with relish. He and Leila were both perched on the stairs in their pyjamas, looking thoroughly delighted by the prospect of a soap opera unfolding before their eyes. 'She said . . .'

'Yes, all right, you two,' Clare said, hearing their voices and bustling through the hallway. 'That's ancient history now. Jay and I sorted the whole thing out ages ago.'

'But you said you were going to kill him,' Alex said.

'Chloe in my class is *still* going on about it,' Leila said, folding her arms across her chest.

Polly looked from their stern, disapproving faces to Jay's uncomfortable expression, feeling as if she'd missed something.

'I can explain everything,' he said, as much to the children as to Polly. Then he addressed them directly. 'Did your mum *really* say she was going to kill me?'

'Too right I did,' Clare said. 'But anyway. Don't let us hold you up. Come on, kids, let's go and brush your teeth. Have a good time, Polly, but don't buy any second-hand goods from this man, whatever you do. Bye!'

Chapter Twenty

Polly's mouth fell open as she stared up the stairs after them. 'What the hell,' she murmured, turning back to Jay, 'was all that about?'

Jay held up his hands. 'A completely legitimate misunderstanding,' he said. 'I swear! Come on, let's get out of here, before the reinforcements turn up; I'll explain in the car. You look great, by the way.'

'Thanks. You're not looking bad yourself. Proper shoes and everything – I'm flattered.' She snatched up her handbag, then shut the door behind her, feeling jittery. It was just a *drink*, she reminded herself. Just a drink and a chat, nothing else on the agenda. But all the same, her and Jay, out on the town together again? Who would have predicted *that*?

Her phone beeped and she checked the text surreptitiously as she walked down the front path. *Have fun + see you 2moro. I won't wait up! C x*

Not waiting up? They were only going for a drink, for goodness' sake.

Ha-ha, she texted back quickly. *Prob back by 9, having driven each other mental x*

'Everything all right?' Jay asked. He was waiting in the road by a battered old Land Rover, with mud liberally sprayed across its lower half. Cinderella's golden coach it was not.

'Yeah, sure,' she said. She raised an eyebrow. 'Borrowed this from one of the farmers, did you?'

He put a protective hand on the bonnet. 'Oi. This is a classic, thank you very much.'

A classic old wreck, she was about to scoff, but stopped herself, noticing the hurt look on his face. Oops. 'It's lovely,' she said demurely instead.

He laughed. 'You hate it, don't you? Not your style at all. I should have brought the company Beamer along instead, just for you. Then again, I don't want to get drunk and plough it into a hedge.'

She clapped a hand over her mouth, remembering him doing just that with his dad's Toyota, three days after he'd passed his driving test. 'Oh my God! I'd forgotten about that. Very naughty. Weren't you grounded for about a year?'

'It felt like it at the time.' He opened the passenger door for her and walked around to the driver's seat. 'He's just about forgiven me now.'

She clambered inside and fumbled with her seatbelt, suddenly conscious of the small, contained space they were now in. She could smell his spicy aftershave and the distinct pong of wet dog coming from an old red blanket in the back. 'I hope your driving's a bit better these days,' she teased. She felt safer taking the piss out of him than actually talking about anything serious.

'Nah, still crap,' he said, starting the engine. 'You're literally taking your life in your hands now, you know. You all right with that?'

'Well, I used to work in the risk industry,' she told him archly. 'I've never been scared to take a gamble.'

'That's lucky then,' he said accelerating away. 'Because tonight feels like one of those nights when anything could happen.'

She didn't know what to make of that. 'Oh yeah?' she said breezily. 'I knew I should have worn wellies.'

'There's a spare scuba-diving set in the boot,' he said. 'And I took the liberty of packing a tent.'

She laughed. She was starting to feel a bit giddy. 'Where *are* we going?' she said. 'Don't tell me it's The Green Man in Amberley, otherwise I might have to perform an emergency stop and get out of this old banger. I mean, out of your extremely nice car.'

'Damn,' he said. 'I'll just cancel that booking I made for the table for two near the skittles alley, then . . .' He glanced sideways at her, then back at the road. 'Not really,' he went on. 'Actually, I'm a bit pubbed out, if you know what I mean. I spend half my time driving round them, it feels like a busman's holiday when I go there in the evening as well.'

'Fair enough,' she said. 'So . . . ?'

'So I've had a better idea,' he said mysteriously. 'You didn't seem all that thrilled about being back in the countryside when we met in the meadow that day, so I thought I'd remind you just what a gorgeous place Hampshire is.'

Oh. What did that mean? Were they going on some kind of hideous evening hike? Polly's heart sank as she looked down at her shoes. Her gorgeous high-heeled shoes, which were totally impractical when it came to countryside walks of any description. 'Er . . . *should* I have worn wellies?' she hazarded.

A smile twitched at his lips. 'You'll be all right,' he said, as they left the village behind.

They talked about trivia for twenty minutes or so, including, at last, an explanation of Leila's reaction to Jay at the front door earlier. 'I swear on my life I didn't know the bike was nicked,' he said, thumping the steering wheel for emphasis. 'I swear! I got it from a mate's brother. I thought he was a decent bloke – honest. I felt so shitty when Clare harangued me about it the next day. Right in the middle of the street, as well.'

'Oh dear,' Polly said, trying not to laugh. 'She can be quite ferocious, can't she, when she's in a bad mood.'

'Tell me about it,' he said, and groaned. 'That kid of hers — Leila, is it? She's never going to let me forget it, is she?'

'Never,' Polly replied confidently.

Jay indicated to turn off the main road. 'Not far now.'

Polly frowned, trying to orient herself. They were driving along a dirt track through woodland, with a swollen, bosomy hill straight ahead. 'I think I've been here before,' she said, scrolling through her brain, trying to locate the memory.

'You have,' he said, then slowed and steered into a small deserted car park. 'Don't you remember?' He cut the engine and Polly could hear the wind rustling through the leafy trees all around them.

'Er...' she said, playing for time. She was beginning to feel on edge, being in the absolute middle of nowhere with this man. Anything could happen, he'd said. This wasn't some grim dogging venue, was it? She sneakily reached down to find her mobile in her bag and kept her hand on it, just in case.

'Whistledown tree-planting day?' he prompted. 'Come on. You must remember that!'

'Whistledown ... Oh! This is Whistledown Hill?'

'Yeah, we're at the bottom of it, anyway. I thought we could go and look at our tree, then take a stroll up the hill to see the sun go down.'

Our tree. Why was he saying it like that? It was only a *tree*, only a spindly little sapling they'd planted on some boring council initiative all those years ago. Images were spooling through her mind now, the memory having been tracked down. They'd been – what? sixteen? seventeen? – and the whole sixth form had been taken out for the afternoon on a coach and split into groups. She and Jay had been together with Carolyn Dawson, Polly's best friend at the time, and her boyfriend, whatever his name was . . .

'Who was Carolyn seeing back then?' she asked, getting out of the car.

'Donno,' he replied. 'Ian Donnelly?' He was looking at her as if hoping for a better reaction to the excursion he'd arranged.

'Donno Donnelly, that was it. It seems so long ago.'

'Twenty years,' he said, heaving a small rucksack onto his back. 'Provisions,' he explained when he caught her staring at it. 'Come on, I'll show you.'

They went through the car park together, and it was like stepping back through time. She half-expected to see glimpses of her teenage self running ahead, ponytail swinging, not a care in the world.

After a short walk along a stony path, they emerged into what Polly had remembered as being a field. 'Oh,' she said faintly, blinking and staring around.

The field they'd been sent out into all those years ago,

with their spades and compost and weedy little baby trees, had been transformed. Polly and Jay were standing at the edge of dense, dappled woodland, with broad oaks and ash trees forming a high canopy above, and smaller trees planted between them to make a second tier of light and shade. The evening sun shone warm and golden through the leaves, lending the woodland an almost magical serenity.

'Wow,' she said, gazing around. 'A lot can happen in twenty years.' She could still visualize how puny their sapling had been, with the little plastic tubular surround protecting its young, vulnerable trunk. And now ... 'We planted an oak, didn't we?' she said, recalling the distinctive jigsaw-piece leaves. 'I wonder which one was ours.'

'It's down here,' Jay said, and took her hand. 'Ours was the very furthest one, do you remember? We deliberately went for it so that we could have a crafty fag away from Mrs Morris.'

He was right, but she was distracted by the sensation of Jay's warm, strong fingers wrapped around her own. Her heart thumped as they walked between the trees together, and suddenly she wasn't sure if they should venture any further into this memory forest. She'd left the past behind for good reason, after all.

They passed spiky hawthorns and pretty hazels, then Jay stopped in front of a tall, sturdy oak that towered over their heads. 'This is it,' he said, slapping its trunk.

Polly put a hand to it wonderingly, gazing up and up at the broad, strong branches arranged like the spokes of a wheel above her. She could hardly believe the tree had been standing here, quietly growing all this time, after the half-arsed way they'd bunged it in the earth. She'd been more interested in trying to look cool in front of Jay, she remembered, lying back on the grass with her sunglasses on, watching as he bent over to dig a hole for the sapling. And now look at it. *Our tree.*

'Wow,' she said again. Then she tried to laugh it off, not wanting Jay to see how vulnerable the flashback to their teenage years made her feel. 'Well, you can tell it was brilliantly planted, just looking at it. Excellent horticultural skills we had, obviously.'

Jay was smiling at her, his eyes soft and amused. He had a hand on the rough bark too, and his gaze felt worryingly, yet thrillingly intense.

A shiver went through her – was he about to kiss her? – and she quickly pulled away from the tree, rubbing her arms, which were prickling into goose-bumps. 'It's a bit cold in the shade, isn't it?' she said, taking a step back to break the spell. 'Shall we go and have that drink then?'

There was a moment of silence. 'Sure,' he said. 'Let's take a wander up Whistledown.'

Whistledown Hill was a well-known local beauty spot, famed for its views over the county. Polly had been dragged up there many Sunday afternoons *en famille* when she'd been young, usually moaning about wanting to stay indoors and sulking about how *boring* going for walks was, but she hadn't been back since she'd become an adult. How come she had never noticed just how lovely it was around here? Her parents had always droned on about the beautiful views and how lucky they were to live in the valley of the hill, but at the time Polly had been unable to see any beauty. She'd just whinged on about wanting an ice cream, and attempted to amuse herself by pushing her siblings into the bracken wherever possible.

'Gorgeous,' she said, with a little sigh as they walked up its steep slope, the grass freckled with daisies, their heads closing up for the night. It was still light and clear, and you could see far out into the distance, towards Andover and Salisbury Plain, with mile after mile of rolling hills, old flint churches and lush farmland. 'It's your quintessential English countryside scene, isn't it?' she added, then stumbled as she put her foot in a rabbit hole.

Jay caught hold of her arm and she fell sideways into him.

'Oops,' she said, aware of how close they were. 'Sorry.'

'That's your quintessential rabbit hole,' he joked, steadying her. 'Don't get many of them in London, do you? Mind you, you don't get views like this, either.'

'No,' she said, and kicked off her sandals. The ground

was cold under her bare feet, but it felt safer that way. 'I'd forgotten about this place. It's beautiful.' The words seemed insufficient somehow. It was *so* beautiful. She felt as if she hadn't looked properly at the world for the last ten years. She hadn't stopped and gazed at a panoramic view like the one that was unfurled so gloriously before her. It gave her the creeping, unnerving sensation that maybe, just maybe, her priorities had been askew. Maybe the path she'd taken hadn't been the best one after all.

She shook herself briskly, not liking the thought. What was done was done. Regrets were for losers, right?

They'd reached a bench and Jay gestured to it. 'Shall we?' he said and then, without waiting for an answer, unhitched his rucksack, plonked it on the aged wooden seat and opened it. 'I have wine,' he said, producing a bottle swathed in a freeze-pack, 'I have glasses – mercifully unsmashed – and I have raspberries that are only a bit squashed.'

Polly smiled at him dazedly. The whole evening was starting to feel surreal. There was a fluttering sensation inside her and she felt like a kite whose string had been cut loose and was floating up into the air, going who knew where. He'd done all this for her. She couldn't remember a man ever doing a sweeter thing. Why was he being so nice? 'Sounds lovely,' she managed to say, sitting next to him. There was a clump of bobbly-headed dandelion clocks at the side of the bench and she kicked a bare foot through them, shaking the gossamer-like seeds from their stalks, and sending them floating away into the evening, like wishes on the breeze.

Jay uncorked the wine with a pop, then unwrapped two wine glasses from a tea towel and poured. 'Cheers,' he said, passing her a glass. 'Good to have you back in town, Polly.'

'Cheers,' she said, clinking her glass against his. 'It's good to *be* back.' But as she said the words, she could feel herself shrinking away. Where was this leading? she wondered in sudden alarm. Perhaps a drink in The Green Man would have been safer after all. It felt too soon and too intimate for them to be sitting side by side in the middle of nowhere, drinking wine and eating raspberries on their first evening out together in twenty years. And Polly hadn't done intimate for a long, long time. Intimacy scared the hell out of her. If you let your guard down for a second, you could lose everything.

She swung her face away, remembering Michael. Her own brother had died the last time she and Jay had been in such close proximity, and all of a sudden the thought of history repeating itself between them felt like it would be a betrayal, as if she hadn't learned anything from her mistakes. 'Well, it's good to be back for the time being, anyway,' she found herself amending hastily, edging away a fraction and tucking her skirt around her legs. 'Just until I can get back to the wonderful pollution and crime stats of our glorious capital city, of course.'

He looked at her quizzically, then recovered himself in the next heartbeat. 'Of course,' he said. 'Do you miss London then?'

'Miss it? God, all the time,' she said, swigging at the wine without tasting it. She felt a pang of loss for her flat, now with a SOLD sign above its picture on the website. 'I feel like one of my limbs has been hacked off, not being there. I can't wait to go back.'

She could feel his gaze still upon her, but couldn't bring herself to look at him. 'Must be difficult,' he said after a while.

And then because she felt guilty for going cool on him when he was trying so hard, and muddled because she no longer knew what the hell she wanted, she clicked into flirtatious mode by default. 'Well, it has its compensations,' she said, tilting her head coquettishly.

He looked confused and sipped his wine, and she felt like the biggest faker ever.

The evening she and Jay had broken up had been imprinted so vividly in her memory, it was as if it only happened the week before. Churned up with guilt and grief in the wake of Michael's death, she'd pushed him away from her, telling him she hated him and never wanted to see him again.

He'd looked at her helplessly as she railed furiously at him, blaming him, shouting at him, weeping and wild-eyed, punching at his chest like a madwoman.

'I know you're upset about Michael . . .' he kept saying, grabbing hold of her fists.

'Upset? UPSET?' she'd screamed, thrashing in his grasp. 'You have no idea how . . .' And then the fury had vanished, like a flame snuffed out, and she'd broken down in sobs, shaking and unable to stop.

'Oh, Polly,' he'd said, patting her gingerly as if scared she would erupt again. 'It'll be okay.'

'It'll never be okay,' she'd said, the savageness returning to her voice. 'Don't you see? Don't you get it? That's why we've got to split up. Because it'll never be okay again.'

Well, she'd got that one right, at least. They'd gone their separate ways, had seen out the rest of their A-level year in haughty silence towards one another. He'd gone off with bloody Big-Tits two weeks later and she'd simmered for the rest of the term, her face a permanent scowl. The sooner she could get out of Elderchurch and leave the revolting pair of them behind, the better.

And she thought she'd managed it, she thought she *had* left him behind. But spending the evening with him now, sharing wine and raspberries and memories with him . . .

whoa. It had brought her up short, given her a jolt. It turned out that she still had strong feelings lurking just beneath the surface, after all, which had sent her spinning back twenty years to happier times, before everything had gone pear-shaped. Perhaps she hadn't left him behind as successfully as she'd thought.

When Jay dropped her off later on, she felt herself stiffening as he parked the car. What now? A kiss, an embrace? A smouldering look as he leaned over and took her hand?

Her heart skipped a beat as he pulled on the handbrake, but he merely smiled. 'There,' he said politely. It was barely ten o'clock.

She swallowed. 'Jay, about what happened...' she began haltingly. 'I'm sorry about ... you know. How it turned out between us. The things I said.' There was a massive lump in her throat as she spoke. 'I was just ... upset. I think I went a bit mad.'

His eyes softened. 'Don't worry about it,' he said gently. 'Really. I know it was a horrendous time for your family. And...' Now it was his turn to look awkward. 'For what it's worth, I'm sorry too. I was insensitive, I was selfish, I didn't know how to comfort you. I couldn't handle the situation, either.'

She nodded, her lips pressed tight together, terrified she might do something awful like let out a sob.

He patted her arm. 'No hard feelings, yeah?' he said.

'No hard feelings,' she echoed hoarsely, trying to smile.

God, it was hard being a grown-up, Polly thought to herself as she lay in bed that night. Why was it all so complicated?

Her whole life she'd tried to do the right thing, she'd tried to be someone her family would be proud of. And for so long she'd been absolutely sure of herself, convinced that she'd been on the best path forward. Returning to Elderchurch this summer had muddled everything up, though, thrown her whole life up in the air. Completely unexpectedly, she had come to regret severing herself so brutally from the people she loved, all because of a guilty conscience and the conviction that, deep down, she was a bad person who didn't deserve any better. With hindsight, that didn't seem to have been the best course of action after all.

From now on she would try a different way to make amends for what had gone so wrong in the past, she decided, rolling over and putting her arms around herself. She'd start rebuilding the bridges she'd smashed down all those years ago, attempt to put things right again as best she could by being a better daughter and sister, a nicer friend. And maybe, just maybe, she could even be the sort of woman that a man like Jay could fall in love with again . . .

Chapter Twenty-One

Clare hadn't heard anything from Steve since his strange phone call the weekend before. She'd quizzed the children when they'd come home from his place, to try to pin down exactly what they might have said that he could possibly use against her, but they'd both looked blank.

'The thing is, Daddy seems to have got it into his head that me making soap and bubble bath in the kitchen is some kind of health hazard,' Clare said, trying to sound as light-hearted as possible about it. 'I was just wondering why he would think that. Might you have said anything that gave him that impression?'

Leila bit her lip. 'I might have said the smells make me sneeze,' she confessed warily. 'But that was all.' She glanced at her brother. 'Oh, and he asked about Alex's leg too . . .'

Alex's leg? Clare felt nonplussed until she looked down at the limb in question and saw the purple bruise blooming there just above her son's knee. 'How did you get that?' she asked.

'I was chasing Leila and tripped over a box of stuff in

the kitchen,' he shrugged, looking as if he couldn't care less. 'Dad went on about it for ages, though.'

I bet he did. 'Right,' Clare said, rolling her eyes. 'Well, it sounds like one big fuss about nothing to me, but never mind. Thanks for telling me.'

Alex darted off down the garden to dangle dangerously from the apple tree, but Leila was more hesitant. 'Is Dad ... cross with you?' she asked after a moment.

'I think so,' Clare replied, 'but he shouldn't be. I haven't done anything wrong.'

Leila's head was bowed. 'I'm sorry I told him about the sneezing,' she said. 'I didn't mean to get you into trouble.'

Clare hugged her. 'I'm not in trouble, love,' she said, crossing her fingers behind her daughter's back. 'Dad's got the wrong end of the stick, that's all.'

Comforting words, hopefully spoken. But then the bomb dropped the following week, when a letter landed on the doormat one morning. The headed paper from Steve's solicitor and the formal language he used were merely the velvet glove for the iron fist within: *My client has instructed me to convey his unhappiness at the unsuitable living conditions of the children's dwelling place ... Does not want the children's home to become 'a factory' environment ... Is the council aware that the domestic residence is being used as business premises? ... My client hopes the situation can be resolved immediately ... otherwise will be forced to contact social services and the housing department in order to take this matter further ...*

She read it once, and then again, because her eyes and brain couldn't take it all in the first time. The fucking bastard, she thought. The miserable, spiteful, petty, shitty bastard's threatening me. But why?

'Honestly, what a complete prat,' Polly said, scanning the letter when Clare silently passed it to her over the breakfast table. 'Ignore him. It's a load of meaningless flannel. He's just trying to scare you, the pillock.'

'Who's a pillock?' Leila wanted to know, from where she was sitting on the floor, trying to teach Fred to play dead.

'What *is* a pillock?' Alex asked with interest, sauntering in wearing nothing but a pair of pyjama bottoms, his hair tousled from being in bed.

Your father, Clare wanted to reply, but merely clenched her jaw and said, 'Nobody', before stuffing the letter into the dustbin where it belonged.

'Come on, Fred, you pillock, roll over,' Leila said to the dog, lying down next to him. 'Like this!'

The hairy pillock wagged his tail delightedly, but didn't move otherwise. Another time Clare might have laughed as Leila started pushing at his body, trying to make him obey, but laughing didn't seem possible. She didn't know what Steve was up to, but she didn't like it one bit.

*

The summer rumbled along, with a bright sunny July morphing into a thundery, muggy August, and Steve continuing to be a jerk. When he'd next come to the house to pick up the children he'd made a point of barging through to the kitchen, as if to inspect the premises. Clare's hackles rose as he strode around her kitchen looking for evidence of her 'factory' in action, no doubt. Little did he know that she'd temporarily relocated the so-called factory to the shed at the bottom of the garden so that, as far as he was concerned, she'd toed the line and done what he'd asked.

Not that he had any *right* to attempt to lay down the law, but sometimes you had to jump through hoops for a quiet life.

He'd sniffed theatrically – obviously hoping to detect polluting fumes of vanilla or lime, or perhaps even bring on his very own sneezing fit: proof! – but she'd already thought ahead and had flung the windows and back door wide open hours before he was due to arrive. The only thing he could smell was the fragrant grass clippings, from where she'd mown the lawn earlier that day.

So up yours, Steve.

'Good,' he said after a moment, as if satisfied with his inspection, and it was all she could do to stop herself from braining him with the rolling pin. Self-righteous idiot.

But if she thought that would be the end of his problem with her, she was wrong. The next morning he telephoned to say that actually he'd decided to have the children for an extra day, given that they didn't have to rush back for school.

He'd decided. Just like that.

'Obviously, as we have joint custody, I am entitled to have them fifty per cent of the time,' he'd reminded her smugly, 'and so that's what we're going to do. I'll bring them back tomorrow.'

'But—' she said, although he'd already cut her off.

She stood there in the living room with the buzzing phone to her ear, feeling incensed that he was behaving so childishly. She hated that he was using Leila and Alex as pawns to get at her like this. *I am entitled to have them*, he'd said, as if they were things you could pick up and put down when you wanted to, things you had some divine ownership over. It made her feel sick. If he'd bothered to ask, she could have told him that Leila was meant to be going pony riding with a friend the following morning. Not any more, obviously. Now Clare would have to phone and rearrange. Thanks a bunch, Steve.

The worst thing was that there wasn't much she could do about it. He was right: he was entitled to look after them for half of the time. It wasn't down to her to dictate when he could have them each time, either.

She'd prided herself previously on how grown-up she and Steve had been about divorcing, how they'd managed to spare the children as best they could, how they'd maintained some civility towards each other, even when he'd first gone off with Denise and she felt like gouging his eyes out. But now he was acting like a petulant child who wouldn't share nicely any more. And even though two could play at that game, she didn't want to stoop to his depths. Not yet, anyway.

Given all this, and her full workload, it wasn't surprising that her nightmares had come back with a vengeance. She was waking several times a night, shocked awake by her racing heart. Then she'd lie there for ages, worrying that she would be too tired for work, angsting that she'd never fulfil the Langley's order, and beating herself up for not spending enough time with the children. She'd already blasted through all the money from her loan and was broke again, with the bitter knowledge that there was no chance of the situation letting up until September.

Honestly! Summer was meant to be a fun time, a happy stretch of relaxed family days out, not a nightmarish series of run-ins with one's ex-husband, or a marathon of sweating over a cauldron of scented goo night after night. Clare was usually pretty good about looking on the bright side of things and making the most of a tricky situation, but right now she felt as if she was on the verge of cracking up, clinging onto her last shreds of sanity by her fingernails.

In the end she became so desperate for a good night's

sleep that she booked an appointment at the surgery on her day off to see Dr Copper. Hopefully Angela would sort her out with some sleeping pills, which would zonk her into oblivion every evening. Surely then she'd be able to cope a bit better with everything and wouldn't end up so ratty all the time.

But when she reached the surgery Roxie beckoned her over. 'Angela's phoned in sick, so Luke's covering her appointments today,' she said. 'That okay?'

'Oh,' Clare said, wanting to groan with dismay. Oh *no*. It was one thing to pour her heart out and beg for sleeping pills from kind, no-nonsense Dr Copper, but quite another to have to go to *Luke* with her worries. Yes, technically, he'd sworn his Hippocratic Oath not to gossip to anyone about patient information, but it was going to be horribly embarrassing having to discuss her problem with him in the first place.

She was about to cancel the appointment and go home, but the thought of another night tossing and turning stopped her. She couldn't bear the insomnia any more. She *had* to get some kind of prescription today or she'd officially lose the plot. She'd just have to swallow her pride and go through with it. 'Okay,' she said, defeated, and took a seat in the waiting area far away from Roxie so that her friend couldn't start grilling her about why she was there.

If Luke was surprised to see her in his office, he gave no

sign of it. 'Hello Clare,' he said, ushering her to a chair. 'How can I help?'

She took a deep breath. 'I'm having trouble sleeping,' she said. 'I was wondering if you could prescribe something that would knock me out at night.'

A small frown creased his forehead. That wasn't a promising start. 'Is there anything in particular that's stopping you sleeping?' he asked, not seeming in any rush to type out a prescription. 'Is it noise, perhaps, or is the early-morning sun waking you up . . . ?'

She shook her head. 'Just old-fashioned worries,' she said lightly, reluctant to launch into any further details unless she absolutely had to. 'Life, you know.'

He took her blood pressure and typed it into the computer. 'It's a bit low, if anything,' he said. 'Have you been feeling lethargic lately?'

That was the understatement of the year. 'Yes,' she said heavily. 'I'm knackered. That's the annoying thing. I'm exhausted, but every night I lie awake, unable to drop off.'

'I see,' he replied. 'Well, insomnia is very common, but rather than go straight to sleeping tablets, there are other things you can try first.'

She tried not to sigh. She'd read enough helpful magazine articles on the subject to know that he was going to suggest soothing lavender baths and hot milk. She didn't want soothing lavender baths and hot milk, though. She just wanted a nice white pill that she could pop into her mouth, which would block out all the racing anxieties and sweep her into a black hole of sleep. 'Right,' she said glumly.

'How much exercise are you doing at the moment?'

'Exercise? Um ... None,' she confessed sheepishly. Great. Now he would think she was a slob. 'Walking the dog, I suppose, but I've been so busy lately that even that's been a bit rushed.' Poor Fred. Even Polly was paying him more attention than she was these days.

'Hmmm,' he said. 'Well, you could certainly try taking more regular exercise. If you're physically tired, that will help you sleep better. Thirty minutes every day could make a real difference – walking the dog is fine, but you could also think about jogging or swimming.'

She flinched at the word 'swimming' and he broke off and looked at her curiously.

Her face flamed. Don't go there, Luke. 'I can't,' she said helplessly.

'Can't swim? It's nothing to be ashamed of. There are some excellent learn-to-swim classes at the leisure centre in Amberley,' he went on, and she found herself laughing mirthlessly at the well-meaning kindness in his eyes. If only he knew.

'I can swim,' she interrupted him, 'that's not the problem.

The problem is . . .' She hesitated, feeling the weight of the silence between them. Oh God. Step away from the can of worms, Clare. 'It's not important,' she lied.

Silence again. He was waiting for her to spill, but her lips were clamped shut now. 'Is it something I can help with?' he asked eventually.

'No,' she replied, so bluntly that it was on the verge of sounding rude. 'Thanks,' she mumbled as an afterthought.

There was another awkward pause before he spoke. 'Okay,' he said. 'Then I'd prescribe you plenty of fresh fruit and vegetables, reduced caffeine and alcohol, fresh air and exercise. And try winding down in the evening with a bath and a hot milky drink ... What? Did I say something funny?'

'No,' she said, smiling weakly. 'Thank you.'

'If you're still having problems in a fortnight, come back and we can try something else,' he added. 'And of course you can always talk to me as a friend, as well as a doctor, about any worries, okay?' He hesitated as if he was about to say something else, but she was already getting to her feet. 'Take care,' he said.

'Thanks,' she muttered again, walking out of there as fast as she could. What a complete waste of time *that* had been.

*

That evening, to celebrate now having made three-quarters of the stock she needed for the Langley's order, Clare gave herself and Polly a night off and opened a bottle of wine. It was bliss padding out into the garden, glass of wine in hand, she thought gratefully. She had been so busy recently that she'd barely been out there, only rushing to let the chickens out in the morning and put them to bed every night, her mind elsewhere. Now she noticed that the plants had exploded in one of those mad jungly rushes of growth, where everything was suddenly twice its previous size, flowering, lush and heavy with scented blooms. The roses were the colour of poured cream, their curled petals forming glorious velvety rosettes. The sunflowers beamed out like friendly golden beacons, and the lawn was thick and springy, tickling her bare toes as she walked across it.

Marjorie and Babs seemed drowsy, so she shut them in the coop, then dragged a couple of cobwebby deckchairs from the shed and brushed them clean. She clicked their wooden frames into place, lowered herself carefully into one of them and took a sip of cold wine. Ahh. It was utterly delicious; like an elixir, restoring her sanity. She shut her eyes for a moment, enjoying the flavour in her mouth and the gently cooling evening air around her. God, she needed this. She hadn't realized just how much until now.

Polly joined her shortly afterwards and they sat enjoying

the last of the day's sunshine in companionable silence for a few moments. Polly was a very different house-guest these days from the one she'd been at first, it had to be said. She insisted on cooking dinner and washing up every other night, and even though some of the earlier blackened offerings had been barely recognizable as shepherd's pie and salmon fishcakes, Clare had eaten every last scrap in gratitude. Polly had become more thoughtful too – doing the supermarket run, taking her turn at cleaning the bathroom and hoovering, and reading stories to the children in the evening or playing long games with them. And yesterday Karen had phoned Clare in astonishment to say that Polly had turned up out of the blue with some flowers for her, 'just because', and had spent the afternoon in the garden with Graham, weeding the vegetable patch and talking about birds of prey, of all things. 'She even wanted to get out the old photo albums and look through all our family holidays,' Karen had said. 'It was lovely, Clare. Really lovely.'

Not everything had changed, though. Much to Clare's disappointment, Polly was still tight-lipped about her private life. There had been that call she'd tried to make the other week, when she was trying to apologize to someone – some bloke, Clare was sure of it – but had Polly divulged a single smidgen of information about who? No, she had not. Even more frustratingly, Clare hadn't been able to get a thing out of her about her date with Jay, either. Not a bloody thing!

'How did it go at the doctor's today then?' Polly asked conversationally. 'Did you get some nice strong druuuugs?'

Clare cringed and gestured up at the open window above their heads. The open window of Leila's bedroom, where both children were probably still wide awake, having only just gone up there, complaining bitterly about it still being light, and why should they have to go to bed *already*?

'Don't say that,' she hissed. 'The last thing I need is one of them telling bloody Steve that I'm "on drugs". Just think what a shit-storm he'd create about *that*.' She grimaced, imagining the carnage that would ensue, the letter from Steve's smarmy solicitor that would arrive next: *Some concern for the mother's fragile mental health ... Children openly concerned about her drug-taking ... My client feels he would be the more suitable parent to have residence ...*

'Sorry,' Polly replied in a stage whisper. 'What did she say, though? Did she prescribe you a magic potion to cure all ills?'

Clare rolled her eyes. 'No,' she said. 'Angela – the doctor I'd booked to see – wasn't there. I had to see Luke instead.' She found herself blushing. 'He just gave me the hot-baths-and-physical-exercise line. No magic potions. Told me to take up swimming – like that's going to happen.'

The words were out of her mouth before she could stop them, and Polly leaned forward with interest. 'Why not? I've been meaning to ask why you don't swim with the kids. Don't you enjoy it any more?'

'Something like that,' Clare mumbled, not wanting to elaborate.

Polly was watching her closely. 'You like him, don't you, this Luke,' she said, not even bothering to make her words a question. 'What's he like?'

Clare blushed even deeper. 'Oh, he's lovely,' she said – or rather, the wine must have said it for her. She'd never have admitted as much to her sister otherwise. 'He's just ... a really good bloke. Nice, friendly, funny, kind...'

'Good-looking? Sexy? Please don't tell me he's in his fifties with a comb-over.'

'No, thank God.' Clare laughed. 'But...'

'But?' Polly prompted.

Clare shrugged. 'Where do I start? BUT he's got a girlfriend whom he lives with. BUT he's way out of my league. BUT ... oh, I don't know, millions of reasons. It's just a crush, that's all. Nothing's ever going to happen.' The conversation was making her uncomfortable, so she turned it back on Polly. 'What about you, anyway? When are you going to start telling me what's going on with Jay, after you went out the other night? You've kept your cards very close to your chest so far.'

Now it was Polly's turn to sigh and look awkward. 'It's because I don't know what sodding cards I've *got* yet,' she moaned. 'And I don't even know how to play the game, which is even more of a problem. The last time I had any kind of relationship that lasted longer than two weeks was . . .' Her expression was shifty and she pulled her glasses back over her eyes to hide them.

'Was . . . ?'

'Well, it was with him, Jay, back when I was a teenager. How sad is that?'

Clare was taken aback. Whoa. Seriously? She licked her lips, not knowing how to react. 'Well . . .'

'It's okay, you don't have to pretend it isn't weird,' Polly said quickly. 'I know it's awful. I know it makes me some kind of . . . freak who can't form attachments.' She raised an eyebrow. 'Classic psychopath material, apparently.'

'You're not a psychopath—'

'I know I'm not a psychopath, but you must admit, it's not exactly normal.' She sighed, looking small and vulnerable as she sat folded in the depths of the deckchair.

'Why do you think it's been like that?' Clare asked carefully, tiptoeing around the edges of the subject. 'I mean, what do you think has stopped you from falling madly in love with someone?'

Polly shrugged again. 'I guess I'm a bit . . . scared,' she confessed, gazing into the distance. She sipped her wine, frowning. 'I'm not usually scared of anything,' she said with a self-conscious laugh, 'but that opening-up to another person thing – I find it terrifying. What if you, you know, hand yourself over to them, say here I am, this is me, and ... they reject you?'

Clare could hardly believe what she was hearing. She'd never seen Polly like this: so uncertain, so anxious. 'Well, then they're an arsehole and it's their loss,' she replied. 'And you slag them off to your mates, and you pick yourself up and carry on, and you thank your lucky stars that not everyone in the human race is such a prat.'

Silence thickened between them, and Clare felt her face prickle with heat. She was making herself sound far more confident and carefree than she really was, when it came to the thorny subject of relationships.

'I know I was just a teenager, but when me and Jay split up, it was so monumental I felt completely ... well, annihilated by it,' Polly said. 'Like nothing would ever be the same. And it hasn't been.'

'Oh, Polly,' Clare said helplessly.

'And after that, I sort of closed myself off,' Polly said, barely seeming to hear. 'I was like: right! Never again! Independence all the way – nobody else will ever make me feel so unhappy.' She sniffed. 'And of course it was all mixed in with Michael dying too. I was massively beating myself up for that, totally blaming myself, and ...'

Clare stared at her in surprise. Had she just heard that right? Polly's face had turned ashen and she looked stricken at what she'd just said. 'Blaming *yourself*?' she echoed. 'Why?'

Polly finished her wine with a single gulp. There was a long, highly charged silence. 'I think I need another drink if we're going to talk about this,' she said shakily.

Chapter Twenty-Two

Polly retreated to the kitchen and filled their wine glasses, feeling the rush of adrenalin as it pounded around her body. Oh God. Why had she blurted that out? Now she would have to fess up to Clare about the terrible thing she'd done, and Clare would hate her for it. She'd tell their parents, and turn them against her. Polly would be evicted from the village — from the family, more like — within hours.

No. She couldn't do it. Why had she even started down that road in the first place? All that honest, emotional stuff that had gushed out of her about men and her crap track-record of non-existent relationships. How embarrassing could you get! Clare was probably chortling to herself about it right now, texting her mates or posting it on Facebook. *You'll never guess what a saddo my big sister is. Only ever had one proper boyfriend. At the age of thirty-seven!*

No, she wouldn't. Clare wasn't like that. Clare was sympathy and kindness, not taunts and sniggering. But finding out that your own sister was responsible for your brother's untimely death was enough to test anyone's sympathy and kindness to their outer limits.

What a mess. What a complete and utter mess. She'd really gone and dumped herself in it this time, letting slip her deepest darkest secret like that. It would poison the new confidence that had bloomed between them recently, smother the tender shoots of friendship in an instant.

'Are you trampling the grapes yourself in there, or what?' came a shout from the garden. 'Hurry up!'

'Just coming,' Polly called back and picked up the full glasses unsteadily. Well, this was it, then.

Nice knowing you, kitchen, she thought, gazing around at its familiar friendly clutter. Chances are I'll be kicked out of here before the night's over and I'll never see you again. But thanks for everything. You've been a great place to sit and not get a job all these weeks.

She pulled a face. Talking to the kitchen now? God, Polly, have a word with yourself.

Every step she took back to her sister was heavy with trepidation. 'Here you are,' she said, passing Clare her glass and sitting down again. *So, where were we? Oh yes. I was just about to wreck everything between us, wasn't I?*

'What did you mean when you said you blamed yourself for Michael's death?' Clare asked in the next second.

Polly felt herself sag. Shit. There was no getting away

from it. No convenient memory lapse on her sister's part in the last two minutes.

'Only, the thing is . . . Well, I've always blamed *myself* too,' Clare went on.

Polly stared. 'What do you mean? You weren't even there!'

'No,' Clare said. Her mouth had puckered as if she was trying not to cry. 'But I had a horrible teenage whinge that night – don't you remember? – about wanting Mum and Dad at the swimming championships. I was competing,' she added needlessly. She pressed her lips together tightly, her fingers knotted around the stem of her wine glass. 'I knew Michael wasn't well,' she went on, 'but I was such a selfish, attention-seeking cow, I basically forced Mum into coming along. Just so that they could both watch me. And if I hadn't—'

Polly leaned heavily against the canvas of her deckchair. 'No, you've got it wrong,' she said. She swallowed and looked at her lap. *Here goes.* 'I behaved even worse, Clare. I stayed at home and was meant to be keeping an eye on him, but ended up shagging Jay on the sofa. I even heard Michael cry out, and I didn't go up to him. I ignored him. And he . . . he died. Because I was having sex with Jay.'

There. She'd done it. She'd actually said it.

'Oh God,' Clare said, her voice becoming a sob.

'I know,' Polly said, shame burning its way through every cell. 'I've never been able to forgive myself. I feel so bloody awful about it. If I could turn the clock back and make things right, I would. I so would.' She hung her head. 'I'm so, so sorry.'

There was a moment of deafening silence. Polly's blood drummed through her veins as she waited for Clare's face to screw up in hatred, for the accusations to come flying. It was only what she deserved.

Instead, Clare reached across the divide between their deckchairs and took Polly's hand. 'You don't have to apologize,' she said. 'It wasn't your fault.'

For a second Polly wasn't sure she'd heard correctly. But Clare's fingers were around hers, and her eyes were full of compassion. Polly squeezed her sister's hand and swallowed hard, not trusting herself to speak at first. 'It wasn't your fault, either,' she said eventually.

They sat like that for a few minutes and it was as if a spell had been broken at last by their mutual confession and mutual forgiveness. Polly could practically feel the weight of her guilty secret sliding off her shoulders. The black bile that she'd feared would reside in the depths of her soul forever seemed to drain away and vanish, as if Clare had finally given it permission to go. To think that all this time they'd both tormented themselves with similar loadings of guilt and self-hatred; to think it had taken them so many years to finally have this conversation, this really important, game-changing conversation. What a waste of time.

'Shit,' she said after a while, trying to lighten the intensity. 'What are we like?'

'I know,' Clare said. 'So I never let myself go swimming again, and you never let yourself love anyone again. The psychiatrists would have a field day with us two.' She pretended to dial on an imaginary phone. 'Get me Dr Freud on line one, please . . .'

'You never let yourself . . . Oh, *that's* why you don't go swimming.'

'Yeah. I know it sounds mad, said out loud like that.' Clare wrinkled her nose. 'It *is* mad. A stupid mental block that has stopped me for so long.' She sipped her wine. 'I should let it go now really, shouldn't I?'

'You should,' Polly told her. 'You really should.' She gave a small smile. 'God. This is some conversation we're having tonight, eh? No chit-chat for us two. Straight in there with the love and death.'

'It's good to talk,' Clare said in a rubbish Bob Hoskins imitation, and they both laughed, louder and longer than her words really necessitated. 'Seriously, though,' she went on, 'I get why this thing with Jay is messing with your head. But do you know what? Sometimes you've just got to take a chance. Allow yourself to be vulnerable. The worst that can happen already did happen. So why not treat this as a holiday romance, a fling to enjoy while you're here for the summer?'

'You don't think I'd be ... betraying Michael somehow?'

Clare shook her head. 'No,' she said. 'Definitely not. Michael wouldn't want you to sabotage the chance of something that might make you happy. He wasn't the kind to bear a grudge, was he?'

Polly shook her head. It was true. Michael had been one of those people who could shake off a bad mood in an instant, rather than wrap it around themselves in a sulk for days on end. And, in all honesty, she would love to remember how to go about having a relationship with an attractive, funny, interesting man without running for cover. That was, if she hadn't already put Jay off, of course. She hadn't heard from him since the Whistledown evening. 'Okay,' she said slowly. 'I will, if you will.'

'What? Go out with Jay? Thanks for the offer, but...'

'No, I mean, take a risk yourself. With Luke.'

'Ahh.' Clare's smile fell from her face. 'Well, that's different. He's already with someone. And I *am* taking a risk anyway, with the business. One risk at a time is enough for me.'

'Hmmm,' Polly said. She wasn't about to let her sister off the hook that lightly. 'We'll just see about that.'

*

The following Monday Polly had arranged to have the morning off her pub job. She got up at the same godawful early hour, but instead of chucking on her tatty denim shorts and a bleach-marked T-shirt as she usually did, she slipped into a crisply ironed short-sleeved white blouse and some smart grey pin-striped trousers. She scraped her hair back into a chignon and carefully applied a full face of make-up. Then she picked up her jacket and her favourite ruby-coloured Mulberry handbag and rifled through it to check her essentials. Lipstick, mini *A–Z*, phone, wallet, pocket mirror and tissues.

'London, here I come,' she said to her reflection, tucking a loose strand of hair behind her ear. It was like looking back in time, seeing herself scrubbed up and ready for action again. Looking back in time ... with a difference, though. She was tanned and freckly from all the hours she'd spent outdoors in Clare's garden, and her eyes seemed brighter than they had for years. The bags and worry lines had gone from her face too, and her cheeks had filled out a little from home-cooked meals every night.

Maybe the old saying was right: a change *was* as good as a holiday. She certainly looked more relaxed these days, and since she and Clare had had their almighty, no-holds-barred conversation, she was sleeping better than she'd done for years. Clare knew her secret and yet was still on her side. That felt like the most amazing gift she'd ever received.

She was absurdly excited about going back to the capital; had dreamed of nothing else all weekend. After weeks of exile she was well up for kicking some recruitment-agency butt. She would not return to Elderchurch until she had made some kind of progress, she vowed, whether it was an interview, an introduction or even just a tip-off about something coming up.

Over the last few weeks she'd let her job-hunting drift; she'd become caught up with village goings-on, and helping Clare get her business up and running. Now it was time to focus back on herself, be proactive again. She'd bloody well elbow the recruitment agents aside and go through their databases herself, if that was what it took to bag a new opportunity. After all, time was ticking by. There were only a few weeks before summer would start its gradual turn to autumn. If she was to keep up the story she'd spun to her parents about her sabbatical, she needed to get something lined up, and fast.

Clare and the children were still asleep when she crept out of the house. She caught the bus from Elderchurch to Amberley, then walked the short distance to the old-fashioned red-brick station. It didn't seem to have been modernized since it had been built in the Victorian era, with its aged iron-fretwork decorating the platform shelters and the dusty-windowed shop selling cups of tea and newspapers. Children had been evacuated to Amberley and its surrounds during the Second World War, and Polly could imagine the old trains puffing into the station amidst clouds of steam; hordes of soot-smudged London urchins spilling out onto the platforms with their little suitcases, blinking in the sunshine.

Thank goodness she was going the other way today, returning to the heaving metropolis she loved, with its streets paved with gold. Bring it on!

When the train pulled into Waterloo ninety minutes later, Polly wanted to run at the city with her arms open wide. Hello, people with laptops and suits and takeaway frappuccinos, talking urgently into their mobiles as they strode to and fro. Hello, overpriced shops and snack bars. Hello, wide-boys and hustlers; hello, streetwise teenagers with jeans around their arses; hello, harassed tourists trying to make sense of their pocket maps. God, she'd missed them all.

She bought a copy of the *Financial Times* to brush up on the day's news and pored over the main stories as she took the Tube to Piccadilly Circus. The pound was up against the dollar and the markets seemed to be shaking themselves out of their recent torpor, which was good news. There was just time to check her own investments – mostly still flat-lining unfortunately, although Morton's, the UK software company in the North-East, did seem to be rallying slightly at long last – before she reached her stop.

Emerging into the blare and blast of Shaftesbury Avenue, she smiled as she took in the good old bendy buses, the black cabs, the reckless motorbike couriers all streaming past. Soho lay ahead with its saucy shops and Italian coffee bars; behind her stood Fortnum & Mason and Mayfair and the Royal Academy . . . Oh, London, I have *ached* for you, she thought joyfully, heading for the first recruitment agency with a spring in her step.

Okay. Here she was at her first port of call, Finance Professionals UK, and she was going to dazzle them if it killed her. 'Cover me, I'm going in,' she muttered under her breath and pushed open the door.

It was a gruelling marathon of a day. She'd arranged five appointments – two in the West End, one in Chancery Lane and another two near Liverpool Street – so there was hardly time to draw breath, let alone meander around the shops or grab a decent coffee. Still, it had definitely been worth her while. And what a treat it had been too, just sitting in an office environment again, talking banking jargon and financial opportunities, slipping back into her native tongue as if she'd never left that world.

Polly knew she interviewed well – she was sharp-witted and articulate, she knew her stuff, she was precise and smart and polished. The only slightly precarious subject was the area of her CV that had been left fallow for the last few months. Every interviewer had, of course, asked what she'd been doing since being made redundant, as she'd expected them to. Luckily she had rehearsed her answer.

'The redundancy came as a huge shock,' she admitted briskly, 'but I'm not one to panic or give up. I've taken some time out recently to help with the family business – I've advised them on financial matters, for example – and I've also taken the opportunity to pursue some research into banking law, an area that has always fascinated me.'

Funnily enough she didn't mention her job at the pub, her new-found expertise in Ginger Ninja bubble-bath-making, or the long depressing afternoons in front of her laptop staring blankly at the complete dearth of job vacancies on the screen, with only Agatha and the mad chickens for company.

Her explanation seemed to pass muster, though, thank goodness. Finance Professionals had immediately come up with two possible vacancies for which they'd promised to put her details forward; the woman at Compass had told her there was a great maternity cover coming up at Arthur Andersen, which could lead to something permanent; and the other three agencies had all spoken of a new confidence and buoyancy about the current jobs market, and said that they were confident they could find her something within the next few weeks. It just went to show that it was all a matter of being in the right place at the right time. She doubted these vacancies would even get put on the website.

It was almost five o'clock now, and London was on the verge of swinging into Happy Hour. Computers would be powered down for the day, and out would pour the worker ants into the bars and restaurants, the buses and trains. Already there was a buzz in the air as the lucky few slunk away early with alcohol and freedom on their minds.

Polly's day was not over yet, though. There was one more place she had to go. She plunged back into the sweating depths of the Underground towards the address she had in London Bridge. She hoped she wasn't already too late.

The company's name, Domestic Angels, might have suggested a heavenly address with Doric columns, harp-playing cherubs and fluffy clouds, but the reality was far more down-to-earth: a small, dingy office block with tinted windows and a reception area that sported a nicotine-stained ceiling and an old beige sofa. It was approaching six o'clock by the time Polly tracked the place down, her feet now hot and blistery in her heels after all the pavement-pounding she'd done.

'Hi,' she said to the sallow-faced girl on reception who was gawping at her Facebook page and blowing small pink gum-bubbles through pursed lips. 'Have I missed Magda? Only I was meant to be meeting her here at half-five and I got stuck in traffic. We're going to that new wine bar, but I thought I'd hang around for her, if she hasn't already gone.' She pulled a funny face. 'I hate walking into those places on my own, don't you? Always feel a right plonker.'

Blind the girl with unnecessary facts, that was Polly's tactic, and hope she'd be taken in. It was a gamble, yes, but she'd already tried the polite telephone request and that had got her precisely nowhere.

The receptionist blinked at the information overload and shifted her gum to the side of her mouth. 'Magda? She's still at the Kipling Street job,' she said.

'Oh, my mistake,' Polly said, pantomiming a silly-me reaction. 'Lucky I checked. I'll come back later, cheers.'

'Who shall I say was looking for her?' the girl called after her, but Polly pretended she hadn't heard and went quickly out of the door again.

Her heart was racing. The gamble had actually paid off. Magda was still working for the agency and was somewhere on Kipling Street right now. Polly flicked through her *A–Z* and then went to find her.

As luck would have it, Kipling Street was only a short road. Polly perched on a wall where she could see all the way along the street, and waited. Twenty minutes later she saw Magda emerging from a terraced house. That slight, slim figure with the straight back and neat bobbed hair, carrying a yellow bucket of cleaning materials. 'Magda,' Polly called, jumping off the wall and waving. 'Magda!'

The woman stopped and stared at her in surprise. Then her expression changed to one of suspicion. 'Miss Johnson,' she said coldly as Polly ran towards her. Her cat-like eyes had narrowed and her body language was unfriendly. 'What are you doing here?'

Polly swallowed. 'I came to say sorry,' she replied. They were standing a few metres apart on the pavement and she felt hot and awkward, aware that her hair had worked its way loose from that morning's elegant chignon, that there was sweat under her arms and in a line down her back, that her feet probably stank in the crippling heels she had on. 'I'm really sorry. I was an idiot. I hope I didn't get you into trouble.'

Magda exhaled slowly, her eyes giving nothing away. 'I

got in trouble, yes,' she said, putting the bucket down. 'Bad trouble. They want to sack me, I had to . . .' Her vocabulary ran out, and she pressed her hands together as if praying.

'You had to beg,' Polly translated. 'I'm sorry. But you kept your job at least – yes?'

Magda folded her arms across her chest. 'I lost best clients,' she said. 'They tell me I am . . . not to trust. They give me shitty jobs instead.'

Polly bit her lip. 'I'm so sorry,' she said again. And then, all of a sudden, she wondered what on earth had possessed her to come and do this. What was the point? What could she possibly do to make it up to this woman whom she'd wronged in a fit of spite all those months ago? 'I tried to phone, to give you a message, but they wouldn't let me,' she said weakly after a moment.

Magda stood there mute. *Big deal*, her eyes flashed scornfully. *So what?*

'You know, I am a cleaner now,' Polly began, 'and . . .'

Magda started with shock. 'You? You clean?'

Polly nodded. 'I clean,' she said. 'And it's really hard work. I never knew.'

'Yes. Is hard work.' Magda gave a snort suddenly, her eyes bright with amusement. 'You really clean? You?'

'Yes. I know it's hard to believe,' Polly replied. 'And I know now how hard you worked for me all those weeks.'

'Months.'

'All those months,' Polly corrected herself, eyes downcast. 'I just came to say sorry anyway,' she finished. 'If you want, I can write to the manager at the agency, tell them I was wrong.'

Magda nodded. 'Yes. You tell them. Tell them I good cleaner, you wrong.'

'I'll say I was unfair and that you don't deserve the shitty jobs.'

'Is true.'

'And that they should give you a pay rise and lots of free holidays.'

Magda was at least smiling now. 'Is true,' she said again and punched Polly lightly on the arm. 'Is okay. Thank you.'

Polly smiled back. 'Thank *you*,' she said. 'You were so kind to me when everything got on top of me. I didn't appreciate it at the time, but ... you are a good person. I didn't deserve you.'

'Is true,' Magda said again. 'All true.' And then they were both laughing, and Magda had put her arms around Polly, patting her back, as if comforting a child. 'You have new job now?' she asked after they'd disentangled.

Polly shook her head. 'Not yet,' she said. 'But I'm trying.'

'I wish you good luck,' Magda said. '*Dobre szczęście*, as we say in Poland.'

'Thank you,' Polly said. 'Thank you so much, and the same to you. It's nice to see you again, Magda. Take care.'

'You as well,' said Magda. 'You are different now, I think. Good-different.' She held up a hand. 'Goodbye.'

Polly watched her pick up the bucket of cleaning sprays and bottles (not dissimilar from her own white bucket of bleach and disinfectant that she used at the pub) and then walk away down the street.

You are different now, I think, she'd said. *Good-different.* Polly found that she was nodding to herself, right there on the pavement like a nutter. She *was* different, she *had* changed since she'd acted so appallingly back then. And Magda had noticed – even better.

Mission accomplished, Polly thought, setting off to the Tube. With a bit of luck she could catch the 18.57 back to Amberley and be home for nine o'clock. It had been a long, tiring day, but her legs didn't feel so heavy any more. She was going to make things right for Magda: she'd write the letter absolving her of any fault – why hadn't it occurred to her before? – and everything would be okay.

Just at that moment her phone started ringing. An unfamiliar London number was on the screen. Her heart leapt. 'Hello?' she said, jabbing at the button to accept the call.

'Is that Polly Johnson? It's Anne-Marie from Finance Professionals here. Hi. Just to say I sent your details to the Walkley Group for the Risk Manager role, and they've come back already to say that they'd like to meet you. How are you set for next week?'

Polly's mouth hung open and she stopped dead in the middle of the street. 'You mean . . . I've got an interview?'

'That's right. They sounded very keen – said you were just what they were looking for.'

She wanted to laugh. The hours and weeks of fruitless searching, the times she'd ploughed through websites and newspapers, trying to stay optimistic as she emailed her CV and job applications, to no avail. She had begged and pleaded for a chance at times, making herself cringe. And now it turned out that all she'd needed was Magda's blessing of good luck, and along came the very call she'd been waiting for, minutes later. It felt as if the universe was giving her another shot.

'That's wonderful,' she replied, joy rising inside her like bubbles. 'Oh, that's really great news, Anne-Marie. And I'm free to come in for an interview any time. Any time at all.'

Chapter Twenty-Three

Polly was on the train thundering back to Amberley with a celebratory gin-in-a-tin when her phone rang again. Jay, this time. A frisson went through her as she remembered the conversation she'd had with Clare. Take a chance, she reminded herself. Be open to something happening. And don't be afraid!

'Hi there,' she said cheerfully, swirling her ice cubes around the plastic cup and draining the last drops. 'How are you?'

'All right, thanks. Where are you? Sounds noisy.'

'I'm on the train, been up in London for the day,' she said, gazing out of the window as they rattled along the tracks. They'd already left the bustling terraced streets and looming council blocks behind and were now moving into the suburbs: Esher and Hersham with their bigger gardens and leafier streets. *Goodbye, big city. See you again next week. Looking forward to it already.*

'Oh yeah? Wheeling and dealing?'

She hesitated for a second. 'Just catching up with some old mates,' she said in the end. What a lie. She didn't even have any old mates to speak of. But something had stopped her from telling him the truth nonetheless. It was almost as if by speaking about the interview, she might jinx this brand-new seam of luck she'd just struck.

'Sounds good. What time are you due back?'

'Um . . .' Her brain was already pleasantly addled by the gin; she frowned at her watch, trying to remember. 'About half-eight, I think. Why?'

'I'll pick you up. We could go for a drink maybe.'

'That would be great. Although . . .' She remembered, too late, her stickiness, the grime in her pores, her collapsing hairdo.

'Although . . . ?' he prompted.

'Well, I'm a bit scruffy and dirty,' she admitted, wincing as the words came out before she could stop them. Telling a man you were 'a bit dirty' was practically asking for trouble. Damn that gin for being so delicious that she'd necked a double already.

He laughed softly. 'Even better,' he said. And before she could think of any witty comeback to *that*, he'd added, 'See you later, then' and had hung up.

Hmmm. Time to check out the train loos and hope that she could make herself look halfway presentable before they crossed the Hampshire border. She also had to hope that

Jay wouldn't wonder why she'd got all dressed up in a suit merely to hook up with her imaginary 'old mates'. She was smiling, though, as she picked her way along the swaying compartment. Somehow having the prospect of her job interview floating tantalizingly ahead of her made things with Jay seem less important. She'd be out of Elderchurch before she knew it anyway; what was the point of getting her knickers in a twist over him? They could have some fun together without any need for emotional dramas.

At last it seemed as if everything was falling perfectly into place.

Jay did a loud, embarrassing wolf-whistle when he saw her. Which was ridiculous, seeing as her patch-up attempts in the Ladies hadn't been quite as successful as she'd hoped; her hair felt too dirty to style as perfectly as she'd managed that morning, and there was no disguising the grit and grime on her clothes after her long day in the capital. But she had managed a stripdown wash in the tiny cubicle, so that she smelled clean at least, and she'd put on fresh lipstick and mascara and had tidied her hair as best she could.

Still, the way Jay was looking at her so appreciatively made her feel as if her efforts had been rewarded. In fact she was quite tempted to wolf-whistle back at him, seeing him there in a gleaming white shirt and jeans, his face smooth-shaven and tanned.

'Evening,' she said, smiling shyly. 'How are you?'

'All the better for seeing you again,' he said and pulled her to him for a second. The fresh, lime-scented cologne he had on made the hairs on her arms prickle, and something flipped over inside her. God, she shouldn't have drunk that second gin; it had made her feel alarmingly carefree. Stay in control, Polly, she thought desperately.

'Have you eaten?' he asked as he let her go.

'Um . . .' She *was* kind of hungry, now that he asked. The buffet car on the train hadn't had the most appetizing array of food, and she'd only eaten a bag of crisps since midday. No wonder the alcohol had gone straight to her head. 'Not really,' she confessed. 'I might have to swing by the chippy on the High Street, if it's still there.'

'Oh, I think we can do better than that,' he said. 'Why don't you come back to mine? I'll make you something there.'

Back to mine? Eek. 'Sounds perfect,' she said, with faux casualness. 'I hope you're a better cook than you are a driver, that's all.'

'Well, I haven't killed anyone yet,' he replied. 'Although there's a first time for everything, I suppose. The car's just round the corner.'

As Jay started the Land Rover, she realized that she had no idea where he lived, or what sort of home he would have made for himself. Growing up, his family had lived in one of the modern semi-detached houses near the primary school with the bog-standard rectangle of lawn outside, but where had the adult Jay chosen to hang his hat? She tried to picture him in a bungalow like her parents, but couldn't see it somehow. Would he have plumped for one of the houses on the new estate just outside the village? Polly hadn't been inside them, but she remembered her parents muttering about them being eyesores and a blight on the village, some Christmases ago. She was curious to see his taste, his style, she realized. What if she got there and it was a hideous bachelor pad, decorated throughout in black and chrome, with leopardskin throws on the leather sofas, like you saw in footballers' houses in *Hello!* magazine? She stifled a laugh at the thought, and Jay looked over quizzically.

'What?' he asked.

'Nothing,' she said. 'I'll just send Clare a text, so she knows where I am,' she added, getting her mobile out of her bag. 'Don't want her staying up worrying about me.'

Hiya, she typed. *Hope all okay. Gr8 day – interview next week! Just nipping to Jay's 4 drink. See you later.*

A reply pinged back seconds later. *WELL DONE! PS Don't 4get our deal, will you? TAKE A RISK. SNOG HIM FFS!*

She gave a snort and stuffed her phone back in her bag.

'Now what?' Jay asked. 'You can't keep sniggering like that. It's the sort of thing that makes a bloke anxious.'

She laughed again, partly at the thought of laidback Jay being anxious about anything. 'Sorry,' she said. 'Ignore me.'

He raised his eyebrows. 'Like I've ever been able to do *that.*'

He was joking, of course, but his words made her feel hot all over. 'Jay Holmes, you're not flirting with me, are you?' she said primly.

He glanced across at her and winked. 'You think that's flirting? I haven't even started yet,' he said, slowing to thirty as they approached the 'Welcome to Elderchurch' sign.

'Is that so,' she bantered, trying to keep her cool. 'Well, I hope you're up to the job. I hate to see a grown man in tears.'

'You know me, I love a challenge,' he replied, then turned off the main street and into a small lane lined with banks of lush, long grass and leggy, looming cow parsley. 'Nearly there,' he said.

'Mill Lane – is this where you live?' Polly asked in surprise. Well, she hadn't been expecting that. Mill Lane was the oldest part of the village, where the original farm and grain mill had once stood. The farm had been sold off long ago and the mill-house converted to a gorgeous five-bedroom property, she seemed to remember, bought by an eccentric businessman who'd upset the locals by shooting the rooks out of the rookery at the bottom of his garden with an air-rifle. 'Bally things kept waking me up in the morning,' he'd explained, as if this made it acceptable.

'Yep,' Jay said. 'Not the mill-house, before you get excited, though. I bought one of the outbuildings from the farm, turned it into a house.'

'So you live in a shed, is that what you're saying?'

'Yeah, I live in a shed,' he said, slowing to a crawl as they crossed the humpback bridge over the mill-stream. 'That shed over there.'

He pulled up on the gravel drive outside his 'shed' and Polly fell silent. It wasn't a shed at all, it was a gorgeous barn conversion, with great slabs of oak forming the front porch, a slate roof and a white-rendered front. Two silvery-leaved olive trees in terracotta pots stood on either side of the entrance, and a clematis with small white flowers had been planted further along. She could hear his dog barking excitedly from within at her master's return. *This is the house that Jay built.* And bloody lovely it was too.

'Oh, wow,' Polly said, still gazing at it. 'It looks amazing. And there was me thinking you'd be living in a horrible, tacky bachelor pad.'

'Cheeky cow,' he said, getting out of the car. 'Come on then. It's even better inside.'

He wasn't joking. The front door opened into a long, open-plan living space with vast windows looking out over the fields and hills beyond. There was an open fireplace at the far left with herringbone brickwork, and the furniture was simple and rustic: a big red sofa, a chunky wooden coffee table, an aged black-leather footstool, and a solid wooden bookcase filled with paperbacks, with his beloved guitar propped in one corner. Overhead were the original beams, great thick timber struts, rising to a central horizontal peak. It felt spacious and airy, but she could just imagine what a cosy space it would be with a roaring log fire in the winter. Not that she'd get to see that, of course.

'The kitchen's this way,' he said, kicking off his shoes and walking towards the other end of the house, the dog at his heels, tail wagging furiously. Polly kicked off her heels, dropped her bag and followed him.

The kitchen was simple and stylish. There was a brick-built surround housing a wood-burning stove, and the worktop was a single slab of wood above plain white units. 'It's amazing,' Polly said, leaning against the worktop as she gazed around, noting the tangle of copper pans hanging from a rack on one wall, and the spice rack full of jars that actually seemed to be well used, rather than merely there for decorative purposes.

Jay smiled and slapped the worktop. 'Recognize this, by any chance?' he asked.

Polly shook her head. 'Should I?'

'It came from one of the labs at the comp,' he confessed.

'They were refitting the science block and I got a tip-off that they were chucking all the old workbenches out. I rescued a couple of them out of a skip and sanded this one down. Reclaimed teak – would cost a fortune new.'

'It's lovely,' Polly said, running a hand along its smooth surface. She smiled. 'Funny to think of all the Bunsen burners and tripods that must have stood here over the years.'

'I know, and us as vile teenagers sitting at it, carving graffiti into it too,' he replied. 'Well, not me, of course, I was far too well behaved to do anything like that.'

She grinned. 'Of course.'

'Anyway – food! Will pasta and salad do you?' he asked. 'I've got a bottle of white in the fridge over there, if you want to pour us both a glass.'

'Sounds brilliant, thanks,' she said, pulling open the fridge door and peering in nosily. Eggs. A packet of bacon. Some chicken breasts. Salad. Her hand closed around the neck of the wine bottle and two things popped into her head at the same time.

One: if he started drinking, he wouldn't be able to drive her home again. Sure, she could *walk* back to Clare's later on, in theory, although finding her way down the dark lane in her heels was going to be a complete nightmare, but he might very well suggest that she stayed over. In which case she'd say . . . Well, what *would* she say? She had absolutely no idea.

Two: she was in such a fizzy mood already from her day

up in London, and all the gin, that even a single glass of wine was likely to tip her over the edge and then she'd lose *all* her inhibitions. And, with Clare's encouraging text message in the back of her mind – *SNOG HIM FFS!* – there might be no stopping her. Oh God. It was terrifying ... but kind of exciting too.

She poured them each a large glass and raised hers to her lips. 'Cheers,' she said demurely. She didn't have a clue how tonight was going to pan out, but she had a feeling she might enjoy herself all the same.

After they'd eaten platefuls of pasta in a garlic, cream and bacon sauce and an enormous green salad, the sky was darkening into sombre shades of purple and navy. They were sitting outside at a small iron patio table around the back of the house, and it was so quiet, Polly felt as if they were the only two people left in the county.

'That was delicious,' she said tipsily, pushing her plate back. 'So what happens now? Is this where you start serenading me on your guitar?'

'You should be so lucky,' he replied. 'No. What happens now is ... this.' And then, before she could say or do anything else, he'd leaned across the table and was kissing her full on the lips. Her heart almost stopped in shock. 'Excuse *me!*' she was on the verge of bleating, but then she noticed just how soft his mouth was against hers and how tenderly he was holding her. The words slipped away, unspoken and she felt the blood rush first to her head, and then to various other sensitive areas around her body.

Oh my goodness. Her nerve endings were tingling. I am kissing Jay, she thought in a daze, and it's okay. In fact, it's better than okay. I'm enjoying it. I want to keep right on kissing him actually.

'Mmm,' she said, rising to meet him halfway. Her fingers circled his arm, and she could feel his bicep taut through his sleeve. 'Anything else?' she whispered, before she knew what she was saying.

'Perhaps ... this,' he murmured, moving a hand around to unbutton her blouse. She gasped as she felt his fingers brush against her skin, the sensation star-bursting through her entire body. It felt amazing. Stay in control, Polly, her last shred of sanity managed to squeak, but she ignored it. Oh, sod staying in control, she thought, with a sudden yearning hunger. Sod being scared.

'Why don't you show me your bedroom?' she said breathlessly.

'I thought you'd never ask,' he replied.

It was without a doubt the sexiest sex she'd ever had, the slowest, gentlest, most sensual experience of her entire life.

He looked even better naked now than he had done at eighteen, although her fingers traced a new scar on one arm, a faded Celtic tattoo on one shoulder, and firm abdominal muscles that definitely hadn't been there twenty years ago. It was all so different, yet wonderfully familiar. It felt as if she'd come home.

To think of all the crap sex she'd had since she'd last slept with him: all those awful, disastrous encounters with completely unsuitable men, which had stemmed from her loneliness and her need to feel another person's arms around her. The last guy had been a ruddy-cheeked, slightly overweight fellow delegate at the dreary Future of Mobile Banking conference she'd attended back in the spring – Patrick Someone-or-other. He'd had clammy hands, he'd grappled with her bra as if he'd never encountered one before, his kissing had been one enormous probing tongue thrusting in and out of her mouth, and as for the act itself, he'd barely put the condom on before he'd exploded into it, puffing like a beached whale.

Whereas Jay, on the other hand ... He made her feel beautiful. She could see the desire shining out of his eyes. He'd held her, touched her, looked at her all over. And she hadn't felt afraid, not for a second.

It was only afterwards, when they were lying together, that doubt and anxiety crept back. Oh God, she thought, as her pulse returned to normal and the heat between them cooled. Now what? Whose life had she just jinxed this time?

He was stroking her hair and she could feel herself starting to panic. She shouldn't have done that. Her and Jay: it was a terrible idea. However much she had fancied him in that crazy drunken moment, however much she'd enjoyed having sex with him, she needed to get out quickly before things became too complicated. Quit while she was ahead. Because she was hopeless at relationships, period. And with him – well, it hadn't exactly worked out the first time, had it?

'I'm falling in love with you,' he said at that moment, and it was like a needle screeching horribly on a record.

She stiffened, jerking away automatically. 'Don't say that.' *Don't say it, don't say it, don't say it.* He couldn't possibly mean it. Couldn't they just leave it at sex? She wasn't sure she could cope with anything else.

'Why not? It's true. I always wondered about you, wondered what might have happened if we'd stayed together, and . . .'

She couldn't bear to listen. 'Yeah, well, we didn't, did we?'

He propped himself up on an elbow to look at her and she pulled the sheet over herself, suddenly aware of her cellulite and lumpy bits, and the – yikes! – single black hair that appeared to be sprouting under her nipple. 'What's up?' he asked, frowning.

She rolled over onto her front and began pleating the soft cotton of the pillowcase between her fingers. 'I don't think there's any point talking about *love* when...' She shrugged. 'Well, I'm only here for the summer, aren't I?'

'Are you?'

'Yes. I thought you knew that?'

Now it was his turn to look away. 'I suppose I was just hoping...'

'No.'

'What?'

'Whatever you were hoping, it's not going to happen.'

There was an uncomfortable silence, then Polly heard a threatening rumble of thunder in the distance. A storm was brewing outside the house, as well as right there in the bedroom. 'What makes you so sure?' he asked after a moment. 'How can you possibly know?'

He was running his fingers up her back and it was distracting her. Mustn't get distracted. She swallowed. 'Look, I'll be gone in a few weeks,' she said, turning to face him. 'Let's not make more out of this than there really is.'

She was being deliberately harsh, she knew, but it was the best thing for both of them if she was upfront. Nothing was going to come of this – how could any kind of relationship work when she'd be back in London again so soon? What was the point of pretending otherwise?

He looked as if she'd slapped him; the hurt was visible

in his eyes. 'Well ... okay,' he said eventually. 'I suppose you're right. Thanks for the shag, though. Kind of you to give me that much.'

'Don't be like that,' she said wretchedly. 'I've had a lovely evening. I do really like you, and it's been great getting to know you again. But ...'

'But *what*? Why does there have to be a "but"?'

'You *know* why there has to be a "but". Because you're you, and I'm me. We want different things – we've got nothing in common.'

He was staring miserably at the ceiling and said nothing.

'Look, it's not you—' she began.

'Don't.' His tone was savage now. 'Just don't. If you start on the "It's not you, it's me" crap, I'm actually going to have to ... I dunno, go outside stark-bollock-naked and start bellowing obscenities into the night.'

She laughed. Nervously. 'Sorry,' she said. 'It *is* me, though. I'm rubbish at lovey-dovey stuff. Makes me want to run for the hills.'

He waved a hand. 'Go ahead. I won't stop you.'

God, she'd really wrecked this now. Or rather he'd wrecked it first, by saying that horrendous L-word out loud, and then she'd double-wrecked it by freaking out.

She felt sober and embarrassed and tired. And if he was saying 'Go ahead' in that offhand way, there was really no reason not to do precisely that.

She sat up, reached for her clothes and began dressing herself just as torrential rain started hammering against the skylight above them.

'What are you doing now?' He sounded completely exasperated by her. It was definitely time to vamoose.

'What does it look like? I'm going back to Clare's.'

'Oh, for heaven's sake, don't be such a drama queen. How are you planning to do that? We're both over the limit and you'll never get a cab around here.'

She glared at him. 'I'll walk.'

'In the dark? In the pouring *rain*? Jesus, Polly.' He smacked the heel of his hand against his head. 'Just stay. I'll sleep on the sofa, if you can't bear to share a bed with me.'

She put her head in her hands, wishing she could rewind the whole evening. 'Wait,' she said feebly, but he was already storming out of the room, bristling with irritation.

Well, that had gone absolutely brilliantly ... *not*, she thought, collapsing back onto the bed. Bloody Clare and her texts. Take a risk! Snog him! Yeah, she'd done that, and look what had happened — it had trashed everything, and he hated her.

Great. She punched the pillow and listened to the rain, feeling thoroughly confused. Why did other people have to be so *complicated*?

Chapter Twenty-Four

The following day was Clare's last shift at work for two whole weeks, and she already felt in a holiday mood as she turned on her computer and glanced through the morning's appointments. She'd worked so hard lately, day and night, that she was definitely ready for a break. Debbie's parents had a static caravan in Bournemouth, and they'd said Clare and the children could stay there, rent-free, for a week. Clare planned to pack up and set off on Monday, after a last blitz on her Langley's order. With a bit of luck, she'd be able to deliver the goods early then leave for a well-deserved holiday with a clear conscience. Whoopee! The weather was forecast to be beautiful, and Clare could envisage day after day of sunny beach fun. She'd even bought herself a new swimming costume, just in case she dared take her first dip in years. Or maybe she'd just paddle. Whatever. She was going to have a great time.

First things first, though: she had today to get through. And before she could even *think* about work, she had to uncover what exactly was happening with her sister. She'd been so deliciously excited for her the previous evening, as hour after hour had ticked by with no sign of Polly returning. And then this morning her bed hadn't been slept in, which could only mean one thing. Get in! Clare had known all along that Polly and Jay were perfect for each other. At last it seemed that they might just have realized the obvious truth too.

Oi, dirty stop-out, what time do you call this?? she texted. *Ring me when you get a mo. I need to know EVERYTHING!*

'Morning,' Roxie trilled just then, chucking her pea-green bag under the desk and pushing her shades up on top of her head. She was wearing a denim playsuit with a lilac broderie-anglaise vest underneath, and had dyed her hair a rather brassy shade of copper. It was fastened at the side by one pink polka-dot Hello Kitty hairslide and one diamanté flower clip. 'Sorry I'm a bit late,' she said. 'George just wouldn't take no for an answer and insisted on one last quickie over the kitchen table before he'd let me out.'

Clare giggled. 'George?'

'Clooney,' Roxie said airily, switching on her computer. 'You know what he's like.'

'Bit old for you, Rox, isn't he?' They both swung round to see Luke standing there, looking bemused.

Roxie tossed her hair. 'I share him with my mum,' she said, as if that made everything all right. 'I have him

Mondays, Wednesdays and Fridays, she takes the other days. He has Sunday off to catch up on his sleep in a luxury hotel.'

'Ahh,' Luke said solemnly. 'Of course.'

'Talking of luxury hotels,' Roxie went on, and then stopped, as if noticing Luke properly for the first time. 'Sorry, did you want something?'

'I can't find my notes on Mrs Ellington,' he said. 'She's coming in today and I know we had a letter from the hospital about her recently, but it doesn't seem to be on the system.'

'Ah,' Clare said guiltily, pointing to the tray in front of her, which was stuffed full of papers. 'Sorry. I've been meaning to scan those in, it's probably in there. Bear with me.' She began rifling through, still half-listening to Roxie's wittering.

'So, yeah, as I was saying, luxury hotels – well, Aunty Kate came round for tea yesterday and she said Langley's is nearly ready for the opening. She took us for a sneak preview of it: whoa, wait till you see it, Clare. The bedrooms are just stunning. And the pool – oh my GOD, it's to die for. There's a waterfall in it, and a jacuzzi area, and best of all—'

'Here we go,' Clare said, fishing the letter out and passing it to Luke. His fingers brushed against hers and she felt her skin tingle a hot pink. She looked like the proverbial village idiot, no doubt. Great.

'Thanks,' he said.

'Clare, are you even *listening*?' Roxie said peevishly, hands on hips. 'I'm trying to tell you something important here.'

'Yes,' she replied, trying not to sound impatient. 'I am listening, Rox, but it's not all that relevant to me, is it? I'm only going to be a supplier, not a guest, more's the pity.'

Roxie was pouting. 'Fine,' she said. 'Well, I'll give my complimentary vouchers to *Luke*, then, shall I? He might want to take his girlfriend there for a dirty weekend, if *you're* not interested, Clare.'

Clare swung round at the mention of complimentary vouchers, wishing she'd sounded more enthusiastic. 'I didn't mean—' she began, but Luke was already holding his hands up.

'Don't drag me into this,' he said. 'Besides, there is no girlfriend any more, so...' He shrugged and walked away with the letter.

Roxie raised an eyebrow at Clare, inclined her head sideways after his departing figure and licked her lips suggestively. 'In-ter-est-ing,' she purred.

'Shut up, Roxie,' Clare said, going crimson. 'Don't even go there.'

Roxie mimed zipping her lips, then pretended to turn a

key in them and toss it over her shoulder. Then she began demurely typing away like a model employee, although when Clare glanced over she appeared to be on the Lonely Planet website rather than actually doing any work.

Clare laughed despite herself. 'Thank you for the voucher,' she said. 'My sister might fancy a dirty weekend at the hotel with her new bloke, even if I've got nobody to go with.'

'No worries,' Roxie said lightly, peering at a map of central Peru on her screen.

As Clare took the sheaf of letters over to the scanner and began working her way through them, she felt unexpectedly downcast. For the first time since she and Steve had split up, she found herself wishing she *did* have someone to take to the hotel, someone to dress up for and hold hands with over the dinner table. Would there ever be such a person in her life again?

There was no word from Polly all morning. Strange. Maybe she was sleeping off the shagathon. Maybe she had already embarked on shagathon number two. Maybe she was in the process of moving her stuff into Jay's house right now and ... No. Calm down, Clare.

Her phone rang while she was sitting out in the sunny

courtyard garden on her tea-break and she pounced on it eagerly. Then paused. It was Steve. What did he want?

'Hello?' she said warily.

'Hi. Steve here.'

'Hi. Are you all right?'

'Yes. Just ringing to say I've taken a few days off next week, so I thought I'd treat the children to a bit of a holiday.'

She passed a hand through her hair, feeling tired by the conversation already. 'Ah. Well, the thing is, I'm already—'

'Thought we could get the Eurostar to Paris, see the sights. Maybe even have a day at Disney World.'

'But Steve—'

'So I'll pick them up on Thursday and—'

'Steve, wait!' she all but shouted. 'We're going to be away next week; I'm taking them to Bournemouth.'

There was a lengthy silence. 'You haven't cleared that with me, though,' he said.

The pompous arse. 'What do you mean, I haven't cleared it with you? I don't *need* to clear it with you. I'm their mother, and I'm taking them on holiday.'

'Yes, but it's my weekend to have them. And seeing as I've got a few days' leave and I'm entitled to half the week, then—'

Clare could feel her holiday collapsing before it had even

started. 'Can't you take them next week?' she said, trying not to lose her temper. 'I mean, don't get me wrong, they'd love to go, but—'

'No, I can't.'

'But I've already sorted this out. We're leaving on Monday.'

'Well, you should have checked with me first. You're disrespecting my rights as a father by—'

'Steve, stop, this is ridiculous.' She practically had to yell again to make herself heard over his ranting. 'Why are you behaving like this? Why can't we just talk about this reasonably?'

'Because you're not playing fair, that's why. And—'

'*I'm* not playing fair?' She couldn't believe the nerve of him. 'Look, I'm at work, I don't want to have a shouting match about this now. Let's talk later on and we'll get it all sorted out, okay?'

'God, Clare, you're so bloody sanctimonious, aren't you? What do you think the kids will say, when I tell them you wouldn't let me take them to Disney World? How will that make them feel?'

Her jaw dropped open. If it wasn't for the fact that Hilary Manning had just walked out with a steaming coffee and plonked herself down on the bench nearby, she would probably have started screaming at him. 'I don't want to talk to you when you're being like this,' she managed to say, anger boiling up within her like a volcano about to blow. 'We'll discuss it later.' And she hung up before he could say another word and sat there, red-faced and furious.

'Everything all right, Clare?' Hilary asked, peering over her glasses.

Clare gritted her teeth. 'Men,' she said, walking back towards the main building. 'Bloody men!'

She sat down at her desk again, then noticed the text from Polly which had just come through. *Total disaster, ruined everything, Jay hates me. MEN.* ☹

It was obviously catching.

When she arrived home with the children, Clare found Polly typing away on her laptop at the kitchen table with a murderous look on her face. 'Hi,' she said, opening the fridge and wondering what she was going to make for dinner. 'Are you okay?'

'Yep.' Polly's reply was so brusque that the word was like a bullet shot from her mouth. 'Just swotting up for my interview next week.'

'Oh yeah, you mentioned it in your text. Nice one.' She hesitated. 'And ... Jay?'

'Never happened.'

'Okay. Well, if you want to talk about it later—'

'Nope.'

'Right.' Ahh. It had gone *that* well. Clare gave up looking in the fridge, feeling uninspired by the contents. There was a pile of muddy beetroots on the worktop (a new offering from Agatha, no doubt), but they didn't inspire her either.

'Beans on toast all right, kids?' she bellowed, putting a pan on the hob without waiting for the answer. Beans on toast was always all right, luckily. Then she glanced at Polly again, who was still mutinously stabbing at the keyboard. 'So, what's this job then?'

At last something other than 'pissed off' appeared on Polly's face. A smile bloomed. 'Oh, it's really good, Clare,' she said. 'Similar to what I was doing before, but with more responsibility. Better pay even.' Her eyes had become starry. 'It would be perfect. Hence –' she gestured at the laptop. 'I want to give the most impressive interview ever known to mankind. I've got to convince them that I'm their dream employee.'

'That's great,' Clare said. 'Well done. You deserve this, all the effort you've put in.' The next moment she was struck with a pang at the thought of Polly vanishing back to London. She didn't want to lose her again, this smart, loyal sister she'd only just found. 'I'd miss you, though,' she added. 'We'd have to pledge not to lose touch again, see each other at weekends and phone more often . . .'

'Definitely.' Their eyes locked for a moment and Polly

smiled. '*Definitely*,' she repeated. 'Let me just save this lot, and I'll give you a hand with dinner. Even I can help with beans on toast.'

Later that evening Clare braced herself for another argument, took several deep, calming breaths, then picked up the phone to ring Steve. She'd only dialled two numbers, however, when she heard footsteps and then Alex's face appeared around the door.

'What's up?' she asked. She knew he found it difficult to get to sleep when it was still so light outside, but lately he'd got into the bad habit of reappearing after bedtime almost every night with some excuse or other.

'I can't sleep,' he said.

She held out her arms to him and he came and sat on her lap. 'You've hardly tried yet,' she said, holding him close. 'Go on, go back up to bed and just lie quietly with your eyes shut. And don't come down again, okay?'

He shuffled off her knee. 'What if my tooth falls out?'

'Well, you can come down, if your tooth falls out.'

'What if I'm sick?'

'You won't be sick, but if you are, just shout for me.'

'What if the window smashes?'

'It won't. Go up to bed now.'

'What if I have a bad dream?'

'Then think about something funny and go back to sleep.'

'What if—?'

'Alex, just go, okay? Everything will be fine. Go and have a lovely long dream about our holiday next week.'

He hovered in the doorway. 'But what if there's a burglar?'

Clare rolled her eyes. 'Alex . . .'

'But what if there is?'

'Fred will savage him, don't worry,' Polly put in, coming into the room just then and overhearing. 'And I'll whack him over the head with a rolling pin until he starts crying for his mummy.'

Alex glanced down at Fred, who was lolling on the carpet, looking about as ferocious as a banana. He grinned. 'Okay. Goodnight.' And off he went.

Clare and Polly both laughed. 'Comedy violence, that was all it took,' Clare said, as they heard him scampering back up the stairs. 'Boys!'

'He's so gorgeous,' Polly said, sitting down and opening a library book called *Answering Tough Interview Questions for Dummies*. 'They both are. Such lovely, funny, adorable children – I can't believe it took me so many years to realize, the stupid, blind dunce that I am.'

There was a lump in Clare's throat, and a sudden

fuzziness around the edges of her vision. She'd always felt a stab of pain inside whenever Polly, her own sister, had displayed a total lack of interest in Leila and Alex. Thank goodness those days were over. 'Thank you,' she said. 'They *are* gorgeous.' She eyed the phone with a little sigh. 'Which is why I've got to sort out their crap dad before I lose my bottle.'

'Do it,' Polly urged. 'And tell him if he doesn't start behaving soon, there's a rolling pin with his name on it. We could take turns whacking him with it.'

'Or shove it somewhere even more painful,' Clare muttered grimly. She steeled herself, then dialled. His mobile number went straight to voicemail, so she tried the landline. It rang and rang and she was just about to hang up when a breathless-sounding Denise picked up the call. 'Hello?'

'Hi, Denise, it's Clare. Is Steve there, please?'

Denise hesitated. 'Er ... he's in the shower,' she said. 'Um, listen, Clare,' she went on after a moment. Her words came out in a rush, as if she'd only just decided to say them. 'I know it's none of my business, but he's been really upset lately. I don't want to interfere, but I can't bear to see him so low. Is there any way you can change your mind about ... well, you know. What you've said.'

Clare was perplexed. 'About Disney World?' she ventured.

There was a pause. 'No,' Denise replied, sounding every

bit as confused. 'About not letting him see the children if we move.'

What? thought Clare, the words making no sense to her. Before she could reply. though, Denise was saying in a rather panicky voice, 'Oh! He's here, he's out of the bathroom. Babe, it's for you, sorry, I didn't realize you'd come downstairs.'

Clare was still so disarmed by what Denise had just said that she barely registered the puke-making 'Babe'. 'Hi,' she said when Steve came on the line. 'What's Denise talking about? Why does she seem to think I wouldn't let you see the children any more? And what's all this about you moving?'

She heard him groan and then the line became muffled, as if he was holding his hand over the receiver. 'Den, what have you *said*?' he snapped. 'I told you to keep out of this!'

'What's happening?' Polly hissed from across the room.

'Dunno,' Clare replied, stroking Fred distractedly with her foot. This was all a bit weird. 'Are you there, Steve? Steve?'

'Sorry,' he said, coming back on the line. 'Ahh ... I think there's been a bit of ... er ... a misunderstanding.'

'What sort of misunderstanding? You've lost me. Are you moving house?'

Again there came that groan: a low, weary noise of

dismay. 'I can't do this over the phone. Can I come over? We need to talk.'

She pulled an agonized face at Polly. 'O-okay,' she said. Then she remembered the kitchen was full of her business equipment and decided she couldn't be bothered to go through the palaver of clearing it out again, in order to keep up appearances. The strange mood he was in, it might be better to talk on neutral territory. 'Why don't I meet you somewhere in the middle?'

He sighed. It was starting to make her feel concerned, the way he was behaving. 'Steve, you're not ill, are you?' she asked when he didn't say anything.

She could hear Denise twittering on in the background – anxious, apologetic. 'What? In a minute,' Steve snapped and then, in a more conciliatory voice to Clare: 'Yes, okay. Let's meet in the Red Lion in Nettleside. I'll be there in an hour.'

She didn't even have time to say goodbye before he hung up.

Nettleside was about twenty minutes' drive to the east of Elderchurch, and the Red Lion was a cosy pub just off the main road, with a large beer garden and an enormous menu. They'd gone for dinner here many times as a couple because Steve had a particular hankering for the generous steak-andale pie with flaky pastry; he'd order it every time, and always ran his finger around the pie pot to get the last of the gravy. Funny the silly little things that stuck in your head, Clare thought to herself as she parked the car.

She'd fretted the whole way there, worried about what Steve was going to say. He'd been acting so oddly the last few weeks; there was obviously a big story waiting to tumble out. Thank God Denise had opened her gob and given her some hint of it on the phone, otherwise she'd have been kept in the dark until Steve had decided he was man enough to tell her himself. There was something about moving house, that was for sure. But why spin Denise a lie about her not letting him see their children? As if she would ever say that, for goodness' sake!

His BMW was already in the car park, she noticed, as she walked towards the pub entrance. He'd parked slightly askew — unheard of, for the man who prided himself on his immaculate driving skills. Just the sight of the angled wheels, the way the car had been left impatiently there, gave Clare cause for concern. It was so out of character.

Steve was at a table in the corner of the pub, nursing a glass of red wine with an air of self-absorbed gloom almost visible around him like a mushroom cloud. She bought herself a Diet Coke and took a deep breath. Next stop: into the lion's den.

'Evening,' she said coolly, sitting down opposite him.

Prince Charming that he was, he'd hogged the comfortable padded armchair for himself and had left her a sticky-looking bar stool, but she didn't comment on this, merely steepled her fingers together on the table and looked at him expectantly.

'Hi,' he said. God, he looked rough. *Was* he ill? There were huge bags under his eyes and he had a general air of unkemptness, what with the creases in his T-shirt and the stubble around his jaw. 'Look, I'm sorry about this,' he began, fidgeting in his seat. 'I've had a difficult time lately.'

Clare sipped her drink. 'What's happened?' she asked after a few moments, when it seemed as if the conversation had already ground to a halt.

'Well, work's been ... tricky,' he said, swilling his wine around in the glass, his focus seemingly on the whirlpool he was creating.

Come on, out with it, she thought. How long was he going to drag this out?

'The big boys in head office decided last year that we'd save a lot of money if we relocated,' he said at last, 'but that's gone down like a lead balloon with most of the workforce. Not least with me.'

Relocation. Ahh. Steve worked in the accounts department of a large insurance firm that was based in Reading, a short hop up the A33 from Basingstoke. 'Where do they want to move to?'

He sighed. 'Liverpool,' came his answer, pronounced so miserably it was as if he was reading out his own death sentence. 'Miles away from here, and the children.' He put his head in his hands. 'I don't know what to do.'

'What does Denise think?'

'Oh, she's over the moon. Half her family are in Stockport, so she'd love us to live up North. But . . .' He shrugged.

'But you don't want to,' Clare finished for him. She leaned back in her seat, eyes narrowing. 'So, what? You told her I wouldn't let you see the children if you went? Was that your plan?'

'I'm sorry,' he said. 'I didn't know what else to do.'

'Er, you could have told her the truth?' she said witheringly. 'That you didn't want to move hundreds of miles away from Leila and Alex?'

There was guilt all over his face. 'I tried that,' he muttered.

Not hard enough obviously, Clare thought. 'It doesn't make sense,' she said. 'Even if Denise had come round to your view, had said, "Okay, if Clare's playing hardball, then of course we can't move", what would you have done? Surely the point is: you're relocating? You *have* to move?'

'I don't have to,' he replied, plucking at the beer mat and tearing shreds off one corner. 'There's a voluntary redundancy package, so . . .'

She stared. 'What, so you'd rather lose your job than

move away?' She hadn't been expecting that. Steve loved his job; he loved the office banter and the sales targets, loved wearing a suit and tie every day, loved the self-importance that his laptop and smartphone gave him.

He shrugged again. 'It's a big decision,' he said. 'All I know is that I don't want to lose touch with my own children.'

Seeing him looking so grey-faced and beaten-down, Clare realized she was actually feeling sorry for him. For a whole split-second anyway, until she remembered the full extent of his weird behaviour. 'Hang on, though,' she said. 'What about all that shit from your lawyer – that bloody pompous letter? – not to mention you springing this Disney World trip on me, all that emotional blackmail about "What will the kids think of you, when I tell them you won't let them go"? What was all that for?'

He hung his head. 'I ... I let things get to me,' he said hoarsely.

Was that it? Was that the sum total of his explanation? She stared at him, dumbfounded. 'Yeah, I'll say you did,' she replied sarcastically. 'And you took it out on me. What was that: a little power trip to make yourself feel better?' She suddenly remembered Polly's words the night she'd moved into the cottage: *I never liked the way he tried to put you down. He seemed to hate it when you had any kind of success or triumph.* At the time Polly's comment had irritated her; who was her sister to criticize Steve, when she'd barely bothered getting to know him? Perhaps she'd had a point, though.

'I'm sorry,' he said. 'Leila said something about you getting this new business up and running and . . .' He wrung his hands. 'It just felt like a kick in the teeth: you doing so well, when everything was going so badly for me.'

What a wanker. 'Right,' she said coldly. 'So you thought you'd try and mess everything up for me, did you? Keep me in my place? How big of you, Steve. How generous.'

'It wasn't like that, I—'

'How was it then? Do explain, I'm all ears.' She felt like strangling him, great bungling idiot that he was.

'I'm sorry,' he said again. 'I've been a prat. I thought if it turned out we did go up North, I might be able to . . . take the children with me.'

Her heart seemed to stop beating. 'You *what?*' She was stunned that he could stoop so low. 'What were you trying to do: prove I was an unfit mother or something?'

Silence fell. Yes. Apparently that was exactly where he'd been going. She wrapped her arms around herself, wanting to wrap them around Leila and Alex protectively too. 'Over my dead body. There is no way on earth that is going to happen,' she said, loud and clear. She wished that looks really could kill, or at least maim someone very painfully. 'Do you understand?'

'Yes.'

'Don't you dare do anything like that again,' she said, rounding on him with genuine venom in her voice. 'I mean it. It's below the belt, Steve. It's just ... nasty.'

'I'm sorry,' he said for the third time, but with a meekness she'd never heard before. And then, to her horror, his bloodshot eyes filled with tears and he was scrubbing at them with his fists. 'Like I said, it's been tricky.'

'Mmm,' she said without a flicker of compassion. She got to her feet, wanting to get home to her cottage, her warm sleeping children, her sister and a glass of something stronger than Diet-frigging-Coke. 'Well, let me know what you decide to do,' she said frostily. 'And, Steve, for crying out loud, I'd never deny you access to the children if you move,' she added. 'We'd work something out, okay? Just don't try to shit on me in the process. Ever again.'

She walked out of the pub before he could say another word to her. This holiday could not come soon enough, that was for sure.

The encounter with Steve might have been a bruising one, but equally it seemed to fill Clare with a new kind of strength. She couldn't trust him any more, that much was obvious, but rather than getting her down, the realization gave her a feeling of autonomy and control. It was up to her to ensure that she and the children had happy lives; and, boy, was she going to do her best to make that happen.

With this in mind she worked like a Trojan for the rest of the week and was able to deliver her Langley's order by Saturday afternoon, with the most glorious feeling of accomplishment. Once the last box of soaps had been taken from her boot and signed for, she felt lighter than air and drove home, singing at the top of her voice, stopping only to splash out on a celebratory bottle of Prosecco for her and Polly to drink that night. She'd done it! *They'd* done it rather, the wonderful Team Clare of friends and family.

I am a businesswoman, she'd thought deliriously as she drove, and she couldn't stop smiling. *I fulfilled my contract. I've just delivered some fantastic hand-made products to a brilliant, upmarket hotel chain.* What was more, she knew none of this would have happened if she'd still been married to Steve.

Later that evening, flushed with her success and slightly squiffy on Prosecco, she decided that, as a liberated businesswoman of the twenty-first century who'd definitely washed her hands of her ex-husband, there was something else she needed to do. Hadn't she urged Polly just the other week to take a chance in love again? Well, it was high time she followed her own advice.

'Luke? Hi, it's Clare,' she said when he picked up the phone. 'Listen, I've been thinking. When I get back from holiday, I was wondering if you fancied going out for a drink one night?'

She held her breath. Polly, who was loitering supportively, held hers too.

'You would?' Clare beamed in delight, and tried not to laugh as Polly started bouncing up and down like a demented kangaroo in the background. 'Cool. So, when would suit you?'

Chapter Twenty-Five

With a huge hullabaloo and hoo-hah, Clare set off on holiday with Leila, Alex and Fred the following Monday and the house was plunged into silence.

Polly spent the next few days rather pleasantly. Once her shift at the pub was over, she revised her interview notes in the garden, met her parents for lunch one day, took herself off for long walks in the meadows and woods, and stretched out on the lumpy old sofa watching some excellent trashy television in the evenings. (The first thing she was going to buy for her sister, when she had a decent pay packet again, was a proper sofa that didn't have springs poking out everywhere.) Secretly she was hoping she'd bump into Jay during her long walks – indeed, she found that she was accidentally-on-purpose steering her route so that it went quite near his house – but he must have been at work or busy elsewhere each time, because she didn't glimpse so much as a hair on his head. The cold war between them showed no sign of thawing any time soon.

Better news came on Wednesday when the contracts for the sale of her flat dropped through the letterbox. She signed her name with a flourish and tried not to feel too sad when she posted them straight back to Vince. There. The last tie to her old life severed. Now it was time to throw herself into the new.

By Thursday Polly felt fully prepared to steam into the interview on full dazzle mode. Excitement beat through her as she caught the train to London, dressed for business in her smartest summer suit and shiniest shoes. She had her answers pat, knew the company history backwards and was fully prepared for the toughest of questions. If it went well – and it *would* go well, or her name wasn't Polly Anne Johnson – then she'd already promised herself that she'd head straight to the Jo Malone shop near Bond Street and splash out on a new bottle of Pomegranate Noir. And hell, she might just treat herself to a late lunch at Carluccio's too, with a celebratory glass of vino. Bring it on, she thought happily, as the train rattled over Waterloo Bridge and delivered her into the cavern of the station.

Two hours later she walked out of the boardroom feeling as if she was floating on air. It had been one hell of a grilling from a panel of six interviewers, but she'd barely faltered for a second. She'd kept her composure throughout, been able to reel off reams of data when they'd asked technical questions, and had even made them laugh a few times. The only unexpected thing had been her answer to their question about her personal interests. In the past, she'd often invented a list of imaginary hobbies that sounded suitably intellectual to answer this particular enquiry – she'd talked about how much she loved the theatre, for instance (even though she'd only been once, in the entire time she'd lived in London, to see *Mamma Mia* for an office night out) and opera (never been), and she'd always faked an interest in current affairs, even though she usually only read the business and financial pages in the newspapers. Today she'd been about to blurt out the usual tripe, but found herself coming out with something completely different instead.

'I'm part of a close-knit family, so I love spending time with them,' she'd said. 'I've got the coolest niece and nephew, who've taught me roller-skating – really bad roller-skating, admittedly' (this had made the panel smile), 'trampolining, and the brilliance of Harry Potter. I love going for long walks in the countryside with my parents, and putting the world to rights. Oh, and I've been involved with my sister's new business venture too – it's a real family affair!'

'Lovely,' said the matriarch of the panel, whose eyes twinkled at Polly.

It was the only time Polly had felt remotely flummoxed.

She didn't usually appeal to the mumsy types. 'I thought about giving you a much more highbrow answer,' she confessed, 'telling you about all the cultural hobbies and pursuits I have as well, but being made redundant has reminded me how important family is. Besides, I'm a firm believer that honesty tends to be the best policy.'

They'd loved that. Appreciation had practically shimmered visibly in the air above their heads. 'A real pleasure to meet you,' the matriarch had said, shaking hands with her at the end. 'We'll be in touch with the agency very soon – hopefully by the end of today.'

She'd not said anything more specific than that, but Polly could tell (she could just *tell*) that the woman had liked her. But had it been enough to swing her the job, or was there an even better candidate on the shortlist?

Sod it, she was going to Jo Malone anyway. *And* she was treating herself to that slap-up lunch. Sometimes you had to be optimistic about these things and take a chance, right?

It was when she was walking out of the office building onto Liverpool Street that she almost collided with two smartly dressed women in pencil skirts and high heels, both clutching laptop bags. 'Polly? Is that you?' said one, raising a cigarette to her mouth and taking two quick puffs in surprise. Oh hell. It was the blonde Sophie; the mean one who'd been so gloating about Polly's downfall, who'd dropped her like the proverbial lump of rock once she'd lost her job. Damn, Polly had forgotten she worked for the Walkley Group as well. 'Fancy seeing *you* here!'

Her voice wasn't friendly, but her eyebrow was arched and her eyes gleamed; clearly she was dying to know the gossip.

'Sabrina!' Polly said, deliberately getting her name wrong. 'What a lovely surprise.'

'It's Sophie,' she snapped coldly. She eyed Polly with renewed curiosity, taking in the sun-kissed natural highlights in her hair, the tan and the freckles all over her nose, which even the last of her Clinique couldn't quite hide. 'You look different. Have you had some work done?'

Polly laughed. 'I *am* different,' she said. 'Thank God. See you around.' And she smiled pleasantly before walking away, head high. But the exchange stayed with her, needling her under the skin. Having survived the traumas of the recent months and made amends with her family, she'd been feeling stronger than ever, full of confidence again. So how come the possibility of having to work in close proximity to Sophie was making her break out in a sweat all of a sudden?

She definitely needed a drink now, she decided. A long cold drink, and a long hard think . . .

*

Back at the cottage, Polly saw that the postman had delivered a red envelope for her. Recognizing Clare's loopy scrawl on the front, she opened it while kicking her shoes off with relief. She could hardly believe she'd worn heels like that, day in, day out, for so many years. Blisters seemed to be popping out all over her feet in protest already.

The envelope contained a card with GOOD LUCK! printed in lurid colours on the front. Inside were messages from Clare, Leila and Alex.

Dear Polly, lots of luck on Thursday. You deserve this more than anyone, and they'd be lucky to have you! Love, Clare

Dear Aunty Polly, you are THE BEST, good luck, love from Leila xxx

Dear Aunty Polly, pleeease get the job so I can have my bedroom back, love Alex. PS Only joking.

Someone – Leila, she guessed – had drawn a doggy pawprint and written *WOOF LUCK from Fred* underneath. She smiled and held the card to her chest for a moment, her mind a tangle of emotions. And then the phone rang.

*

'Hi, Mum. Have you got a minute?'

Karen beamed at the sight of her daughter on the doorstep, and pushed Sissy, who was yapping shrilly, back into the house. 'Of course! Come on in. I've just taken some ginger muffins out of the oven; you can test one for me.'

'Thanks,' Polly said, stepping carefully over the dog, who was still in a frenzy of barking. Ever since the phone call she'd been desperate to talk to someone about what she should do. Of all the times for Clare to be away!

'Hello, love,' Graham said. He was just coming in from the garden as they entered the warm gingery-scented kitchen, a lumpy-looking carrier bag swinging from one hand. 'I've been picking tomatoes; I was going to drop some off for you and Clare later on, and check how those strawberries of hers are doing. Have you remembered to water them? It's been so dry lately.'

'Thanks, Dad,' Polly said, smiling at him. 'Yes, I've watered the strawberries. And the raspberries. And the blackcurrants.'

'They've been lucky with the weather so far, haven't they?' Karen commented, filling the kettle at the sink. 'Clare and the kids, I mean. Must be gorgeous on the beach this week.'

'She sent me a text yesterday saying they were having a great time,' Polly replied, reaching down three mugs from the cupboard without being asked. 'Oh, and get this. She even said she'd been in the sea for her first swim in years!'

Karen swung round, her eyes suddenly wet. 'Really? Oh,

that *is* good news,' she breathed. She and Polly exchanged a look that spoke volumes. Karen obviously knew what a significant event this was too.

Polly took a deep breath. 'Listen, I've got a bit of a confession to make,' she said baldly. 'I haven't been completely honest with you.'

'Here we go. The secret family in London: those three love-children you've kept hidden in a swanky boarding school,' her dad joked, coming to the sink and elbowing his wife aside. 'Budge over while I wash my hands, will you.'

'No, Dad, it's—'

'Ah, then it's those five ex-husbands you've kept quiet all these years . . .'

'No, I—'

'Let the girl speak, for heaven's sake, Graham!' Karen said, elbowing him back impatiently. She flicked at him with a tea towel, then turned to face Polly. 'Go on, love. I'm listening.'

'When I said I'd like to come to Elderchurch for my sabbatical,' Polly began haltingly. 'It wasn't true. I'd actually been made redundant.'

Her parents exchanged a look, but neither made any comment.

'I was too proud to admit it to you, but as well as losing my job, I lost all my money too, and I had to sell my flat. That was why I needed a place to stay.' She swallowed, staring down at the floor. She didn't want to see the disappointment in their eyes, the look that said *You've let us down.* 'I shouldn't have lied, and I'm sorry. But I couldn't bear for you to pity me.'

'Oh, Polly,' her mum clucked. She came over and hugged her. 'Did you really think we hadn't guessed?'

Polly stiffened in the warmth of her mum's embrace. 'You ... knew?'

Her mum squeezed her. 'Of course we knew. You've never chosen to stay here voluntarily before – we knew you must be in some kind of trouble. And then Stuart let slip something about you working at the pub, and ...'

'Oh God.' Polly hid her face in her mum's shoulder as the kettle began roaring its crescendo. Bloody Stuart and his big gob!

'But you were always so defensive, we knew you didn't want us to find out.' Her mum let go of her and looked her full in the face. 'Polly ... You're our daughter. Our clever, talented, beautiful daughter. We're always going to be proud of you, whatever you do. But you could have told us you'd lost your job. We wouldn't have judged you or thought any less of you. We only want you to be happy.'

Her dad cleared his throat. 'She's right, for once,' he said gruffly. 'And being made redundant is nothing to be ashamed of. It happened to Mike Jacks from the golf club last month. Couldn't meet a nicer bloke. Best putter I've ever known.'

'Sit down, let me make the tea,' her mum said, patting Polly's shoulder. 'And tell us all about it, if you want.'

'Well, that's the thing,' Polly said, sitting at the table. 'I've just been offered a new job.'

Her mum gave a squeal and threw her hands up in the air. 'You have? Oh, well done! Doing what?'

'Don't tell us – Stuart's made you bar manager,' her dad teased, dumping the tomatoes in a colander and turning the tap on again.

'No,' she said, pulling a face at him. 'It's back in London, similar to my job before. But better.'

'Oh, that's brilliant,' her mum said, pouring the tea and putting a warm, sticky-looking ginger muffin in front of Polly. 'Well done, you. So, when does it start?'

'September,' Polly replied. 'But...' She fidgeted, feeling uncomfortable now that they'd reached the crux of the matter. 'Well, I don't know if I'm going to say yes, to be honest. I don't know if I want to go back.'

Her parents both stared at her in surprise. 'You don't want to?' her dad repeated, as if he'd misheard.

Polly took a bite of the ginger muffin. It helped. 'I thought I did,' she said through the delicious spicy mouthful, 'but now I'm not so sure.'

'Is it the job you're not keen on, or the thought of moving back to London?' her mum asked. 'Because plenty of people commute from Amberley, you know. And there's a faster train from Basingstoke.'

'Or you could always get a job around here,' her dad added. 'I know it's not as whizzy as London, but there are jobs going for brainboxes everywhere, if you wanted to move into accounting or ... I dunno ... computing.'

Polly was still coming to terms with the fact that they'd known her secret for so long, yet hadn't held it against her. 'The job in London does sound great,' she said. 'It's more that being here for the summer has made me realize I wasn't very happy, the way I was living before.' She chewed thoughtfully, trying to untangle her thoughts into coherent sentences. 'I love it here. I know I was a bit of a pain in the neck at first, but ...'

'No. Never!' her dad joked.

'But everyone's so friendly. I've really enjoyed spending so much time with you two, and Clare and the kids. And I love the countryside too.' She sighed. 'My old job was such long hours, it took over my whole life. I don't want to live like that again. Oh, I don't know what I want!'

Her mum took her hand. 'You'll figure it out,' she said. 'I'd sleep on it. You've waited all these months to get a new job. You can wait a few more hours before you decide anything. And whatever you choose to do, we're right behind you, all the way.'

The answerphone light was flashing when Polly returned to Clare's and she listened to the message. 'Hi, this is Kate Hendricks for Clare Berry. Just to say, Clare, that we are all delighted with the products you've supplied us, and would love to arrange another meeting to discuss a future contract together. Thanks very much.'

Polly smiled from ear to ear. Despite her ambiguity about her own job prospects, there was no doubt at all that this was fabulous news for her sister. She could just imagine Clare's squeal of joy when she heard the news. 'Well done, Clare,' she said into the quiet kitchen. 'Good for you.' She tried to call her, but the phone went straight to voicemail. Clare had warned her that the caravan site had dreadful reception, so Polly sent a text instead, hoping her sister would get the news sooner rather than later.

She mooched around the house for the rest of the afternoon. She watered everything and pulled out a few weeds in the vegetable plot (at least she hoped they were weeds). She fed Marjorie and Babs and locked them in for the evening. She poked a fork around a plate of couscous and peppered mackerel salad, before giving up and throwing it into the compost. She was too confused even to eat. Oh, Clare! She was desperate to speak to her now. Being apart had only made her realize just how close they'd become in recent weeks; Clare was now Polly's go-to person, her confidante, her advice-giver, the person who'd always listen to her.

What was she going to do about this job? She couldn't possibly decide something like this on her own!

Right, Polly, pros and cons, she said firmly. Let's get down to the nitty-gritty.

If she said yes and went back to London, she'd be mentally challenged again, she'd spend her day making interesting, important decisions, motivating and managing a team of staff, advising clients on million-pound deals. She'd be getting paid lots of money for it too, and could swing back into a more luxurious lifestyle: her own home again, new clothes and shoes when she wanted them. What was more, she wouldn't have to snap on a pair of Marigolds and scrub pub toilets for the rest of her life, hopefully. Those elements all sounded pretty bloody great.

It was the accompanying lifestyle she wasn't so keen on, though. The return to the concrete jungle, living in an office where a summer's breeze was replaced by the drone of the air-con unit. It was the macho bullshit, the old boys' network, the bitching and back-stabbing, the shallowness of the social gatherings, and an empty flat waiting for her at the end of the day, however luxurious it might be. It would also mean she'd probably never see Jay again.

She perched on the swing in the back garden and pushed herself gently off the ground, pointing her toes to send her higher. But she'd waited so long for a job like this. Surely she couldn't turn it down?

Leaning back, she let her head fall behind her so that the world was upside down. The sky whirled dizzily above her and the ground rushed to meet her face. What was she going to do?

'Oh! It's *you* on the swing, Polly' came a voice. 'I heard it creaking and thought the children were back.' It was Agatha, waving over the fence, her mismatched gardening gloves on as usual. 'Everything all right, dear?'

Polly sat up again, head rushing as the world swung back to its usual position. 'I'm fine,' she said. 'Just trying to decide on something.'

Agatha pursed her lips. 'If it's money, sex or gin, just say yes,' she advised breezily. 'Everything else, just say no. Best of luck!'

Polly spluttered with laughter. Life lessons from Agatha — what next? 'Wait!' she called, as Agatha wandered away, secateurs in hand, humming to herself. 'Agatha, what if it's love?'

Agatha stopped still and turned, beaming, to face Polly once more. 'Love? Oh, well, love wins hands down in any competition,' she said, blue eyes twinkling amidst the deep wrinkles. 'You say yes, of course. Yes to love!'

Polly smiled. 'Thanks,' she replied. 'Thanks a lot. That's very enlightening.' She scuffed her feet along the ground to slow the swing and jumped off with a little wave.

'I'm going to have to talk to him, aren't I?' she muttered to herself, walking back towards the house.

'Oh yes,' replied Agatha, overhearing. 'You've got to *talk* to him, dear, absolutely. *Then* you can get to the sex. And the gin!'

Polly saluted her and went inside. Damn. She really was going to have to talk to him now, if only to get Agatha off her back.

She left the house before she could change her mind, and set off down the lane.

Chapter Twenty-Six

'Hi.'

'Hi.'

Well, he was at home, at least, even if she wasn't quite sure whether he was going to let her into the damn house. Even his wretched dog seemed to be staring balefully at her, as if weighing up whether or not to start savaging her ankles. After a long, heart-bumping moment he pulled the door wide. 'Come in.'

She could hear the drone of sporting commentary from the television as she followed him into the living-room area; she'd interrupted him watching the cricket. Hopefully he wouldn't hold that against her, she thought, as he turned it off with the remote control. Then there was silence. A clock ticked somewhere, measuring the seconds it took her to speak.

Tick, tick, tick. She didn't know where to begin.

'Have a seat,' he said politely, waving a hand at the sofa.

He perched on the leather cube and looked at her expectantly. Oh God, it was as if they were strangers, as if nothing had ever happened between them.

Tick, tick, tick.

'I'm sorry,' she blurted out at last. 'I'm really sorry. I was completely over the top the other night; I just panicked and handled it all wrong. I'm an idiot.'

'No, you're not,' he said, but there was no real conviction in his voice.

'I am,' she argued. 'I've had my head stuffed up my own arse for years; it's taken me this long to realize.'

He smiled at that. A small, quick smile that flickered on his mouth and then was gone again.

She crossed her legs, feeling miles away from him on the sofa. 'I got offered a new job today,' she said.

His face changed for a second, before he regained his composure. 'Back in London?'

'Yes.'

'Congratulations,' he said dispassionately. 'Just what you wanted.'

She shook her head. 'Turns out it isn't what I wanted, after all.'

Tick, tick, tick. He was staring at her as if he didn't recognize her. 'What do you mean?'

'I mean, I'm going to turn it down.' Boom. She'd said it.

She hadn't even been sure of the decision until that very second. But as soon as the words were out of her mouth she felt a massive relief. Yes. It was the right thing to do.

'You what? Turn it *down*? Why?'

'Because . . .' A million different reasons rose to the tip of her tongue. Because she loved popping round to see her parents for a cup of tea and a ginger muffin. Because she hadn't laughed so much for years as when she'd messed about with the kids. Because she loved hearing the birds and seeing flowers bloom, and spending so much time with her sister. And because . . . 'Because I want to try again with you,' she said simply.

Well, he hadn't been expecting *that*, judging by the way his jaw dropped. 'That doesn't mean you have to turn down a new job,' he said slowly.

Tick, tick, tick. They looked at one another, and it was as if time had been suspended.

Then, 'I want to try again with you too,' he said, his dark eyes on her. 'I really do. I'm so glad you came round tonight.'

Hope burst within her; it felt like a reward for bravery. 'You do? You are?'

He grinned. 'I do. I am.'

Polly laughed. And then she was standing up and rushing towards him, and he was doing the same. They met in the middle and wrapped their arms around each other. She could feel his heart beating through his shirt, could hear the sound of his breath close to her ear.

'I'm sorry,' she whispered again and squeezed him as hard as she could.

'Forgiven,' he murmured, stroking her hair and squeezing back for a long, wonderful moment. Then he pulled away from the embrace. 'I'm opening a bottle of wine,' he said, 'to celebrate you having finally removed your head from that fabulous arse of yours.'

'I'll drink to that.' She felt high and giggly all of a sudden. 'The view's much better this way.'

'And then,' he said, taking her hand and leading her towards the kitchen, 'I want you to tell me all about this new job and why the hell you're going to turn it down. And then . . .' He looked back over his shoulder and winked. Pure cheese, but she loved it. 'Well, after that, we can find something else to do.'

She blushed. 'That sounds like a plan to me.'

Somehow or other, though, the agenda didn't quite go that way. No sooner were they in the kitchen than they started kissing. Tentatively at first, with the gentleness of uncertainty, but then becoming faster and more fervent, their fingers fumbling with buttons and zips, clothes being taken off and blindly discarded around their feet.

Just as Polly was thinking they were about to do it there and then on the kitchen table – and why the hell not, it was as good a place as any – he led her into the bedroom and they fell onto his bed in a tangle of limbs and hot, juddering breaths. It was more frantic than last time, more urgent and passionate, but still felt like love-making.

Love-making. Such a beautiful, romantic phrase, Polly thought dazedly, as the words came into her head. She'd run a mile last time he'd dared mention 'love', but she'd done a lot of thinking since then. The idea of love and intimacy didn't terrify her quite so much any more. In fact, it made her feel ... happy.

Afterwards the world seemed to tilt back around again and fall perfectly into focus, as it had done on the swing. Polly knew for sure that she'd made the right decision.

'As I was saying, before I was so rudely interrupted,' he began, and they both burst into giggles.

She lay curled against his chest, feeling absurdly content. 'You can interrupt me rudely any time,' she growled, tracing a finger across his skin. 'By the way, do you think you can teach that dog of yours to bring the wine in here, please? I can't be bothered to move from this bed ever again.'

'I'll get the wine,' he said, gently extricating himself from her, 'and then you can tell me about this job. I still don't understand why you're going to turn it down, unless it involves a placement in Outer Mongolia or somewhere.'

She watched his gorgeous bare bottom thoughtfully as he left the room. Right now, London might as well be Outer Mongolia, for all the inclination she had to live there again.

He came back and poured the wine, and then she explained exactly why she was going to say no to the job.

He frowned. 'Nope. Still don't get it,' he said, passing her a glass of smoky-smelling Merlot. 'I'm not some caveman bloke who thinks a relationship has to mean that you're here cooking dinner and fetching my pipe and slippers every evening. Why don't you take the job and we can see each other at weekends?'

'It wouldn't work like that,' she said, wrinkling her nose. 'That kind of job, it takes over your whole life. I should know. I've only just recovered from the last one. We'd hardly see each other.'

'It seems so extreme, though,' he countered. 'What about commuting? Or asking if they'd consider taking you on part-time, or as a job-share?'

She hooted with laughter. 'No. It *is* extreme, that's part of the deal. You have to sell your soul to these people. I just don't want to do that again.'

They were propped up cosily against the pillows and there was silence for a few moments.

'So what *are* you going to do?' he said eventually. 'Other than cook my dinner and fetch my pipe and slippers every evening. JOKE!' he added, as she punched him on the arm.

'What am I going to do? Well, that's the big question,' she said. 'I really don't know. I need to find somewhere to live before Clare boots me out, though. And . . .'

'Why don't you move in here? With me.'

She nearly choked on her wine.

'I mean it,' he said. 'Why not? There's plenty of room for two.'

She gulped. This was all moving a bit fast. 'I . . . Thanks,' she said. 'One thing at a time though, eh. I was thinking of asking Stu and Erica if I can rent a room above the pub for the time being.'

He was beaming at her. 'You're serious, aren't you? About staying in Elderchurch, I mean.'

She nodded. 'Deadly serious.' And, with a huge wave of happiness, she realized that yes, this was what she wanted. A life of her own, here in the village. To be here for Alex's birthday in the autumn, to watch the trees turn golden brown, to take the children sledging down Whistledown if it snowed, to be there for every Sunday dinner at her mum's. To be at peace with her memories of Michael, instead of trying to escape from them. And for long, happy days and nights with Jay Holmes forever after. Yes, that really was what she wanted.

He put his arms around her and showered kisses on her head, neck, shoulder. 'Brilliant,' he said. 'This is the best news I've had all year.'

She lifted her head to kiss him right back. Turning down a heavyweight job in London ... Sophie and the like would think she was crazy. Well, maybe she was – maybe she'd live to regret this decision if she still hadn't found a good way to earn some money by Christmas. But right now, at this precise moment, she had never felt saner or more contented.

The future was rosy.

Epilogue

'Is that the lot?' Graham was waiting by the van, his hand on the back door.

Polly nodded. 'That's the lot,' she said.

It was a Saturday, six weeks later, and summer had definitely given way to autumn. The trees on Whistledown were seeing the first tinges of rust-gold edging their leaves, the flowers in the Remembrance Garden were brown and drooping, and all over the country women were digging out pairs of tights they hadn't worn for months and deciding that yes, they definitely needed a new pair of boots and, what the hell, a new coat too. As for Polly, she was on the move again.

Her dad slammed the van doors shut. 'I guess we'd better go,' he said.

She hadn't been there long, but truth be told, Polly was a tiny bit sad to be leaving the bedroom she'd been renting above the King's Arms. It had become a regular love-nest, with her and Jay shacked up there together so many nights.

It was where she'd properly fallen in love with him again, curled up with him in the double bed, talking and laughing long into the night. She gazed up at the upstairs window where she'd stayed, and smiled. This was a special place; one she'd never forget.

'Let's do it,' she said, climbing into the van.

Was it really only six months since she'd left London? It seemed so much longer. Already Elderchurch felt like the home she'd always wanted, the safest place in the world – somewhere she could be herself, and be loved for it. Thank goodness she'd turned down the job with the Walkley Group when she had, even though doing so had made her feel sick with nerves. She'd gritted her teeth and asked Stuart and Erica if she could work some extra hours at the pub instead. Oh, and about the room that was going begging upstairs: would it be possible to rent it?

Clare and her parents clearly thought she'd suffered some kind of breakdown – turning down a perfectly good job and moving her belongings into a poky, beer-smelling room above a pub on the main road. What the hell was she playing at? And while Jay had understood her rationale for not taking the job offer, he didn't get why she wouldn't move in with him, when his house was a million times nicer. But Polly had stuck to her guns and refused to let anyone talk her down. She didn't want to clip the wings of their fledgling relationship before it had even lifted off the ground. She wanted to take things slower this time; to get it right. And she had to take this leap of faith that an even better job would come along – a job that suited the life she wanted to lead now. No more compromises.

Just one week later an even better job *had* come along. 'I'm afraid it's not *exactly* what you were looking for,' the recruitment consultant had said apologetically when she'd phoned with details of the position. 'I know you wanted to be back in London, whereas this is largely home-based, with perhaps two days' travel a week, but I thought I'd flag it up in case you were interested.'

Polly, who'd been collecting dirty glasses in the pub when the call came, promptly sat down at one of the tables, her heart pounding. 'Tell me more,' she said.

This time the job sounded completely different from what she'd done before. Although based within the financial industry, it would be as an outsider, working for a financial watchdog that monitored and regulated the banking world. She'd be poacher-turned-gamekeeper effectively, checking up on all her old colleagues and contacts, advising on best practice and having a good snoop through their paperwork to make sure everything was above board. She'd almost laughed in glee as the consultant filled her in. Let's face it, she knew where a *lot* of bodies were buried . . .

Once again she'd stormed the interview process and had been offered the job. She'd been there three weeks now and was thoroughly enjoying herself. The work was fascinating and called on all her years of expertise and investigative skills, without swallowing up her entire life. She loved having her London 'fix' every week, while still spending most of the time home in Elderchurch. Best of all was the fact that she'd be auditing Waterman's in the next few months. She could hardly wait to see their faces when she walked in there to investigate them. Revenge was going to taste so damn sweet . . .

One thing was for sure, though. She was never going to let herself get in a financial mess again. Her investments were finally on the up, and she planned to tend them carefully from now on, as well as building up a buffer of savings for the future. It was all very well taking risks with one's heart, but when it came to money matters, Polly had vowed to become a new, improved model of prudence. She'd certainly learned from her past mistakes on that score.

Graham started the van's engine and set off down the high street. Polly waved as she spotted Debbie hurrying towards the post office – probably to send her hundredth care-parcel to Lydia, who'd just started at Bristol University. According to Clare, Debbie had got herself a place at college too. Spurred on by the success of the labels she'd designed for Berry Botanicals, she'd started a graphic-design course at Amberley Tech and was having a whale of a time.

Graham snorted as they glimpsed someone else running

along the pavement, beaming and waving. 'What the hell is that batty old woman doing now?' he said fondly, pulling over to the kerb.

Polly wound down her window. 'Are you okay?'

'Is there room for me? I've made you a cake.' Karen had a Family Circle tin swinging in a carrier bag, and Polly could see a potted fern as well. Bless her.

'Of course there's room,' she said, unclipping her seatbelt and shuffling along the double passenger seat. 'You didn't have to bake a cake, Mum. You're still going to see me all the time.'

'I know but ... Well, you know.'

Polly squeezed her mum's arm companionably once she'd clambered in. Yes, she did know. She knew that she had the loveliest, kindest parents in the world, and was truly grateful that she'd finally realized as much.

'Don't start getting muck from that plant in the van, will you,' Graham admonished. 'I borrowed this from Mike; he's not going to be happy with me if I bring it back in a state.'

'Oh, hush, will you,' Karen said, pulling a face at Polly. 'Just drive us there, for heaven's sake.'

Graham gave a long-suffering sigh, then set off again. 'I don't know why you couldn't just *walk* there, Karen, it's not exactly *far*,' he muttered.

Polly smiled to herself. Funny he should use those words. It wasn't far to Jay's house, no, but the journey felt pretty momentous to her right now. She couldn't quite believe she was moving in with him, after all these years of being apart. And yes, okay, maybe this wasn't taking things quite as slowly as she'd initially anticipated, but hey, she couldn't resist any longer. Jay was a hard man to refuse. Besides, whenever she thought about the dark winter months ahead, and Christmas to celebrate at the end of the year, she was certain there was nowhere else she would rather be every night.

And, as Clare had said, sometimes you just had to take a chance.

Meanwhile, on the other side of the village, Clare was trying to hurry Leila and Alex into getting ready, but couldn't help the occasional admiring glance into her hall mirror as she waited for them. She'd had her hair cut the week before, had actually treated herself to a proper salon do after years of snipping haphazard trims herself, and the soft feathery layers fell about her face, framing it prettily. Alison, the hairdresser, had put some colour in too – a cheerful coppery shade that somehow brought out the flecks of green in Clare's eyes. Damn it, it felt good to look after herself for a change. And hadn't she bloody well earned it.

It had been fantastic, signing a new twelve-month contract with Langley's back in the summer. It had been even more fantastic getting the cheque for the first delivery. Once she'd paid Debbie and Lydia for the hours of work they'd put in, she'd taken her parents and friends out for a slap-up curry at the Bombay Brasserie in Amberley as a thank-you. It had been the proudest moment of her life being able to treat all the people she loved with her earnings. Her – a businesswoman. She'd never held her head quite so high before.

Polly had refused to take any money from her. 'Let's call it quits, for you putting up with me in your home for so long,' she'd said, handing back the cheque. 'You have it, Clare. Put it towards that holiday you were talking about.'

'No way,' Clare had argued, trying to press the cheque into her sister's hand again. 'You worked flat out for me all those evenings. Please, I want you to take it.'

After much toing and froing Polly *had* taken the cheque, but had got her own back by ordering her sister the most stupendously comfortable sofa that Clare, Leila and Alex had ever had the joy of resting their bottoms on. As it turned out, Clare still had enough money to book them a week's holiday in Fuerteventura this coming half-term. Leila and Alex were already wild with excitement.

Alex trailed through into the hall, shoes still off, eyes glued to the new Nintendo DS she'd bought him for his birthday.

'Alex, come on, you should be ready by now,' Clare

scolded. 'Polly will be wondering what's happened to us. Leila, where are you? Hurry up!'

She glanced back into the mirror again, peering at her skin this time. It definitely looked fresher and pinker these days, now that she was sleeping so much better. And her face actually looked a tiny bit slimmer too. Must be all the swimming she'd been doing lately with the new club she'd joined at the leisure centre. It was hardly Junior Dolphins – Middle-Aged Whales was more apt – but she'd rediscovered the breathless joy of diving, the exhilaration of butterfly, and the endorphin rush she always got when she hauled herself, dripping, from the pool at the end of a hard session. What was more, she knew Michael would not have begrudged her any of it. He'd have been pleased for her.

'Done!' Leila said, coming through with a gaudy card in her hand. 'Do you think she'll like it?'

The card had a picture of a small rodent on the front cover. 'Is that a guinea pig?' Clare guessed.

'No! A hamster, of course,' Leila said, stuffing her feet into her favourite sparkly baseball boots.

'And you've made Aunty Polly a Moving House card with a hamster on because . . . ?'

Leila grinned. 'She'll know. Just a reminder about something. Are we going then?'

'We are,' Clare said, snatching the DS from her son and

putting it in her bag. 'Don't moan, you can play on it when we get there. Come on!'

She grabbed the bag of potatoes Agatha had dropped round for Polly, then they set off down the road towards Polly and Jay's place. *Polly and Jay's place!* Clare was absolutely thrilled that her sister had decided to stay in Elderchurch for keeps. Who would have foreseen *that* at the start of the summer?

Her phone beeped with a new text message as they walked along. *Still on for tonight? Will pick you up at 8. Lx*

Warmth flooded through her at the simple sentences. *Definitely*, she texted back. She and Luke had met for drinks and dinner several times since that first heart-pounding date. He'd even come out with her and the children for a long, bum-aching bike ride through the gorgeous autumn country-side the previous Saturday. Clare had been worried that they wouldn't like him, or might start making pointed remarks about how wonderful their dad was, but it had been a day full of laughs and fun. The two of them were going to Roxie's farewell bash in The Fox and Goose tonight – her last weekend in the UK before she set off travelling around South America with her mates. The surgery wouldn't be the same without sparky, funny Roxie, but she'd promised Clare postcards galore 'And his-n-hers sombreros, if you're *really* lucky.'

'Oh, I'm feeling lucky all right,' Clare had replied, grinning. 'Very lucky.'

She smiled and pulled her coat tighter around her as she and her children walked through the village together. It had been a strange old summer, all in all. A summer of sisterhood, new business ventures and the first flush of love; a summer when she'd finally faced up to what had haunted her about the past and let go of the guilt. With her family all around her, and Luke in her life, she had a feeling that the future was going to be even better.

Lucy Diamond's
Summer Cocktails

Whether you're sharing these with a sister or not, a cool, colourful cocktail can be the perfect drink at a summer party. Here are some suggestions:

Classic Pimms and Lemonade
(Serves 6)

250ml Pimms No. 1
1 litre lemonade
Half cucumber, chopped
1 apple, cored and chopped
1 orange, sliced
3 strawberries, sliced
Handful fresh mint leaves

Mix all ingredients in a large jug. Serve chilled, or with ice.

*

Mint Julep

70ml Bourbon whiskey
4 fresh mint sprigs
1 tsp powdered sugar
2 tsp water

Muddle the mint leaves, sugar and water in a glass. Fill the glass with crushed ice and add Bourbon. Top with more ice and garnish with a mint sprig. Serve with a straw.

*

Raspberry Champagne Cocktail
(Serves 8)

3 tbsp Crème de Cassis
1 bottle of champagne, chilled
A few raspberries

Divide the Crème de Cassis between 8 champagne flutes. Carefully add the champagne. Just before serving, add a few raspberries to each drink.

*

Citrus Peach Cooler (non-alcoholic)
(Serves 8)

2 lemons (juice only)
2 limes (juice only)
1 lemon, thinly sliced
1 lime, thinly sliced
Peach juice (or peach nectar)
Cloudy lemonade
3 sliced strawberries
Sparkling water
Mint sprigs

Put the lemon and lime juice into a large jug. Add the sliced lemon and lime, and a handful of ice cubes. Add peach juice to fill about one third of the jug, then add the lemonade until the jug is two-thirds full. Add the strawberries, then top up the jug with sparkling water. Garnish with mint sprigs.

★

Lucy Diamond's
Home-made Beauty Products

For Clare's storyline, I did a lot of enjoyable research into making beauty products. Here are a few easy recipes you can try for yourself:

Rose-petal Bath

1 cup of rose petals
½ cup of rose water (you can buy this from health-food stores)
½ cup of coconut milk

Mix the rose water and coconut milk, then pour into a warm, running bath. Add rose petals for extra scent.

*

Avocado, Carrot and Cream Face Mask

1 avocado, mashed
1 carrot, cooked and mashed
250ml double cream
1 egg, beaten
3 tbsp honey

Mix all the ingredients until smooth then spread gently over your face and neck and leave for 10–15 minutes. Rinse with cool water and pat dry.

Packed with vitamin E, avocado also makes a great moisturising hair mask. Simply mash one into a smooth paste and spread on clean damp hair for 20 minutes, then rinse.

*

Natural Shampoo

25ml olive oil
1 egg
1 tbsp lemon juice
1 tsp apple cider vinegar

Blend all ingredients until well-combined. Use like ordinary shampoo and rinse well. (Discard any leftovers.)

*

Soothing Foot Balm

1 tbsp almond oil
1 tbsp olive oil
1 tsp wheat germ oil
12 drops eucalyptus essential oil

Combine all ingredients in a bottle and shake well. Rub into the feet and heels nightly to smooth and soften rough dry feet.